WHERE THE

Pink Houses Are

REBEKAH RUTH

WestBow
PRESS
A DIVISION OF THOMAS NELSON

Dear Diana,
It's been so nice
getting to know you
over the years. As
you move on to a new
adventure — I'm
praying for you!
Love,
Rebekah

WestBow Press books may be ordered through booksellers or by contacting:

WestBow Press
A Division of Thomas Nelson
1663 Liberty Drive
Bloomington, IN 47403
www.westbowpress.com
1-(866) 928-1240

ISBN: 978-1-4497-2983-7 (sc)
ISBN: 978-1-4497-2984-4 (hc)
ISBN: 978-1-4497-2982-0 (e)

Library of Congress Control Number: 2011918968

Printed in the United States of America
WestBow Press rev. date: 11/22/2011

Contents

Acknowledgements. vii

A word about accents ix

Chapter One 1

Chapter Two 11

Chapter Three 17

Chapter Four 23

Chapter Five. 33

Chapter Six 39

Chapter Seven 45

Chapter Eight 49

Chapter Nine. 65

Chapter Ten. 71

Chapter Eleven. 79

Chapter Twelve 83

Chapter Thirteen 89

Chapter Fourteen. 97

Chapter Fifteen 105

Chapter Sixteen 113

Chapter Seventeen 129

Chapter Eighteen 139

Chapter Nineteen 151

Chapter Twenty 155

Chapter Twenty-One 159

Chapter Twenty-Two 169

Chapter Twenty-Three 185

Chapter Twenty-Four 193

Chapter Twenty-Five 203

Chapter Twenty-Six 215

Chapter Twenty-Seven 229

Chapter Twenty-Eight 239

Chapter Twenty-Nine 245

Chapter Thirty 255

Chapter Thirty-One 261

Chapter Thirty-Two 269

Chapter Thirty-Three 275

Chapter Thirty-Four 283

Chapter Thirty-Five 293

Epilogue 301

Author's Note 303

Acknowledgements

First, I must thank my "three musketeers" who read as I wrote and spurred me on by sending me emails demanding the next chapter; Ruthie (a.k.a. Marmee), Leah & Jenn, without your encouragement I may never have gotten past the first chapter.

Thank you to Jocelyn, Candace, Heather & Christine, who also read the first rough, rough chapters and were incredibly encouraging to this novice author.

Thank you to all those who read once the first draft was done: Jordanne, Edie, Sarah, Sammie, Karen, Kellie, Nancy, Rose, Chris, Patti, Tamara, Auntie Joyce and my gram (with the special extra large print copy!)...and anyone else that I may have overlooked. I appreciate all of you taking time to read and give me your input. And to Brenna, my life-long friend, who inspired the name for my main character, thanks for having such a cool name.

Thank you to all those who have been asking me repeatedly when the book will be published and are anxiously awaiting their chance to read it. I love that you are my first fans!

Thank you to Pastor Jerry Gillis. Our church is so blessed to have a man of God who delivers the gospel message unflinchingly week after week. Thanks for telling it like it is.

Thank you to Courtney and Stacey for the use of your photographs.

Thank you to Benji and Jenna Cowart for letting me use your lyrics in my story. Your songs are an inspiration to me.

Thank you to agent extraordinaire, Kelly Mortimer of Mortimer Literary Agency. Without even taking me on as a client, you gave me great feedback and helped me more than you know.

Thank you to editor Christine Moore at WestBow Press who knows where to put all the dots and dashes and spaces, etc. I appreciate all your hard work.

A big thanks goes out to Jordanne, Jacob, Josh and Jonny. Thanks for letting mom spend so much time in front of the computer and for being great cheerleaders! (I mean that in the manliest of ways, boys!)

And lastly, to my number one encourager, Bill. Thank you for telling me to stop reading and start writing. You have been the most supportive husband a girl could ask for and I love you dearly. And I'll tell you one last time, *this is not an autobiography!*

A word about accents

Most of the characters in this book are Irish. I could hear their accents while I wrote the dialogue and I wanted to remind the reader of their Irish lilt without being obnoxious.

Therefore, I tweaked certain words throughout the dialogue as cues. Most of the changes are self explanatory. However, the word *you* requires some explanation. Sometimes it is actually pronounced just like it is in America but when you see it spelled *ya* it is really more of a *yih* sound (same vowel sound as in the word *him*). My hope is that these changes will help you hear the melodic Irish accent as you read.

For my Grandma Pat,
whose love for her Irish homeland
has always inspired me. I love you, Gram!

Chapter One

The instant the plane encountered turbulence, I woke with a start. This was it. After all my worrying about making it through customs in Shannon, I wasn't even going to make it to Ireland. I was going to die in a fiery crash in the middle of the ocean. *How could I have been stupid enough to get on a plane? I hate planes! They're flying coffins!* My hands went numb. Sweat soaked my back. My heart pounded. And my mother-in-law, Anna, seated next to me near the window, slept on. How could she sleep?

Breathe, Brenna. Just breathe. I settled back a little and stared down at Anna's totally relaxed hands. The plane shivered again, and still Anna didn't move. What would I do without her? I used to be so independent ... so strong. I had managed to hide just how weak and needy I felt lately, but inside I was a mess. Anna had no idea she was the only reason I forced myself out of bed most days. She slept peacefully next to me. Maybe we weren't going to crash after all. Still, my imagination spawned all kinds of looming disasters. *What was wrong with me? Why couldn't I control this irrational terror? Breathe, Brenna, breathe.*

Anna woke suddenly. She didn't even ask me what was wrong before reaching over to put her arms around me and whisper a prayer of peace. Wrapped in her motherly embrace, I relaxed. My eyelids soon grew heavy, and I slipped into a dreamless sleep. The next thing I heard was the pilot's voice.

1

"Good morning, ladies and gents. We trust you've had a good night's sleep here aboard Aer Lingus flight 140. We're just beginning our approach to the Shannon, County Clare Airport. Local time is 6:20 a.m. Current temperature is 12 degrees celsius and we'll be landing in plenty of time for you to find yerselves a hearty Irish breakfast. Please enjoy yer stay and as always, thank you fer choosing the simply unbeatable Aer Lingus ... low fares, way better."

"Feeling better?" Anna eyed me with concern as overhead lights blinked on throughout the cabin.

"Yeah, sorry. I'm not sure what happened. I guess the turbulence just spooked me." Panic attacks were new. I'd never experienced anything like that before, not even after the accident. *Was I losing my mind?*

Anna squeezed my hand. "You'll feel much better once you've had a nice plate of eggs and sausage. And despite what the British say, no one makes a cuppa tea like we Irish. You just wait and see!" She glowed with the anticipation of returning home after so many years.

Thanks to Anna's dual citizenship, moving through customs proved to be an easy process. Certainly not worth a panic attack. Anna had suggested that an unhurried day of relaxation was the best way to begin our vacation. And so, instead of driving straight through to Millway, we'd spend a day at nearby Glin Castle in County Limerick.

I spent much of the hour-long cab ride to the castle alternately absorbed in the breathtaking scenery and lost in thought. I'd agreed to this vacation because I couldn't refuse Anna. She so rarely asked for anything for herself, and this trip home meant the world to her. She really missed her family. I'd always wanted to go to Ireland but assumed I'd go with Ben someday. Someday would never happen now. As we traveled along the glistening Shannon River, Anna reminisced.

"People say you can't go home. It's not true. Home always has a soothing effect on a soul."

I nodded as if I understood, but I didn't. I didn't have a home. Watching Anna's face as she took in the countless shades of green blanketing the rolling countryside, I suddenly realized that, if home was a place that had a "soothing effect on a soul," then *maybe Anna was my home.* She'd been a refuge for me since I was fourteen years old. Even when I lived with my gram, Anna was more like a mom to me. Seeing her finally filled with peace, I decided that, in spite of the constant aching in my soul, I would do everything I could to make this the best vacation Anna had ever had. It was time to put the past where it belonged and to make a fresh start. This holiday would be a new beginning for both of us.

The sun gleamed brightly off the parapets of Glin Castle as it came into view, reminding me of another castle I'd visited back in New York. My mom and dad had taken me there when I was a little girl. We'd vacationed in Alexandria Bay, and when I heard my parents call the area "The Thousand Islands," I thought we were literally going to visit a *thousand* islands. We actually visited two or three, and Boldt Castle was my favorite part of the trip. I remember pretending I was a beautiful princess returning to my castle after visiting the people of my kingdom. My mom laughed and played along with my fantasy. I must have been about six years old, and after that trip I dreamed for years of having a Cinderella-type wedding at Boldt Castle. How I longed for that carefree life I'd had all those years ago. If Ireland was a magical land, perhaps I could capture a leprechaun and wish myself back to those innocent days. It was wishful thinking. That little girl at Boldt Castle had no idea how painful and complicated life would become. I swiped at a tear, relieved that Anna was too caught up in her joy at coming home to notice.

"'Tis beautiful, isn't it?" she said, sweeping her hand across the view of castle grounds and gardens.

I agreed. "We'll have to take a walk this afternoon."

The promised Irish breakfast did not disappoint. I stuffed the corner of my napkin into my collar like a three-year old, as I was famous for dropping food on myself. It happened constantly, no matter how careful I was. Egg yolk, in particular, has a magnetic attraction to my sleeves. And if anyone within a ten-foot radius has something sweet or sticky, I'll manage to get it all over myself. We were served two kinds of eggs, sausage, bacon, potato bread, and soda bread ... all with tea, of course. How was it that the local women didn't each weigh at least three hundred pounds? If the meals kept up at this pace, I'd put the fifteen pounds I'd lost back on within the week. I suspected that was part of Anna's plan.

All fifteen guest rooms at Glin Castle were occupied, June being a very popular time for tourists. Our room boasted deep-blue walls with white crown molding and large windows overlooking a magnificent garden. A dizzying abundance of floral patterns danced across the curtains, an overstuffed chair, and the bedding. My recent obsession with late-night home-and-garden shows had me considering how I could update the room for under five hundred dollars.

After a relaxing night at the castle, we hailed another cab and headed to Millway in County Cork where Anna's Aunt Patricia ran the Maloney Bed & Breakfast. Auntie Pat, as she preferred to be called, was close to eighty years old and had helped raise Anna. I had never met her but she had inadvertently paid for this trip. It was a wedding gift intended as a one-year anniversary trip for me and Ben. Anna explained that Auntie Pat was in excellent physical health but she'd become increasingly absent-minded of late. Thankfully, her widowed daughter, Bettie, had moved in several years back to cook for the guests and help with the details of running the B&B. Anna suspected that many people stayed overnight at the B&B just to sample Bettie's Saturday breakfast buffet.

The road to Millway wound through lush emerald meadows and rolling hills. In the past twenty-four hours, I'd seen more shades of green than I had in my entire twenty years of life. In Millway, buildings painted various shades of blue, yellow, red, and pink clustered around the town center. The scene reminded me of an old photograph that my mom had kept on her dresser. I remembered the wooden frame that showcased a photo of the quaint little Irish village where my mom had been born. As a little girl, I particularly loved the pink house in the center. Whenever I asked, my mom told me magical stories of the place in the photograph. Over time, I came to think of Ireland as the place where the pink houses are.

With a charming smile, Anna asked the cab driver to take a roundabout way to the B&B so that she could show me the house on Abbey Street where she grew up. Her eyes glittered with happy tears as she pointed to a charming row house facing the low rock wall that bordered the sparkling river.

I'd expected the Maloney Bed & Breakfast to be a quaint, old-fashioned inn, but as we rounded the bend on Connaught Drive, a thoroughly updated and modern-looking, tan-plaster guesthouse with ivory trimmed windows came into view. Well-tended trees, shrubs and flower beds dotted the grounds. I even glimpsed a satellite dish protruding from one corner of the roof. This was definitely not what I expected.

Anna directed the cab driver to pull around to the back entrance which was used only by family and friends. He helped us with our bags and, before we could knock, the back door opened and a middle-aged woman with close-cropped curly white hair and rosy red cheeks bounded toward us. With her arms spread wide in welcome, the woman I assumed to be Bettie exclaimed, "Oh, Anna, 'tis yerself in the flesh! We're so sorry about what happened, but we're thrilled you've come. How was yer trip, cousin?" While she talked, the woman embraced Anna in a warm hug. Then she turned to me. "And this must be Brenna. What a beauty ya are, dear!" She pulled me into her ample arms and kissed the top of my head as she whispered, "Thank you for bringing Anna home to us, darlin'."

Anna's Irish lilt seemed stronger than I'd ever noticed as she said, "You look as healthy as ever. I hear yer cooking is still the envy of every housewife from here to Dublin!"

Bettie shooed us inside and into a spacious kitchen that smelled like fresh baked bread. It was outfitted with state-of-the-art equipment and yet somehow still exuded a "country kitchen" feel, thanks at least in part to the oversized antique hutch along the far wall. As she showed us around, it was obvious that this was more than just a place to do her job. Bettie loved her cheery yellow kitchen. I looked longingly at the corner where an aged oak table sat below a leaded-paned window overlooking a sunny garden. Any time I stayed somewhere longer than a day or two I would seek out my own cozy book nook. I could definitely picture myself ensconced by the window with a hot cup of tea and a good book.

"Bettie, I can't believe this is the same kitchen. It looks so different... gorgeous!" Anna commented.

"Aye, we've updated the whole place. You'll not recognize much, I expect." Bettie grinned and as she directed us toward the back stairs, she called out, "Mum! The girls are here. Where've ya gone to? MUM!" There was no answer as she shook her head and continued up the stairs. "Yer welcome to use the front stairs if y'like. We usually take this way from the kitchen, though. Kitchen and back stairs are kind of our area, the front rooms and guest rooms are for the guests. But again, yer also our guests so feel free to go where y'like. It's the same as when we were young, Anna. All the doors on the south side of the hallway are for guests, and all the doors on the north side here, are for family and overflow. Mum's is the first door here, mine is the second and you two can choose from the last two."

She pointed down the hall and looked distractedly at her mother's door. "I'd best find Mum, so I'll leave ya to get settled in. Come on down for a cuppa tea when yer ready." With a quick peek into the first room, Bettie was off down the stairs and could be heard calling for her mother yet again.

"Think everything's okay?" I asked Anna.

"Oh, I'm sure it is. Auntie Pat is easily distracted and Bettie worries about her, but she's a tough little cookie, you wait and see. She's probably tending to the garden or scolding the groundskeeper. Don't worry. Shall we choose our rooms?" she asked as she opened the first door.

I stifled a giggle as there was no question that this would be Anna's room. She had decorated her dining room at home with costal accents and a collection of porcelain lighthouses from around the world. She absolutely loved lighthouses, and if each room had a theme, this would be "The Lighthouse Room." The walls were a soft sky-blue, and the sandy-colored hardwood floors were accented with a couple of ocean blue throw rugs. The far wall was dominated by the bed, and above that hung a beautiful seascape picture with a tall blue and red lighthouse prominent in the foreground. The bed was a dark mahogany as was the dresser, and there was a small writing desk by the window. I also noticed little touches around the tidy, uncluttered room—like a basket of extra linens in the corner and fresh cut flowers on the desk. It suited Anna perfectly.

"Should we look at the next room before we decide or would you prefer to stay here?" I asked with a grin.

She grinned back. "Brenna, dear, you know me well. This room is lovely, and I would choose this one even if the next one had a Jacuzzi tub!"

I laughed. Anna was a very tall, blond woman, more Swedish-looking than Irish. She had often complained that taking a bath was more than uncomfortable in a standard sized tub. She'd joked with her late husband, Joe, that she would go anywhere he wanted on vacation, if only he got her a room with a Jacuzzi so she could soak in the tub like "normal-sized women do." On the other hand, I fit quite nicely in a standard tub, being all of five foot, two inches tall. Over the years, Anna had made it clear she was slightly envious of my small stature, to which I would reply, "Yeah, right. Could you hand me that plate off the top shelf?" *Point made.*

To my relief, my room wasn't decorated with any sort of theme. It was very cozy, though. The walls were a warm golden color, and the rest of the room was done in neutral tones. All the rooms were *en suite*, meaning they each had a small bathroom, and, no, mine did not have a Jacuzzi but it did have a small claw-foot tub that would suit me perfectly.

On the east wall, what I initially took for a large curtained window was actually a set of French doors leading out to a charming, private terrace. It overlooked the flower garden, and though I could see a farmhouse down the road, it was not very close at all. This trumped the kitchen corner and would definitely be my little book nook while on vacation.

"Brenna?" Anna found me enjoying the view

"Isn't this lovely?" She scooped me into a sideways hug.

"Better than a Jacuzzi," I teased with a grin.

"Well sure, for you of course," she teased back. "I smell Bettie's famous, fresh-baked scones. Want to have some with a nice cup of tea?"

"Sure!"

We heard Bettie even before we entered the kitchen. She sounded as if she were scolding a naughty child. We paused at the door, somewhat embarrassed to walk in on her ... and even more so when we discovered that the object of her chastisement was her own mother.

"... simply saying, Mum, you should let me know when ya plan on leavin' the house—not because ya can't handle yerself, but because y'never know when somethin' could happen, and I don't like not knowin' where y'are!" Bettie finished in an exasperated, high-pitched tone.

"Nonsense!" said the other voice with authority. "I've been comin' and goin' of my own accord for most of me eighty years, and I don't need some youngin keepin' tabs on me. Why, if I get into a spot of trouble, I'm sure the wee folk will lend me a hand. So never you mind!" She dismissed her daughter outright.

At that, Anna pushed the door open, hoping to end the argument with our arrival. "Auntie Pat!" She rushed over to a frail-looking woman seated at the table by the window. She gave her aunt a gentle hug, looking almost as if she were afraid she'd break her.

Auntie Pat stood with her hands on her hips and responded in mock scorn, "What? I don't see ya in over ten years, and all you've got for me is that poor excuse for a hug? Give yer auntie a squeeze, young lady!"

Anna laughed and replied with a hearty embrace, appeasing her aunt. Then she nodded toward me. "Auntie Pat, this is Brenna."

Auntie Pat turned her piercing gaze on me, and I'll admit I was intimidated. I pride myself on being strong and holding my own, but this tiny woman, who couldn't have weighed much more than one pound for each year of her life, suddenly scared me senseless. I'm not even sure why, except that her presence seemed much larger than the physical space she occupied. This was a woman who was sure of herself and what she wanted, and her confidence made me feel completely transparent. After witnessing her bully both her daughter and her niece in the span of two minutes, I had an almost uncontrollable urge to run back up the stairs and lock myself in my room.

"Well, don't just stand there, girl. Come here an let me get a look atcha!" She waved an impatient hand at me, and I moved in obedience until I stood right in front of her. Somehow, being close up put her back in proper perspective for me. It was not often that I met people shorter than me, and I felt some courage return.

"Forgive me, Auntie Pat, I'm delighted to meet you," I said with what I hoped was a proper, respectful tone. I suspected this was a woman who appreciated, if not demanded, propriety.

She cocked her head to the side as she appraised me. Then she turned to Anna, "Well, I certainly see why young Benjamin took to her so. She's a beauty, she is. A right Irish beauty!" All this was said as if I were not standing directly in front of her with my face rapidly turning varying shades of scarlet. She turned to me. "'Tis a pleasure to meet you as well, dear. I'm so sorry for yer loss … and at such a young age. 'Tis a shame, it is. I know you've been very good to Anna these last many months. We're grateful you've been there for her." She squeezed my hand. "You are family and are always welcome under my roof." Having said that, she reached up and kissed my forehead. Her sudden sweetness touched me and I choked back surprising tears as I thanked her.

Bettie came to the rescue with a plate of hot scones and clotted cream. I listened while Anna got caught up with her family, and Bettie explained that the B&B would be fairly full for the next several weeks. I offered to help, but she wouldn't hear of it. "You're on vacation, dear, and I'll not be havin' you workin' for yer keep!" she said with a no-nonsense tone.

I held my hands up in surrender. "Okay, well thank you, Bettie, I will try to remember that I'm on vacation. So, tell me about what you do here at the B&B." She and Auntie Pat gave me a crash course on the ins and outs of bed-and-breakfast living. Having lived with them as a child, Anna knew what to expect, but it was all new for me. From the early morning breakfasts to the late night snacks, it sounded like Bettie and Auntie Pat never stopped working.

As we were talking, the front bell rang. A new guest checking in effectively ended our afternoon tea, so I headed to my room to get settled. I had two suitcases to unpack. We had not decided how long we'd be staying, so packing had been tricky. I had trouble packing for a weekend, much less an open-ended vacation in a foreign country. I had a sneaking suspicion that Anna was hoping to make this a permanent move. I wasn't ready for that. I'd heard it's not wise to make any major decisions for at least a year after a life-changing trauma.

Nine months. It had been nine months since my world was rocked by a freak storm and a directionally challenged girl. That gave me three more months to put off making any big decisions. I sighed at the thought. At the moment, I was having trouble deciding which drawer to use for my underwear. *Pitiful.* I had to laugh at myself. If this was my progress after nine months, how much help could three more bring?

Chapter Two

The next few days were spent blissfully unplanned. Both Anna and I relished the idea of sleeping-in and adjusting to the jet lag. I put my new reading spot to good use and spent hours out on my terrace, snuggled into a down comforter, finishing the book I'd started on the plane and enjoying the surrounding landscape. The quiet alone-time was refreshing, and it was surprisingly healing too. Still, I can only take so much inactivity before I begin to feel like a worthless lump, so by the third day I was ready for some adventure. I proposed my plan over a delicious breakfast of soft-boiled eggs and soda bread.

"So, Anna, let's go do some sightseeing today," I said, scrubbing egg yolk from my right sleeve.

Bettie chimed in from the other side of the kitchen. "Ya can borrow my car, girls. I won't be needin' it today, anyway."

"Well," Anna hesitated, "I'm sure you've noticed that drivin' is a bit different here. I mean, 'tis true I learned to drive here ... but *most* of my drivin's been done in the States. Honestly, I'm a bit nervous to give it a try so soon without any refresher, y'know?"

I hadn't even thought of that, but she was right, of course. "Well, it's a nice day out. How about we go for a walk into town, and you can show me around your old stomping grounds?

She brightened considerably at the idea. "Perfect! I'll just run upstairs to freshen up, and I'll meet ya back down here in a few minutes."

Maloney's was less than a ten-minute walk from the town center, and all along the way Anna pointed out where different childhood friends had lived. We detoured down a side road off Main Street so she could show me where Joe had lived when they'd met. I saw the little park where they'd spent many sweet afternoons together. This was the first time I'd heard her talk of Joe without tears and sadness since the accident. It seemed as if she was truly settling into a peaceful place.

I wasn't so sure for myself. I knew I'd accepted the reality of it all. I also knew that I missed Ben fiercely, mostly at night when I went to bed. Going to sleep alone seems completely natural before you know anything different. But once you've grown used to the warm, secure feeling of the man you love sleeping by your side, it's torturous to have to fall asleep night after night, knowing he'll never put his arms around you again. I had to admit, though, that sleep had come easier here. Maybe I was healing after all.

"My best friend Mary lived down that way. We lost touch over the years. Bettie says she's still in town," Anna said. "I'll have to look her up while we're here!" The idea tickled her, and as she continued to share stories of adventures she'd had with Mary, I began to think about Ben again. It struck me that Ben was not only my husband and my best friend; he was my *only* close friend. Why was that? This sudden revelation bothered me. I found myself only half listening to Anna while trying to sort out my thoughts.

Ben had been jealous of my time but not in a controlling, freakish way. I *wanted* to spend all of my time with him. Yet, was that normal? To spend so much energy and time on one person that you exclude all other relationships? I couldn't believe these thoughts had never crossed my mind before.

"Anna, were you and Joe best friends?" My question seemed to surprise her, and she took a moment to formulate her answer.

"I'd have to say yes and no."

"How very political of you," I teased.

She laughed and continued, "No, I mean that. Joe was my most *important* friend and one of my best friends, yet I certainly had a number of other close friends over the years, particularly at church. But if you'd asked Joe, he'd have said without hesitation that I was his best friend.

Generally, it's much harder for men to have those close relationships than it is for women. What are y'thinkin' about?"

"Well, it just hit me that I never really had any close friends other than Ben. Is that weird?"

"Actually, Ben and I fought over this exact subject," she confessed, looking uncomfortable.

"What?" My jaw dropped. I'd never even heard Anna raise her voice to Ben, much less argue. Now, Joe … he had the Irish temper people joke about, and I'd heard him lose it before when Ben was being particularly stubborn. But Anna? I couldn't picture it.

"On more than one occasion," she continued. "You and I have don't have a typical 'in-law' type relationship, Brenna. It wasn't long after meeting you that I began to see you as my own daughter. You know that, don't you?" I nodded, still confused. "So, looking out for your best interests sometimes meant going head to head with my strong-willed son. And he did not like it."

"What did you say to him?" I asked, still trying to picture them fighting, but coming up blank.

"I told him I thought you two spent too much time together. Not because I didn't think you should be together, but it concerned me that you didn't seem to have a social life outside of our family." She was absolutely right. *Why had I never noticed that before?* I was making a mental list of any other friends from the past six years that I would consider "close." Not one made the list. No wonder I felt like my whole life had died with Ben. It had. I had *made* him my whole life. "Brenna?" Anna prompted.

"Sorry. I was thinking. You're right. It didn't seem like it at the time, but I think we did spend too much time alone. We didn't hang out with friends much. It was always just the two of us."

"Did you know we didn't speak to each other for a whole week just after he proposed to you?" she asked.

Ben had put a ring on my finger before the first day of college, "so there will be no confusion for the other freshman guys," he'd said. I didn't really think that would be an issue. I'd never even been asked out by another guy. Of course, as Ben proudly pointed out, he had scooped me up on the first day of ninth grade and hadn't let me out of his sight since.

As Anna's words registered, a lump rose in my throat, and I couldn't disguise the hurt in my voice. "Wait … you didn't want us to get married?"

"Oh, hon, no, not that," she reassured me. "No, I just wanted him to wait a little longer. I thought you should have some freedom in your first year of college, meet new people, make new friends, y'know? But he was just so sure you'd go and meet someone you liked better than him. He refused to hold off."

"How could he even think that way? He knew how much I loved him. He always seemed so confident about everything. The guy you're describing sounds so insecure. Why didn't *I* see that?"

"Sometimes I think we see more of what we *want* to see and less of what we don't. I think Ben made you feel very safe?" She knew that was true. He'd always been a bit of a knight in shining armor for me.

"He was very protective of me, and I guess I liked that," I admitted.

"And you're right, he was confident about most things; he just had a blind spot when it came to you. He was terrified of losing you, so he held on very tightly. I thought that might become an issue for you as you got older, and I knew it would be better for you to deal with it before you got married. Ben disagreed."

I was silent, thinking through it all. "You know, none of this takes away from what the two of you had. It doesn't change how much you loved each other or how good you were together," she assured me, even as I could see that talking about Ben was making her sad. I had lost my husband, but she had lost her whole family in one day.

"No," I replied, "it doesn't. I walk a line each day between being thankful that I had him in my life at all and being furious that he's gone. I'm giving myself mental whiplash!"

Anna laughed softly and put her arm around me. "I can relate, love. I don't understand why such horrible things happen. But I am starting to feel like myself again, and I'm thankful for that."

"I can see a difference in you here. Was it just coming home that you needed?" In the months since we'd made the decision to visit Ireland, Anna had done a complete one-eighty.

"I can't say for sure. I think I just got tired of being angry and bitter. What good does it do? Look at you. Widowed at twenty years old. How unfair is that? And yet you picked yourself up and kept moving. I'm so proud of you, Brenna. You have no idea."

I smiled at her kind words, but inside I was aching. I was not as strong as she thought I was. "Thanks," I said absently.

She put a hand on my shoulder. "Are you upset, love?"

"No, I think I'm just a little confused. I need time to sort through some of this."

"Well, that's the beauty of vacation. You've lots of time to think things through, right?" she asked.

"Absolutely. I'm fine. Just realizing that I need to be more intentional about making new friends. I feel like I've been completely oblivious!" Anna still looked concerned, so I reached over and gave her a sideways hug. "Don't worry, I'm fine."

She eyed me skeptically, then switched gears. "Do you think we should grab a bite to eat, then?"

As if in response, my stomach growled loudly, melting away tension as we both laughed. "I think that's an excellent idea."

We ate lunch at Rosie's Pub in the town center. On the outside it was a deep red with white and black trim and ivy climbing all three stories. The dining room was a homey place with dark wood paneling and a polished granite bar on the far wall. I smelled pot roast and grilled onions as we took our seats. The staff was friendly and chatted amiably with the customers. There were definitely some regulars at the bar giving the young female bartender a good-natured ribbing about something. She looked to be about my age, maybe a little younger ... fair skin, green eyes, freckles, and red hair.

"Finally," I quipped, "someone that looks Irish!"

Anna laughed, "What do you think most Irish look like?"

"Like the bartender, there," I pointed toward the girl.

Anna glanced in her direction and responded. "It's true, that look is common, but nowhere near as common as you'd think. Probably well under half the population. You're just as likely to see someone who looks very much like yerself, dear. The dark hair, tan skin, dark eyes ... all very Irish."

I had no idea. I'd always thought I didn't look Irish at all, but apparently I was wrong. Auntie Pat's remark about me being a "right Irish beauty" now made more sense. I guess I fit right in, at least in the looks department. My distinct upstate New York accent, however, gave me away every time.

Lunch was delicious. We both had the special; roast beef and gravy wrapped in pastry and browned to perfection. The gravy made me nervous, but I managed to keep it all either on my plate or in my mouth. Our server, Katie, was bubbly and helpful, checking back at regular intervals. At the end of our meal, I caught Anna staring intently at the bartender.

"Why are you looking at her?" I whispered across the table.

"Hmm?" She looked at me, confused at first. "Oh, well, she looks a lot like my friend Mary. I'm wonderin' if there's any relation."

"Why don't you go ask her?" I suggested.

"Aye, I think I will." She put some cash on the table for our bill and headed over to the bar. I followed slowly, watching the exchange, and walked up just as she was giving the girl a hug.

"Brenna, this is young Tara, just as I thought! Her mum Mary and I were great friends."

I took her extended hand as she said, "Pleased t'meet ya!" with a genuine smile. "I was just tellin' Anna here, my mum will be thrilled when I tell her I've seen ya. The stories I could tell ya, Brenna," she teased.

"Oh, come now, none of that." Anna blushed. "Please tell yer mum to give us a ring up to Auntie Pat's place. It's been years since we've talked. Tara, you were just a wee one!"

"'Tis sure I will," said Tara, "and Brenna, I'd love to chat a bit and show you 'round town more, if you'd like. I'm done here 'round two o'clock every day. Come by tomorrow and see me?"

"Um … yeah, I'd like that," I decided.

She waved as she headed to the far side of the bar to serve some new guests. I waved back and smiled at the thought of making a new friend already.

Chapter Three

Tara was true to her word. She was waiting for me the next day when I arrived at 2:00 p.m. First she introduced me to some of her coworkers. Katie, Sarah, Liz, and Brigit were all servers, and Sam was her boss. Next she took me on a tour of the little village, introducing me to so many people that I'd have no chance of remembering their names. Everyone seemed very pleasant and hospitable, most offering to have me in for a "cuppa tea" one day soon. I lost count at seven tea invites and began to giggle as each new person offered some variant of the same invitation.

As we passed by the Catholic church, a priest was sitting outside on the steps eating his lunch. He waved a greeting, and Tara said, "Hi, Father, this is my new friend Brenna. Brenna, meet Father Tim Gillis."

"Brenna, pleased t'meet ya!" He was maybe in his late forties with salt-and-pepper hair and subtle evidence of a fondness for sweets around his midsection. He had a warm, easy smile, and I liked him instantly.

"And you, Father," I replied while shaking his hand.

"I'm takin' her around to meet the locals," Tara told him.

"Aye, well have a blessed day, and I hope t'see ya at Mass on Sunday."

I didn't know what to say. I wasn't Catholic and wasn't planning on going to his church, but I smiled in response as we moved on to more village shops.

"Is everyone always this friendly?" I asked her as we left the hardware store where I'd met Old Mike and his wife Katherine.

She laughed and answered, "Well, not to say the townsfolk aren't friendly; they are. But yer the talk of the town, y'know. They're all curious about Anna's young American friend and probably all jealous that I'm the one who's takin' ya 'round town and gettin' the scoop."

"Seriously?" I was floored. "Why are they all talking about *me?*"

She had a musical kind of laugh that was contagious. I smiled in spite of myself as she explained, "Brenna, we don't often get a lovely stranger from across the sea movin' into our sleepy little town."

"Moving in? We're just visiting," I corrected.

She smiled again, almost as if she knew something I didn't. "Aye, but it's called the Enchanted Isle for a reason. Sometimes plans change. I'm thinking ya might find it hard to leave before long … and people are saying yer Anna will be a great help to Bettie in managing the B&B as it gets more difficult for Miss Pat."

"Hmm, I hadn't thought of that. We planned to stay three or four weeks, but we haven't talked about moving here."

For the first time, I let myself imagine what it might be like to *live* in this pleasant little town. I knew Anna was probably already thinking of it, but I hadn't seriously considered it. The people were obviously friendly enough. I would need to get a job, though. I didn't have life insurance money like Anna did, and I was already feeling a little strapped for cash.

"What are y'thinkin' about?" Tara pulled me back into conversation. I hadn't realized we'd been walking in silence for a few minutes.

"Sorry. Lost in thought." Before this trip, I never would have thought of moving to Ireland, but it was an interesting idea. "If we did stay, I'd have to get a job, and I'm not sure if I'm even allowed to stay in the country. Guess we'll just see what happens."

"Of course. Nothin' needs to be decided right away. But just so ya know, Sam, the manager at Rosie's? He'll be needin' to hire a daytime waitress as Liz will be headin' back to school in a few weeks. We really need to keep four girls available to cover the shifts. Ever waited tables before?"

"Yeah, actually. It feels like most of my life!" I said. I wouldn't mind checking into it. But for now, I was curious to know more about my bubbly tour guide. "So, have you lived here all your life?"

"Aye, born and raised," she said with pride. "Most of the folks my age move out of town, ya know? They head to the big city for adventure and whatnot, but I really love this town. My two older sisters are here, and they both have wee ones, so I get to sit for them. I'd miss my family too much if I went away." She turned the question back to me, "What about you? Did you live in one place growin' up?"

"Well, I've lived in New York my whole life."

"New York City?" She had a dreamy, faraway look in her eyes now.

"No, not really." People always think that.

"Well, that's one place I've always dreamed of visitin'. Not goin' to live there, of course, but just to go to Broadway and Central Park and all the places you see in the movies," she said.

I nodded. "I lived downstate as a kid. We visited the city, but we lived a couple hours away. Then I moved to Buffalo when I was ten. That's at least six hours from the city," I explained.

"Yer jokin' me! Six hours? Why it only takes four to cross the whole of Ireland!" She shook her head in amazement. "Well, maybe someday we'll go to New York City together then," she smiled.

"You never know," I replied as we rounded the bend toward Maloney's.

"So you married Anna's son?" Tara asked, outing the white elephant that most people avoided.

"Yeah, Ben." I smiled at the thought of him in spite of the painful lump that formed in my throat. "You heard what happened?"

"Aye. Car accident?" She nodded and looked at me sideways. "Are y'dealin' with it okay?"

"I guess so. They say time heals all wounds, right?" I hesitated. "Does everyone know?"

"Well, 'tis a small town. I knew because my mum told me when it happened. Her growin' up with Anna and all, Bettie called her right away. I don't think everyone knew at the time, but when news of you two comin' hit town, the story was passed 'round and 'round. Hard to keep somethin' like that quiet, y'know? How long were ya married?"

"Four months," I answered with a slight break in my voice.

"Ah, that's so sad."

19

We walked in silence while I resisted the urge to cry. I took a deep breath and continued. "Yeah, we'd been together since ninth grade. He was my first and only boyfriend."

"Wow. Well I think yer really brave to come half way 'round the world," she said.

"Thanks. I don't feel brave. Kind of the opposite, actually. Anna's really my only family, and I'm not sure I could have stopped her from coming, even if I hadn't been up for it."

"You have no other family?" she said, surprised.

"No … well, that's not true. I have two half-brothers, but I don't know them well. There were always issues between their mom and mine," I said.

"What about yer parents?" she asked and then added, "I'm sorry. Am I bein' too nosy?"

"No, it's okay. It's easier to talk about my parents than Ben. I've had longer to adjust. They were killed in a plane crash when I was ten. They were on a business trip, and their plane went down over the ocean. A lot of people died. It was all over the news. Really sad." Something clicked at that moment. Telling the story made me think of my panic on the airplane. I'd never flown before, but it would only make sense that I'd freak out a little since my parents were killed in a plane crash. Duh! *Note to self: does not like airplanes.*

"Geez, that's terrible. I'm so sorry," she said.

"Thanks. Like I said, it's been a long time, and I'm used to it. But now, with Ben and Joe dying, it's like the whole thing starts over, with people feeling sorry for me and always looking and whispering. I was so tired of that at home, and I was hoping to avoid it here."

"You probably won't have to worry about it much 'round here. It's in our nature to move on. We're Irish, y'know? Our kind have been through so much hardship over the years, and they're a tough lot because of it. They'll take their cues from you. If you act like you're fine, they will too."

I breathed a sigh of relief and hoped she was right.

We arrived at the B&B, and there was a middle-aged man trimming some out-of-control bushes in the front lawn.

"How's the form, Tom. Are y'well?" Tara called to him.

"Ah, I'm fair to middlin', Miss Tara, and yerself?"

"Grand. Have y'met Brenna then?"

"No." He walked toward us. "I've been down t'visit my mum for the past few days. Just got back. So, yer the young cousin I've been hearin' about?" He smiled at me with warm, weathered eyes.

"I'm Brenna." I extended my hand, to which he chuckled and held up his dirt-caked palms.

"Pleased t'meet ya, love, but I don't think you'll be wantin' to shake my hand." We all laughed. "I'm sure we'll be seein' ya around, lass. If y'hurry, you might catch Bettie with one of her fresh apple tarts!"

We did catch Bettie, and as the apple tarts melted in our mouths, I only found one small spot of apple goop on my shirt.

"Brenna, I've a grand idea!" Tara said through a mouthful of apple filling. "You should come with me to the Millway Street Festival tomorrow night."

"What is it?" I asked.

"They do it every summer ... the whole town comes out for it. There's food and music. Some people sell crafts and stuff. And dancin'. That's the best part." She smiled wide.

"Well, I'm always up for food. I'll probably pass on the dancing, but the rest sounds great."

"Brilliant. We can meet at Rosie's at seven? I'll introduce you to all the cute lads in town." She giggled as I rolled my eyes. Yeah ... that's what I needed. A cute lad. Right.

Chapter Four

I had no idea what one would wear to a street festival, but I went in my favorite jeans and a boring, dark-blue shirt, hoping I would blend in rather than stand out. I hated being the center of attention, and Tara had me worried that I might be just that. My goal was to meet some of her friends and just have fun. She'd said "dancing" and I wondered ... did dancing mean, "Swing your partner round and round," or did it mean, "I like to move it, move it?" Either way, I loved music and was looking forward to a girls' night out.

I met Tara at Rosie's. We were waiting for her friend Shannon, when three guys came into the pub and headed straight for us.

"Tara, aren't ya goin' to introduce us to yer friend?" the first one said with a crooked smile that made my stomach flutter. This one was straight out of some Hollywood movie. He had dark blond hair with natural golden highlights. It was tousled on top with loose curls. He had chocolate brown eyes and a wicked smile. He was so attractive, I couldn't have told you a thing about the two standing with him if my life depended on it. This would have to be the town heartbreaker.

Tara smiled casually, but a faint blush on her cheeks betrayed her, "Hi there, Luke. Are y'well?" She didn't answer his question, and I wasn't sure she'd even heard it. Apparently he had a potent effect on her as well.

"Very well, Tara, very well indeed, at the moment," he answered her without taking his eyes off of mine. I couldn't believe the way his gaze made my heart race. He sauntered toward me and extended his hand. "I'm Luke Dillon."

"Brenna O'Brien," I answered, and as I reached to shake his hand, he gently twisted mine and brought it to his lips in a medieval, prince-like gesture. I felt my cheeks begin to burn as I pulled my hand back, and Tara swatted at Luke.

"Cut that out, Luke. You're embarrassing her!" she reprimanded him in a confident but playful tone and turned toward me. "Pay him no mind, Brenna. He fancies himself a sort of prince in our good town here, I think."

"Well, I'll admit that was a first for me," I said, trying to recover and play it cool.

"Yer first kiss then?" he said mischievously.

"No," I snapped back, beginning to resent his ability to unsettle me.

"Ah, well, good, because I would have shown you a much better kiss if I'd thought it was yer first." I didn't know how to respond to that, but his brutally handsome smile suddenly had me laughing, maybe as a defense mechanism. He laughed in response and continued, "'Tis truly a pleasure to meet ya, Brenna. I hear you've come over with Anna Maloney for a spell?" His use of Anna's maiden name threw me for a moment.

"Oh, yes. We're visiting her Auntie Pat for a little while," I explained.

At that moment, Tara's friend walked in the door. She was tall and slender with curly black hair reaching past her shoulders. Her large, dark eyes held a hint of sadness.

"Shannon!" Tara called out, and I watched Shannon to see if Luke had a similar effect on all women. She visibly stiffened at the sight of him, yet she looked anything but smitten. In fact, a quick look of disgust crossed her face before she swiftly schooled herself and donned a disinterested air.

"Hey, Luke ... boys." She nodded toward all three and effectively dismissed them as she stepped between us and turned her back toward them. "Sorry I'm late, love. My da was a wee bit buckled and needed a digout. So, you must be Brenna, then?" She smiled.

I had no clue what she'd just said to Tara, but I responded politely to her greeting, "Yes, nice to meet you, Shannon."

From behind her, Luke winked at me and waved as he and his "lads" headed out of the pub.

"I hear the music startin'," Tara prompted, and the three of us headed out into the crowded, bustling street.

Traditional Irish music lilted on the air from somewhere down the street. I heard guitars, fiddles, a tin whistle, and some kind of harp or dulcimer. I'd always loved Irish music, and I was drawn to it as we made our way through the mass of people. The aromas of varied treats to tempt the taste buds filled the air. There were sausage rolls and sweetbreads at one booth, dessert crepes at another, and an assortment of smoked meats at a third. Drinks were flowing freely as well, and as the sun slipped away, so did the inhibitions of the townsfolk; laughter and merriment were in abundance.

We finally made our way to the main stage where a motley crew of middle-aged musicians was picking up the tempo, luring dancers out into the square. I saw two ladies doing an Irish jig, while several others seemed to be engaged in a country line dance of sorts. Still others just stirred and swayed to the beat in whatever way the music moved them. It was a pure delight to watch.

Tara and Shannon had been engrossed in a deep conversation since we'd left Rosie's. This left me free to people-watch, which was a favorite pastime of mine. Back the way we'd come, I could see street performers garnering applause and a stilted, eight-foot-tall juggler dressed in green and white from head to toe.

"Do y'wanna grab a snack, then?" asked Tara.

"You're the expert tour guide," I teased. "Lead the way!"

We settled on a potato pesto soup appetizer served in plastic cups with a side of soda bread. It was smooth and filling with more flavor than I expected. Having no desire to tempt fate by eating soup and bread standing up, I found a seat near the square where I could watch the dancers stomping and gliding.

"Are you gonna dance?" Shannon asked me.

"Oh, well, I don't really know how." I laughed at the thought of me out there tripping myself.

"Aye, but that's the beauty of bein' led; the lad does all the work, you just go with the flow. It almost feels like flyin'. Ya never danced with a partner like that?" She pointed to the six or seven couples doing a two-step around the perimeter of the make-shift dance floor. It looked intricate and difficult to me, but I had to admit, it also looked like fun.

I shook my head. "No, I always meant to learn but just never got around to it, I guess." Ben had promised to take lessons with me this summer. The thought made me sad, and that familiar ache thudded in my chest. I hadn't noticed Shannon and Tara getting up from their seats, but the next thing I knew, they were standing before me with three young guys.

"Brenna, these are the O'Conor boys. They are some of the best dancers in town, and they're gonna take us for a spin. Whadya say?" Tara was pleading with her eyes, even as she kept her voice casual.

They all looked like they were in their late teens and were kind-looking boys. I got the feeling they wouldn't laugh at me or embarrass me. So, uncharacteristically, I agreed.

My partner was Jamie O'Conor, who was actually slightly older than me. His younger brothers, John and David, were identical twins with blondish red hair and had been classmates of Tara and Shannon. Jamie was tall and thin, but strong, with black hair and almost-black eyes. I was nervous as we began, but he was a fabulous teacher.

"I know it may be hard to do, seein' as we just met and all, but try to relax and trust me. The closer we stand, the easier it will be to follow me." He positioned our hands and then pulled me close to him and began to move forward, left, right, left. Shannon was right; it felt like flying. The more confident I became, the faster Jamie moved us in a wide arc.

"Look up at my face; don't look down," he cautioned as I began to get nervous and watch my feet. "You'll get more confused if ya look down, cuz you'll try to match what I'm doin'. Just relax and feel the music." He had a warm, engaging smile, and I relaxed in his arms as we flew around the outer loop. Too soon, the song ended and we came to a sudden stop.

"That was fabulous!" I said and gave Jamie a hug. "Thank you so much for teaching me that!" I was truly thrilled. I hadn't had so much fun in a very long time.

"My pleasure, Brenna." He smiled his easy smile again. "Be sure t'save me another dance. I promised my friend Megan a dance, and I see her eye'n me 'cross the way." He waved at a pretty young woman with strawberry blond hair who was shooting daggers at me with her emerald eyes. I waved too, with a big smile, hoping to communicate that I was not trying to steal her man. I didn't know if Jamie knew he was her man, but it was clear she thought so.

"Of course, thanks again, Jamie." I shook his hand this time, to which he gave a hearty laugh and sauntered across to the waiting Megan.

I sat back down to catch my breath during the next song. I was surprised at how out of shape I'd become. How could one dance leave me winded? *I need to start running again.* Running was something Ben and I had done together since tenth-grade track. I didn't have long legs, but I was fast, a good sprinter. I think I made three strides to every one of Ben's, but we enjoyed running together. It was a time to be together without having to talk or think. But I'd given up running when he died. Now I made a commitment to myself that I'd get up early, watch the sunrise on my terrace, and head out for a run. Of course, that was before I was asked to dance several more times by various new "friends."

There was a Patrick, who worked on his family's dairy farm. Sean, who had moved to Cork City to go to school but was home visiting his sister. There was Liam, Tara's older brother, and another Patrick, who went by Paddy and was a banker by day and a fiddle player by night. None were quite as good as Jamie, but I had gotten the idea and had no problem following them.

Jamie did come back for his promised second dance but not before introducing me to Megan as his new neighbor. Turned out he and his brothers were literally my neighbors. The farmhouse I could see from my terrace belonged to the O'Conor family, and apparently their father had gone to school with Joe and Anna. According to Jamie, we were officially invited for tea the following day.

Once more, he whirled me around, and I lost myself in the pure joy of it. He was fairly attractive, but I wasn't attracted to him in that way, so it made things very easy and comfortable. When our dance was done, I walked Jamie back to Megan. "Thank you so much for lending him to me for a bit. I've never danced like that before, and he's a great teacher." I turned to Jamie. "Please tell yer mum that Anna and I will come by for tea tomorrow, and thank her for the invite for me." Megan's smile did not reach her eyes as she nodded and pulled Jamie back onto the dance floor. I thought I had been very sisterly in my approach, but for some reason, she still seemed upset with me.

"Please tell me it's my turn, love." A soft voice came from just behind me, whispering into my right ear. The hair stood up on my neck, and I shivered involuntarily. "Sorry," Luke said as I turned to face him. "I didn't mean to scare ya." That devastating smile had my stomach doing flips yet again.

"No, you didn't scare me, just took me by surprise is all." I looked around subtly, hoping to catch Tara's or Shannon's eye. I wanted to be rescued, and I wasn't sure why, but they were both dancing and didn't seem to notice my deer-in-the-headlights look.

"So," Luke continued, "is it my turn then, Brenna?" I was caught. I couldn't exactly use my old excuse that I didn't know how to dance. I'd just spent an hour dancing with every guy who asked me. I had no rational reason to refuse. So, I gave in. What could it hurt?

"Why not?" I said, desperately trying to sound nonchalant. I'm sure I managed to fool him for about five seconds, but the minute he pulled me to his chest and began to weave us through the other couples, my heart began beating so fast and loud that I knew he must have felt it through his shirt. He smiled at me, and then my cheeks flared. I hated that I couldn't control my stupid cheeks. They always gave me away!

He leaned in and whispered into my ear again, "Relax, Brenna."

Everything happened at once. Chills ran down my spine as my stomach did another flip. Somehow, my legs crossed and tangled in his, and before I knew it, we were on the ground. Luke was actually laughing.

I was mortified. "I'm so sorry," I croaked in a whisper. He continued to laugh, and then I found myself doing the same. Soon I was laughing so hard I was crying, and Tara and Shannon were standing over me with worried expressions.

"Brenna, are y'all right?" Tara asked.

I wiped the tears from my eyes and took Luke's hand as he helped me up. "Yes, I'm fine Tara, no worries. Just lost my balance, I guess, and took us both down. And here I thought I was ready for the re-launch of *Dance Fever.*"

She laughed. "Aye, you may want to hold off on the audition tape for that one."

"Well, seein' as you ended that one prematurely, you still owe me a dance, young lady, and I'll come collectin' one of these days," Luke said playfully as he brushed the grass from his jeans. Shannon rolled her eyes discreetly, and I made a mental note to ask her what she knew about Luke.

"Of course," I agreed, "if my television contract allows for it," at which Tara pulled me away to sit under a nearby tree as the song ended and the band took a break.

"Well, someone's movin' in fast on the new girl, eh?" she said with excitement. I blushed again.

"Who is he?" I asked. "I mean I know his name, but what do you know about him?" Shannon sat down as Tara answered.

"Well, obviously, he's about the prettiest thing in town, but you can see that with yer own eyes, I'm sure. Always has been. He's a good bit older than me ... maybe twenty-five or so. I just graduated secondary this year, so he's a bit outta my league, ya know? Not that I haven't thought of it, don't mistake me, who wouldn't? But his little brother Matt and I have grown up together, so it would be weird."

"So, he's not with anyone?" I wasn't interested in dating anyone, but he definitely had me curious. He had an ability to unnerve me that I couldn't explain and had never experienced before, not even with Ben.

Tara grinned. "Not that I know of. Interested?" I could see she longed to be matchmaker.

"No, actually, I'm not," I said firmly. "But *he* seems to be, so I'm just curious about him."

She looked stunned. "You're not interested? Are you crazy? Do ya know how many girls in this town would kill to have Luke Dillon lookin' at them like he's been lookin' at you all night?"

"I'm not interested in dating anyone right now," I defended myself even as the thought of him watching me had me blushing again. "Besides, I'm on vacation, and I'm not a one-night-stand kind of girl. *If* I were interested," she raised an eyebrow, "and I'm not, I wouldn't want a long distance relationship, so there's no point."

"But have ya *seen* him?" she half pleaded.

"Yeah, it's completely cruel that a guy can be that gorgeous," I admitted. "But I'm really not interested."

Shannon absent-mindedly piped in, "You're better off," to which Tara raised her eyebrows.

I had to ask. "You don't seem to like him, Shannon." She seemed surprised that I'd noticed.

"Oh, I don't really know him well, just heard stuff." She dismissed it quickly and stood up. "I see a friend ... I'll catch y'later!"

I looked at Tara. "Was that weird?" They were friends, and I figured she could read Shannon better than I could.

"Um, yeah, I'm not sure what that was all about. I've never heard her say a cross word about Luke before. I always thought she had a crush on him. Although she seems pretty into David lately." She motioned toward Shannon who was obviously flirting with one of the twins across the street. "Still, probably sour grapes, right?"

"I guess," I agreed, but I wasn't so sure.

Well, if Luke comes collectin' for that dance, you'd better take him up on it, y'hear?" she said with feigned authority.

"Hmm ... maybe." I shrugged. "But like I said, I'm not really interested."

She sighed. I was doing my best to convince her, all the while trying even harder to convince *myself*. I knew I could play my widow card and get her off my case instantly, but I was the one who said I didn't want people pitying me, so it hardly seemed fair. We wandered around meeting more of Tara's friends and sampling more local flavors. Eventually I had to admit that I was ready for bed. So we headed back toward Rosie's, keeping an eye out for Shannon.

"Was she gonna meet you back at Rosie's?" I asked as we arrived at the pub.

"Aw, she's probably snoggin' David in some dark corner. I was hopin' we'd at least run into John, and he could walk us home." Tara lived a five-minute walk past the B&B. I was beginning to catch on to her interest in the other twin, John.

"Did he know you wanted him to walk with us?" I wondered aloud.

"Yeah, I asked him to meet us back here when the band stopped playin'." She paused to listen. "Course, they haven't stopped yet have they?" The fiddle and guitars could still be heard. At that moment, Jamie and Megan came around the bend.

"Jamie, have y'seen yer brothers?" Tara inquired.

"Not since they were spinnin' you and Shannon round the dance floor," he replied with a grin. "Would y'like to walk home with us, then?"

"You go ahead, Brenna," she said, completely oblivious to Megan's suspicious stare. "I'm goin' t'look for Shannon and the lads."

I was torn. My feet were sore from dancing, and I was dying for a good soak in the tub, but walking alone with Jamie and Megan was not appealing in the slightest.

My obvious hesitation prompted an unexpected response from Megan. "Come on, we'll walk y'home. 'Tis no big deal. Ya look tired."

I was surprised by her sudden change in attitude, but I was grateful because I had no desire to go back with Tara to find her friends.

"Okay, thanks. Go on, Tara. I'll walk with them." I said as I gave Tara a quick hug and thanked her for inviting me.

The walk back was surprisingly pleasant. Jamie oozed a quiet confidence that made conversation easy and comfortable. I noticed he looked at Megan differently than he had just a couple hours earlier, though. My guess was that she'd made it quite clear to him between then and now that she was certainly more than just his friend. He seemed pleased with their new understanding, but she continued to keep herself between us, just in case there was any confusion. Anna was waiting for me when I walked into the kitchen.

"So, did ya have a great time?" She smiled from her seat at the table. I joined her.

"I really did," I answered and knew I was beaming. "I had a blast. I danced all night long. Can you believe that?"

"I'm so glad," she said with misty eyes. "You deserve to have a blast, darlin'. So, who'd ya dance with?"

"Who *didn't* I dance with is more like it!" I laughed. "These Irish boys are all so friendly. I've never had so much attention in all my life. You'd think they'd never seen a girl before, but I know that's not true, because I saw plenty of very pretty girls. It's just weird." I told her about my numerous dance partners while avoiding any details about the one dance that landed me on my butt.

Anna laughed delightedly and put her hand over mine on the table. "Oh, Brenna, dear, you are such a riot!" I was confused.

"Me?" I asked.

"Yes, you. Ya have no idea what a beautiful girl you are, do ya?" She put her head in her hands and laughed again.

"Come on. I know I'm not ugly—but beautiful? I don't think so. I'm scrawny and short. I have huge lips that don't fit my face and goofy dimples. I'm no beauty," I insisted.

"You're wrong, dear. You are a beautiful girl, inside and out. We're taught to stress the importance of inner beauty, and that *is* more important, but you are one of the lucky ones who has both, dear. Did my son never tell ya how stunning you are?" she asked skeptically.

"Well, of course he did, but he *had* to think that. He was in love with me," I explained.

She shook her head. "So you think the twenty boys who lined up to dance with you were all in love with you?" She grinned.

"No." I shook my head.

"Did someone pay them to ask you to dance so you wouldn't feel bad, then?" She was thoroughly enjoying herself.

"Of course not." I rolled my eyes.

"Well, I'd say the most likely explanation is that you were the most striking young woman in town, and they couldn't help but ask you to dance." She rose from the table before I could argue and kissed my forehead. "Sleep tight, love."

I dragged my aching feet up the stairs and ran the water for a bath. As I immersed myself into the steaming tub of water, I mentally revisited my day. In all, I was very pleased with myself, if slightly embarrassed by Anna's conclusions. It felt like I had made more friends in one day than I had in the past six years. Later, as I drifted off to sleep, a certain twisted smile kept intruding on my thoughts. "Go away," I said aloud, but he didn't listen; he just slipped into my dreams.

Chapter Five

The next two weeks were a blur. Anna and I visited both Jamie's mom Elizabeth and Tara's mom Mary. Tea with Auntie Pat became a daily routine, and I laughed when I recalled my initial fear of her. She was a feisty yet precious old woman. I don't know if it was our similar size or what, but we connected in a way that surprised me. It was as if she understood me at times better than I understood myself. I was now under strict instructions to refer to her simply as "Patsy" and as far as I could tell, I was the only one allowed to do so.

We had in-depth talks about her life growing up in Millway. She talked of what things were like "in the old days." She'd gone to Cork City at fifteen to apprentice at a bakery, coming home on weekends but spending all week living above the bakery. She worked in the Millway bakery for a few years until she married Jack Maloney, the new young doctor in town. He had bought a cookie at the bakery every day for months before he got the nerve to ask her to a dance. She almost said no just because it had taken him so long. But she really did like him, so she went to the dance. They were engaged two weeks later and married two months after that. Talk about a whirlwind romance!

I loved hearing all her stories. She talked about marriage: how you had to work at it every day. She talked about having babies and raising them right. She took the opportunity more than once to tell me I should be getting myself to church on Sundays. I always laughed and told her I wasn't Catholic. This never satisfied her, but she'd drop it until the next time.

I did begin to see her lapses in memory, though. She'd often tell me stories she'd already told. Her long-term memory seemed excellent, as each time she told a story it was exactly the same. But she'd routinely forget things we'd just spoken about or done together. I knew this was extremely frustrating for her. She was fiercely independent, and the thought of growing dependent on anyone was a thorn in her side.

I empathized with that sentiment completely, which was why I spoke with Sam about the waitress job at Rosie's. I had agreed to stay in Millway another month due to Anna's puppy dog eyes and the fact that I was enjoying myself immensely. Because Sam was in a bind and I had a lot of experience, he agreed to take me on temporarily. It was a little sketchy, because I didn't have any kind of work permit, but Sam didn't seem to be looking over his shoulder for immigration officers, so I decided not to worry about it either. Bettie fussed over me getting a job when I was supposed to be "on holiday," but Patsy told her to mind her own business—with a wink in my direction.

I shadowed Liz, the girl who was leaving, for two mornings, and then I was on my own as she went off to Limerick to prepare for school. I was surprised to realize that I had no desire at the moment to return to school. I had been an art education major, but that seemed like a lifetime ago. I found it refreshing to not have everything planned out for the next year. It was a new experience for me to be "flying by the seat of my pants," but I rather enjoyed it.

A great side benefit of working at Rosie's was getting to know the locals. While we did a decent breakfast business, lunch was the specialty. There were three servers on for lunch, including me, and some days that was barely enough. Katie, Sarah, Brigit, and I covered the six lunch shifts between us (Rosie's was closed Sundays), and Tara alternated behind the bar with a guy named Danny. I had worked everywhere from a greasy spoon to a country club, so I was up to speed in no time. Apparently I was doing well because Sam routinely told me I was not allowed to leave the country anytime soon.

Several of my "dance partners" stopped in regularly, and more than one asked me out. I laughed, as Anna's unlikely theory seemed more plausible by the day. Either these Irish boys were crazy, or I was using a broken mirror. The one guy that I both wanted and didn't want to see was Luke Dillon. The other ones were easy to say no to. I just explained that I was "on a break" from relationships. But Luke was more persistent and, unfortunately, much more tempting. He didn't care that I was on a break. He came by every few days with his dazzling smile just to "check and see if yer break is over yet."

It was annoying and thrilling at the same time. I knew Tara thought I must be made of stone to keep resisting him, but something told me I should be very careful around Luke. So I continued to brush him off and did my best to focus my attention on my job. I had to be at Rosie's by 7:00 a.m., so I began getting up with the sun each day, spending some quiet time on my terrace and getting in a quick run before getting ready for work.

The craziest days were when a tour bus would stop in town, headed for the famous Blarney Stone. One day, two tour busses rolled in around 11:00 a.m., and within fifteen minutes we were swamped. Each of us had seven tables, and Sam himself was bussing and filling drinks for us. Tara was completely weeded at the bar until Tommy, a regular, stepped in and gave her a hand.

By 1:00 p.m., however, the rush was over and the busses were gone, so we all sat down and ate lunch together before we cleaned up and readied the pub for the dinner crowd. Apparently, most of the locals stayed away for lunch on "tour bus days" but then came out in force for dinner. Fortunately, my shift was over at 3:00 p.m., and I had made plans with Tara to do some sightseeing of my own, after tea with Patsy, of course.

At my request, Tara took me to see the Blarney Stone, which she warned was mostly a waste of time. She appreciated the history of it all, but as a tourist attraction she said it was "kinda lame." Sadly, I had to agree. I basically paid ten euros to walk up one hundred plus steps. The view was beautiful, and the 600-year-old castle was amazing to look at, but the Blarney Stone itself was uninspiring. If I wanted to actually kiss it, which I did not, I would have had to hang upside down from the castle tower to reach it. No, thank you. Still, it was entertaining to watch the tourists from a local girl's perspective. Although I was technically a tourist, as Tara entertained me with stories of goofy tourist mishaps, I was stunned to realize how much this already felt like home.

As usual, Anna was waiting for me when I returned. I told her about our night and filled her in on the eventful day at work.

"You really seem to be enjoyin' yerself, dear," she prompted.

"I am," I agreed. "I can see why you were so glad to come home."

"Have you given any thought to how much longer you'd like to stay then?"

"Not specifically. What about you?" I asked.

Anna paused. "Well, I have thought a lot about it. Brenna, you are my only family left in the States. My family is here; my history is here. I've decided I'm goin' to stay."

She looked at me with an unreadable expression. The way she said it, I wasn't sure what that meant for me. Was she asking me to stay, or was she assuming I'd go back to New York? I couldn't tell, and I was almost afraid to ask. I looked away as unexpected tears burned hot in my eyes. I told her I needed to run to the bathroom, and I literally ran to my room and locked the door. What was wrong with me? *"Get a grip!"* I scolded myself, but it did no good. I put my face into my pillow and began to sob.

A short time later there was a soft rap at my door and a jiggle of the handle. "Brenna, open up, dear," Anna quietly pleaded. I wiped my face with the back of my hand and unlocked the door. She wrapped her arms around me and, against my will, I began to cry again. I hated myself for being such a weakling. I had no idea why I was crying, yet I couldn't stop myself. Anna held me for a few minutes until I calmed down, and we sat down on the bed to talk.

"I don't know what's wrong with me," I whined with a sniffle. "I'm not a crier. What's my problem?"

"You don't know why you're upset?" she questioned.

"Not really. I don't know what your decision means for me, so I feel a little unsettled, I guess. But it's not a reason to cry like a baby!" I was so confused.

"What do you *think* my decision means for you?" she prodded.

"Are you saying I should go back?" I asked with a lump in my throat.

"I'm sayin' you should do what you want to do, and I'm doin' what I want to do. I don't want to influence you one way or the other. I want you to make the decision that's best for you. You have brothers in the States." I rolled my eyes. I hardly knew my brothers. "However," she continued, "you will always have a home with me if you desire." Yet again, the waterworks began. I hated not having control of my emotions. "Do you want to go back then?" She misread my tears.

"No," I answered quickly and knew it was true.

"Then why are y'cryin' again, dear?" she asked.

"Relief." It was the first word that came to my mind. I wasn't even sure what I meant by it. Anna seemed to figure it out before I did.

"Ah, I see. I'm an idiot for not seein' it sooner. Did you think I didn't want you to stay with me, love?"

I thought about it, then nodded. "Yeah, I guess that's why I got upset. I thought you were telling me you were staying but I should go."

She nodded. "I'm so sorry. You've had so many loved ones leave you." The hard truth stung, and I felt the hot tears yet again. "But as long as I have any say in it, I'll never leave you, Brenna." Tears streamed down my cheeks, and she pulled me into a warm embrace.

"Thank you," I whispered. "I love you."

"I love you, too." She pushed me back to look me in the eyes. "God gave me the daughter I always wanted." She wiped my tears with her hands, and I couldn't help chuckling at the thought of how my red, blotchy, tearstained face must look. I was still troubled by something, though.

"You're an Irish citizen, right?" I asked, and she nodded. "So, you won't have a problem staying, but am I allowed to stay here? My visa is only for three months. Every time I think about staying, I get stuck with the legality of it all. I'm not even supposed to be working, you know?" I chewed my lip, a nervous habit.

"I've done some lookin' into that. You've never talked much about your mum and dad, but I seem to remember you sayin' your mum was born in Ireland, right?"

"Yeah, I think she was born in a small town somewhere outside of Dublin."

"Excellent!" She smiled widely as if she was about to watch me open a present. "Congratulations, my dear, you are already an Irish citizen."

"What?" I was lost.

She leaned in closer to me as if to emphasize her point, "Because yer mum is Irish, you are already, by Irish law, a citizen!" she explained. "We'll have to figure out what kind of paperwork is required. But the law is clear, love." She paused to let it sink in. "So, welcome home then!"

I felt warm all over. There was nothing holding me in New York and so many things were pulling me to this enchanted little island. Once, I had said that my home was where Anna was. And while that was still true, I knew I was beginning to put down my own roots here, and for the first time in almost a year, I was excited for whatever the future held.

"Yes, home, where the pink houses are," I smiled.

Chapter Six

"Warning, Brenna!" Tara said in a hushed tone. "Look who's just showed up." She nodded toward the door of the pub. It was Luke. For the first few weeks I'd worked at Rosie's, he had been a constant fixture, coming in every day for lunch, sitting in my section and unashamedly flirting with me. He was relentless and I enjoyed it, but I truly wasn't ready for a relationship. My refusals didn't seem to bother him, but one day he just stopped coming. It seemed he had left town altogether. I missed him at first, but it had been a good month now, so I was surprised to see him.

"Hey, stranger." I smiled as I sat down in the booth opposite him.

"Ah, Brenna, sure an yer a sight fer sore eyes!" He grinned, and I discovered that his absence had increased the potency of his smile. My stomach fluttered once again in his presence.

I returned his smile with practiced ease, though. "What have you been up to lately, Luke? I haven't seen you in a while." I acted casual, as if it had been a couple days instead of a month.

"Oh, this and that," he evaded, and I raised my eyebrow in dissatisfaction at his answer.

He noticed and added, "My brother lives up in Limerick, runs a pub up there, and he was short-handed for a while. I just helped him out is all." It seemed a reasonable enough explanation. "Why Brenna, dear, if I didn't

39

know better, I'd think ya missed me!" He smiled full on now, obviously pleased with the thought. I realized I'd missed his attention, and that embarrassed me. My cheeks flared without my permission.

"Of course I did, Luke. You're my best tipper!" I recovered and shot a mischievous grin his way as I stood to take his order. "Now what do you want today?"

He grinned back, and I knew my wording had been a mistake. Quicker than I could react, he stood and wrapped his arms around my waist and peered into my stunned eyes. "You know exactly what I want, Brenna. Won't ya give me a chance? Let me take y'out tonight?"

His sudden intensity caught me off guard, and without thinking, I said yes. Before I could change my mind, he quickly kissed my cheek, said he'd meet me at Rosie's at seven, and was gone.

"What was that all about?" Tara rushed to my side, her eyes lit with excitement.

"I guess I just agreed to go out with Luke." My stomach began to do somersaults again, and this time it was not due to Luke's striking smile. I had never been on a date with anyone but Ben, and I was suddenly scared silly.

"Finally!" she said in mock exasperation. Her expression suddenly turned to one of concern as the color drained from my face and I took a seat.

"I don't feel well," I managed as I put my head down on the table.

"What on earth is wrong with you?" Tara asked. "Are y'worried about the date, then?"

"No," I lied. "I just feel sick all of a sudden. Maybe something I ate?" I did my best to throw her off the scent of my fear, and she bought it.

"Sam!" she called out. "All right with you if Brenna takes off early? She's not feelin' well."

"Ya gonna cover for her then, Tara?" Sam yelled from back.

"Aye, got it covered." She clutched my arm and pulled me from the booth while whispering, "Listen here, missy, you get home and take a nap. You've got a hot date tonight, and I don't want ya missin' it, hear?" With that I found myself walking home, taking deep breaths to calm myself. Why was it that a person could have a firm command on her emotions for years and then abruptly lose all sense of control? I despised this relatively new defect and wanted desperately to have my old, steely nerves back.

Bettie and Anna were having tea in the kitchen when I walked in. "Yer home early," they said in unison followed by laughter. They'd been raised almost as sisters and had grown very close again over the last couple months. Both were also widows now and likely took comfort in each other's empathy. The fact that they were now saying the same things and finishing each other's sentences was humorous to us all.

I smiled weakly. "Not feeling too great. Just gonna go lie down for a bit," I said as I strode through the kitchen without a pause.

I splashed cold water on my face and did indeed curl up under the covers. I'd always found it difficult to take a nap during the daytime. But with guests coming and going all the time, I had recently discovered I'd fall asleep within minutes if I covered my head with a dense pillow to block out all noise and light. Even when I had a lot on my mind, it usually knocked me out in no time.

Three hours later, I had almost left the house without notice, when Anna's voice pulled me up short. "Brenna, are y'feelin' better, love?" she said as she entered the kitchen.

"Yeah, thanks. Must have been something I ate," I assured her.

"Yer headed out then?" she asked.

"I'm meeting friends at the pub for a bite," I was afraid to tell her the truth. One of the reasons I had resisted Luke's prior advances was that while I didn't think I was ready to date yet, I also wasn't sure if *Anna* would be ready for me to date yet. How would she feel about it? I didn't know and certainly didn't want to discuss it at the moment.

"Well, have fun, dear. We won't wait up," she joked with a smile.

I waved as a pang of guilt rippled through me: Guilt over lying? Guilt over dating? I wasn't sure which, but I quickly switched gears as I headed down the path toward town. I had to mentally prepare for this. What was Luke expecting? I didn't even know where we were going. I had dressed casually in my typical jeans and T-shirt. I didn't want to appear to have put much effort into it. I did, of course, do my hair and spend a ridiculous amount of time primping in front of the mirror. I wanted to play it cool, but there was no reason not to look good doing so. Besides, Luke really was one of the best-looking guys I had met. I didn't want people whispering as we walked by: "What in the world is he doing with *her*?"

I gulped as I caught sight of Luke at the bar. So this was the result when *he* put effort into it. His hair looked much like it normally did but had a bit of gel or something in it, giving him a more polished look. He had on a lime green button down shirt that set off his brown eyes. He was wearing jeans and, oddly, a pair of cowboy boots. But the overall effect was almost intoxicating. Not for the first time, I cursed his ridiculous good looks.

However, watching him smile and head directly toward me, apparently oblivious to all the eyes on him, gave me a rush of exhilaration and maybe pride? *That's right girls. He's with me.*

"I was afraid ya might not show." He eyed me with a rare vulnerable look that was quickly replaced by an appraising stare. "Yer lookin' mighty fine t'night, love." He smiled wickedly, and I felt inclined to slap him for whatever thoughts he left unsaid.

"Thanks," I said as I rolled my eyes, and he laughed, fully guessing my violent thoughts. I held back a compliment of my own on the suspicion that he knew exactly how good he looked. It was a powerful tool that he used, and while I enjoyed the view, I didn't like the power it held over me.

"So, where are we going?" I asked.

"Y'don't know?" he said with a fake surprise.

"Umm, dinner and a movie?" I guessed.

"Boring." He frowned.

"Rodeo?" I quipped with a glance at his boots.

"Ah, now yer gettin' close. Do y'remember, I said ya owed me a dance the night we met?"

I was suddenly excited. I had loved dancing, and while the thought of doing so with Luke all night was somewhat dizzying, I couldn't help but show my enthusiasm. "Really? That's a great idea, Luke!" I was smiling from ear to ear like a kid on Christmas.

"Geez, Brenna, if I'd known you'd react like this, I'd have tempted y'with dancin' ages ago!" He guided me toward the door, his hand hot on my lower back. Again, my heart pounded relentlessly.

Luke drove us to Cork City where a friend of his was having a party in a place called The Attic. It was a loft space that was rented out for private parties. There was a large dance floor, various couches and chairs scattered about, and a bar at one corner. The DJ was saying something into the mic when we walked in, but all I noticed was the sea of cowboy hats. This was obviously a theme party, and I was severely underdressed.

"Why didn't you tell me?" I turned toward Luke, who was now wearing a hat of his own and holding one out toward me. "Where...?" I stammered.

He interrupted. "I had the hats stashed here, but these took more connivin'." He pulled a pair of brown leather boots from a bag he'd slung over his shoulder at the car. I sat down and pulled on the perfectly fitting boots.

"How did you manage this?" I said, duly impressed.

"I called Tara, she guessed yer size, and I borrowed these from a friend."

"Impressive, Luke. Very impressive." I smiled, genuinely pleased. He had put in a lot of effort to impress me, and it was working. He set down his bag and whirled me out onto the dance floor. I faltered at first. "It's been a while," I mumbled, embarrassed.

"You'll pick it up again," he assured me. "Don't they say it's just like ridin' a bike?" And there was that wicked smile again.

I laughed and rolled my eyes. "There'll be no 'bike-riding,' Luke." I tried to look stern but it was hard to do just inches from those eyes.

"No, no, just dancin'." He pulled me close and reminded me, "'Remember, look at my face, not down. And it really does help if ya relax and lean into me. Just to make the dancin' easier, of course," he teased.

I followed his instructions, and we began flying around the floor. I found it hard to believe I'd never known how much I loved to dance. This had become one of my absolute favorite things to do, and I had to admit that dancing in Luke's arms was more than pleasant. He introduced me to a number of his friends. Several asked to cut in, but Luke refused each one and told me he was going to be selfish with me and there was nothing I could do about it. I laughed. I had no desire to dance with anyone else. I was having way too much fun with him, and he knew it.

Eventually my feet gave out. I wasn't used to the boots, and I knew I would pay tomorrow for abusing my feet tonight. Luke offered me a drink several times, and each time I opted for Coke. Finally he asked me, "Are y'opposed to the drink then?"

"You mean alcohol in general? No, I don't think so. I'm not much of a drinker, that's all. I'm not even legal in the States, you know."

"Ya are here, love. Have a pint!" He pushed again.

"No, thanks," I said firmly. "I really don't like the taste." He looked disappointed but acquiesced. He watched as I looked around for a clock. "What time is it?" I was worried about getting home too late and arousing Anna's suspicions.

"'Bout ten. Old Miss Patsy give ya a curfew?" he chided.

"No," I said with a smirk. "But I have to work in the morning, and I don't want to be out too late." It was true, but my main concern was getting home before my willpower to resist Luke failed me.

We said our goodbyes and headed back home. As we drove, I asked him more about his brother in Limerick and his other family members. I was relieved he didn't ask me about my family, and before I knew it, we were pulling into town. He parked on the street near the B&B but didn't pull in the driveway. I thought at first he must have picked up that I was hiding our date from Anna. That thought vanished when he leaned over and planted his mouth on mine. I could taste the beer and instinctively pushed him away.

"No, Luke … I'm not ready for this …" was all I managed to say before he wrapped his hand behind my head and pulled me back to him. I tried again to push him away, but I could tell he was hungry. His intensity shocked me, but even more shocking was my response. For a few seconds I gave in and kissed him back urgently, until a cohesive thought ran through my brain and I realized what I was doing. I had never kissed anyone but Ben. I was unprepared to *enjoy* kissing someone else. I pushed him away harder this time and immediately opened my door and staggered out. As I turned around to apologize and say goodbye, I was met with a furious glare, and before I could say a word, he peeled away from the corner with the passenger door still hanging wide open.

Chapter Seven

"So he didn't say *anything?* Just drove away?" Tara was shocked with my story. I got the impression she was beginning to see me as her own personal soap opera. I had managed to sneak into the house the night before and go to bed with no one the wiser, but there was no avoiding Tara at work the next morning. She had insisted I tell her everything, with no detail left out. So, while we set up for lunch, I spilled it… the whole story. She was entranced until I got to the part about me getting out of the car. I could tell she didn't like that part. Yet she also seemed to disapprove of Luke's hasty departure and was dying to know what might happen next.

"Swear you will tell me if he calls or somethin'?" she pleaded.

"Of course," I promised. "I hope he does. I still want to apologize. I wasn't trying to lead him on or anything. I just lost control for a minute … but I *did* try to tell him no." I had replayed the scene in my head a hundred times since. I truly didn't think I was teasing him. Maybe he'd had more to drink than I'd realized. Maybe he wouldn't even remember. I had a feeling that was wishful thinking.

That evening, Tara and I came back to the pub for karaoke night. I had no intention of singing, but Tara was a regular participant, and I was amused just listening to the various would-be Sinatras and Celine Deons. I hadn't noticed him come in, but I saw Tara's eyes widen as she was belting her way through some twenty-year-old Whitney Houston song. As I turned to see what she was staring at, I caught sight of Luke with his arm draped around some pretty blonde girl I'd seen at Rosie's before. They were whispering to each other and laughing. I suppressed a wave of jealousy that I had no right to feel. I watched several pairs of female eyes follow the couple's movement toward the bar.

I was on edge from that point until the singing stopped and people began to filter out into the street. Tara was talking with John O'Conor in a corner booth. Jamie and Megan had stopped over to say hi to me but had now headed out, and I was left sitting alone. I took a deep breath and headed toward the bar where Luke and his date were still sitting.

"Hey, Luke," I interrupted. "Can I talk to you for just a second?" I asked. He looked at me coolly and turned toward the blonde. He whispered something to her and she did not appear happy as she shot a killer look my way.

"Yeah, sure. This is Char." He nodded toward his date.

"Hi, I'm Brenna." I smiled and she did not. Then Luke got up from the bar and followed me over to the corner.

"Whaddya need?" he asked in a neutral voice.

"I just wanted to apologize for last night," I began.

He shrugged. "No big deal."

"Well, I just …" I hesitated, unsure of how to say what I wanted to say. I didn't want to take all the blame, but at the same time, I felt bad for how I'd acted and wanted to make sure he knew that. "I wasn't trying to tease you, ya know? I tried to tell you I wasn't ready for that," I explained.

"Like I said, Brenna,"—he was playing it *way* cool—"it's no big deal. I'll see y'round."

He headed back to Char, who'd been boring holes into his head with her laser-like stare. I stood rooted where I was, shocked by his complete brush-off. I expected him to be upset, but he was acting as if he hadn't just spent months pursuing me. I hated the feeling of someone being angry with me, but shouldn't *I* be the one upset with *him*? He was the one acting like a jerk, so why did I have the urge to run back to him and beg him to forgive me? *Don't be such a people-pleaser!* I silently scolded myself. It was ridiculous, and I refused to give in to such a pathetic desire.

Instead, I found Tara and told her I wanted to leave. She was so absorbed in conversation with John that I knew she hadn't seen a thing.

John walked home with us, and my house was first, so I didn't even have a chance to tell her what had happened. But all of the night's drama left my mind as soon as I walked in the kitchen door. Bettie was yelling at the top of her lungs, "Mum! If ya can hear me, *answer me!*" Her voice had a hysterical edge to it.

"What's going on?" I asked Anna, who was on the phone.

She put her hand over the receiver and whispered with wide eyes, "Auntie Pat's missin'."

Chapter Eight

They had been looking for her for over an hour before I got there. Anna was on the phone with the police but filled me in when she hung up and knew the police were on their way. No one had seen Patsy for at least four hours. When Bettie realized she was gone, she searched the house, searched the gardens, called friends … but no one had seen her.

Apparently she'd gone missing once before, but she had just been over at Elizabeth O'Conor's house having tea and was furious with Bettie for making a big stink about it. This time was different. Tom, the groundskeeper, had seen her in the garden that afternoon, but he'd been the last to see her. Now it was dark, and everyone was very worried. Tom had already been scouring the back acreage with a flashlight, with no luck.

The police arrived quickly and set up in the kitchen. They laid maps of the surrounding area across the counters and asked Bettie several questions about people that Patsy might think to visit as well as places she may have an emotional attachment to. All this was done with great speed, and before I knew it, we were outside looking and shouting her name.

Each of us went with one of the four officers, searching in a pattern that appeared random but was really planned precisely. They had divided the search area into grids on the map and each group was searching a particular grid. Our biggest concern was a large stream that ran through the back of Patsy's property. It was all I could do to keep from running straight to it to make sure she wasn't there, but I understood the rationale behind the officers' organized search. Before long, all the neighbors had come out with flashlights and joined the search effort.

We looked for what must have been at least an hour when the signal horn was blown somewhere to our left. We took off running toward the noise and found a crowd gathered and a disheveled and disoriented Patsy yelling for Tom to get out of her way so she could find her fishing pole. If I hadn't been so frazzled from the search, I would have burst out laughing at the sight and sound of her. Bettie and Anna hadn't arrived yet, so I hoped she'd recognize me in her current state.

"Patsy!" I shouted as I ran toward her. "Hey, I have your fishing pole back at the house. I didn't know you were looking for it." I played along and she relaxed.

"Well, what are ya doin' with my fishin' pole, young lady? Here I was, blamin' the wee folk, mischievous little leprechauns that they are. But I'd have lent it to ya if ye'd just asked me." I'd never been so glad to be scolded by the old dear before. I wrapped a blanket around her, and we led the procession back toward the house. Bettie and Anna both caught up with us before we got home and, despite all her protests, gave Patsy several hugs before we could begin walking again. Surprisingly, Bettie held her tongue and just walked in silence next to her mother, deep in thought.

At home, Bettie took her upstairs to bed, and Anna and I helped the policemen gather their things. We thanked them repeatedly and both collapsed together on the couch when everyone had finally left. Bettie came into the living room with downcast eyes. When she sat down, the brave face she'd put on for her mum crumpled into a tearful mess.

"What am I supposed to do with her?" She was desperate for an answer.

Anna put an arm around her. "We'll figure somethin' out. We'll just have to take turns keepin' an eye on her right now, and we'll go from there. Do you think she'll remember this?" I wondered the same thing.

"She's already forgotten it." Bettie sighed. "She went into the bathroom to tidy up and get ready for bed, and when she came out, she looked surprised to see me and asked why I was in her room." She put her head into her hands and slowly shook it back and forth. For the first time, I understood the lock I'd seen high up on the outside of Patsy's bedroom door.

"That's why you installed the lock?" I asked.

"Aye, just this past year. She won't admit it, but she's in the early stage of Alzheimer's, and I was worried somethin' like this might happen. I lock her door at night and wake up early to unlock it before she notices. It's the only way I can actually feel comfortable enough to fall asleep. At least I know she can't wander in the night. Did y'notice she has trouble with her words from time to time? She forgets things that have just happened. The other day she started tellin' me to get ready for school, for Pete's sake!"

I felt guilty. I'd been so focused on myself lately, I hadn't noticed how quickly she was declining. We hadn't even had our daily tea in weeks. "I'll do some research online … see if I can find some ideas on how to keep her safe," I said. "Should we make a schedule of who will keep an eye on her when?" I determined to be more vigilant and even put my now-flourishing social life on hold as a penance for my lack of attention to Patsy. Bettie didn't respond but stared off with a blank look.

Anna answered, "I think we can just make sure someone's always here. If any of us leave the house, we just connect with each other beforehand so we're covered. For now, I think we all need to get to bed."

We agreed and headed to our rooms. I was exhausted, but of course I couldn't sleep, even with my usually infallible pillow trick. After tossing and turning for an agonizing hour, I gave up on sleep, grabbed my laptop, and began looking up info on Alzheimer's.

The next morning, it was as if nothing had happened, at least on the surface. Patsy, Bettie, and Anna got ready for church as always. And while Patsy had habitually badgered me to go, today, to her surprise, I relented. Something about almost losing her the day before had me feeling both a little scared and sentimental. I hadn't gone before because I wasn't Catholic, and the few times I'd gone to Anna's church at home, I felt really awkward. I never attended church as a kid, although my mom had been raised a strict Catholic. She had some horror stories about parochial school and stopped going to church before I was born.

Ben had started going to a non-denominational church when we were in high school. A friend of his invited him to the youth group, and he loved it. I didn't go at first. I wasn't real big on God, blaming him for the death of my parents. I teased Ben about becoming a "Jesus freak," but I eventually broke down and went with him. I could see why he liked it; it was young and vibrant. Most of the kids seemed genuine and different from the kids at school, and I always left feeling better than when I arrived.

It took me longer than Ben, but I eventually came to the point where I truly wanted a relationship with God. I let go of the anger I had carried toward Him and asked Him to be a real presence in my life. That was when I started going to church regularly. It was just before we got married, and Ben was thrilled. Anna was glad that both Ben and I were going to church, but I knew she would have preferred that we went to a Catholic church.

She had gone to St. Patrick's at least twice a week ever since I'd known her, but Joe was strictly a "holiday attender." I remembered Anna telling the story of the one Easter he went to Mass, stuck his hand in his suit pocket, and pulled out the program from the previous Easter. *Busted!* We all laughed about it, but I always suspected that it bothered her that he didn't share her commitment or enthusiasm.

That wasn't the case here. Both Bettie and Patsy were devoted Catholics. I'd walked in on numerous religious discussions between the three of them, but always felt completely unqualified to join in. According to Anna, the Catholic Church here was a little different from the one she was used to and that concerned her at first. She seemed to have adjusted, though.

I stopped going to church when Ben died. I just couldn't find it in me to go alone. I did miss it, but I didn't think I'd find anything like it here in Millway ... certainly not in a Catholic church. So I had avoided going altogether until now.

Just for Patsy, I found myself putting on a skirt and sweater and walking the short distance to Sacred Heart of Millway. It was a beautiful, old building made of dark-brown stones and stained glass. The ladies apparently had regular seats on the fifteenth pew. I just followed along and took in the sights. There were plaques on the walls with Roman numerals on them, all depicting some part of Jesus' life, it seemed. Patsy noticed my interest and told me they were the "stations of the cross." She seemed to think that was enough of an explanation, and I was fine with that.

Before long, the part I dreaded began. It was up, down, cross yourself, kneel ... I felt self-conscious and out of place because I didn't know what to do when. I was pleasantly surprised by the music though. It was still formal but also a little bit folksy, and the woman leading the singing had a beautiful voice. She wasn't easy to see, as she was off to one side, but when I finally did get a better glimpse, I was shocked to see Jamie's girlfriend, Megan, who I had met at the street festival, standing at the microphone. That would explain Jamie's beaming smile a few pews ahead of us. I took a better look around and noticed many familiar faces. Tara and Liam were near the front with their mum, Mary. I saw most of my regulars from Rosie's as well as most of the friends Tara had introduced me to over the past few months.

Now I was feeling guilty. I had been sleeping in every Sunday, not even trying to make it to church. I thought of it as something for the older women, and yet clearly I was wrong. It appeared that at least half the congregation was under thirty.

Once Father Tim began his homily, I knew why. He was fantastic. I'd met him before, but I had no idea he could preach like that. What a speaker! He had everyone on the edge of their seats for twenty minutes. He mixed in storytelling with humor while explaining a passage from the Bible so that it made complete sense to me. From the corner of my eye, I could see Patsy smiling at me. She knew from my expression that I was hooked. I would look forward to going to church from now on. I figured it would be worth learning all the up-and-down stuff because just being there made me feel better than I had in a long time.

Toward the end of the service, they did communion, and I stayed in my seat. I didn't fully understand it and wanted to make sure I did before I walked up there and stood face to face with the priest. Besides, I had the feeling I had to be an official Catholic to do that. I'd just take it one step at a time—like getting to church two weeks in a row.

"Well," Anna asked as we left the church, "what did ya think?"

"I'm surprised," I admitted. "I liked it a lot."

Anna looped her arm through mine as we walked. "I'm glad. I thought ya would. It wasn't what I expected either. It's pretty different from St. Patrick's. It's more alive, more ... I don't know. He's quite a preacher, isn't he?"

"Yeah, honestly I always had trouble following the pastor at home. But I really got what Father Tim was saying. He kind of made the Bible come alive," I responded.

"Well, of course he did!" quipped Patsy. "That's his job!"

I chuckled as Bettie rolled her eyes behind her mum's back like a teenager. Some habits don't die with age.

Patsy added, "Not to say he hasn't gotten in trouble before for his newfangled ways. But it suits me just fine. The church has grown so much since he came, he must be doin' somethin' right!"

We walked in a thoughtful silence. I was digesting more of what I'd heard that morning. The message was about the "Prodigal Son." I'd heard the story before of the selfish son who squandered his inheritance, while the dutiful older brother stayed by his father's side. When the runaway son hit rock bottom and woke up, he went home, hoping to be a servant in his father's house. Instead, his father welcomed him with open arms and celebrated his return. The older brother was jealous and furious. All of this was familiar to me, but Father Tim had made it personal.

"Who are you in this story?" he had asked the congregation. I didn't know. I certainly wasn't the father; the priest had been clear that he symbolized God. That left only two options, and I didn't like either of them. I pictured myself before I went to Ben's church and decided I probably was like the prodigal. I had been trying to do everything my way. And it was hard to change that. I had made strides until Ben died. Then I kind of stalled. As I was mulling all these things over, my thoughts were interrupted by a whispered argument to my right.

"You may not remember, Mum, but it happened, and I have many witnesses!" Bettie hissed in annoyance.

"Hogwash!" replied Patsy in full voice.

"Brenna?" Bettie pleaded with her eyes, and I sighed. Lately, Patsy seemed to listen to me better than she did to Bettie or Anna. This was especially frustrating for Bettie, but she was learning to use it to her advantage.

We stopped walking so I could get Patsy's full attention. "Patsy, I know you don't want to hear this, but you *have* been forgetting things, and last night was horrible. We couldn't find you for hours, and it was getting so cold outside." She peered into my eyes looking for a lie. "When we did find you, you told me you were looking for your fishing pole. Patsy, do you even have a fishing pole?" A spark of remembrance lit her eyes.

"Used to," she mumbled and lowered her eyes in defeat. I hated to break her spirit, but this was important. We had to figure out how to keep her safe. I'd found some ideas online but wasn't ready to share them with her. I wanted to discuss them with the others first. "I don't do it on purpose, and I don't remember, so how am I supposed to stop it?" she said in an angry but defeated voice.

"We don't know yet, Auntie Pat, but we're workin' on it," Anna said. "Just please let us know if ya want to go somewhere. We'll make sure someone goes with you."

Patsy began walking at a brisk pace, mumbling something about babysitters and effectively ending the conversation.

Over the next few weeks, Patsy seemed a little subdued and was quieter than normal. She didn't have any more "wandering" episodes, but we were all on heightened alert just in case. I discovered a company called LifeSave that offered a bracelet with a tracking device, which was intended to avoid the exact kind of incident we'd had that frightening night. It could be worn on the ankle or wrist, and while it was slightly cumbersome, bracelets like this had saved numerous lives worldwide. There was a monthly subscription fee that kept everything active, and if ever Patsy turned up missing, we would simply call LifeSave, and the authorities would be notified with her GPS location.

We had expected her to rail against the idea of wearing a tracking bracelet, but she'd surprised us all by taking to it without issue. I realized later that she figured we'd ease up on the "babysitting," as she called it, if we felt she was safer with the bracelet. And she was right, as the tension did ease up, and life became a little more normal again. I met more of the extended family. Cousins from near-by towns came to visit with Anna and reminisce. She was helping Bettie and Patsy with the B&B and I was dividing my time between hanging out with Patsy and working at Rosie's.

I had intentionally put the brakes on my social life for a bit. I still hung out with Tara some but I stuck close to home more often than not. I was no longer a novelty so the guys in town seemed to have lost interest, which was fine with me. Luke seemed to be dating Char but he began acting more normal toward me. He wasn't quite as flirty as he had been, but he was at least friendly, and I was polite in return.

One day at work, Father Tim specifically requested to sit in my section. "Hello, Brenna, how are ya?" he asked as I approached the table.

"Great, thanks for asking. How about yerself? Are y'well?" I almost laughed as I heard myself slip into Irish brogue. Apparently, it was contagious, and I was suddenly self-conscious, worried he'd think I was poking fun at him.

"I am blessed, that's fer sure," he replied with a grin. "I've seen you at Mass these past few weeks. Glad you've joined us."

"Yeah, Patsy finally got me there. I had no idea I was missing such an incredible speaker all this time, or I would've come sooner!"

He looked down at the table, apparently uncomfortable with the praise. "Well, if yer hearin' anythin' special, it's not comin' from me but from the Master, y'know? Still, I appreciate the compliment. I'm doin' my best to share what he's done fer me." He paused. "Yer not Catholic, though, are ya?" he asked without a hint of accusation, just curiosity.

"Uh, no. I guess I'd be Protestant," I responded.

He chuckled and whispered, "Y'might not want to say that too loudly. Bit of bad history, so to speak, between the Catholics and Protestants 'round here." Then, no longer whispering, he said, "No, I just noticed ya hadn't come up for communion, so that meant either yer livin' in sin or yer not Catholic." Again he chuckled.

I wasn't sure if he was serious or joking, but he moved on. "I hear yer from New York, then?"

That again. Everyone assumed New York meant the city. "Yeah, but far from the Big Apple," I replied.

"Aye," he said, "My sister lives in Rochester. That's not too far from where you lived, is it?"

"Oh, no, that's very close. 'Bout an hour or so," I answered.

"So you've got no family back there?" he inquired. Although I probably would have regarded these questions as a bit nosy, he was so genuine that I felt like he truly cared. I answered several more questions before I finally got his lunch order from him. It was a very slow day, so I had a bit of time to chat with him before he left. By the time he did, I'd tentatively agreed to come to the Thursday night college group called Veritas, which, he explained, was the Latin word for *truth.*

"Well, you and Father Tim were talkin' up a storm, there," Tara said as she wiped down the bar before we left for the day.

"Yeah, he's very nice," I responded. "He invited me to a college group on Thursday. Do you go?"

"No, I help my sister with her kids on Thursdays. But I think Jamie and Megan go," she answered.

That was a pleasant surprise. Having someone that I knew there would make me a little less nervous to go. Maybe I could even walk into town with them. I'd have to remember to call and ask.

When I arrived home, I noticed a few extra cars in the family driveway as I headed for the back door.

"Brenna," Anna smiled as I walked into the kitchen. "Would ya like to join us? The girls and I have started a book club." She beamed. "You remember Mary and Elizabeth?" There were three other ladies besides Anna, Bettie, and Patsy. I recognized Tara's and Jamie's mothers. The third was new to me.

I nodded and said hello to them as Bettie said, "Brenna, this is my sister-in-law Patti. Patti, this is Brenna."

The striking blonde woman extended her hand and said in a slightly cool tone, "Nice to meet you, Brenna. Please, call me Patricia." I noticed Bettie and Patsy simultaneously rolling their eyes behind Patricia's back.

"Nice to meet you, Patricia." I matched her tone without meaning to and then quickly turned to Anna. "What are you reading?" I asked.

"Well, we thought we'd start with somethin' easy and classic." She held up a copy of Jane Austen's *Pride and Prejudice.*

"Great book!" I replied. "But I'm a little tired today. Can I take a rain check?"

"Sure," she and Bettie said, speaking in unison and then bursting into laughter.

"You two sure you're not twins?" I asked as I headed toward the back stairway. Laughter and conversation slowly faded as I climbed the stairs toward my room. I might have thought I'd imagined Patricia's attitude toward me if I hadn't seen Bettie and Patsy's reaction. However, I'd never met the woman before and had no idea why she'd have an issue with me. I chose not to care for the time being. I was looking forward to some quiet time.

I had recently started journaling my thoughts again. Even as a kid, I had found it to be very therapeutic after my parents died. But for some reason I'd stopped doing it years ago. Since I'd come to Ireland though, my desire to journal had returned. So I changed out of my work clothes, donned sweats and a hoodie, and headed out to my terrace to spend some time writing about my day. Before I knew it, the sun was going down and the temperature with it. I saw Elizabeth walking back to her house, so I figured it was safe to head back downstairs for a bite to eat and a hot cup of tea.

The next day was a tour bus day—very busy very quickly—and I had been swamped for a couple hours, so he had probably been there for a while before I noticed him.

"Who's the guy at the bar?" I asked Tara in a whisper. He was smiling and talking with one of the regulars. He had short, dark hair that was a bit longer and messy on top, and he was wearing a dress shirt and an ice-blue silk tie that matched his eyes. He was very good-looking, but that's not what made me want to stare. He just had such a warm, compelling vibe about him that I was suddenly jealous that I wasn't the one sitting there talking with him. It was completely irrational and took me by surprise.

"Oh, that's Ryan Kelly. Ya haven't met him yet?" She looked confused.

"No, is he a regular?" I asked, wondering.

Tara giggled. "Yeah, I guess ya could say that. When he's in town, he's a regular. He owns the place. Owns a number of places here in Millway. I guess he has been out of town for several months, so ya wouldn't have met him yet. C'mon, I'll introduce ya." She started to walk toward him. Instinctively, I grabbed her hand and pulled her back.

"No!" I said, suddenly embarrassed. I felt the color rising up my cheeks. "I'm sure I'll meet him at some point, but I would feel silly if you took me up and introduced me."

With a shrug, Tara gave up for the moment, and I went to clean up my tables. I tried to keep from watching him, but it was much harder than it should have been. As I cleared the corner booth, I thought I might catch another quick glimpse of his face. I kept my head down but chanced a fleeting look through my lashes. My heart skipped a beat. He was looking directly at me!

His piercing blue eyes held a sparkle as he lifted his hand into a small wave. My cursed pink cheeks were blazing. *Excellent, Brenna!* I looked away quickly, but not before I caught the slightest upturn at the corner of his mouth. Was he smiling? He had me so curious, but I forced myself not to look at him, even out of the corner of my eye as I finished cleaning my section. I was done for the day, and I didn't stick around to chat with Tara. I dropped my apron off in the kitchen and scooted out the back door to avoid any more I'm-trying-not-to-look-at-you moments.

The walk home was just long enough for me to clear my head and persuade myself that most of what had happened at the pub had been in my mind. The guy probably wasn't even looking at me. That happens all the time, right? You think someone's waving at you, and you wave back—only to realize they were looking behind you at someone else. I was almost sure that was what had happened, so I put it out of my mind.

We had new guests at the B&B, but I wasn't in the mood to be polite and engage in small talk. I really just wanted to soak in a hot bath. I made my way through the kitchen with a quick hello to Bettie. I begged off of afternoon tea with Patsy, who didn't seem to mind, as one of the guests was an old friend and they had catching up to do. The piping hot bath hit the spot perfectly as I eased in and laid my head back on a rolled up towel.

A light knock at the door woke me. *Ugh.* I'd fallen asleep in the tub and was way past the prune stage, not to mention freezing cold. I grabbed my towel and dried off as I called out, "Anna, that you?"

"Yes, hon, are ya comin' down for dinner? Bettie's been workin' her magic in the kitchen again tonight, but she's headin' out and wants to get dinner on the table. And I'd like ya to meet my cousin Finn. He's just come from Limerick, and Auntie Pat invited him for dinner."

"Um …" I stalled. I would have loved to just crawl under my covers and read a novel, but I could tell by her voice that Anna would be disappointed if I didn't come down. "Yeah ... I'll be down in a couple minutes," I said, surrendering.

I had met a few of Anna's cousins over the past couple months. They were all like long-lost uncles who had great stories to tell about Anna as a "wee lass." While I suspected most of the stories were probably wildly exaggerated, they often made Anna and Bettie laugh so hard that they cried. Apparently, they'd been mischievous little cousins and had driven Patsy crazy on rainy days when they'd been cooped up inside.

Their cousin Paddy had told the story of how Anna and Bettie had hidden a year's worth of sandwich crusts from Patsy. Apparently, they were under strict orders from her that if they didn't finish all their lunch, there'd be no afternoon tea and cookies. Well, they both vehemently hated eating the crusts. Anna's dad, a traveling salesman, always cut them off for her when he was around, but Patsy would have none of that when he was gone—which was most of the time. So Anna had devised a plan. Just behind the small table where they ate lunch was a miniature door that led to the empty space under the back stairs. Each day when Patsy wasn't looking, they'd toss their crusts through the door and close it back up again.

The ruse had been successful until one rainy day when Paddy came over and they were all playing hide and seek. He discovered what he thought was a great hiding place under the stairs. Unbeknownst to him, he was quite allergic to mold and began sneezing uncontrollably after a few minutes of hiding. Patsy came to investigate and found him sitting in the dark on a mound of moldy bread. While I suspected no one had laughed at the time, even Patsy had laughing tears streaming down her face as Paddy recounted the tale. Maybe Anna's cousin Finn would have a story to top the bread-crust caper.

I pulled on a comfy green sweater and jeans, fastened my damp hair haphazardly atop my head, and put on a little mascara and lip-gloss. I wasn't one for much makeup, but a little bit always seemed to help me wake up. I didn't know how hungry I was until the aroma of pot roast and mashed potatoes hit me like a wave on the back stairs. Bettie was humming to herself as I walked through the kitchen.

"Oh my! Ya startled me, dear! Hope yer hungry. You could use a good hearty meal, ya know!" She was always commenting on the lack of "meat" on my bones. I stuck my tongue out at her in fun. She knew as well as I did that I'd managed to put a few pounds back on since I'd arrived, and I was no longer looking to add any more. But I reconsidered as I got a fresh whiff of her pot roast gravy.

"Actually, Bettie, I just might eat seconds tonight if that tastes as good as it smells," I confessed. She smiled a self-satisfied little smile and went back to stirring her gravy.

On most days, we ate at the kitchen table in front of the large, lead-paned window and left the dining room for the guests, but apparently Patsy always used the dining room when family came in from out of town, if there were no guests staying overnight. The table was set for four, as Bettie had other plans for the night, but no one was seated yet.

I heard laughter coming from the front sitting room. More "wee Anna" stories, no doubt. I rounded the corner and froze. It was the guy from the pub, looking even more gorgeous than he did earlier, in jeans and a steely-blue sweater that set off his eyes. He immediately got to his feet and walked with his hand extended toward me while Anna made the introduction.

"Ah, here she is. Brenna, this is my cousin Finn. Finn, my daughter-in-law Brenna." He made no indication that he'd seen me before. He shook my hand and smiled a warm greeting. "My family has always called me Finn, my middle name. Friends call me Ryan." He spoke in that melodious Irish lilt that I now heard all day long but never grew tired of hearing.

"Hi, Ryan." I recovered quickly, but I knew the pink was obvious in my cheeks again. I didn't know if he truly didn't recognize me from earlier or he was just being gracious. I suspected the latter. Confused, I turned to Anna, "I thought you said Finn—er, Ryan—was your cousin." I had been expecting someone much older. He didn't look much older than me.

"Oh, yes, you know, second or third cousin … which is it, Finn?" She turned to Ryan.

"Well, let's see. You and Da are first cousins, so that makes us second cousins, right?"

"Exactly, but family, any way y'say it. I think last time I saw ya, though, ya had to have been just a teenager. Ben was about six when we came to visit." There was a touch of sadness in her voice as she said Ben's name, and I felt an involuntary lump in my throat. It was part sadness and part guilt at having been thinking how handsome Ryan was. First Luke, now Ryan.

I hadn't thought I'd ever be okay with thinking of someone else in the way I'd once thought of Ben. Now it was becoming too easy to do, and that somehow seemed wrong to me. Silently berating myself for it helped me get my thoughts under control. We continued to visit in the front room until dinner was served, and it was, of course, every bit as delicious as it smelled.

As dinner conversation flowed, I began to suspect Patsy had ulterior motives for inviting Ryan to dinner. She'd made it clear through our tea-time discussions that she thought the best thing for me would be to find a good man, get married, and start a family. To my shock, in the last couple weeks, Anna had chimed in and begun to agree with her. They had already hinted at all the available locals. I had even considered going out with a few of them just to be polite and get the matchmakers off my back.

But this was different. Now they were bringing in possible "suitors" for dinner? They spent the first ten minutes of dinner peppering me with questions they knew the answers to. It was as if they were doing it simply to give Ryan more of an idea of who I was without being obvious enough as to offer him a printed resume. They were beginning to get on my nerves. Not because I didn't appreciate the thought, but because they were embarrassing me, and I was never good at covering up embarrassment. They were also getting on my nerves because they'd finally hit on a "prospect" that was very appealing to me, and that just ticked me off. Unfair, I know, but it annoyed me anyway.

As the conversation turned to Anna and some of her memories of Ryan as a kid, I tried to discern if he was in on the setup or not. He didn't appear to be. He looked at me when I was talking, but he didn't linger. He didn't "appraise" me like most of the town boys did. Oddly, I found that fact both refreshing and disappointing at the same time. Luke and the other guys had been so easy to read, so obvious in what they wanted, that I'd become overly confident in my ability to read the opposite sex. This guy was giving nothing away. He didn't act uninterested, but he also didn't act too interested. I decided that he probably was not in on the matchmaking plan. He just didn't act like someone who was trying to score a date.

He did entertain with stories of his various business travels and adventures. He had started working in real estate as a very young man and had made some savvy choices along the way, allowing him the opportunity to purchase a number of local properties here in his hometown. He now spent most of his time in Limerick but came home to visit from time to time.

"How did you get your start in real estate, Ryan?" I asked a safe question midway through dinner. He smiled wistfully as if he were remembering a particularly fond memory.

"Well, I guess it goes back to when I was a wee lad," he grinned. "I was always by my da's side when he would make repairs or additions to the house. Even as a kid I loved the smell of the fresh-cut wood and the satisfaction in my da's eyes when the job was well done."

"He was a fine carpenter, yer da," Patsy chimed in.

"Aye," Ryan agreed. "Still is. And he taught me everythin' I know, startin' as soon as I could safely handle a hammer."

"Does he live around here?" I asked.

"Limerick, actually. He and Mum moved there when my sister got married ... what, ten years ago, Patsy?"

"Aye, ten or eleven," she replied. He'd called her "Patsy" and she hadn't flinched. Apparently, I was *not* the only one allowed to call her that, but he was the only other person I'd ever heard attempt it. "Go on," she urged him. "Finish yer story. Tell her about yer grandma's place."

"Right. So when I was maybe sixteen or seventeen, I began restorin' an old cottage on my grandma's property. She'd given up on it, but once I was done, it was a different place. 'Simply stunning,' she called it. She was very pleased." He smiled again, lost in a memory.

"Does she still own it?" My question seemed to bring him back to the present.

"No. Well, she passed later that year, actually."

Good job, Brenna. "I'm sorry," I interjected.

"No, 'tis fine. She was ready to go. But she left her land and home to me and specified she wanted me to, quote, 'fix it up and sell it for all it's worth.' He chuckled, having said the last part in a fierce Irish brogue, a likely imitation of his grandma.

"Wow. So that was your start? What an awesome grandma!" I turned to Patsy. "Was she your sister?"

"No, his mum's mum," she replied quickly, absorbed in the retelling of a story I was certain she'd heard at least a few times before. "Go on," she commanded again.

Ryan took her impatience with practiced ease. "Well, I got to work on it right away and sold it as she'd wished. It fetched a very handsome sum and got me started on buyin' older homes, fixin' 'em up, and then sellin' 'em. Some folks call it *flippin'* houses."

"Yeah!" I remembered. "I've seen people do that on TV, with all the *before* and *after* photos and stuff. I *love* that." He seemed genuinely pleased by my interest. And he was friendly, but in a very brotherly sort of way.

"So, Finn," Anna queried in not-so-subtle fashion, "ya haven't married in all this time?" I couldn't help rolling my eyes. *Typical.* I quickly found my potatoes fascinating, so I wouldn't have to look up as he answered.

"Ah, well, my busy work schedule has made it difficult to do much settling down these many years." He politely put her off.

"Now, that's no excuse!" Patsy chimed in with a stern, motherly tone. "What, ya must be thirty-five years old by now Finn—time to put some of that time and energy into findin' a wife!"

He laughed graciously. "Oh Patsy, don't go agin' me. I'm twenty-eight, actually, so I guess that gives me seven more years, in yer estimation, to get the job done?" He winked at me, a good-natured gesture. That wink would have meant something else entirely with Luke. There truly didn't seem to be any extra meaning behind it with Ryan.

I was quite sure of Anna and Patsy's motives, but he didn't look uncomfortable in the least. So I took my cue from him. If he didn't think we were being set up, then I wouldn't concern myself with it either. Especially having discovered that he was eight years older than me! Maybe I had imagined the set-up in the first place.

The rest of the evening passed with no more hints or pressure from the *yentas*, and the conversation was easy and constant. I found myself disappointed when Ryan had to leave and was secretly thrilled when he mentioned he'd be in town for a while.

Chapter Nine

🐾 "Would ya like me to introduce ya now?" Tara said as I walked up to the bar.

"To who?" I asked.

"Ryan Kelly. He's sittin' in yer section," she answered.

My stomach did a flip as I stared at Tara. "Is he looking this way?"

Tara looked confused. "No. Do ya want to meet him?"

"No, I actually already met him last night. He's related to Patsy, and she invited him for dinner." I casually glanced toward my section, and sure enough, he was sitting in the corner booth looking over the menu.

"Oh, yeah. I didn't even think about that. Does that make you cousins or somethin'?" she asked. I turned away quickly so she wouldn't see the blush on my cheeks.

"Does it?" I said over my shoulder as I walked toward Ryan.

He looked up and smiled. "Well, good mornin', Brenna. It was nice to meet ya last night. I didn't know who ya were yesterday when I saw ya here, or I would have introduced myself then." *So he* had *seen me looking at him.*

"Oh, yeah, same here. I had no idea. When you didn't mention it last night, I was thinking maybe I imagined seeing you here." I said it with a laugh while trying to muffle the excitement I felt at seeing him again so soon.

"So, how do ya like workin' here?"

"It's been great. I've met so many people, and everyone's really friendly. But I heard the owner's in town, so I'd better get your order. I don't want to be accused of being too chatty with the guests." I smiled and he laughed.

"Of course not! Okay, my order, hmm …" He perused the menu again, as if he didn't know it by heart already. "Think I'll have the ham and cheese omelet with a glass of orange juice," he said as he handed me the menu.

"Excellent choice. Would you like any coffee with that?"

"Aye, was it the dark circles that gave me away?" he asked.

"No, it just seems to be the drug of choice for most people who wander in before eight." I smiled again and headed back toward the kitchen. Soon I was swamped with tables and truly had no time for chatting. He left a generous tip, though, and said he'd see me again soon.

He wasn't joking. Just as the lunch crowd was thinning, there he was again. This time, to my secret disappointment, he was in Brigit's section. He waved and smiled from across the room, but that was all, and I felt like a jerk for indulging my little crush. I analyzed our conversation from that morning for the tenth time. Did he show any interest, or was he just being friendly? I couldn't tell, and that irritated me. I wanted to ask Tara more about him, but I didn't want her to know I had any interest, so I would have to be clever about it. As we walked home, I asked her how long she'd been working at the pub.

"Well, Liam has been workin' nights in the kitchen for four years, and I came in to see him so much that they started puttin' me to work on busy nights just to get me out of his hair. I was probably fifteen or so," she guessed. "Why d'ya ask?"

Be subtle. "Just curious. You're very good at it, and you're kinda young, so I figured you'd been there awhile. It almost has the feel of a family-run place. Are you and Liam related to Sam or Ryan?"

"No, Liam's friends with Sam's son Joseph. I think that's how he started workin' there. Ya know, Liam's been askin' me to set you two up on a date," she said with a sideways grin.

"Me?" I asked with surprise.

"Yeah, half the town has a crush on you, but you've got a reputation, ya know?"

"Huh? No, I *don't* know. What do you mean?" I didn't like this turn of the conversation. Not only had I gotten no information about Ryan but now I had some sort of town reputation?

"Oh!" She took in my shocked expression. "No, not *that* kind of reputation. Kind of the opposite. Guys are afraid to ask ya out 'cause you've shot so many of 'em down, ya know?"

"Oh, yeah, I guess I have, haven't I? Well, I've tried to be really nice about it. And no one's asked me since Luke."

"Yeah, that probably adds to the problem," she said, almost under her breath.

"Why?" I was confused.

She hesitated while formulating her thoughts. "Well, number one, Luke's kind of top dog around here, and if *he* couldn't win ya over, what chance do they have? My mum says guys are terrified of rejection, y'know?" I had never thought about it, but I nodded as if it was common knowledge. "And number two, I don't imagine Luke was very gracious when he had to explain why he didn't score a second date with ya." She said this sheepishly as if she'd already heard rumors and was hoping I wouldn't ask her to spill it.

"What have you heard, Tara?" I stopped walking and looked her in the eye so she couldn't wiggle her way out of explaining.

"Aw, Brenna, it's all just rumor mill stuff, ya know? I shouldn't have mentioned it."

"No way, you're not getting off that easy. Don't worry; I'm a big girl and I can take it," I assured her.

She hesitated, "Okay, well, Brigit is friends with Char—ya know … Luke's girlfriend, Bettie's niece? And Char told—"

"Wait a minute," I interrupted her. "Char is Bettie's niece? How is that?"

"Uh, let's see. Bettie's late husband Danny has a sister named Patti. Her daughter is Char. That makes her Bettie's niece, right?" She looked upward as if she were doing math in her head.

"Yeah, I guess it does," I said as she casually tried to start walking again. Something was tickling my memory, but I wasn't gonna let her go without telling me what she'd heard. "Oh no, you don't get away that easy, darlin'. Spill it. What did she say?"

Tara rolled her eyes and continued. "Okay, so Char said that you were a …" She scrunched her nose as if she smelled something unpleasant. "… a psycho. That you were all over Luke and then told him to get lost when he tried to give ya what you said ya wanted." She blurted out the rest in one breath.

I was enraged. "That is such a lie! You know that's not true. What did you say to Brigit?"

"I told her it wasn't true, I did! She said she had considered the source and didn't think it sounded like you anyway."

"Is that all?" I asked after I'd taken a few deep breaths to calm down.

"That's all I've heard," she said with certainty.

"I can't believe Luke would lie like that."

"Well, I don't know that he did. Char says whatever she needs to in order to make herself look good," Tara reasoned.

"What did Brigit mean 'she considered the source'?"

"Just that she knows Char's reputation. Brigit's never been stung by her personally … but she's seen Char in action and knows she's manipulative. She and Luke have been on and off for years. When they're 'off,' she's always with another guy … like she can't handle bein' on her own. Don't worry about her. People know she's a connivin' witch, and few people believe a word she says. I've never understood why Brigit stays friends with her. They grew up together, I guess." Something clicked when she said that.

"You said Char's mom was named Patti?" I asked.

"Yeah."

"Is she blonde and really pretty?"

"Yeah, you've met her then?" she asked.

I nodded. "She's in a book club with Anna and your mom?"

"Yep, that's her," she confirmed. "My mum tolerates her but doesn't like her much."

Now Patricia's oddly cold attitude toward me fell into place. I may not have known who she was, but she'd obviously had an earful about me. *And she'd made up her mind about me before ever laying eyes on me. Classy.* I noticed Tara looking at me.

"Are y'okay?" she asked tentatively.

"Yeah, I'm ticked, but I'm okay." I let her off the hook. "I wish you'd told me sooner, but thanks for saying something."

"I'm sorry. I should have told ya, but I didn't want to hurt yer feelings or make ya mad, and I saw no way to tell ya without doin' both."

"I know … you were in a hard spot. Just so we're clear, though, in the future I'd rather you tell me than spare my feelings, okay?"

"Got it." She smiled as she raised her hand to her forehead in a mock salute. "Feel free to hurt yer feelings." At that, I playfully smacked her arm, and we began walking toward home again.

Chapter Ten

Anna joined Patsy and me for tea because she was all excited to tell me her good news.

"Well, it turns out the lady who's been part-time church secretary is needin' to take an extended break to watch her granddaughter. So, I went in and met with Father Tim, and I've got the job!"

"That's awesome! I didn't even know you were looking for a job," I replied.

"Aye, I'm wantin' just a little more to do. I've enjoyed doin' the gardening when Tom's away helpin' his mum, but that doesn't take too much time. Bettie has things in hand here, although I've offered to Auntie Pat here to take over the book-keepin' …"

"I've got that under control, young lady." Patsy raised an eyebrow as she made herself clear.

"Yes, I know, so you've said, but the offer is always there, ya know. I realize you're capable of handlin' it, Auntie Pat. I just thought ya might like a break from it is all." Anna lied through her teeth. I knew that she and Bettie were secretly going through the books and fixing Patsy's mistakes after she went to bed at night. Patsy was still sharp at times, and she narrowed her eyes and just stared at Anna for a moment. Then she gave a "harrumph" and stuck out her lip in a pout as the conversation moved on.

"So, what will you be doing?" I asked.

"Well, mostly answerin' the phones and office work. I'll be helpin' with the bookkeeping and with organizin' the church programs and the like." She smiled with delight.

"It sounds perfect for you." When she mentioned church programs, I realized it was Thursday, and I had to decide if I was going to check out the college group.

"Yes, I think it will be great. I start next week. Oh, that reminds me … we got a package from Sue. There's some stuff from yer old jobs and from school." She handed me a stack of mail. Anna's friend Sue was subletting her apartment in Buffalo. She was gathering up any mail that came for us and sending it to us periodically.

"Thanks. Same old boring stuff." I sifted through the envelopes.

"Aye, no lottery checks or anything?" she teased. "Now, how are things going for you at work? See anyone special today?" She and Patsy exchanged obvious glances. I decided to play with them. I knew what they were fishing for, and I'd make them work for it.

"Anyone special? No, not that I can think of," I said innocently. Anna frowned.

"Really? No one stopped in that you've met recently?" she said, so blatantly talking about Ryan.

"Oh, yeah," I continued to tease. "Actually, I ran into Father Tim the other day." I had to disguise my giggle as a cough as I watched both their faces light up and then extinguish with disappointment. They were playing right into my hands. I would not bring up Ryan's name, but I knew *they* would, and then I'd be able to ask some questions without having to initiate the conversation.

"You mean ya hadn't met him before?" Patsy asked.

"Well, I met him when I first got here, but I hadn't really spoken to him since I started going to Sacred Heart. We had a nice little chat."

"Hmm, that's nice dear." *Here it came.* "So, did ya see my cousin Finn today?" Anna asked casually.

"Yeah, I think he was in a couple times, actually. Tara said he's the owner. That true?" I said with as little interest as I could manage.

Patsy answered, "Aye, he's a very good businessman, y'know. He owns the pub, the hardware store, and a few apartment buildings. He also owns half of the building yer sittin' in right now," she said proudly.

This was news to me. "I thought you owned the B&B?"

"Aye, I have for years, but I wanted to update it, make it more modern, and Finn helped me do that. That's why you can use yer laptop thingy up in yer room, cuz he put in the satellite and the hi-fi or whatever it's called. He paid for Bettie to make the kitchen just like she wanted it. He was wonderful." She smiled when she talked about him. He was definitely a favorite.

"Wow, that's great, Patsy. So, has he just come to Millway to check on his properties?" I had been here for months and never seen him.

"Oh, he comes and goes. He has a place in Limerick where his company is located. Sometimes he's here a lot; sometimes we don't see him for months, as was the case lately. You'll be seein' plenty of him for a little while I imagine." She smirked.

"I will?" I said with too much enthusiasm. I forgot to play it cool, and she noticed.

"You would like that, Brenna?" She eyed me with a knowing stare.

"Sure, I had a nice time talking with him last night." I again tried to act nonchalant about it. Why did she think I'd be seeing him? Did he say something to her? Oooh … I wanted so badly to ask, but my pride would not let me. "I've enjoyed meeting all Anna's cousins," I added with a smile.

"Did ya know he has an apartment above Rosie's?" Anna asked me.

"No." But that explained why he was in twice in one day. "I knew there were apartments up there, though." Luke lived in one with a couple friends.

"Well, tell him he's invited for dinner on Sunday, next time ya see him," Patsy said with a mischievous grin.

"Will do." I stood to head upstairs but remembered I had forgotten to call Megan and Jamie to see if they were going to the church tonight. "Patsy, can you give me Elizabeth's number?"

"Sure, but what do ya want to call her for?" She looked confused.

"I don't, I want to ask Jamie for Megan's number."

"Ah, sure, well, it's just on the speed dial thing on the phone. Show her how that works, Anna. It's number two," she said as she headed toward the back stairs. "I'm gonna go watch my soaps," she said with a little giggle and headed upstairs.

Jamie wasn't home yet, but Elizabeth gave me Megan's number, and she answered on the second ring. "Heya?" she said.

"Hi, Megan," I said. "This is Brenna."

"Oh, hi, how are ya?"

"I'm good, thanks. I have a question for you."

"Aye, work away," she replied and waited for my response. I assumed this meant *go ahead.*

"Well, Father Tim invited me to the college group tonight, and Tara said she thought you might be going."

"Sure am! Would y'like to go with me?" She sounded excited.

"Yeah, would you mind?" We hadn't started off on the best of terms, but whenever I'd seen her since, she was fine.

"Not at all. I'd love it. Jamie's not goin' tonight anyway; he's outta town, so I'm glad for the company. Can I pick y'up?" she offered.

"Oh, yeah, that'd be great, thanks." I certainly didn't want to walk alone in the dark.

"Right, well … would y'want to get a bite to eat first?" she asked.

"Yeah, I'd love that!"

"Brilliant! There's a cute little place called the Tea Shoppe with sandwiches and stuff just on the edge of town. I'll have to get ya soon. Is half an hour enough time for ya?"

"Yep, see you then." *There goes my shower.* I ran upstairs and freshened up as best I could, and I was waiting outside when Megan pulled up.

"Thanks so much for picking me up," I said as we drove toward the Tea Shoppe.

"Oh, it was my pleasure, really." She hesitated for a moment. "Brenna, I have to apologize to you," she said with a sheepish look.

"What for?"

"Well, I should have been friendlier to ya from the start. I've felt guilty about it all this time, and I'm embarrassed that you had to reach out to me. It should have been the other way around. You were new in town, and I was just bein' petty."

I was stunned. "Megan, thanks, but I don't see what you have to apologize for. It's not like you've been rude or mean or anything." I felt bad that *she* felt bad.

"No, that's not true. You know I was rude to ya that first night at the festival. I was jealous because I was finally startin' to get Jamie to notice me, and then he's dancin' with this gorgeous American girl." She chuckled as she recounted the night we met. "I was just bein' a silly girl, but you were very gracious about it; and then I was embarrassed to try to get to know ya, cuz I figured ya probably thought I was a jerk." She looked at me and then added, "Cuz I was."

"No you weren't," I protested.

"Really, ya know I was," she replied.

"Okay, maybe a little." I laughed. "But you know I wasn't trying to steal Jamie from you, right?"

"Well, I know that *now*; at the time I had no idea. But that's no excuse. So will ya forgive me?" she asked with a hopeful smile.

"Of course I will." I cleared my throat and put on an official sounding voice. "I, Brenna, hereby forgive you, Megan." She gave me a playful shove as we pulled into the parking lot.

"Thanks," she said, "Now we've got that outta the way, I can relax and enjoy our meal!"

We had a great time at dinner. Sometimes when you're getting to know someone new, conversation seems forced or erratic. This was not the case with Megan. We talked for an hour straight and were almost late to Veritas (the college group) because we lost track of time. She *got* me and I got her—as if we'd known each other for years.

Veritas met in a building that was joined to the church. It was set up like a coffee house with warm, soft lighting, café tables spread throughout, and a small coffee bar in the corner. One end of the room had a slightly raised platform with sound equipment and an oriental rug covering the floor. I estimated there were fifty or sixty people in the room—I thought it a very impressive turnout.

"Are there always this many people?" I asked Megan as we found a seat at a table near the front after grabbing some coffee.

"Ah, no. We're a little small tonight; there's some big conference goin' on at UCC this week."

"UCC?" I asked.

"Aye, University College in Cork. A lot of the kids that come here go to school there."

I was surprised. I had expected a much smaller group for some reason. It was nice. I saw a few faces I recognized and many more that I didn't. Shannon, Katie, and Sarah came walking in and pulled up chairs to our table.

"Hey, Brenna!" said Katie. "I can't believe I never thought to invite ya! Good job, Megan."

"No, kudos to Father Tim. 'Twas himself that invited her," she said with a nod toward the priest who'd just walked in the door.

"Ah, well, glad he did. Welcome!" Sarah piped in. I felt like I'd just joined a sorority.

"Shannon, I haven't seen you since you started school. How's it going?" I asked. She was living with some friends near the campus in Cork.

"It's fabulous. I'm lovin' school and the freedom of bein' on my own."

"I'm glad. I know Tara misses you, though," I said. "So, what's the setup here?" I motioned to the front platform.

Shannon answered, "We usually chat for the first fifteen minutes or so. Then Megan here leads worship with Jamie on guitar; then Father Tim gives a talk on whatever topic he chooses. That's pretty much it."

Katie added, "Sometimes we do a series on a particular subject; like we just finished one on the book of Revelation."

"Aye, that was some deep stuff," Shannon said.

"I think now he's doin' a series on relationships," Katie said. The other three confirmed this with a nod of the head.

"I need to go find Ryan and do a quick sound check," said Megan. At the sound of his name, I got instant butterflies. I remembered feeling the same way when I first met Ben. Every time I saw him in the hall, I'd get the same butterflies I now had dancing in my belly.

"Ryan?" I asked, thinking it could be another Ryan.

"Aye, he's a friend of Father Tim's, and he's fillin' in for Jamie tonight," she said as she got up and left the table. I looked toward the others.

"That's the same Ryan who owns Rosie's?" I asked.

"Aye," said Katie. "Have y'met him then? He's a sweetheart."

"Yeah, he was over for dinner with Patsy earlier this week," I answered. "He's older than college age, though, right?"

"Well, I don't think he's attendin' so much as he's helpin' out. But we don't really have an age cut-off. Father Tim says we're a group for the 'young and the young at heart.'" Sarah chuckled at her own impression of the priest.

"How long has Father Tim been here?" I asked.

Sarah and Katie both looked to Shannon to answer. She'd grown up here, but they'd both been here only a few years.

"Hmm, I think I was about six or seven years old when he came," she recalled. The church was really boring when he got here. I remember me mum talkin' about it. I mean, there were plenty of people who came but it was more out of duty. Now I think people look forward to Sundays."

"I know I do." I smiled.

"Oh, Brenna, you've got coffee on yer sweater." Sarah pointed to a pea-sized coffee drop that dribbled down my torso. I grabbed napkins to try to blot it out but knew from experience it was pointless.

"Yeah, that's not unusual," I said with a roll of my eyes.

Both Brigit and Sarah laughed. "We know," they chimed in unison, which made us all laugh. We were interrupted by the sound of Father Tim's voice.

"Glad you could all make it tonight," he said into the microphone. "We have a special guest tonight. My friend Ryan is gonna play and sing alongside our lovely Megan."

The room erupted in a rowdy applause. Then Ryan started playing, and Megan spoke: "Hey, guys, why don't y'stand? We're gonna teach ya a new song tonight."

As she and Ryan sang, I stood transfixed. I loved music to begin with. I was already a fan of Megan's voice, and now Ryan adding the harmony was almost too much for me. Both of them had absolutely gorgeous voices, but they didn't come across like they thought they were great or anything. If a person can ooze humility, that's what they did, odd as that sounds. They just were completely focused on bringing the group into a place of worship. It was simply beautiful. I completely forgot about the butterflies and found myself wiping unexpected tears from my face as they moved from one heartfelt song to the next. Sunday morning worship was more formal. This was so fresh and real that I was disappointed when it ended.

"That was beautiful," I said to Megan as she took her seat.

"Thanks." She smiled and gave my hand a squeeze as she turned her attention to Father Tim at the microphone.

He spoke for about thirty minutes on what he called our vertical relationship with God, or our "Number One Relationship." As always, he was humorous and engaging. I found his talks to be more than thought-provoking; they were *action*-provoking. He inspired me to try to be a better person. I didn't always feel very successful at that, but each week I felt encouraged to try. I wasn't a horrible person or anything, but I knew where I fell short and what things I had to work on. Sometimes it was as if Father Tim knew too! That was scary.

The night came to a close, and the butterflies returned when I saw Ryan staring at me from across the room. The instant my eyes locked with his, he looked away. I could have sworn he blushed, but that was probably just wishful thinking. I wanted to go tell him how much I enjoyed his music, but I felt suddenly shy, and by the time I worked up my courage, he was gone. *You snooze, you lose, Brenna.*

Megan drove me home afterward. "Thanks again for the ride and the company," I said as I gave her a quick hug and got out of the car. I added, leaning back into the window. "I really had fun tonight and your music was amazing."

With a beaming smile she asked, "So ya want me to pick ya up next week then?"

"Absolutely! See you Sunday," I replied as I waved and walked toward the back door. I couldn't wait to get upstairs and write about my day. One of Father Tim's sermons had inspired me to keep a list of things I was thankful for. This was one of the best days I'd had since I moved here, and I was especially thankful for my new friendship with Megan.

Chapter Eleven.

I wasn't scheduled to work Friday, but Brigit was sick and Sam called me in. I got in later than normal, around 8:00 a.m. We had a fairly busy breakfast crowd going, and the other girls were already swamped so I took the next three tables that came in to the restaurant. The third table was none other than Ryan and Father Tim. Once the other two tables were done, I had a chance to talk with them a bit as they finished their breakfast.

"Father Tim, thanks for inviting me to Veritas last night. I really enjoyed it." I intentionally spoke to him first. I didn't want to seem eager to talk with Ryan, even though I was.

"Aye, dear, so glad ya came out. I usually have to invite someone at least two or three times before they show up. Very impressive," he said with a wink toward Ryan.

"Well, it helped that Megan picked me up. I don't have an Irish license yet, and actually, the way I've seen some people drive around here, I'm not sure I want to," I whispered from behind my hand. They both chuckled at my joke.

"I'm sure Ryan here could give ya a ride next time if y'need one." I may have imagined it but I could have sworn Ryan kicked the priest under the table when he said this.

"Absolutely," Ryan replied, contradicting his body language. I had never in my life met someone who sent such incredibly mixed messages, and I had no clue what to make of it.

I shrugged. "I usually walk most places, and it's no big deal. But I don't feel really comfortable walking at night, you know?"

"Aye, don't do that," said Ryan. "Seriously, if ya need a ride at night, you can always call me. I've just finished a large project in the city, and I'm basically on vacation right now." At that, he handed me his number, freshly written on a napkin. I took it as I saw a Cheshire grin spread across Father Tim's face and a definite blush creep up Ryan's cheeks. I wanted to laugh. It was the first time I'd been on the other end of telltale cheeks.

"Well, thanks, Ryan. I just may take you up on that." And I'd have to come up with an excuse to do just that. "Oh, by the way, Patsy asked me to tell you you're invited for Sunday dinner. Would you like to come?"

"Aye, well, an invite from Patsy is more of a summons, now, isn't it?" he said with a knowing smile. "Of course I'll come. After church then?"

"Sounds good. Father, I'm sure you're more than welcome," I added.

"I do appreciate that, Brenna, but I've already been asked to the O'Conor's place. I'll take a rain check, though. Only a fool would pass up an opportunity to eat Bettie's home cookin'."

"All right, then, I'll tell her you're coming, Ryan. Can I get you two anything else?"

"We'll just take the check when ya get a chance," Ryan responded.

I went to get their check, and as I stood at the bar waiting for Tara, I watched Ryan from the corner of my eye. He and Father Tim appeared to be having some type of disagreement, but the priest kept laughing, and occasionally Ryan did too. It was an odd type of argument. I was dying to know what they were talking about, and it did not escape me that they looked in my direction several times.

"Just cuz yer paranoid doesn't mean people *aren't* talkin' about ya." Tara startled me with her comment. I didn't realize she was standing there and wondered exactly how long she'd witnessed me watching their table. I decided right then that I needed an ally, and I let her in.

"It does look like they're talking about me, doesn't it?" I asked her.

"Aye, and they were doin' it before, too," she confided.

"Really? Weird," I said.

"Geez, Brenna, you don't aim low, do ya? First Luke, now Ryan Kelly!" She said this quietly enough that no one else would hear, and she said it with no malice at all. I knew my cheeks were now blazing.

"I didn't plan it," I said, looking down at the bar.

"Oh, I'm not sayin' ya have bad taste, friend. Just that you've picked a tough one. He hasn't dated anyone that I know of in the whole time I've worked here," she said in a hushed whisper.

"Well, he lives in Limerick too. Maybe he has a girl there?" I would be surprised if he didn't.

"Maybe, but I don't think so. I've seen Father Tim tryin' to set him up before like he's doin' now with you. And he'd know if Ryan had a girlfriend back in Limerick. They're good friends."

"You think Father Tim's trying to set us up?" My heart started beating faster. What better ally could I ask for? "Why?"

"Beats me, but I'd bet my tips that's what they're talkin' about. Here." She handed me their check. "Better go deliver this before they realize we're talkin' about them." I'd completely forgotten the check. Even though he owned the place, he always asked for the check.

"Thanks," I said, grateful for someone to talk to about Ryan.

I delivered the check and smiled and waved when they left. I knew Tara would be waiting to walk home with me today.

"I can't figure him out," I confessed as we walked. "He's not like anyone I've met. He's sweet and funny, but he kind of keeps his distance. Then, when he gave me his number, he—"

"He gave ya his phone number!" Tara interrupted, obviously shocked.

"Yeah, but it wasn't like he was saying to call him or anything. Father Tim had offered him, I think against his will, as a driver for me if I needed one. I think he kicked the priest when he said that!" I chuckled at the memory.

"Wow, still … he wouldn't give out his number if he didn't want ya to call him, would he? Seriously, think about it. If the tables were turned, would you give out yer number if ya had no interest?"

She had a point. I continued, "Well, that's what I was gonna say; when he handed me the number, he blushed!"

"Oooh," Tara squealed. "That's a good sign!"

I rolled my eyes. "I know, cuz I can't keep my cheeks from turning red most of the time when I'm around him; but other than that, he gives no normal signals. Like he doesn't flirt *at all*. It's weird."

"Hmm … yeah, that's weird. But maybe he's just shy," she offered.

"That doesn't fit, though. He talks to everyone," I complained.

"Yeah, but he doesn't ask everyone out. Maybe he's just shy when it comes to that kind of relationship," she said.

"Maybe," I conceded. "Well, just do me a favor and keep an eye out when he's around. Maybe you'll notice something I don't."

Tara giggled. "Well, I would have been watchin' anyway. May as well keep ya in the loop, right?"

"Funny." I smirked as we approached the B&B. I knew Patsy would be waiting with a steaming pot of Earl Grey. "Thanks, Tara. And I don't have to ask you to please keep this between us, right?"

She feigned offense. "Of course not!"

"Thanks," I said again.

"Sure thing. My eyes and ears are at yer service, dear. See y'tomorrow?"

"Yep, I'm not in till nine." As I watched her walk away, I realized that I had unintentionally made a brilliant decision by taking her into my confidence. If I hadn't, she'd be blabbing her suspicions to everyone. This way, as my confidante, she'd be much more likely to keep it to herself.

Chapter Twelve

The weekend couldn't go by fast enough. I jumped every time the pub door opened on Saturday, hoping I'd see Ryan walking through it. But he never did. The heart is so fickle. A week earlier, I'd never even met the man, and now I was consumed with trying to figure him out.

Luke came in for lunch, which wouldn't have been as bad if he hadn't brought Char with him. She was always openly hostile toward me, so I always did my best to completely ignore her. That was easier to do when she wasn't sitting in my section. Everyone else was slammed, so I had no choice but to wait on them.

"What can I get for you?" I directed my question to Luke. His wicked little smile still made my stomach flip, but its power was growing weaker, to my immense relief. He opened his mouth to answer, but Char cut him off.

"Why can't Brigit wait on us?" she asked disgustedly while crinkling her nose as if she smelled something rotten.

"I'm sure she'd be thrilled to take care of you if you'd like to come back in half an hour. Right now she has more tables than she can handle. Would you like to leave?" I said this with a polite, professional voice, but I saw Luke stifle a smile as Char's eyes grew wide with indignation.

"Of course we aren't going to leave," she snapped. "I'll have the grilled chicken sandwich, no tomato and no onions. And I want water with a lemon."

"Certainly. Luke?" I asked. I could see that he was amused by her irritation, and I wondered what he saw in her.

"Ah, let's see. I'll have the usual. Same thing I always want, Brenna." My eyes narrowed. His double meaning was clear to me, but thankfully Char was oblivious. If she had any idea what he was saying to me, she probably would have scratched my eyes out. Again, he hit me with that twisted smile.

"That's no longer on the menu," I said with a smile. "Would you like what Char's having?" *A hissy fit with a side of jealousy?*

"I'll just have a roast beef sandwich then," he answered. As I walked toward the kitchen, I felt the heat of her stare on my back. Brigit was in the kitchen, and I knew she was friends with Char.

"What is the deal with her? She's so nasty to me." I motioned through the little window toward Char, who was giving Luke a piece of her mind.

Brigit rolled her eyes and answered, "Ah, Char, she's always wanted Luke, and he toys with her. She knows he still wants you, and since she can't bring herself to hate him, she hates you instead."

"Oh." I considered that for a moment. "Well, I guess in some twisted way that makes sense." I felt sorry for her, actually, and told Brigit so.

"Yeah, me too," she said. "We've been friends since before we started school. I keep holdin' out hope that she'll change. She's not really all that bad underneath. Ya want me to trade tables with ya?"

I thought about it. "No, I'd rather not give her the satisfaction." I winked at Brigit, and she shook her head and smiled as she left the kitchen. I did do my best to be kind and polite every time I went to the table. Not that it thawed the ice queen, but I felt better about myself that way.

I was done before Tara, so I walked home on my own. I was chilled to the bone by the time I got home and I headed straight to my room for a piping hot bath. We had guests for the weekend, so I made myself scarce. I was perfectly capable of small talk, but I really didn't enjoy it. Anna was good at it. She could carry on a three-minute conversation with anyone about anything. Not me. I found small talk boring. Put me in a room full of people, and I'll be the one sitting in the corner talking to one person all night long. So, after working all day where small talk was the norm, I rarely ventured out of my room at night. On my days off, I did my best to be more hospitable, but not on workdays.

I went to bed early like a kid on Christmas Eve. I was so looking forward to Sunday dinner that I did everything I could to hasten its coming. Church dragged on like never before. We had a visiting priest, and he did not have the speaking ability that Father Tim did. Old Mike from the hardware store was snoring two pews back; it was hard not to giggle, but I didn't blame him. I had slept for nearly twelve hours, and I still had trouble keeping my eyes open. I could see Ryan sitting near the front with Megan and Jamie, but staring at the back of his head was not particularly satisfying, so I instead took to counting down the minutes to the end of Mass.

As we walked out the church doors, Ryan walked up behind us and asked if we needed a ride. Patsy answered for us, "Oh, thank you, dear. Bettie drove us today, but ya know, it is a bit crowded in her little car. Maybe y'could drive Brenna home?" *Oh, very subtle.* She winked at Anna as she said it, and although I wanted to spend time with him, I was embarrassed by her tactics.

"Sure." He smiled. "We'll be there soon. I need to go pick somethin' up first." He led me to a green pickup truck and, in true gentlemanly fashion, opened my door for me and helped me into the cab.

As we pulled away from the church, I apologized. "Sorry about that. I could have ridden with them." I knew I was blushing.

"It's no problem, really," he said with a genuine smile.

"So what do you have to pick up?" I asked.

A mischievous grin spread across his face. "Nothin', really, but since they're so determined to set us up, I figured we'd let them have their fun, speculating about what we're doin'."

I turned to him in shock. Did he really just say that, or did I imagine it? He laughed at the look on my face, and I chuckled nervously. "So you know what they're up to, then?" I asked, feeling completely mortified.

He looked at me sideways. "They're not exactly subtle."

"No, I'm sorry. They've been doing this to me for months now." *Oh, what I wouldn't give to read his mind right now!*

"I've got ya beat. Patsy's been doin' it to me for years." He laughed again.

"Really? Well, what should we do about them then?" I asked, not sure I wanted to hear his answer.

"I've actually been tryin' to figure that out all week long," he admitted. "Here's what I'm thinkin'." He hesitated. "See, I'm really not lookin' for a relationship right now, and I imagine you aren't either." My heart sank, but I just nodded and smiled. "But I'm always open to new friends. Why don't we just hang out some, get to know each other. I can even help ya get yer license. If they see us spendin' time together, maybe they'll ease up."

"That's brilliant." I smiled in spite of feeling queasy. It was not an outright rejection, because I had not given any indication of how I felt, but it stung regardless. Still, I figured I could settle for friendship with Ryan, since he seemed adamant that nothing more would happen. Better that than no relationship at all and I wasn't sure I was ready for that kind of relationship again, anyway.

We pulled in behind the pub and took the back stairs to the apartments above. "Well, I do have a plant I bought for Patsy. We'll just run up and get it quick," he said as he took the stairs two at a time. I'd never been up to the apartments, and I was curious. There were two on the second floor and one on the third. That was Ryan's place. It was a typical bachelor pad, I guess. It was cleaner than I would have expected, but then again, he'd only been back in town for a week. He still had suitcases sitting in the living room and a laundry basket full of clothes on the dining room table.

"How long are you in town for?" I asked while looking at a picture of what I assumed were his parents.

He answered from the kitchen where he was wrapping up the potted plant. "I don't really know. I mentioned the big deal I just finished?"

"Yeah, the other day," I responded.

"Well, it was a highly detailed project, and it took months of nights and weekends to get it wrapped up, so I'm a little burned out. I needed a break, and I haven't given myself a time limit, really. I'm just gonna play it by ear, I guess." He came back into the living room.

"Hmm, sounds familiar." I smiled. "That's exactly what Anna and I said when we came here for a vacation."

"Really? Ya didn't plan the move ahead of time?" he asked as he sat on the couch and motioned for me to sit down.

"No, it was an open-ended vacation. I really had no intention of moving. It hadn't even crossed my mind, but I think Anna was thinking of it all along. I'm glad, though. It was a good idea." I wasn't sure if he was keeping the conversation going just to be polite. "Should we get going?" I wondered.

"No, it's more fun this way." His eyes twinkled as he laughed. "We'll keep 'em guessin'."

He was right; it was fun. "You're awful," I said with a grin.

"I know," he confessed. "So, why did ya decide to stay?"

I considered my answer. "Well, several reasons, really. I guess mostly because Anna is like a mother to me. I didn't really have a reason to go back, once she decided she was staying."

"Wow. Ya have no family back in the States then?" he asked. I proceeded to give him a bit of my sad history ... starting with my parents, all the way up to Ben, which he knew about already. He asked a lot of questions and I found it very easy to talk to him. When I finished my "tale of woe," he had a strange look in his eyes that I couldn't read.

"What?" I asked.

"I'm just impressed, Brenna. Yer a strong woman," he said with a tenderness that made me melt. This friendship thing was gonna be hard.

"I don't know about that. I've had a lot of bad stuff happen, true, but I've also been blessed all along the way. I never would have survived if it weren't for Anna. She was God's gift to me. Which reminds me, we really should get going. Dinner's probably ready." He looked at the time and agreed.

I could see the curtains move as someone was watching out the window for us when we pulled up to the B&B. We were giggling as we walked in, knowing that they were having fits, wondering what we'd been doing for an hour.

"Sorry we're late, ladies," was all he said, which was hysterical. I could see they were dying for more information as they looked at each other and shrugged.

"Well, come on then; dinner's gonna get cold," Patsy scolded as she headed to the dining room.

Dinner was delicious, as always, and the conversation was even better. Ryan's plan was genius. Not only did it have the ladies stumped, but it also took all the pressure off of us, and we just had fun getting to know each other. Anna brought out a deck of cards, and we played random games after dinner until Patsy began to nod off and Ryan stood to go.

"I'm gonna let you girls get on with yer evenin'. Thanks for dinner." He hugged Bettie and Anna. "I'll see ya tomorrow at the pub then?" he asked as he gave me a quick, brotherly hug. My stomach did a flip, regardless of his intentions.

"I'll be there bright and early," I replied with pink cheeks. "Speaking of early," I said to Anna, "I'm gonna call it a night now so I can get up when that alarm goes off!" With that I managed to get myself into my room before I could be grilled once Ryan left. I read for a while and then drifted into a sweet dreams.

Chapter Thirteen

"So, I'm dyin' to know what happened at dinner. I saw ya drive away from church in his truck!" Tara was practically drooling.

I laughed. "Well, it's nothing exciting. Calm down, girlfriend. Ryan says he's not interested in dating anyone right now."

"He came out and said that to you?" She was offended for me.

"Yeah, but it wasn't like I professed undying love for him and he shoved it in my face or anything. He doesn't have a clue that I like him. He just knows our family is trying to set us up. It was really funny, actually. He wanted me to go with him to make them wonder what we were doing and maybe get them off our backs."

"Really? Did it work?" she asked.

"Like a charm." I laughed as I saw Patsy's face in my mind. "They stopped making silly comments and trying to set us up, because as far as they can tell, we've already taken the bait. The plan is to hang out and get to know each other ... as friends." I grimaced.

"Ouch, the 'let's be friends' line." She grimaced too.

"Yeah, I know. It's not what I was hoping for, but I still get part of what I wanted, which was to get to know him better, right?"

"Sure. At least he's not sayin' *Get lost!*" she consoled.

We had the bar stocked for the day by the time we finished talking. There were a few regulars already eating breakfast when Ryan walked in and sat down at the bar. "Hi there, girls," he said with a smile.

"Hey, Ryan. Orange juice this mornin'?" said Tara.

"Aye, and some coffee too, if ya don't mind." He looked tired.

"I'll get that for you," I chimed in. "What would you like for breakfast?"

"I'll have the ham and cheese omelet again. Thanks, Brenna."

I brought his coffee and breakfast, and my section started filling up, so I didn't get much of a chance to chat with him until he got up to leave.

"Last night was fun. Yer quite the card shark," he teased.

"Yeah, right. I always lose; I've just accepted it." I shrugged and smiled.

"Well, I'm gonna head out, but what time are y'done today?"

"Um, usually by around two. Why?"

"Because I was serious about helpin' ya get yer license. If y'like, come upstairs after yer done, and we'll go to Cork to get ya signed up for the exam and start studyin'. Sound good?"

"Sounds great!" I was thrilled. "See you then." I waved as I headed back to the corner booth to deliver a check. Tara winked at me as I walked by, and I gave her a beaming smile in return.

I ran into Luke going up the back stairs. *Awkward.*

"Were ya comin' to visit me, Brenna?" he asked with surprise. He shared one of the second-floor apartments with a couple friends.

"Oh, hi, Luke. No, actually Ryan's going to help me get my license. We're going to Cork City," I said coolly as I slipped past him. He quickly grabbed hold of my hand and stepped up to stand face to face.

"Brenna, I'm sorry. I acted like an idiot. Can ya give me another shot?" I was stunned. His closeness already had my heart beating faster, and now he decided to apologize?

"I heard that I was a psycho," I said sarcastically, using anger to control my beating heart.

"I never said anythin' like that. Who told ya I said that?" He acted sincere.

"No, it was Char that said it, I guess," I admitted.

"Figures," he said. "I'm sorry, Brenna, really. Whaddya say to a fresh start?"

"Luke, thanks, but I ... wait, what about Char?" I suddenly had a vision of her jumping on my back and pulling my hair out.

"I broke it off with her. We've tried to work things out a few times, but we're just not right together. As you know, she has some growin' up to do besides."

"And you don't?" I raised my eyebrow. He chuckled and nodded.

"Aye, me too. So, what do y'say to another date?" Standing so close to him, it was tempting, but something inside me was frantically trying to get my attention. Maybe the voice of reason? I hesitated, and he liked that.

"I need to think about that, Luke," I stalled.

"Don't ya forgive me?" he pouted, his chocolate brown eyes turning puppy dog-like.

I rolled my eyes. "Yes, of course I forgive you, but I'm not ready to say I'll go back out on a date with you. I just don't know right now. I'm sorry."

He was about to say something when Ryan called from the top of the steps. "Hey, Brenna, I was just coming down to see if you were done yet." I wondered how long he'd been standing there. I almost felt guilty, but there was no reason to be. I was interested in Ryan, but he'd made it clear he was not interested in me. Yet as he came down the stairs I suddenly felt relieved, like I was being rescued.

"Hi, yeah, I finished a little late. You know Luke?"

"Aye, how are ya Luke?" He smiled a very neutral smile.

"Fine, Ryan. Yerself?" Luke returned the same smile.

"Fine, thanks. Am I interruptin'?" Ryan directed his question to me.

"No, we were just catching up. Ready to go?" Ryan nodded and stepped between Luke and me, swiftly putting his hand behind my back to lead me down the stairs.

"I'll see ya soon, Brenna," said Luke as we walked away.

"Okay, bye, Luke," I replied. Again, Ryan opened the door for me and helped me into the cab.

"You don't, by chance, have yer passport on you, do ya?" Ryan asked as we pulled away from Rosie's.

"No, do I need it?"

"Aye. We'll stop by the B&B so ya can grab it. Did ya have lunch?"

"Yeah, you?" I replied.

"I'm all set. So, are you and Luke together?" he asked with a surprising edge to his voice.

"No, we went on a date once a couple months ago, that's all," I answered with a shrug.

"Hmm." He smiled a sideways smile.

"What?" I asked.

"Well, ya know *he* doesn't see it as 'that's all.' Right?"

"How do you know?" I asked.

He laughed. "Guys can tell things like that about each other."

"Really? Well, yeah … he was just asking me out again," I confessed.

"I thought so. So are ya gonna go out with him?" he asked with a forced lightness to his voice. Part of me wanted to tell him it was none of his business, but a bigger part of me increasingly *wanted* it to be his business.

"I don't think so … I don't know really," I evaded. We pulled up to the B&B, and Ryan stayed in the car so we wouldn't lose any time talking with the ladies.

"Hey, Patsy, I'm gonna have to bail on tea today," I said as I strode through the kitchen to the back stairs.

"What for?" she said with irritation. I waited until just before I stepped up onto the first stair to drop the answer. I wanted to see her face but not let her see mine.

"Ryan's taking me to Cork City." Her eyes grew as big as saucers, and as she looked my way, I bounded up the stairs with a huge grin on my face. Ryan was right. This was too fun!

We sped out of town and the conversation was light. He told me some about his mum and dad, and I shared several stories of living with my gram. She had been sick for the last few years I was with her, but before that she was a riot. She had a great sense of humor and was always making me laugh. That was the part of her I chose to remember—not the frail, thin woman lying on the bed in the hospice center. (I could still smell the sickly sweet, decaying smell of that hospice room.) From the sound of it, his grandma was very similar to mine. Feisty, in a word. I could tell he missed her all these years later, and talking about it made me miss my gram too.

Conversation with Ryan was refreshingly easy. I'm not sure if it was because of our "arrangement" or because we just communicated well, but either way, awkward silence was never an issue. The green, rolling countryside was stunning as it flashed by, and even the roads were quaint with the little stone walls that ran along them for miles (or kilometers) at a time. Before I knew it, we were in Cork City. Ryan pulled off into an abandoned warehouse lot.

"What are you doing?" I asked as he sat there grinning.

"Yer gonna drive for a bit," he stated.

"I can't drive; that's why I need to get my license!"

"Well, technically you can drive, since you've got a valid US license. You have a year as a visitor that yer allowed to drive. Now, since you've settled here, it only makes sense to get you an Irish license, but strictly speakin' it's not yet necessary."

"Are you sure?" I was confused. I guess I had assumed I couldn't drive because I was scared to try—with all the driving-on-the-wrong-side-of-the-road stuff.

"Aye, I'm sure. So, let's just give it a go here in the parkin' lot. There's lots of room, and no one's gonna be in danger. Well … except maybe us." He chuckled.

I glared playfully and hopped out of the truck. "Okay, but just remember this was your idea!" Thankfully it was an automatic. I'd driven a stick shift before, but I didn't need the extra pressure. I had to move the seat all the way forward to barely reach the pedals. Learning on a pick-up truck might not have been the best idea.

"All right, I assume ya know how to drive in general. We just need to get you used to the whole opposite-side thing," he said. It was so odd. I'd barely gotten used to riding as a passenger on the left side of the car. Now I was driving from the right. "Just keep in mind that, even though yer sitting and driving on the opposite side than yer used to, you as the driver should always be in the middle of the road, next to the center line, right?"

"Okay, got it," I said with confidence I didn't feel.

"Great, let's take this row of parkin' spots and use that line as the center of the road. Drive up that way and make a left turn at the end of the row."

He directed me turn by turn. The lesson went on like this for a good half an hour before he congratulated me and we switched sides again.

"That's not too bad, once you get the hang of it," I said with relief to be the passenger once again.

"Y'did quite well, Brenna." He chuckled.

"What?" I asked.

"Nothin'." He tried to cover his amusement about something.

"What, was I that bad?"

He shook his head and asked, "Did ya know that when ya concentrate you stick out yer tongue?" He laughed again.

I rolled my eyes. "Yes, I've been told that before. I only stick it out a little bit." I was blushing. "And I don't do it on purpose." I'd been concentrating so hard on driving that I'd forgotten to watch myself for that annoying little habit that had plagued me since I was a kid.

He put his hands up as if he were under arrest. "I'm not laughin' at ya, really."

"Yes, you are! Brat." I swatted him on the arm and couldn't help but notice he was hiding strong biceps beneath those long sleeves. He laughed again.

"Sorry, it was funny. I'll be good now. Ya really did do an excellent job. I've helped a number of Yanks transition to UK drivin', and you've picked it up quicker than most."

"Well, thanks, but it's only a parking lot, and I'm nowhere near ready to try driving in traffic," I admitted.

"Aye. All in due time. We need to hurry, though. The Testing office closes soon," he said. We headed to the Penrose Wharf building in Centre City. Cork City is one of the largest cities in Ireland, he explained. It was built on the River Lee, and the center of the city is an island where the river splits for a while and then comes back together. That was where we were heading now as we crossed the Lee. We pulled up to a long building with a wide, yellow stripe along the top and red and green windows covering the length of it. I was so glad Ryan was with me. He knew exactly where to go, and I would definitely have gotten lost without him.

Inside the Theory Testing office, we set up my appointment for the following week, and we were given the materials to study on a CD.

Along the wall was a bank of computer stations where several people were currently taking the Theory Test. I hoped it wasn't too different from the US permit test.

"Thank you so much for taking me," I said to Ryan as we walked back to the car.

"My pleasure," he said. "Honestly, I'm glad to have somethin' to do. Havin' so much time on my hands is completely foreign to me. Any other errands we need to run?" he asked playfully.

"Nope, not till next Wednesday at 10 a.m.," I said.

"Great, then let's go get dinner!" We drove further onto the island and stopped at a little restaurant that Ryan assured me served excellent American-style burgers. My mouth was watering at just the mention of a cheeseburger and fries. Bettie's cooking was phenomenal, but to go without real American pizza or burgers had not been easy.

The restaurant was called Gourmet Burger Shoppe or GBS for short. It was the type of place with a cafeteria-style set up. We faced an enormous menu behind the counter, from which we chose our burger size, toppings, and condiments. We both ordered a side of "fresh cut chips," which meant "fries" in UK lingo. And the topper was a large chocolate milk shake.

"I'm in heaven," I said with my first mouthful. "Can we come here every day?" I joked. He hadn't tried his yet. He was just watching me eat without realizing it. He had a slight smile on his face, and for the first time since he blushed at the college night, I saw a glimpse of something other than friendship in his eyes. "Are you gonna eat?" I asked.

"Absolutely!" He recovered from his momentary lapse, and the guard I'd finally realized he was using snapped back into place. Now he had me totally curious. I wanted to know why he wasn't interested in a relationship right now—and apparently hadn't been for several years, if Tara's information was correct. But I didn't know how to approach the subject without giving myself away. So, I focused on enjoying every bite of my American dinner and figured that if we spent enough time together, I'd get him to talk sooner or later.

After dinner, we stopped at a cell phone place where I signed up for a local plan and got myself a cell. My US cell plan had lapsed and would have been too expensive to use anyway. I had been using the phone at the B&B for months, so I was thrilled to have my own phone again. We didn't pull into the driveway until after 10:00 p.m.

"Well, what are the odds they're waitin' up for ya?" he asked with a sly grin.

"Why don't you come in and find out instead of sending me to the jackals alone?" I teased.

"Oh, I'd love to, but ya know, it's late, and I have so much to do in mornin'." He stretched and faked a yawn.

"Liar." I'll admit I intentionally hit him in the arm again. He never said flirting wasn't allowed, just because he didn't partake. I got out of his truck, said good-bye, and headed in to face the inquisition. To my amazement and relief, the house was dark with just a small light on at the kitchen counter. There was a note from Anna.

Hey Brenna,

Hope you had a nice day. We all spent the day working in the yard and we're exhausted. I start my new job tomorrow!! See you in the morning.

Love ya,
Anna

"Excellent!" I thought to myself as I headed up to my room with one of Bettie's homemade cookies and a tall glass of milk. *No inquisition and fresh-made cookies. A perfect end to a perfect day.*

Chapter Fourteen

I'd dodged my matchmakers the night before, but to expect to do so twice was unrealistic. All three were sitting at the table waiting for me when I came down for breakfast.

"Good morning," I said cheerily.

They responded in kind, and Bettie rose to get me some fresh eggs and sausage.

"Sit down, Bettie. I can get my breakfast. Really," I emphasized.

"Well, ya know I don't mind, dear," she said in a slightly wounded tone.

"I know, I know. But we're not guests here anymore, right? If you're already making something for everyone else and you want to include me, that's great; but I don't want you to have to wait on me. Okay?" I replied.

"Aye, alright then," she responded.

"Oh, enough of this jibber-jabber," Patsy suddenly pounced. "Tell us about yer day out with Finn!" No subtlety there. I found it oddly irritating that they insisted on calling him by his boyhood name. It was obvious he preferred Ryan, but I didn't think quibbling over name preference would get me off the hook.

"We had a nice time," I responded.

"Well, what did ya do all day?" she continued to prod.

"He offered to help me get my Irish driving license, so we went and registered for the theory test next week." I was trying to give enough information that they'd be satisfied without my having to lie about the nature of our relationship. The idea was to let them think what they wanted to think.

"He's such a sweetheart, that boy is," Anna chimed in. "So when are y'seein' him again?"

"He'll probably be in for breakfast," I said as I buttered my toast and applied a thin layer of Bettie's homemade strawberry jam. "Which reminds me, I'm gonna be late if I don't scoot. Have fun today, Anna. Good luck!" I grabbed my coat and left before they could ask another question. The ruse was fun, but all this evading was already getting old.

As always, I helped Tara get the bar stocked for the day. She didn't really need to bartend much for the breakfast crowd. She set up for lunch and then did paperwork for Sam at the bar and filled juice orders for us when needed. Just as we finished setup, the door opened, and to my dismay, it was Char and her mother, Patricia. And of course, I was the only waitress at the moment. Both Sarah and Katie were late, and Brigit wasn't on the schedule. I gave Tara a look of dread as I went to seat them.

"Hi, ladies. Would you like a booth or a table?" I asked. They didn't respond. They just stood there for a moment as if I hadn't spoken. I'd had some weird experiences waiting tables, but I'd never waited on someone who completely ignored me. I felt a quiet fury rising up in my chest and did my best to squash it.

I repeated myself, and this time Patricia looked at me and said, "We'd like a different server, *if* you don't mind." She was the ultimate ice queen— and I had thought *Char* was good at it. *Kill it with kindness,* I told myself over and over.

"No problem. You're welcome to take a seat wherever you like, and I'll send Katie or Sarah over as soon as they get here." I forced a smile.

They just stared at me and didn't move. I so wanted to smack Char's nasty little face as she glared at me. Instead I took a deep breath, surprised myself by saying a quick, silent prayer, and tried one more time.

"Ladies, is there anything else I can do for you?" I ran a mental list of things I'd like to do *to* them but scolded myself immediately.

"Actually, yes," Char began as she focused her hate-filled eyes on mine. "You can stay the hell away from Luke, that's what ya can do."

I shouldn't have been, but I was stunned. What could I say to that? I had hardly seen Luke, and *he* was the one still pursuing *me*. I knew she wouldn't see it that way, no matter what I said, so I did the only thing I could think to do, which was to turn around and walk straight into the kitchen. Liam was on the back line, prepping for lunch while waiting for any breakfast orders to come in. From the look on his face, I must have appeared to be ill. He rushed over to me.

"Are y'well, Brenna?" He looked truly concerned.

"Sure, I'm okay, Liam. Thanks. I just had a little run-in with Char. Oooh, that girl does *not* like me, and I have to say the feeling's mutual."

He smirked and replied, "I'd be lyin' if I said that was the first time I'd heard someone say that about her. Don't let her get to ya, Brenna. She's not worth it. How 'bout a hug?" He walked toward me with open arms.

I smiled and pushed him back lightly on the chest. He'd been trying to get a hug from me since I started at Rosie's. "No, I'm fine, really."

Just then Tara burst through the door. "What was all that?" she cried.

"Are they gone?" I asked before I answered.

"Of course, that's why I waited."

"Did they say anything?" I asked.

"No, they just whispered to each other for a few minutes, glared at me, and then walked out," she answered.

I took a deep breath. "Good." I filled her in on the parts she wasn't able to hear, although body language had told most of the story, and she already knew the gist.

"Have ya been seein' Luke then?" she asked suspiciously.

"No, I only ran in to him yesterday, and he told me he broke up with her," I said.

"Hmm. Well, she wouldn't believe ya no matter what y'said."

"I know. That's why I just walked away. I'm getting my picture done for my license next week, and I don't need to have a black eye!" I giggled at the thought.

Just then we heard the bell ring over the front door. We both scurried out into the dining room, and I was overjoyed to see Ryan standing there, looking handsome as ever.

"Well, hello, ladies. I thought maybe we were closed," he joked. It struck me funny all of a sudden that he was our boss. I began laughing uncontrollably and looked to Tara for help. I couldn't stop laughing and Ryan, rightly so, was looking at me as if I'd lost my mind, which only made me laugh harder. I turned around and headed right back into the kitchen. I'd only just stopped laughing when I caught sight of Liam's face as he watched me stumble into the kitchen, and I started laughing all over again.

Tara came in seconds later, and by then tears were streaming down my face. I could barely speak. "I … so … sorry." I laughed. "Maybe I've … lost my … mind." Laughter again. Next, Ryan came through the kitchen door, looking both amused and irritated at the same time.

"Are ya okay, Brenna?" He was completely puzzled.

I nodded and took several deep breaths before I could speak. "I'm really sorry." More deep breaths. "I think … have you ever had a time where you were so angry with someone that you just started laughing?" I was finally calm.

"I don't know," he said as Tara went back into the dining room at the sound of more customers coming in. He had a strange look on his face that I couldn't read, even after I wiped the tears from my eyes. "Are ya mad at me?" he finally asked.

"You?" I exclaimed. "No, not you. I'm so sorry. You just happened to come in right after I, well, there's this girl who doesn't like me, and she had just left after being really nasty. I think I just lost it for a second there. I stayed so calm the whole time she was here that once she was gone, I really just … lost it." I felt bad for making him think I was mad at him. Nothing could be farther from the truth.

"Who is it?" he asked with an intensity that surprised me.

"Do you know Char?" I asked.

He rolled his eyes. "Aye, enough said. I suppose this has to do with Luke?"

"I guess. But she's whacko. She told me to stay away from him when I haven't had anything to do with him, except seeing him on the way up to your place yesterday. She's crazy."

"Y'okay now?" he asked with a crooked smile.

I took one more deep breath. "Yeah. Thanks. Again, I'm sorry."

"No problem. I'm just glad it wasn't anythin' I did."

"Nope, nothing at all. So, you probably came in here for breakfast, right? Go have a seat, and I'll bring you an omelet. Sound good?" I took him by the arm and pointed him toward the swinging door.

"Perfect." He winked and left the kitchen.

After several more deep breaths to steady myself, I put the order in with Liam and headed back to the dining room. Ryan had seated himself in my section, and two more tables were seated as well, but thankfully I could see both Katie and Sarah half-running up the sidewalk toward the pub. By the time I greeted the newcomers, Sarah and Katie were in and ready to take over their sections.

"What happened?" I asked. They both looked flustered.

Katie flashed an uncharacteristic scowl my way as she grumbled, "Flat tire." Behind her I saw Sarah suppressing a grin while shaking her head. She was giving me a silent hint: *Don't ask!*

"Well, glad you're here!" I replied and made a beeline for the kitchen. As I delivered Ryan's breakfast, he motioned for me to take a seat. I looked around, and since no one else had come in, I sat across from him.

"What's up?" I asked.

"Well, Father Tim mentioned that Anna's fiftieth birthday was comin' up soon.

"Yeah, September twentieth—less than two weeks away now."

"So what were ya plannin' on doin'?" he asked.

"Me and Bettie were going to invite her friends over. We thought we'd make her favorite meal and play games or something." As I said it aloud, it sounded so lame.

"Well, that sounds nice." He was being gracious. "But I had an idea; I wanted to run it by ya."

"Tell me."

"I thought it would be neat to have a sort of birthday bash-slash-reunion here at the pub, but a surprise." His eyes glinted mischievously. My heart melted at how sweet he was, and I wanted to strangle him at the same time for insisting he wasn't looking for a relationship.

"That's a great idea! She would love that."

"Brilliant. Let's do it then." He slapped the table as if to seal the deal. "Okay, so you've got some studyin' to do for yer exam. Ya wanna come over after work, and we'll study some and get to plannin' Anna's party?"

The evil part of me was tempted to say I was busy, just because it was unfair that he could be so fabulous and yet take himself off the market. But the biggest part of me, the part that was falling harder for him each day said, "Absolutely!"

I expected the morning to drag on, but it didn't. Luke came in for lunch and was his old self again, flirting and leaving a big tip. Thankfully, I was slammed and had no time to talk with him. I knew that wouldn't be his last attempt, though. Then, just after Luke left, Ryan was back again. "I thought I'd order us some lunch that ya can bring up when yer done. Sound good?" he said.

"Sounds great. What do you want me to bring?" I asked.

"I'm gonna surprise ya," he said with a grin. He headed into the kitchen where he must have taken the back exit, because I didn't see him again until I brought the "secret" lunch up around 2:00 p.m. Ryan had the table set for two.

"Okay," he said as he revealed the contents of the bag. "What I have here is a samplin' of the menu for Anna's party." He was too cute. He was having so much fun with this thing, you'd think she was *his* mom. He served four or five sample-sized portions on each plate, and we got down to business. I liked everything but the fish, and I cautioned him that Anna was not a big fan of seafood either. "Right, so no seafood. Got it. Everything else is good?"

"Great, actually!" I said. "Liam can really cook. Where are the recipes from?"

"Well, Rosie's has been around for years but was more known for its happy hour than its kitchen until more recently. When I bought it, the owners were strugglin' to make ends meet. I figured if we could get some consistently tasty food comin' outta the kitchen, we could build up the restaurant sales considerably."

"That seems to have worked. We're always busy," I chimed in.

"Aye, I have some friends in Limerick who own a couple restaurants. They gave me some recipes to use and even let a couple of the guys come train with them—Liam included."

"Ah, well the food is always fabulous. We get comments all the time about it … especially from the tourists."

"Good. That was the plan," he said with a modest smile. "Now, we have work to do. I grabbed a copy of the testing materials on CD yesterday. My laptop's over by the couch. If ya want, you can start lookin' over the stuff, and I'll quiz ya when yer ready."

"Good idea," I replied and settled myself into a big comfy chair near the couch. The afternoon flew by. Once I was ready, he quizzed me on my traffic theory, and then we moved on to planning Anna's party. We decided that Bettie and I should go on preparing our get-together as planned but should tell Anna that we wanted to take her and her friends to the pub for dinner rather than have Bettie cook for everyone. Then, of course, we'd surprise her once she got to the pub. We made a guest list and agreed that I'd take care of calling and inviting and he'd take care of everything on the pub end of things.

I noticed that throughout our planning and organizing time, Ryan was very careful to keep a safe distance between us. I couldn't remember if this was new or if he'd done the same thing before but this was the first I'd noticed it. I even tried testing him. I'd move closer to him on the couch, and within minutes he'd find an excuse to get up and do something in the kitchen, and then he'd take a seat on the chair when he came back. This was frustrating, to say the least. It was more than being attracted to him; I felt a physical pull toward him. And yet from all appearances, I had the opposite affect on him—like the wrong side of a magnet.

I started to get angry. Here he was being so friendly and darn cute, and I'm not supposed to feel anything for him? What did he expect? But that wasn't fair. I knew the ground rules. He'd been very clear that we'd hang out and get to know each other, but a romantic relationship was not part of the equation. I had stupidly agreed, so this was my fault, not his. He was being honest all along; I was the one hiding how I really felt. But I had a strong feeling that if he suspected how I felt, he'd end the friendship.

So, if I wanted to be around him, I had to play along and pretend I just wanted to be friends.

He had dinner plans with friends in Cork City, so he dropped me off at home around five. I realized I'd blown off Patsy as soon as I stepped into the kitchen.

"Where've you been?" she said with an air of indifference.

"Oh, I'm sorry. I forgot to call," I apologized.

"Well, I guess that's fine for *some* people," she quipped. "If I did that, they'd have a swat team assembled by now."

Ouch. "Really, Patsy. I'm sorry. Ryan asked me to come up after work and work on studying for my test next week, and I just completely forgot about our tea. Will you forgive me?" I pleaded.

"Of course, I was just worried about you is all," she softened. "I realize ya may want to be spendin' more time with Finn now. How about we just have tea a couple times a week then?"

I felt guilty letting her think there was more going on than there was, but I took the easy out. "That'd be great, Patsy. Thanks for understanding," I replied as Bettie walked into the kitchen with her arms full of groceries. "Need help?"

"In the boot," she replied. I'd learned this meant the trunk of her car, so I went and retrieved the rest of the bags.

"Where's Anna?" I asked.

"She's gone over to Mary's fer dinner. A celebration for her new job," said Patsy.

"Oh, right. How'd her first day go?" I asked.

"Fine. She seems happy," Patsy replied.

"Well, this is perfect timing then." I filled them in on Ryan's plan, and they loved it. We worked out more details, and Bettie offered to call some of Anna's friends from high school who were within driving distance. I had the next day off, so the three of us made plans to go shopping in Cork City while Anna was at work.

Chapter Fifteen

Megan had called Wednesday night. "Hey, Brenna, wanna do dinner again tomorrow?" I was glad she'd asked. I worried that with Jamie back in town she might not be as friendly, but my concern was unnecessary. She added, "Jamie will meet us there, but I told him I wanted some 'girl time' with you beforehand." I was all for it, and she said she'd pick me up at five.

It was now 5:20 p.m. on Thursday, and I was starting to get worried.

She pulled into the drive in a rush and ran to the door. "I'm so sorry. I hope ya weren't worried," she said.

"Well, I was getting worried," I admitted. "But I see you're okay?"

"Aye, I stopped by Jamie's to drop off his guitar that he'd left at my place. But when I got there, he was in the barn helpin' one of the ewe's who was givin' birth. And then she was havin' trouble, and he needed my help." I noticed her sleeves for the first time. They were rolled up, but I could see bloodstains, and her hands, although they'd been washed, were still stained with blood. Suddenly dinner didn't sound so appetizing.

"Ya wanna come see the lamb?" she asked.

"Sure, I guess," I shrugged. I'm not a big animal person, but she was so excited, I didn't want to tell her that. We drove right up to the barn, where I could see a lantern swinging back and forth in the wind. Jamie was cleaning up and had made a fresh bed of straw for the new mother and her baby. I had to admit, it was a beautiful sight. I was glad I'd missed the blood and all, but the little lamb was precious. "You helped deliver him?" I looked at Jamie with wonder.

"Well, if it weren't fer Megan here, the mamma might not have made it, and the little guy there definitely wouldn't have. He was turned wrong, but my hand was too big to fit through. Megan was the hero."

He looked at her with bright, proud eyes and gave her a squeeze. She beamed back at him, and for the first time in a while, I desperately missed Ben. He used to look at me like that, and watching them I began to get emotional as those memories returned unbidden. I saw Ben's face as I walked down the aisle toward him. I felt his arms around me as we cuddled on the couch watching TV. I imagined the look on his face when he wanted more than cuddling.

"Are y'okay, Brenna?" Megan's voice brought me back from my memories.

"Yeah, sorry. I was somewhere else for a minute," I said. She looked at me for a moment with a thoughtful expression.

"Well, we'd better get goin'." She gave Jamie a kiss, and we headed back to her car.

"Do ya mind if I run into my house to change and freshen up?" she asked as we sped down the road.

"No, of course not," I answered, and she pulled into a driveway on the left. I stayed in the car as she ran into the cozy, cottage-type home. It was painted blue and white with flower boxes in all the front windows.

She was back in no time, and we headed off to the restaurant. After a few quiet moments, she asked, "Is it still really hard?"

"What?" I didn't catch on.

"I mean, dealin' with yer husband bein' gone. Is it still really hard, like every day?" Oh, she was a perceptive thing, wasn't she?

I took a deep breath. "Sometimes," I answered. "It's nowhere near what it was like in the beginning. Most days I only think about him in the back of my mind. But once in a while ..." I was getting choked up and couldn't finish my answer. She reached over and squeezed my arm but said nothing.

When I was able, I continued, suddenly wanting so badly to talk with her about it. "Back there in the barn, it was like I could see him, smell him, even feel him. It's so strange. After the accident, my brain knew what had happened and that he was gone, but at the same time, I kept expecting to see him in the kitchen or sitting on the couch, you know? It's like it wasn't real." I let it pour out. "Then after a while, it was all too real. He really wasn't coming back. Everything was changed in a split second, and I had no control over it. It was hard."

"I'm so sorry. I can't imagine how ya dealt with it," she said.

"Yeah, I guess I went into survival mode, ya know? Anna was in worse shape than I was, so I just put all my energy into helping her. I moved in with her and got a second job to help out until she got her finances figured out. At first, she was so messed up she couldn't even deal with the funeral arrangements. I did all that myself."

"That must have been really difficult," she whispered as we pulled into the parking lot of the restaurant.

"No, it really wasn't. When I'm overwhelmed, I look for things to do. I'm not good with just curling up and being alone. I need a job to do, so I think Anna's inability to do what needed doing was actually helpful for me. It gave me a purpose, something to do each day."

"She's so bubbly and outgoin'. It's hard to picture her like that," Megan said.

"Yeah, she stayed in her room for weeks. She barely came out to eat. I had to force her to drink those protein shake things. She dealt with it all very differently from the way I did. She was very bitter for a while. But everyone grieves in their own way, right? She really wasn't herself until we decided to come here," I explained. "She's been a new woman since we stepped off the plane."

"Wow. It was really kind of you to come with her," she said.

"Well, honestly, what would I have done with her gone? I probably would have lost it. No, this trip was just as much for my healing as it was for hers, I think." It was true, and I was thankful for it. "But we should get in there if we want to get a bite to eat before the meeting."

"Yeah. Thanks for bein' so open with me. If ya ever want to talk more, I'm available, okay?" She gave me a hug as I nodded, trying once again not to get choked up.

We ate a quick bowl of soup and arrived at Veritas halfway through the mingling time. Sarah and Katie were already there and had saved us seats.

"Thought maybe you were ditchin'," said Katie as we sat down.

"Aye, but then I realized it meant Jamie would have to sing, and I couldn't to that to you all," Megan said with a wink at Jamie as he walked up to the table.

"Oh, that hurts." He feigned insult.

"I know, I know. It says to make a joyful noise to the Lord, but I think the footnote says 'in the privacy of yer own shower,' or somethin' like that," she quipped back. He wrapped his arms around her from behind and whispered something that made her laugh—before putting her into a fake headlock. "I'm just teasin', y'big lout!" She smacked his arm. "Let go." He did, and they walked off to prepare for the worship time. I told the girls about the new little lamb, and they sighed.

"They're so perfect together," said Sarah.

"Truly," agreed Katie.

"Well, I'm hopin' our turn comes along soon, cuz I'm gettin' sick of waitin' for Mr. Right to show up, ya know?" Sarah looked to us for agreement.

"Preach it, girlfriend," said Katie as I nodded in agreement. I was distracted by the sight of Ryan walking in the door. He looked flushed and freshly showered, like he'd just gone for a run or something. Just seeing him walk in made my heart flutter. I watched his eyes scan the crowd and stop on mine. I smiled and waved as he walked over.

"Hey, ladies," he said with a radiant smile. I could see I wasn't the only one who enjoyed his attention. Sarah and Katie beamed back at him and said, "Hi, Ryan!" in unison.

"Have ya been runnin'?" asked Katie.

"Aye, just gettin' a little exercise," he replied and pulled up a chair next to me. "How're y'doin? Brenna," he asked with a hint of concern. I was suddenly worried that my eyes were still red from my emotional dinner with Megan. Or that maybe my cheeks were blotchy. I should have checked in the mirror before I came in.

"I'm fine," I smiled. He didn't look convinced, but Megan started the first song, so he dropped it. I recognized the song from the week before, and I sang very quietly. I didn't like to sing in front of people, but I still wanted to be a part of the worship, so I compromised by almost whispering the words. I enjoyed standing next to Ryan, as I could hear his clear tenor voice singing harmony and blending with Megan, even from a distance. I noticed Jamie was singing but didn't have a mic in front of him and had to chuckle. Apparently Megan's teasing had roots in reality.

Megan spoke, "Okay, this next song talks about majesty. I think that's somethin' we probably don't fully understand. We're no longer in a time where we have a high king that we bow down to, so some of the imagery in the Bible is lost on us. Picture the most powerful leader in the world and imagine he's invited ya to come into his throne room. How would ya feel about that? I'd like ya to close yer eyes and keep that image in mind as we sing." It was a powerful song, made more so by Megan's explanation.

Father Tim was up next. He reminded us we were in a series on relationships and explained that his topic for tonight was the most requested one: "Relationships with the Opposite Sex." It was a subject with built-in humor. He had us laughing for the first ten minutes as he made jokes to warm us up for the main message. He had many relevant points, but what stood out most to me was the idea that too many people go around *looking* for the right kind of person instead of *becoming* the right kind of person. He said that if we put half the energy into becoming who God wants us to be that we did into searching for "the one," we'd be much more likely to have a successful, lasting marriage relationship.

I found that interesting and wondered what God wanted me to be. What were his plans for me? I didn't know, and I was slightly embarrassed with myself for spending so much mental energy on Ryan, and even on Luke. I watched Ryan from the corner of my eye and wondered if that was what he was doing ... working on himself before looking for a relationship. It was something to consider.

Sarah and Katie invited me to go out for coffee, but I'd had a long day and was ready to crash. I promised them I'd go next time, and they said they'd hold me to it. So Megan and I said good-bye to the others and headed home.

"What did ya think of Father Tim's talk?" she asked.

"It was interesting. I think I need to figure out what it means to become who God wants me to be. I don't know how to do that."

"Well, I don't think any of us know exactly how to do that. But I find just askin' God to help me grow is really helpful. Just that simple prayer is enough to start with," she answered.

"Hmm. I'll try that," I promised.

We said good-night, and I headed straight to my room. Getting all emotional earlier had exhausted me. I could barely keep my eyes open, but I took a few minutes to journal. I thanked God for Megan again and wrote a little prayer asking him to show me how to grow into the woman he wanted me to be. I fell asleep with pen in hand.

The weekend was a blur. I had both Ryan and Luke in the restaurant several times, sitting in my section, wanting my attention, but amazingly never at the same time. Of course, Ryan was all business, and Luke was something else entirely. I wished so badly that I could switch that around. But that was not in my power.

By the end of the weekend, Ryan had the dinner menu planned and ordered for Anna's big night, and Bettie and I had called through the guest list. She and Patsy were so cute, sneaking around and acting all suspicious. I worried that Anna would catch on, because they were so obviously trying to act innocent that their faces screamed "guilty!" But she was so focused on her new job that she missed all the clues.

Ryan helped me study again on Monday and Tuesday, so by Wednesday I felt fairly confident. We had planned to go for a run early that morning before leaving for Cork City. He arrived by 6:30 a.m., and we took a long run up into the hills outside of town. It was a stunning sight, looking down at the river valley from high above, and I was especially glad the rest of our run would be downhill. I'd had no idea he was such an advanced runner, or I never would have agreed to go with him.

"This just about killed me," I admitted as we arrived back at the B&B. "You've been running a long time, haven't you?" I asked between taking deep breaths.

"Aye, for years. I find it clears my head and refreshes me, not to mention it's good exercise."

I nodded. "Ben and I used to run together. But we were novices. You're like a marathoner or something." I rolled my eyes.

He laughed. "Good idea. We should train for a marathon!"

"Yeah, sure. You go right ahead. I'll just stick to my wimpy two-mile run, thank you very much."

"What's a mile?" he joked.

"Funny," I smirked. "So, I imagine you're heading home to take a quick shower?"

"Aye, I'll be back for ya in twenty," he said.

"Okay, I'd better hurry then," I said as I waved and ran into the house. Anna was eating breakfast.

"Hey, stranger!" she said. I had hardly seen her in over a week.

"Hi, there! I'd give you a hug, but ..." I pinched my sweaty shirt away from my body, and she got the hint.

"Yeah, we can hug later. That was a longer run than normal," she noticed.

"Yep, Ryan showed me a road that took us up into the hills. It was so pretty. But I've gotta get a move on, cuz he's coming back to get me soon. We're going to Cork for my driving exam." She couldn't help smiling.

"Good luck!" she yelled after me as I ran up the stairs for a quick shower.

We headed off to Cork City right on time after checking to make sure I had all the needed paperwork.

"Okay, you've got to listen to this," he said as I buckled up. "I made a special CD just for the drive."

The first song came on. It was an old rocker song that I couldn't place until it hit the chorus: "I can't drive fifty-five!" I laughed as he pressed the skip button to the next song; "Baby You Can Drive My Car."

"The Beatles!" I exclaimed. "I know that one!"

He nodded. "The first one was Sammy Hagar, early eighties. Okay, guess this one."

I listened for about two seconds before shouting, "'On the Road Again' ... Willie Nelson!"

"Two points!" he congratulated.

I giggled as he sang through a medley of driving songs like "Mustang Sally," "Proud Mary," "Take It Easy," and "Truckin." The list went on and took us all the way into Cork City Centre.

"That was perfect," I said as we parked the car and headed up to the testing office. "Listening to all those songs kept me from worrying about the test."

He grinned and nodded. "That was the plan."

The test didn't take long. I sat at a computer screen and answered the forty questions. There were only a couple I was unsure of, but apparently I guessed right because I aced it. To celebrate, Ryan took me back to GBS for a fabulous burger and chips, a.k.a., fries. Next, we headed to my eye exam appointment, as that was needed for my provisional license.

By 2:30 p.m., we were back in Millway at the Local Motor Taxation office, above Mike's Hardware. I provided all the necessary paperwork and identification, and within the hour I had my provisional license, which was like a learner's permit in the United States. We scheduled my driving test for early October. Then Ryan drove me home and walked me to the door.

"Thank you so much. You've been a prince, driving me around and helping me get all this taken care of." Standing right in front of him, looking up into those sparkling blue eyes, I lost my head. Without even thinking about it, I reached up and kissed him on the cheek. We simultaneously blushed.

"No problem, really," he said, looking at the ground and putting his hands in his pockets. "I have to go. I'll see ya around."

As he waved and drove off, I stood there wondering if I'd just pushed him away. I agonized over it for about thirty seconds before thinking to myself, "Screw it. I'm not going to tiptoe around him. I'm going to be myself, and if I want to kiss him on the cheek, I'll kiss him on the cheek; and if he wants to stop being my friend because of it ... well, he can try."

Chapter Sixteen

❧ With just two days left before Anna's party, we went shopping at the Mahon Point Farmers' Market in Cork City. Bettie went every Thursday morning to get fresh ingredients for her kitchen, and on this day I joined her and Patsy because I was hoping to sneak off into the mall to find a gift for Anna. She had always been quite a shopper before but hadn't bought herself any new clothes in over a year, so I was determined to find her a pretty dress and some new jewelry to go with it. I told Bettie I'd meet them at a place called Eddie Rockets for lunch, and I headed off on my own into the mall.

I entered through a warehouse-like store called Tesco. I had told Ryan I'd pick up some party decorations and paper products, and this was the perfect place to do it. I ended up running everything back to Bettie's car so I wouldn't have to walk around the mall lugging the huge bag. But that also left me with a time crunch. I headed into a store Tara had mentioned called River Island, but it was definitely geared to the younger crowd, and I didn't see anything Anna would wear.

Further down, a store named Carraig Donn caught my eye. They had very pretty dresses, and I had a good feeling I'd find what I was looking for. In the end, I decided on a faux-wrap dress with a purple, green, and black pattern that I thought would suit Anna's tall frame and blonde hair. I grabbed a silver and pearl beaded necklace and bracelet, and I was done.

I wasn't the type to shop for hours on end. I'd been told before that I shopped like a guy. Go in, hunt down the dress, get out.

I even made it to Eddie Rockets before the ladies did. It reminded me of one of my favorite lunch places at home called Johnny Rockets. I asked if there was a connection, but they weren't affiliated. Bettie had never eaten at this American-style fifties diner, and she was suspicious of the food; but I had chosen it specifically because they made all their food fresh, and I knew she'd appreciate that. Patsy was just happy to be having lunch.

I ordered the same thing for all of us: a smokestack burger loaded with onion rings and barbecue sauce, fries, and a chocolate milk shake—classic fifties diner fare. To her surprise, Bettie liked it and said she'd consider making it at home for me sometime.

While Patsy slipped off to use the ladies room, Bettie and I disagreed. She wanted to invite Patricia to Anna's party because they were all in a book club together, but I knew Patricia hated me, and I didn't trust her to be civil. Upon her return, Patsy overruled Bettie when I told her how Patricia had treated me at the pub. "I've never liked that woman anyway!" she said.

"Well, that will be an interestin' book club meetin' next Tuesday then," Bettie mumbled.

"If she's got a problem with Brenna here, she can join a different book club," Patsy said firmly. I loved the way she stood up for me. I didn't fault Bettie; she was a people-pleaser and always looked for the good in everybody, not to mention that she was related to Patricia and Char. But I was just relieved I wouldn't have to deal with them at the party. By the time we arrived home we had everything in order. All the guests were invited and confirmed. It looked like we'd have a full house. We even had some old friends coming in from other parts of Europe. She was going to be so surprised, and we couldn't wait!

Saturday morning, Anna's birthday, I got up early and helped Bettie make a special birthday breakfast. We made homemade waffles with strawberries and fresh whipped cream. By the time she came downstairs, everything was piping hot and ready to eat. She was beaming as she walked into the kitchen.

"I think the smell of those waffles woke me up from a sound sleep!" she said. "Of course, I'm so excited to go see the lighthouse, I didn't sleep much anyway!"

I had taken the day off, and the plan was to go to Mizen Head Signal Station at the south-westernmost tip of Ireland. One of the world's most famous lighthouses, Fastnet stood a few miles offshore, and Anna had always wanted to visit. It wasn't possible to actually go out to the lighthouse, the Mizen Head Signal Station was as close as it got. They offered a museum of sorts with a tenth-scale model of Fastnet Lighthouse. Anna had been beside herself with excitement when I told her Ryan had offered to take us there for her birthday.

"Ryan will be here in half an hour," I reminded her, "so eat up! Oh, and Happy Birthday." I gave her a big hug before she sat down to eat.

"Thanks, girls," she said to Bettie and me. "This looks absolutely delicious." And it was, if I do say so myself. We finished just as Ryan knocked on the kitchen door and then let himself in.

"Happy Birthday, cousin!" he said with a wide grin as he walked over and gave Anna a big hug. He'd been away for days and I'd almost forgotten how gorgeous he was. I hadn't seen him since I kissed him on the cheek, and I wasn't sure how he was going to act toward me, so I was shocked when he walked over and kissed my forehead. "Hello, Brenna, dear," he said with a wink.

I willed my cheeks to stay flesh-colored and said a feeble hello in return. I guessed that he was putting on an act for Anna and Bettie, but he'd never done that in such an obvious way before, and I wondered what that meant for our day together. We'd be in Anna's company all day long; were we really going to pretend to be together? That could be fun!

"Where's Patsy?" he asked, looking around the room.

"She's been sleeping-in lately." Anna answered the question casually, but there was more meaning behind it than the answer alone. Patsy had never been the type to sleep in. Anyone who knew her would realize that it meant she was not herself. In most other ways, she was doing fine. She hadn't wandered off at all since the big scare, and her memory didn't seem to be getting drastically worse. Actually, she seemed to be in a holding pattern: no worse, no better. But I knew the sleeping-in thing had them more worried than they let on.

"Oh." Ryan answered with full comprehension. "Well, Bettie, would ya give her this for me?" He handed her a box of chocolates. "I picked them up for her in Limerick. I know she loves them." They were deluxe milk-chocolate fruit and nut bars. I thought they were gross, but he was right; they were Patsy's favorite.

We were on the road by eight, and Ryan had made a new CD for our road trip—songs from the seventies, when Anna would have been in high school. She loved it and used the songs as a springboard to tell us stories from those years. Each song would bring a new memory and a new story. I laughed to myself and winked at Ryan as she mentioned a couple high school friends who we knew she'd be seeing that very night.

We arrived at the Mizen Head peninsula just after the visitor center opened at 10:00 a.m. We paid admission, and while there was plenty to see and do at the visitor center itself, we opted to start with the walk down the ninety-nine steps to the signal station.

"Are you sure you can handle this, Anna? I mean, at your age and all?" I teased as we set out. She looked at me through narrowed eyes and set off ahead of Ryan and me, just to prove she could do it faster than we could. We let her have her lead and set a relaxed pace, enjoying the view. It was breathtaking. Everywhere I looked, I saw rocky cliffs and outcroppings. We came to the fabulous white arched bridge that took us over the water from the mainland to the island that housed the Mizen Head Signal Station.

We had been told to watch for dolphins, seals, and even sharks from the bridge. As we stopped to take in the sights, I took a deep breath and said to Ryan, "So, you kind of surprised me with that forehead kiss this morning."

He looked at me sideways and replied, "Yeah, I guess I surprised myself too. Sorry about that. I think I just missed ya." He looked lost in thought.

I swallowed a lump in my throat. I had missed him terribly. After spending so many days in a row with him, three days apart had felt like an eternity. I was falling fast and hard, and I knew it; but what did he mean by it?

"You did?" I asked.

"Of course," he replied. "You've become a really good friend in a short amount of time."

Ouch, that stung; there was the "friend" word again. My chest suddenly felt like it had a bowling ball lodged in it. I looked away, for fear he'd see me tearing up. It didn't work.

"Y'okay?" he asked as he turned me toward him by my shoulders. My tears were obvious, and I could only manage to nod. "I'm sorry, Brenna. Have I upset ya?" He lifted my chin. "Was it wrong of me to give ya a kiss, then? I know yer dealin' with so much, and I can't imagine how ya must feel, havin' lost Ben and all. I'm so sorry."

He was way off! He had no idea, and I wanted to smack him; but instead I buried my head in his chest, and he slowly put his arms around me. "Shh, it's okay," he said as he stroked my hair. It felt so right to be in his arms. If Anna needed a show, she was getting it now. She'd been far ahead of us, but I was sure she would have looked back by this point, and our ruse would be even more confirmed.

I wanted to stay right where I was, but I couldn't. I could have told him how I truly felt, but I knew that if that drove him away from me, I wouldn't be able to handle it. So I lied as I pushed away from his embrace. "I'm sorry, Ryan. You didn't do anything wrong. I've just had an emotional week. Thanks for the hug."

"No problem," he said as he patted my back in a brotherly way. *Ugh!* He seemed relieved that he'd not been the one to upset me, though. Of course, he *was* the reason I was upset but for exactly the opposite reason from what he thought! I would probably never be completely over Ben. He would always hold a very special place in my heart. But this man standing next to me had swept me off my feet without even trying, and I was terrified to tell him. What a mess.

Anna was impatiently waiting for us at the other end of the bridge. "What took ya so long?" she asked, exasperated.

"Sorry, Anna, my fault," said Ryan. "I wanted to look for dolphins and sharks." He looked sheepish, and she took the bait instantly.

"Oh, no problem," she said as she smiled at him. *Yeah,* I thought to myself, *he has that effect on me too, Anna.*

"But we did see some seals." I pointed out as we continued on to the signal station. Anna was in "lighthouse heaven." We took the tour of the barracks where the lighthouse crew had lived. We went through every room, and Anna took pictures galore. It was essentially an "all things maritime and lighthouse" museum.

Between the signal station below and the visitor center above, we learned all there was to know about the stunning and slender white granite lighthouse at Fastnet Rock. It could be seen in the distance, but the paintings of it were a stunning portrait. The rocky island and lighthouse combined to form what looked to me like a medieval castle with an elegant white tower glistening high above the rest. It was, by far, one of the most beautiful lighthouses I'd seen, either in person or pictures.

We had lunch at the Mizen Café, and Anna bought a framed print of the lighthouse to hang in her bedroom. We then headed out to tour some of the coast on our way back toward Millway.

"So, what are yer plans this evenin', ladies?" Ryan played it up as we arrived back at the B&B.

"We're goin' for dinner at Rosie's with Mary and Elizabeth," Anna answered. "Would ya like to join us, dear?" she asked as we got out of the car.

"Thanks. I would, but I've already made plans. I'm sure I'll see ya tomorrow at church though, right?" He was a good liar. I made a mental note of that.

"Of course. Thanks for an absolutely perfect birthday trip, Finn." She paused for a moment and added, "Would ya prefer I call ya Ryan?"

"Anna, my family has called me Finn my whole life. My friends call me Ryan. You can call me whatever ya like."

"Got it. It's hard to teach an old dog new tricks, so I'll stick with Finn," she said with a smile and gave him a hug good-bye. "The girls will be here in less than an hour, Brenna, so don't take too long sayin' good-bye!" She winked and went inside.

I turned toward Ryan. "I'm starting to feel like we're being dishonest. What is our endgame here?" I asked. I had surprised and stumped him.

"Ya know, I never really thought that far. I guess … I don't know. It was a good plan at the start, though. It did get them to leave us alone, right?" he asked.

"Yeah, I know. It's been fun, and it did work, but now it just feels like we're lying. Doesn't it?" I looked up at him, trying to figure out what he was thinking.

"Yeah, yer right, of course," he said. "What should we do?"

"I have no idea. I don't want to stop hanging out with you, though." It was the closest I'd come to telling him how I felt.

"No, me neither." I felt some small seed of hope from the way he said that. "Well, we're not really lyin', y'know. They're assumin', and we're lettin' them. That's not exactly the same thing. Do we have to do anythin' differently than we are right now?" he asked.

I thought through his reasoning and replayed the day in my head. He was getting antsy as I stood there thinking it over. "No, I guess not. We can just continue hanging out. As long as it doesn't come to lying. I can't do that. Which means if Anna asks me outright what's going on between us, I'll tell her we're just friends." Even saying the words made me angry, but it was obviously what he wanted.

"Of course! I never intended to lie to them, just let them think what they wanted to think."

"Okay, glad that's settled." I laughed to ease the tension. "Now, you have to get to Rosie's to help them get set up, right? We'll be there in an hour."

"Yep, on my way. See ya soon." He waved and drove off. I stood there wishing things could be different between us, until I heard Anna calling me from the kitchen.

"Coming!" I yelled as I ran to the house.

Mary and Elizabeth arrived right on time and played along with the charade expertly. I had asked them to dress up so that Anna would want to change into something more festive. It worked like a charm.

"Look at you girls. Ya look so fancy!" she exclaimed as they walked in the door. She looked down at her slacks and sweater with a frustrated frown.

"Oh, I forgot," I chimed in. "I wanted to give you your present before we go out to dinner." I handed her the gift box with a grin. "I wrapped it myself."

"I can tell," she replied with a wry smile and went to work opening it.

It had been a joke for years that I wanted to be an art teacher but couldn't wrap a present to save my life. Anna was the Martha Stewart of present-wrapping. She perfectly folded each corner, and like magic, no tape ever showed. She coordinated ribbons and bows so that I never even wanted to open the gifts she gave me; they were like works of art. On the other hand, I was happy to be able to cut the paper the right size. I even put more effort into this one. I'd bought wrapping paper with lighthouses on it and a blue bow, but somehow it just looked sad. I had to laugh. I had tried.

"Oh, Brenna, this is gorgeous! I love the color and the fabric. Should I put it on?" Her eyes were lit up.

"Yes!" Mary and Elizabeth said in unison.

As Anna ran upstairs to change, Patsy came into the kitchen dressed for dinner. We were worried she'd ruin the surprise, but she seemed to have forgotten all about it.

"Pasty, you look lovely," I said as I took her aside. "Do you remember we're gonna surprise Anna at the pub with a party? She doesn't know, so don't mention it, okay?" I felt bad treating her almost like a child, but she didn't appear to notice.

"All right then, but let's get goin'. I'm starvin'," she replied in her trademark blustery tone. Bettie gave me a furtive "thumbs up" from behind the counter, and Anna came back into the kitchen looking marvelous and beaming.

"Hey, hot mama!" I exclaimed, and they all laughed while chiming in with similar compliments. Anna began to blush and gave me a big hug.

"You did great. Thank ya so much, love. The jewelry, the colors—everything's perfect. You'd better watch out, though. I think ya may have just jump-started my shoppin' gene!"

I rolled my eyes in mock exasperation, and Patsy remarked, "That's lovely. Now let's go eat!"

All was going according to plan, and Anna had no clue.

"Oooh, the place looks like it must be packed," she said as we pulled into the parking lot behind the pub. "Do ya think we'll get a seat?"

"Anna," I replied, "it's your birthday. I called ahead and asked Sam to save us that big corner booth."

"Good thinkin'!" she responded with relief. As planned, I saw Ryan peeking out from his kitchen window, and I knew he'd be calling Tara to let her know we were about to come through the door. I gave him the slightest nod and continued following the chatting ladies. As we rounded the corner, I asked them to hold up while I faked having a rock in my shoe. This was just to give Ryan time to get down the stairs and into the back door of the pub so he wouldn't miss the big moment.

We all dropped back at the last moment so Anna was in prime position to open the door.

"*Surprise!*" The loud chorus greeted her as she entered. She turned around and looked at me with shock on her face and then turned back to the crowd and laughed. For the next half hour Anna was hugging old friends and catching up on the past thirty years. She kindly introduced me to everyone as her daughter, and no questions were asked. When we'd invited the guests, we'd been sure to fill everyone in on Joe and Ben's passing so that there were no awkward questions, only quick condolences. Everyone commented on how young and beautiful she looked. I heard more than a few comments like, "Are y'sure it's not yer fortieth?"

I left Anna to continue mingling and took a seat at the bar. I was exhausted already, and the night had barely begun. I laughed at Patsy sitting in the corner by herself, eating a plateful of appetizers. I could tell Anna was having a blast, and I was so glad that when Ryan walked up, I threw my arms around him for a quick, friendly hug.

"Thank you so much for suggesting this!" I looked up at him and nodded toward Anna. "She is loving it."

"Aye, it's great to see her havin' so much fun," he agreed. "We did do a brilliant job. Well done, Brenna," he congratulated me.

"And you too, Finn!" I joked.

"Watch it!" he warned. He might have told Anna it was fine, but I could tell he disliked being called Finn. "They're bringin' out the dinner buffet now. Father Tim said he'd say grace." Ryan waved Father Tim over toward us.

"Ah, Brenna, you two have done an excellent job. Yer mother-in-law is a delight to work with, and she talks about ya all the time, y'know," Father Tim said.

"Well, thanks. She deserves a great party," I replied. "You're going to say grace for us?"

"Aye. Would ya like to say a few words first?"

"Sure." I had planned what I wanted to say. Ryan motioned for us to follow him to the karaoke stage.

"Can I have yer attention?" he said into the mic. "Folks, we want to thank everyone for comin' out tonight to celebrate such a big night with Anna. I'd like to make a toast, if you'll raise a glass with me?" He waited for a moment. "Anna, we're so glad you've come home to us. To homecomings! Sláinte!" The crowd echoed his toast, and he handed me the mic.

"Well, yeah, thank you so much for coming. Anna, I just want to tell you in front of all these people that you—" The waterworks were back again. I looked at Anna, and she was all teary, which didn't help me gain control of myself. I had so much I wanted to say, and all I could manage to get out was, "I love you." The crowd roared with applause, which allowed me to make a hasty exit to the kitchen to gather myself while Father Tim said grace.

Tara came through the door with Megan on her heels to check on me. "Are y'okay?" she asked.

"Yeah, I'm fine now. You know, must be that time." I raised my eyebrows, and they got my meaning. "I've been blubbering like a baby all day, it seems." I laughed at myself.

Dinner was delicious, as I knew it would be. Soon after, the band started up, and the tables were cleared to the sides of the room to create a larger dance floor. The playlist was similar to what Ryan had played on the way to Mizen Head, so all her high school friends were dancing and cracking up. We had asked Jamie's dad ahead of time to make sure he got Anna out on the dance floor, and he didn't disappoint. Thanks to the free-flowing wine, she was easily persuaded, and before long, she was the one pulling others out to dance with her.

Eventually the band switched to some more traditional Irish tunes, and I watched from the corner booth as Jamie grabbed Megan and swung her around the dance floor. Several other couples joined in, and I was shocked to suddenly hear Luke's voice once again tempting me out onto a dance floor.

"Brenna, would ya do me the honor?" he said with his hand outstretched. I deliberated. I was tired. But I loved to dance, and no one else had asked me. Of course, that could have had something to do with me hiding myself in the corner. Still, he knew how to tempt me, and I grabbed his hand.

"I don't recall seeing your name on the guest list, Luke," I razzed him as we headed to the dance floor.

"Ya know, it was the strangest thing. I was leavin' my flat when I took a wrong turn and wound up in the kitchen over there. Then, of course, I had to come see what all the ruckus was, y'know?"

"Mm-hmm," I replied.

"And what travesty do ya think I chanced upon as I came through that kitchen door?" he asked as he began weaving us through the other dancers with expert ease.

"What?" I played along.

"Why, the most beautiful girl in the room was sittin' all by herself in the corner while everyone else was dancin'," he said in mock horror.

I rolled my eyes. "Not everyone else is dancing, Luke."

"Aye, true, but I know how ya love to dance, and it would have been wrong of me to leave without at least offerin' my services." He was so smooth. I did notice that he didn't have quite the powerful effect on me that he used to. But he was still gorgeous, and my heart still raced when he pulled me close and led me around the dance floor. We danced to two songs before I needed a break. But before I could drag him off, Ryan was standing in front of me.

"May I cut in?" he said to Luke, who smiled his wicked smile and passed my hand into Ryan's waiting one. The look on Ryan's face almost scared me. It was intense and almost angry. If he'd looked at me that way, I would have wilted, but Luke just laughed and walked away.

"What was that about?" I asked as he pulled me closer and we began to dance.

"Hmm?" He looked down at me. "Oh, nothin'. Luke's just not one of my favorite people is all." This surprised me, as I didn't think they really knew each other.

"I didn't know you could dance," I said.

"I didn't know ya wanted to," he replied with a grin, while I began to pray for a slow song. And God does answer prayers, because the next song was a beautiful, slow Irish tune that had all the partners easing into a slow

123

dance. I expected him to end our dance, but he didn't, and I said a quick prayer of thanks. For a few short, sweet minutes, I let myself believe that we were the only ones in the room and that Ryan wanted to be with me as much as I wanted to be with him. I laid my head on his chest and let him glide me around the dance floor.

I cursed to myself when it was over, and I knew we'd go back to the "friend" routine. But as I looked up into his eyes, I saw something unexpected. It was an intense gaze that Ben had given me when we first started dating, and it stunned me. As quickly as it had come, it was gone; but I had seen it, and I was no longer fooled. There was something between us, and he could say whatever he wanted, but I knew now that he wanted the same thing I did. Before I could even say a word about what had just happened, he said he had to check on something and took off toward the kitchen.

I considered following him, but Megan and Tara came up to me, giggling. "What's so funny?" I asked, distracted.

They didn't answer at first, so I looked at them more deliberately. Tara had a guilty look on her face, and Megan's eyes were lit with excitement. I knew immediately that Tara had told her about my secret crush. I dragged them to the ladies room without a word. Once I was sure there was no one else inside, I leveled a killer look at Tara, and she folded.

"I'm so sorry. I thought she knew!" She held up her hands as if to defend herself. I looked at Megan.

"It was an accident, really," Megan defended Tara.

"Explain," I said to Tara in a stern voice.

"Well, I was watchin' you two dance, when Megan came up and said, 'Aren't they a cute couple?' So I totally thought you'd talked with her about it, so I said …" And here she looked sheepishly at me.

"Go on," I prompted.

"I said, it seems to me Brenna always gets her man," she admitted.

At this point, Megan joined in, "So I asked her what she meant, and she realized I had no idea, but I pushed her to tell me what she knew. It's my fault. Blame me."

I put my head into my hands as the fatigue truly sank in. "Honestly, I would have told Megan anyway." I let Tara off the hook and turned to

Megan. "So, am I crazy?" I really valued her opinion and was worried she wouldn't approve.

"No, not at all. I think you two would be fabulous together. Jamie and I have even talked about it."

"You have?" I was taken aback.

"Aye. He's known Ryan for a long time, and he thinks yer perfect for each other," she assured me.

"Really? Even with the age difference and all?" I asked. Surprisingly, it didn't bother me at all, but I did wonder what other people would make of the eight years between us.

"Well, if you were ten years old, maybe it would be a concern." She grinned. "But I think yer both adults and can determine for yerselves whether or not that's an issue."

I felt an incredible sense of relief wash over me, and I suddenly became like a giggling, giddy schoolgirl. "Isn't he just adorable?" I asked.

"He's the genuine article, and don't tell Jamie I said so, but yes, he's very handsome," Megan concurred. "So how long has this been goin' on then?"

Instantly my euphoria evaporated as I was brought back to reality. "It hasn't been going on," I said and watched confusion bloom on their faces. "I mean, there's officially nothing going on." I tried to explain, but a woman walked in to answer the call of nature, and our private conference was over.

So we headed back through the crowd of people, who were laughing at a man attempting a three-pint karaoke version of a Sinatra song. We made our way out onto the sidewalk in front of the pub, where I proceeded to fill them in on the maddening situation I found myself in. I ended by telling them what had happened on the dance floor. They agreed that something was up and practically pushed me back into Rosie's to find Ryan and ask him what he was thinking. But I couldn't find him. I searched the kitchen and the dining room and even had Liam check the men's room for me, but no Ryan.

The party was dying down by this point, and the crowd was thinning when Father Tim spotted me and flagged me down. "Brenna, I was lookin' for ya," he said with an odd look on his face. He almost looked guilty, though for what, I couldn't fathom. Then he handed me a folded sheet of paper. "Ryan asked me to give this to ya, dear. He had to run out." He patted me on the shoulder as he handed me the note and headed out of the pub. Tara and Megan found me minutes later, sitting on the kitchen floor, fuming.

"Ya didn't find him?" Tara asked.

I looked up at them and handed Megan the note. "Go ahead, read it," I said.

Dear Brenna,

I'm sorry ... I couldn't find you to say good-bye. I have a business emergency in Limerick, and I have to go. Sam's got a cleaning crew coming in at midnight, so no need to worry about that. Great job with the party. See you soon.

Your friend,
Ryan

"Seriously?" Megan said with such ferocity that I felt slightly cheered up.

"What is he playing at?" I asked, knowing they didn't have an answer. The anger started bubbling up again. "I know what I saw tonight, and then he has the audacity to sign it 'your friend,' as if ..." As I fumbled with my words, my kind friends sat down next to me and let me rant. "Does he think I'm stupid?" I wanted to scream. "He's running away, and I don't understand why." I rested my head on my knees and focused on breathing slowly. I felt Megan's hand rubbing my back, and then the hot tears came. She pulled me into her arms and let me cry. After a few minutes, I heard her whisper something to Tara who got up and left the kitchen. All the emotion of the past couple weeks came pouring out in the form of tears, and Megan just sat there comforting me until Tara returned.

"All set," she said. I looked up to see Jamie standing there behind Tara, and I was mortified. I covered my face with my hands and turned away.

"What are ya doin'?" Megan asked him with an edge of irritation in her voice.

Jamie answered, "I wanted to see if ya needed any help." He sounded worried.

I heard Megan take a deep breath. "No, that's why I asked Tara to tell you I'd meet ya back at yer place in half an hour," she said through gritted teeth. I could only imagine what her face looked like, but I didn't want to look up.

"I told him not to come in. He didn't listen to me," Tara said in an exasperated whisper.

"I know," Megan replied. "Jamie, everything's fine. Brenna's just not feelin' well, and I'm gonna take her home, okay?"

Jamie hesitated and then said, "Okay, I'll see ya soon."

"Is he gone?" I asked after a moment.

"Yes," said Tara as she handed me a towel for my tear-soaked face.

"I'm sorry, Brenna. That was not what I intended," Megan apologized.

"I know. I don't know how I'm going to get out of here now, though. I must look horrid." I sniffled.

"I trust yer other errands went better?" Megan addressed Tara.

"Aye, I told Anna that Brenna was sick, and we were gonna take her home," Tara answered. "She wanted to see her, but someone else came up to say good-bye to her, and I was able to sneak away. They're all still out there, so if we leave now, we can beat them home and get her up to her room."

They helped me get to my feet, and we left through the back door. Tara had grabbed my coat and purse for me, and I let them lead me to the car and all the way back to my bedroom. They proceeded to help me wash my face and get ready for bed. We heard the ladies get home, so Tara went down to stall them, while Megan tucked me in. It was all kind of foggy and dream-like. I guess I was just emotionally spent. The last thing I remember was Megan giving me a kiss on the forehead and saying she'd call me the next day.

Chapter Seventeen

I had left four messages for Ryan since I'd gotten out of bed. I'd missed church altogether. I guess Anna thought I was still sick and needed to rest, because when I woke, the house was quiet. We didn't have any guests this weekend, so with the ladies all still at church, I had the place to myself. I took a look at myself in the mirror and winced. It was not a pretty sight. My puffy, swollen eyes were confirmation that it had not just been a bad dream.

I wandered downstairs, took some ibuprofen to ease the pounding in my head, and made myself some tea and toast. I began to replay the night's events in my head. Now, with a night of sleep between me and the dance with Ryan, I was beginning to doubt what I thought I'd seen in his eyes. Maybe I was simply insane. Still, he wasn't answering my calls, and that was odd in itself. I did have a message on my phone from Megan, though. *"Hey, Brenna, I know it's early, and I hope this doesn't wake ya up. Just wanted to let ya know I'm thinkin' of ya, and I'll stop by after church."* I was once again so thankful for her friendship.

With my tea in hand, I went back upstairs and sat down with my journal to put my thoughts down on paper. I'd always found that to be the easiest way to sort out my emotions when they were jumbled up inside of me. What did I know for sure? Well, on my end of things, I knew I was in deep. I missed him when I wasn't with him. I thought about him without even trying. When we were together, I felt more alive and more myself.

129

He made me laugh with no effort, and he also inspired me to grow and try new things. Until now, I had also trusted him. But with his disappearing act the previous night, I wasn't sure what to think.

On his end of things, I knew a lot less. I did know he enjoyed spending time with me. That was obvious, because he had initiated all our time together in the first place. I knew he didn't want to lose our friendship, because he had said as much. And I knew that I'd seen a couple glimpses of a man who wanted more than friendship but for some reason refused to admit it. None of this helped me decide where to go from there.

I had always been the type to take care of myself. I had been described as "fiercely independent." Whether that was a result of losing my parents young or just part of my nature, I didn't know. But at this moment, I found myself unable to make heads or tails of my situation. I felt helpless, so I tried something new. I wrote out a prayer:

Dear Lord,

I'm not sure how to do this. I know you know what's going on, even though I don't. I need your help. I need you to guide me, because I don't know where to go from here. Should I leave him alone? Should I keep trying to reach him? Does any of this even matter to you? I've heard you know the number of hairs on my head, so I think that means you do care about the details of my life. Help me to do what's right in your eyes, even if it I don't understand it.

Amen.

As I finished my prayer, my eyelids grew heavy, and I curled up in my chair and went back to sleep. I woke to the sound of Anna's voice.

"Brenna, love. Wake up, dear." She was gently rubbing my arm as I opened my eyes.

"What time is it?" I asked as I noticed long shadows spanning the floor of my room.

"It's almost three," she answered, and I bolted upright.

"Seriously? I just closed my eyes for a second!" I'd slept for four hours in my chair? But I did feel refreshed, and a little stiff, as well.

"Are ya feelin' any better then?" she asked.

I nodded. "Yeah, I am now, thanks. Actually, I'm starving. Did you all have dinner already?" Sunday dinner was usually served by 2:00 p.m.

"No, Bettie was runnin' behind, and that's why I came up to check on ya. It'll be ready in about fifteen minutes."

"Okay. I'm gonna grab a quick shower, and I'll be down," I promised, and Anna nodded and headed back downstairs.

"Dinner was fabulous as always, Bettie," I said. She'd make a pork roast with homemade applesauce, roasted potatoes, carrots and parsnips. It was melt-in-your-mouth good, and I ate too much. This pleased Bettie, of course, who reminded me of Mrs. Clause in a Christmas special I'd seen, saying, "Eat, Papa, Eat!"

"I think I just gained five pounds." I rubbed my belly and the others smiled.

"Well, I'm glad to see yer feelin' better," Anna said with a curious look on her face. I could see she didn't buy the "sick" story, and I knew I was in for a grilling at some point in the near future. I suddenly remembered Megan.

"Did Megan stop by?" I asked.

"Aye, after church. I told her you were sleepin' and I'd let ya know she stopped," Anna replied. "Sorry, I forgot to mention it."

"No, no problem. I'm just gonna go give her a call. Thanks again, Bettie. You outdid yourself." I headed back up to my room for privacy. Megan picked up on the first ring.

"Brenna?" she said.

"Yeah, it's me. Sorry I missed you earlier," I said.

"I'm glad you were restin'. How are y'doin?" she asked.

"I'm okay at the moment. You wanna come over?" I didn't really want to be alone, but I also didn't feel like telling all to Anna just yet.

"Absolutely! I'll be there in ten."

Megan stayed for the whole evening. We talked some about Ryan, but mostly we just hung out. Eventually, though, she had to leave, which left me a sitting duck for Anna. As I expected, she knocked on my door within five minutes of Megan's departure.

"So …" She leveled me with a look that said she meant business. "What's goin' on with you?"

I took a deep breath and patted the bedside next to me to offer her a seat. I knew this was gonna be a long one. She had seemed to be totally okay with the idea of Ryan and me, but now that I was about to talk with her about it, it felt so awkward. Was she really okay with me being interested in someone else? What was an acceptable amount of time to grieve? I didn't know, but I had to tell her the truth. So I did. I filled her in on everything. She laughed when I told her about Ryan's idea to get her and Patsy off our backs and admitted it had worked well. I told her everything, right up to the dance at her birthday. As I recalled the details, I saw his eyes in my mind and was convinced once again that I had not imagined it. He was hiding how he felt, and I knew it.

"Ya like him a great deal, don't ya?" Anna said with a tender look in her eyes.

I looked down at my blanket to avoid looking at her. "Is that really weird for you?" I asked.

She grabbed my hands. "Look at me, Brenna." I obeyed reluctantly. "I thought it would be strange, but it really isn't. I've tried to explain to ya before how I see you as my own daughter. I think about Ben and Joe every single day. My heart is still broken that they're gone. But keepin' ya from livin' a full life won't bring them back in any way. No, you need to move on. Ben would want that, wouldn't he?"

"I don't know … I guess. I mean, he wouldn't want me to punish myself with a life of solitude, I do know that."

"No, he wouldn't. Not only that, he would have liked Ryan. I'm sure of it." I noticed she didn't call him Finn today. Maybe she was seeing him as something different than her young cousin.

I looked up at her. "You really think so?" Somehow it was important for me to believe that. Almost like I wanted Ben's approval, as impossible as that was to achieve.

"I know so. Ryan is a gem. I don't know what's wrong with him. I don't know why he's actin' so weird, but I think yer right about him. He's just as into you as y'are into him." She said this with a confidence that I found comforting.

"I hope you're right," I sighed.

"Well, I have the benefit of havin' seen his face while ya danced with Luke. He was not happy at all," she said.

"Really?" I was giddy at the thought of Ryan being jealous of Luke. "Tell me what you saw!"

Anna chuckled as she recalled it. "Well, I had noticed ya sittin' in the corner, watchin' everyone dance, and I wondered why you and Ryan weren't dancin', seein' as I thought there was already an understandin' between you two." She raised an eyebrow, and I smiled sheepishly. "So, when I saw Luke walk in and make a beeline for you, I found Ryan in the crowd and watched him for a reaction. He didn't see ya at first. He was in a deep conversation with Father Tim. You were already on yer second dance when he noticed. He stopped mid-sentence when he saw ya in Luke's arms."

"Really?" I would have loved to have seen that reaction.

"Really. Ryan's jaw tightened up, and he took off across the dance floor to cut in."

My heart soared as my suspicions were confirmed with Anna's story. "I know the story from there." I smiled.

"No, not fully," she replied. "You were dancin' with yer eyes closed. He wasn't. He was lookin' down at ya the whole time, and it was so precious, Brenna. I can't understand why he won't share how he feels, because it was obvious to anyone watchin' the two of ya, includin' Luke." My eyes grew wide with that revelation.

"Luke?" I'd forgotten about Luke the minute Ryan had taken my hand. "What did he do?" I asked.

Anna smiled. "As soon as ya put yer head down on Ryan's chest, the smug little smile of his vanished. He watched for a minute and then took off." I felt kind of bad. I wasn't trying to hurt Luke.

"You knew he liked me?" I was surprised.

"Well, I knew ya didn't want me to know you'd gone out with him." I was guilty as charged. "But it's a small town. News travels fast and rumors even faster." I suddenly thought of Patricia blabbing at their book club.

"What do you think you know?" I asked skeptically.

"I know ya went out with him to Cork City that one night. Of course, I didn't know at the time, but it was mentioned to me later, and I played along like I knew," she said with a tone that made it clear I'd hurt her feelings by keeping her in the dark.

"I'm sorry," I said quietly.

"Yer forgiven," she replied. "Anyway, I knew you'd been out the one time, but I didn't think you'd seen each other since, at least not in a datin' type situation. If ya had, I'm sure I would have gotten an earful from Patti." She rolled her eyes.

"She doesn't like me," I said, annoyed.

"I know, dear. She's all prickles, always has been. Don't worry about her. I know how to filter what she says to get the truth."

"Really?" I decided to test her. "Okay, then, tell me what actually happened with me and Luke, since I'm assuming you got the story from her."

"Aye, that I did. All right, I'll tell ya what I gleaned. Mind ya, this is not what she said; it's how I interpreted it. I think Luke was pursuin' ya for quite some time, and ya finally broke down and agreed to go out with him. I think he's a very smooth operator who was hopin' to dazzle ya with his good looks. How am I doin' so far?" she asked with a grin.

"Spot on. Continue," I replied.

"So, he takes ya to a dance at some club or somethin' in Cork. He brings ya home and expects somethin' in return for his charmin' company, and yer tempted but refuse him. He gets mad and goes runnin' back to Char, which is his pattern, and she calls you the villain."

"Wow." I was impressed. "You are good!" I laughed as she nodded smugly.

"So, I'm guessin' that since he broke up with Char again last week, he's set his sights on y'again, right?"

"Yeah, he's been coming in every day for lunch, asking me for another chance. He's hard to resist, you know," I confessed.

"I can imagine. A girl can only be so strong. I've often wondered why God gives such beauty to those who would squander it. Anyway, I know he's a temptin' distraction for ya. For what it's worth, I think you've been wise to steer clear of him," she encouraged.

"Well, I don't know how clear I am. It's a lot easier to resist him when he's not around." She laughed at that, and I realized it did sound funny. "What I mean is I don't think about him when he's not around, like I do with Ryan. But when he's standing in front of me asking me to dance … it's like I have no willpower at all," I admitted. "How is it that I can have feelings for two guys at the same time? Is there something wrong with me?" I was so confused. She laughed again. "I'm glad you find me so amusing."

"Brenna, ya do make me laugh. No, there's absolutely nothin' wrong with ya. As a matter of fact, you're quite normal. But I can relate."

"You can?" I'd never seen her look at anyone but Joe.

"Aye. When I was a newlywed, I had an experience that scared me. I was on a trip for work, a tour to Greece actually. I worked for a tour company, and it was the first time I'd been apart from Joe since we'd gotten married."

"I didn't know you did that," I said.

"Aye, I got to visit Greece, Turkey, Egypt, Italy. It was a great job for a young girl. But anyway, on this one trip, there was a young man that I just couldn't take my eyes off of. It was like that high-school-crush thing when ya see the person everywhere ya go and just want so badly to go talk with them."

"That's how I felt about Ben," I agreed.

"Well, it freaked me out, because I was happily married. Joe and I were doin' great, and here I was completely attracted to someone else."

"What did you do?" I asked.

"I prayed and asked for help, for one thing. I wasn't sure if it was a sin or not, but I knew it wasn't good thing. Then I did my best to avoid him. Of course, part of me didn't want to, because I enjoyed how it felt to talk with him. I think the attraction was mutual, and that was part of what scared me."

"Wow, so what happened?" I prompted.

"Nothin'. He knew I was married, and most of the struggle was takin' place *within* me, not on the outside. There was nothin' external happenin' at all. No one would have looked at us and noticed anything—except maybe a slight blush on my cheeks when he was around. But I was scared to death by it."

"'Cause you felt like you were cheating?" I asked.

"No, not exactly. Because I realized I could be *capable* of cheatin'. I had assumed that since I had very strong views on marriage and fidelity that I would never be tempted. That was an ignorant assumption."

"So you never saw him after that trip?"

"Nope. I got home and went straight to Bettie to ask her what was wrong with me. She was older and had been married longer, plus I knew she wouldn't judge me."

"What did she say?"

"Just what I'm tellin' you. That I was normal. Stayin' true to yer spouse is not about the absence of temptation, it's about the presence of commitment."

"Well, yeah, that's easy to say, but what if he had been someone you saw all the time, like someone you worked with or something?"

"Aye, that would have been more difficult, but the idea is the same. You will have occasions when yer attracted to different men at the same time. It's not the attraction that's wrong; it's what ya do about it that is important."

"So, the fact that I can be interested in both Luke and Ryan doesn't take away from what I had with Ben?"

"Yer askin' if the fact that yer fallin' for someone else means that Ben wasn't the right one for you?"

"I don't know. Maybe. It just seems like I shouldn't be able to feel like this for someone else if Ben was the one for me. And he was. So what's my problem?"

"Yer lookin' at it wrong. If ya had visited here with Ben and met Luke, do ya think you wouldn't have found him appealing?"

That was a weird thought. "No, I guess I would have, but it would have scared me," I replied.

"Right, but what I'm sayin' is that ya can't let it scare you. Just be wise to it. I think that's how most affairs get started. Someone meets a person that makes them feel all jiggly inside, and they begin to question whether or not they married the wrong person. That's dangerous. Marriage is a commitment, not a feelin'."

"So, do you think Luke is dangerous for me?"

"Well, that depends. Through no fault of yer own, you've been released from yer first commitment. Is Luke someone ya could see yerself marryin'?" she asked.

"*Definitely not*, no. I mean, I like the way he makes me feel. It's like when I'm around him I'm … desirable, maybe? Ben made me feel like that, too. But other than that, there's really nothing there with Luke," I admitted.

"Well, then, yes. I'd say he's dangerous for ya. Now, what about Ryan?" she asked.

"You think he's dangerous?"

"No. I mean, is he someone ya could see yerself makin' a commitment to?" she clarified.

"Oh." I knew I was blushing. That probably sufficed for an answer, but I attempted to reply anyway. I was embarrassed. "Yeah. Definitely."

"Well, then, I don't think he's dangerous for you. That's the kind of relationship you should pursue."

"And just because Luke still makes me dizzy, it doesn't mean my feelings for Ryan are any less valid?"

"Exactly. Just watch yerself around Luke," she said with a smile.

"I'm trying," I assured her. "But what should I do about Ryan? How can I pursue a relationship when he won't even return my calls?" My frustration returned instantly at the thought of the many messages I'd left that day.

"I don't have an answer, dear. I truly don't know what's goin' on with him. But I can tell ya what I'd do," she offered.

"What?"

"I'd take the next few days and just ask God for wisdom. Ask him to help ya know what the next step is."

"But I just want to *do* something. I feel like I should go hunt him down and make him tell me what's going on," I explained.

"Sometimes the best thing y'can do is just be still," she said. "Can I share a favorite verse of mine?" she asked.

"Sure."

"It's from Proverbs 3: 'Trust in the Lord with all yer heart and lean not on yer own understandin'. In all yer ways acknowledge him and he will make yer paths straight.' I've taken comfort in that verse countless times in my life. I was in such a dark place after the accident that I hardly remembered how to breathe but somewhere in the back of my mind, that verse comforted me even then."

"It sounds familiar, I think you may have mentioned it to me back then. I guess I can try to trust that God has a plan in all this," I agreed. But being still would be a challenge for a control freak like me.

"Good." She stood up. "Thanks for bein' honest with me, love. Ya know you can tell me anything, right?"

"Yeah, I know. I forget sometimes. I worry that you'll be upset with me," I admitted.

"Well, I still want ya to know you can come to me if ya need to talk," she reassured me.

"Thanks." I stood and gave her a hug. "Love you."

"You too, sweet girl. You too." She headed to her room, and I got ready for bed. I wrote a prayer in my journal before I turned out the lights and took special care to make sure I thanked God for blessing me with such a fabulous surrogate mother.

Chapter Eighteen

I woke up early Thursday morning and took a long run up into the hills. I had given up on leaving Ryan messages. He had gone absolutely off the grid, and I couldn't do anything about it. It was refreshing to run and not think about anything important.

I had been in Ireland now for almost four months, and still the beauty of the land was breathtaking. It was as if I'd never seen green before I'd come here. The color was so vibrant, so alive. And it carpeted everything. There were low stone walls that lined the roads, and even those were covered by a mossy blanket.

I had learned to carry a small umbrella in my purse due to the frequent rains, but that wasn't possible when I went running. So when the rainfall began on this particular morning, I headed straight for a stand of poplar trees by the roadside. There were three trees that had grown so close together they were intertwined. This created a thick canopy of leaves that had begun to change color but had not fallen yet, keeping me fairly dry. If this had been the typical light and fleeting drizzle, I would have just run through it, but this was a soaking rain. I sat in the crook of a branch to wait it out.

My cell vibrated in my pocket, and my stomach did a summersault as I looked at the caller ID. "Hi, Ryan," I said.

"Hi, Brenna. Sorry it took me so long." Just hearing his voice made my anger dissipate.

"What happened?" I asked.

"I just had to leave town for a little while. Sorry it was so sudden," he answered. That was all I was going to get? The anger began to grow again.

"Why?" That was all I could manage while controlling my temper.

"I'm really sorry but I'm gonna be gone for a while." He was evading my question.

"When are you coming back?" I was suddenly scared he was going to hang up.

"I don't know yet." He sounded so sad.

"I miss you, Ryan. I want to see you." I choked back tears. "Can't you come visit me?"

He was silent for what felt like forever. "I want to see you too," he admitted softly. "Maybe I can come out next week."

I couldn't wait that long. I had to talk with him face to face. "No, sooner. I need to see you." I was more vulnerable with him than I'd ever been.

He paused again and finally agreed. "Okay, I'll come by tomorrow night and pick ya up around six?"

"Thank you," I replied through tears of relief.

"See ya soon," he said and then hung up. I stared at the phone for a minute before I realized that the rain had let up and the sun had come out. By the time I arrived back at home, I'd convinced myself that everything was going to be fine. I would make Ryan see how we should be together, and he would stop being foolish, and all would be fine. My mood was so altered that Patsy couldn't help but ask me what was up as I hummed my way through the kitchen.

"Oh, nothing really. It's just a beautiful day," I replied. "You wanna walk into town and get lunch with me, Pasty?"

She was taken aback. "Well, that would be nice," she said, while her tone said, *It's about time you stopped neglecting me.* I laughed and told her I'd be down after my shower.

"So, are you and young Finn an item or what?" she asked as we headed up the footpath that would take us to town. Subtlety had never been her strong suit.

"I don't know, Patsy. It's kind of complicated," I replied.

"What's complicated? Either yer together or yer not," she replied.

"Well, I like Ryan very much," I said, and my cheeks confirmed it. "And I do think he feels something for me, but he won't admit it."

"Blast, I thought fer sure you'd do the trick!" she exclaimed.

"What?" I was lost.

"You have no idea how many lovely young women I've paraded in front of that boy over the years, and he doesn't show the least bit of interest. Now, with you, I finally saw a reaction. That first night at dinner, I could tell he was intrigued by ya."

"Really?" I had seen nothing but brotherly behavior until Saturday night.

"Aye, he hid it well, but I could tell ya lit a spark in him. But ya say he won't admit it," she said with exasperation. "I'm about to give up on that boy."

"What are you talking about, Patsy?"

"Do ya know that he hasn't dated anyone in ten years?" she asked.

"Seriously?" I was stunned. "How do you know that?" My mood began to deflate quickly, as I considered this new information.

"Talk to his mum all the time," she answered. "She's worried about him too."

"Why hasn't he dated anyone in so long?" I asked.

"No one knows! Well, except Father Tim. He probably knows, seein' as they've always been good friends."

Lunch was not nearly as enjoyable as I'd expected when we set out. I couldn't concentrate on a word Patsy said, and she knew it. All I could think about was going to talk to Father Tim. Maybe he could help me figure out what was going on. Finally, she reached across the table and grabbed my hands to get my attention.

"Listen, how 'bout we go visit Anna at the church, and you can see if Father Tim has time for a little visit." She was perceptive.

"Thanks, Patsy. I'd like that," I said as I pulled out money for the bill.

Anna was pleasantly surprised to see us. "Now, was there a girls' day out and no one invited me?" she teased.

"Brenna here needs to speak with Father Tim," Patsy said with no small talk, as usual.

Anna looked at me with concern. "Are y'all right?"

"Yeah, I'm fine. I'll tell you all about it when I get home," I assured her.

She popped out of her chair and, after a quick knock, slipped into Father Tim's office. She was out a moment later.

"Go on in, love." She motioned toward the still-open door.

"Thanks," I replied.

"I'm about done here. Do ya want us to wait for ya?" she asked.

"No, you go ahead. I'll come straight home, though. I promise."

Father Tim's office was cozy and warm, if a little disheveled. There was a large fireplace on one side, and the walls were lined with bookshelves. There were so many books, I couldn't even make out what color the walls might be. The only free wall space was above the mantle where a stunning painting of a lion and a lamb hung center-stage. Father Tim was seated behind a large oak desk, but when I walked in, he stood up and directed me over to two wingback chairs set in front of the hearth.

"Thanks for meeting with me without an appointment or anything," I began. "I wanted to ask you a few things about Ryan." I got right down to business.

"Sure, 'tis no problem. Been expectin' ya," he said with a warm smile.

"You have?"

"Aye, ever since I had to give ya that ridiculous note at Anna's party." He rolled his eyes, and I thought I just might have an ally.

"Can you tell me why he left?" I asked.

"No, that's up to him, Brenna. This may be difficult. I'll tell y'anything I can, but that'll be limited. Whatever people tell me, I have to keep in confidence, ya know?" he explained.

"Like attorney-client privilege?" I asked.

"Aye, or doctor-patient," he added.

"Okay, so what *can* you tell me?"

He thought for a second. "Hmm, I think it'll be easier if ya ask what ya want to know, and if I can answer, I will. If I can't, I won't."

I was overwhelmed with all the things I wanted to ask, so I started with something simple that I knew he'd answer. "How long have you known Ryan?"

"It's been about eleven or twelve years, I guess." He smiled at the softball I'd thrown him. "Pretty much since I moved here."

"So you knew him when he was still dating?" I asked.

"Aye," he replied. That was all, nothing for free. Okay, this was going to be hard.

"Do you know why he stopped dating?"

"Aye, but I can't tell ya," he replied.

"How long has it been?"

"Well, I can answer that, as it's not somethin' he specifically told me. Hasn't dated anyone for ten years," he answered.

"Do you think he will ever date again?" That was an opinion; he should be able to answer that one.

He looked at me with tender eyes. "I certainly hope so," he answered and paused. "Aye, I think he will."

"But you can't tell me why he won't date?" I tried again.

He was silent for a moment. "I will tell ya this; for reasons only Ryan can tell ya, he made a vow of sorts not to date anymore. And he has been rock solid on that vow until now." *Until now.* That meant until he met me.

"So he left because of me?" I asked.

"Hmm, can't answer that." He didn't answer in words, but I knew the answer was yes, anyway.

"What should I do?" I needed help. I didn't know where to go from here.

"Just pray for him, dear. Give him time, and be honest with him about how ya feel," he answered.

"I don't know what to pray. He's shut me out." I was feeling panicky.

"Pray that he will see himself as his Maker sees him," he responded. "That is what I have been prayin' for a long time, and I think you may be part of God's answer to that prayer."

"Me? Why?"

"Do ya think Ryan cares for ya?" he asked.

My cheeks flared. "I think so. I hope so," I answered.

"That's important," he said. "And I think yer right, so take heart. I believe Ryan will make the right decision. Keep prayin'."

He rose from his chair, indicating he'd said all he could—probably more than he should have—and I was so grateful. I left his office without all the answers, but at least I had a little more to go on. *Ten years.* No wonder he was so hard to read. I was desperate to see him, and Friday night seemed years away. I went right home, as I'd promised. I told Anna that Father Tim really couldn't give me much more information than Patsy had, but that he confirmed that Ryan had not been dating for ten years. I asked her to pray for him, and then I told her I was going to my room for the night.

Megan called, offering to pick me up for Veritas, but I declined. I told her I wasn't feeling well, which was true, but mostly I just wasn't up for light-hearted mingling and banter. Apparently, Anna and Luke weren't the only ones who'd taken notice of my dance with Ryan. Speculation had been running rampant all week in town, and I had no energy to field those questions. If I could have, I would have gone to sleep right then and not woken up until an hour before Ryan came the following night. I considered trying, but I knew I'd be lucky to sleep at all, much less for twenty-four hours. I felt physically exhausted, but my mind was constantly racing.

I passed the time that evening by staring glassy-eyed at HGTV repeats. I didn't know exactly what I watched, as my mind was elsewhere. I tried imagining how our conversation would go, but since I had no idea what his end of it would be, it was a futile exercise. I eventually dozed off with the TV on. Sometime in the night, I realized it and forced myself out of bed to change and turn off the lights. I woke in the morning with an odd, queasy feeling in my stomach, coupled with a pounding headache. I wasn't feverish, but I just felt completely useless. For the first time since I'd started at Rosie's, I called in sick.

It was still very early, and I couldn't go back to sleep, so I turned the TV on for a rare glimpse at the news. I generally didn't watch the news, as it was almost always depressing. But as I flipped through the news channels and paused on one that caught my eye, I was suddenly blindsided. There across the bottom on the ticker was the date—September twenty-fifth—exactly one year since Ben and Joe had been killed.

I jumped out of bed, threw on my robe, and headed straight for Anna's room. I knocked lightly. "Anna?"

"Come in, love," she said in a soft voice.

I opened the door to see her sitting in her bed surrounded by crumpled tissues. Without a word, I crawled under the covers with her and pulled her into my arms. She wrapped hers around me, and we sat there crying until the tears dried up and I said, ashamed, "I forgot. How could I forget?"

"I didn't want to remind ya," Anna replied. "Y'have so much on yer mind right now. But ya didn't forget. Yer sittin' here, first thing in the mornin'. Better that ya weren't dwellin' on it all week long. Besides, I'll always have the reminder of my birthday—just six days later," she explained.

"I feel awful today," I said. "It's like my body knew before my brain caught up."

"Aye, I've a headache myself. But I need to get ready for work," she said as she got out of bed and headed toward her shower.

"You should call in, Anna. They'll understand," I encouraged.

"No. I thought about it, and Father Tim told me it was okay, but Friday's a busy day. We get everything set for Saturday and Sunday Mass. Besides, I'd like to be busy; it's a good distraction." She made sense. That was usually how I dealt with these kinds of things, too. But today was just too much. I felt horrid. It was September twenty-fifth, and I had Ryan coming at six. Too much. I was okay with taking the day off.

I headed straight back to my room, crawled into bed, and shoved a pillow over my head to block out the light. I woke to the sound of my phone vibrating on the nightstand. I'd been dreading a cancellation call from Ryan since the previous morning. But caller ID told me this was Megan. She was probably the only other person I would have answered for.

"Hi, Megan." I tried to sound like I had been awake.

"How are ya feelin'? Still sick?" she asked, concerned.

"Yeah, I don't feel well," I answered.

"Well, I'm bringin' ya some homemade chicken soup," she informed me.

"No, Megan, I'm okay. Really." I tried to dissuade her.

"Brenna, ya called in sick to work, yer probably still in bed at one o'clock in the afternoon." I glanced at the clock. Wow, she was right. I had slept through the whole morning. "And I'll bet ya haven't eaten a thing today, have ya?" She had me pegged.

"Okay, come on over," I relented.

"I am. And stay in bed. I'll let myself in," she ordered, and I obeyed.

Within five minutes, she was walking through my door. I looked at the clock again. Had I dozed off?

"How did you do that so fast?" I asked.

"I called ya from Jamie's. I stopped there to pick up the soup Liz had made last night," she explained. Still, the timing didn't add up. How had she known she would need to pick up soup in the first place? I looked at her, confused, and she wilted.

"Okay, I can't lie to ya." She sat down and handed me a steaming crock of soup with a spoon. "I was at the church, practicin', this mornin', and Anna told me. I'm so sorry, Brenna," she said sadly. "Anna was worried about ya."

"She's worried about me? She's in the same place I am," I said.

"Not exactly. She said Ryan was comin' tonight too." She wanted the scoop, naturally. I told her about my conversation with him the morning before. I didn't go into what I'd learned about him from Patsy and Father Tim, though. I wasn't up for talking about it.

"So, it's been a year then?" she asked.

"Yeah," I said, and unbidden tears welled up again. It was suddenly as if it had just happened. I had an immense weight on my chest so that it was hard to breathe. As the tears streamed, Megan pulled me close and let me cry for a few moments.

"I thought I'd used up all my tears already today," I told her through my sniffles.

"Do ya want to talk about it?" she asked tenderly.

I closed my eyes and saw myself sitting in my apartment one year ago. "Yeah," I said, surprised. I recounted for her the details of that horrible night. I had just come home from class, and Ben was excited. His dad had invited us to go to a concert, and he wanted to go. It was a good forty minutes away, and I had an early class the next day, not to mention a boatload of homework. I'd seen the Sweeney Brothers perform before. They were very entertaining, and Joe loved the Irish music they played— said it brought him home. But I had too much to do, and I knew Anna wasn't going. So I encouraged Ben to make it a "male bonding experience." He hadn't seen his dad since the semester had begun, so the father-son thing was a good idea.

His dad drove the hour to our apartment on campus, and then Ben drove them into Rochester from there. A freak storm hit around 9:30 p.m. I heard the thunder and saw the wild and constant lightning from my room. I knew Ben was on his way home, because he'd called ten minutes before to say good-night from the road. He didn't want me to wait up, since he knew I had an early morning. Anna called around 10:00 p.m. to see if they'd gotten back yet.

"No, but they should be here soon," I assured her. She was worried about the weather. Apparently there had been several accidents on the thruway due to poor visibility. I looked out my window and was shocked. The wind had knocked down two small trees in the common area in front of our dorm, and the rain was slicing its way across campus in horizontal sheets. It was then that I got a sick feeling in my stomach. I didn't see how Ben could possibly drive in that. I told Anna I'd call him and call her right back.

His phone rang four times and went to voicemail. I hung up and tried again … ten times. No answer. That was wrong. If he had pulled over to wait out the storm, he would be answering his phone. Maybe the battery was dead? No, he hadn't had his phone with him in class today because he was charging it.

I turned on the news to see if any accidents had been reported. There were many, and the news channels didn't give out any specifics. The phone rang, and I snatched it without looking at the caller ID. "Ben?" I said with an edge of hysteria in my voice. It was Anna. I'd forgotten to call her back.

"I'm sorry. I can't reach him," I said as panic welled up in my chest. "What should we do, Anna?" The storm was so bad and so sudden that a driving ban had been issued. There were small tornado-like sightings, called *microbursts*, all over the western part of the state. That was what was really wreaking havoc. Trees and power lines were down, and authorities were scrambling to assess and minimize the damage.

"I've called the police," she said. "They have so many accidents, they don't have any information to give us. I'm supposed to call back in one hour," she explained. I could tell she was trying to be hopeful, but I had experienced loss before, and I could feel it stalking me once again. This would not end well.

"I need to do something," I told her. I'd considered getting in my car and driving toward Rochester to try and find them.

"Promise me you will stay put, Brenna." She could tell I was becoming irrational. "Brenna, do you hear me? Promise me." The fear in her voice broke through, and I promised. "I'll call you as soon as I hear anything," she assured me.

I kept the news on, watching with a blank stare. Anna's call woke me at 4:00 a.m. They'd been found, and her voice told me it was not good. Apparently, in the confusion of the storm, a young woman had ended up going the wrong way on the highway. It was a head-on collision with no survivors. Our lives had just been turned upside down.

When I finished telling Megan the story, she had tears streaming down her face. "I'm so sorry, Brenna. How horrific," she said.

I nodded. It was strangely therapeutic to tell the story. I hadn't talked about it in so long, and it now felt like I was putting it to rest.

"How are y'not bitter? First yer parents, then yer husband. I don't know how I would have gotten through all that," she said with a transparency that I appreciated.

"Well I guess I just dealt with it. Didn't have much choice, right? As far as my parents, I probably was kind of bitter for a while, but Ben helped me with that. He challenged me when I blamed God for taking my parents. He told me I couldn't have it both ways. Either God was big enough to have been able to save my parents, or he wasn't; and if he was, then he was also big enough to know a heck of a lot more than I did and I should trust him."

"Good point." Megan agreed.

"I know. He was also convinced that it was wrong to assume we had to either blame man or God when something tragic happened. He said we had an enemy that we couldn't see, who took every opportunity to pull us down and away from God."

"He was an amazin' guy, wasn't he?" she asked.

"He was. He was a godsend, truly. I guess I've come to see it as God lending him to me for a while when I needed him most. Ya know?"

"Aye. I admire ya for havin' such an incredible attitude. So many people would be bitter and defeated," she said.

"Well, I guess that's just not me. I don't know." I really didn't know how to respond. "I hear Anna downstairs," I said. "I should probably see how she's doing."

"Aye, and I need to get back over to Jamie's. Thanks for sharin' with me, friend." She gave me a squeeze and turned back at the door. "Call me. Let me know how it goes tonight."

"I will," I promised.

Chapter Nineteen

It was four o'clock. I had two more hours to kill before Ryan got there, and I was driving myself crazy thinking about what to say to him. I'd already showered. Now I just had to get ready. I intentionally took a long time drying and styling my hair. I put some curls in it and put on my minimal amount of make-up. I tried on five outfits before settling for the first one: jeans and a fitted, button-up shirt. I looked at the clock. 4:40 p.m. *Geez.* Time was passing too slowly. What I needed was a good distraction.

I decided a movie would do the trick and loaded one of my favorites, *Pride and Prejudice.* It was the newest version, and I knew the dialogue by heart, but no matter how many times I'd seen it, I always found myself transported into the world of Elizabeth Bennett and the dashing Mr. Darcy. Which was why I was taken by surprise when a knock at my door snapped me back into my own world.

It was Ryan. I was so relieved to see him, I bounded from my bed and practically knocked him over, throwing my arms around him. "Thank you for coming," I said into his chest.

He pulled me off and said, "Brenna, ya have to stop doing things like that." The look on his face was almost angry, and it shocked me.

He turned around and headed down the stairs, and I followed, feelings tumbling inside me like a thousand bouncy balls.

"Where are we going?" I asked as we got into the truck.

"There's a nice little cinema about twenty minutes away," he said.

Seriously? "A movie?" Anger was creeping into my voice.

"Aye, a movie," he said flatly.

I knew then that he wasn't planning on telling me anything. "Ryan, I want to talk. We can't do that during a movie!" I tried desperately to keep my voice calm, even as I was sensing my tenuous control over my emotions slipping away.

"We can talk after," he said quietly as we turned onto the highway.

"Why can't we talk now?" I asked with an edge to my voice.

He slowed the car. "You don't want to go to a movie?" He sounded exasperated. "Yer right. I shouldn't have come at all."

He was scaring me. I suddenly feared he was going to turn around and drop me back off at home, and I'd never see him again.

"Wait, no … I'm sorry. A movie is great. Let's do the movie." I was panicking inside. What was going on? I figured the movie would at least buy me some time. Besides, quietly sitting next to him in the theater was preferable to being escorted home and left alone with no explanation.

I'm not sure what movie we watched. I couldn't pay attention at all. Sitting so close to him and not being allowed to even reach out and touch him was unbearable. I was desperate to know why he was pushing me away but terrified that anything I said would seal the deal. I could see him out of the corner of my eye. He wasn't even pretending to pay attention to the movie. He just sat there staring straight ahead like he was enduring this distasteful time with me and counting down the minutes until he could break free.

As we drove back to town in silence, I searched my brain for a way to keep him with me a little while longer. Just before we reached the turnoff for the B&B, it hit me. "Can we stop and get a bite at Rosie's? I'm starving," I said.

He considered it and agreed. My plan was to get the food and go up and eat it in his flat. That way we'd have a private place to talk. I ordered a sandwich, and he ordered nothing. When the food came, I asked him if I could eat it upstairs, but he wouldn't go for it. He was refusing to be alone with me, refusing to give me any opportunity to find out what was going on. Well, fine. If he didn't want to do this in private, we'd do it in public.

"Ryan, why did you leave like that last week?" I asked him while sitting at the bar, surrounded by people.

He looked at me with a blank stare and then looked away. I felt wretched. I tried again. "Ryan, please!" I pleaded. "Please talk to me." I was feeling the panic return to my voice, and he heard it too. For the briefest moment, I saw pain in his eyes, and then he looked away.

"Okay, let's go upstairs." He gave in, and relief flooded me.

"Ryan," I started when we reached his flat. "I haven't been honest with you." That got his attention, and he looked at me warily.

"What are ya talkin' about?" he asked.

This was good. He was engaging. "When we met, you said you weren't looking for a relationship." He tensed beside me on the couch. "And I went along with that … because I didn't think I was looking for one either. But I was wrong." I tried to look in his eyes, but he looked away. This was so hard. "Ryan, I'm trying to tell you that I *do* want a relationship. I want to be with *you*."

"Stop," he said loudly. "I told ya I didn't want a relationship."

"I know …" I began to get angry. "But I don't believe you. Are you telling me you don't feel anything more than friendship toward me?" I was pushing him. "Cuz I may have bought that before that dance, but I know I saw something—"

He interrupted me. "Brenna, I should never have spent so much time with you. It was wrong of me. I thought it was safe, what with yer situation." So he was playing my widow card?

"What do you mean, *safe*? Safe for who? Why haven't you dated anyone in ten years, Ryan?" He looked at me with wide eyes. Yes, I'd done some homework.

"Don't wanna talk about it." He was literally gritting his teeth. "I told ya that yesterday on the phone. I can't talk about it right now. Maybe someday. Not now."

We were at an impasse. We sat silently on his couch for a few minutes. Finally, in desperation, I played the ace I'd been saving all night. "Did you know today is the one-year anniversary of Ben's accident?"

He looked at me in shock. And then his steely reserve melted. "Aw, Brenna, I'm so sorry. What an ass I am." His quick turnaround brought tears to my eyes. "Are y'okay?" he asked with kindness and sincerity flooding his voice.

I nodded and began to cry—not for the reason he thought but because I so wanted him to stay this way with me. The coldness was gone, and I was terrified of its return. What he did next took me completely by surprise. He reached over and pulled me onto his lap and held me in his strong arms. My reserve shattered into a thousand pieces. I thought I'd cried enough tears today, that there'd be no more left, but I was wrong. I sobbed in his arms. I sobbed over Ben. I sobbed over Ryan. I just sobbed. He held me close and didn't let go.

Finally, when the aftershocks of my sobbing had ceased, he pushed me far enough away that he could see my face. He took the hair that had stuck to my wet cheek and put it gently behind my ear. Then he wiped the remaining tears away with his thumb. Sitting there, looking into his clear, blue eyes, I felt hope stirring once again.

He leaned in and gently kissed my forehead and then moved on to my eyelids and then my cheeks, and then suddenly he was truly kissing me. I was afraid to move. Afraid that anything I did would break the spell. I carefully kissed him back, and it was amazing. I felt my body responding to him on autopilot. I turned myself so that I was facing him and took his face in my hands, and then I kissed him like I meant it. For one ecstatic moment, he kissed me back passionately, and then he froze. The spell was broken, and he pulled away from me.

"What?" I said, confused. "I want this, Ryan, and you do too. You can't deny that now!"

He looked absolutely crushed and defeated. "I'm so sorry, Brenna," he said in a whisper. "I just can't do this. Yer too dangerous for me. I have to go." He got up and walked toward the door.

"No, Ryan," I pleaded.

"I have to go," he said firmly now. "It's gettin' late. You can stay here if ya like." I nodded. He didn't trust himself to be alone with me long enough to take me home. The door closed. He was gone. And I was so thoroughly rejected I could hardly breathe.

Chapter Twenty

"Hi, Anna, it's me," I said, weary. It was 10:00 p.m., and I knew she might be in bed, but I didn't want her to worry.

"Where are ya?" she asked.

"At Ryan's."

"Everything goin' okay?"

"No, not really. He left," I said.

"Oh, dear. What happened?

"I'll tell you tomorrow, okay? Don't worry, everything's all right. Just don't want to talk right now."

"Want me to come get ya? I can drive Bettie's car," she offered.

I considered it. "No, he said I could stay here, and I think I want to. I'll walk home in the morning."

"Okay, love. Try to get some sleep, and we'll talk tomorrow."

I crawled into Ryan's bed and turned out the light. His sheets smelled like his cologne. It was a light, woodsy, kind of spicy scent, and I breathed it in for a few minutes before turning over onto my back to try and fall asleep. I lay there for what felt like hours but was probably only minutes. The bass line of the music at Rosie's was echoing through the walls. I couldn't sleep. I heard people laughing out front on the sidewalk—probably young couples in love, leaving the pub. I rolled my eyes. I pictured Megan and Jamie holding hands and walking down the road. I pictured Tara and John in the corner booth, laughing.

I started feeling sorry for myself. Why can't I have what they have? Why does everyone always leave me? But quickly my self-pity turned to anger. "God, I've tried trusting you. I've tried praying, and I don't hear you answering. If this is your plan, I don't think I like it."

I got out of bed, grabbed my purse, and headed into the bathroom to freshen up. I brushed my hair and reapplied my makeup. I'd decided to take myself out on the town. I was young. The night was young. Why should I be in bed by eleven on a Friday night? Ridiculous!

The pub was crowded. UCC had let out for a long weekend, and the local college kids were taking full advantage. I wasn't used to seeing Rosie's like this. I was more accustomed to the restaurant atmosphere of the daytime. This was a totally different place. The bar now took center stage; the lights were low, and the music was loud. I was hoping Tara was working. She sometimes picked up weekend shifts behind the bar.

I picked my way through the crowd and squeezed into a newly vacated spot at the bar. Tara was there along with two other bartenders. It took me a while to get her attention.

"Brenna! What are ya doin' here?" she asked with a laugh.

"Just wanted a change of scenery, I guess," I said.

"Thought you were sick."

"Yeah, felt horrible this morning. But I'm better now," I lied.

I noticed a cute guy next to me watching our conversation. When I looked at him, he smiled and turned to Tara. "I'd like another pint, and one for the lady," he said, nodding in my direction.

I started to protest but stopped myself. Why not? I was in Ireland, for goodness' sake. Why shouldn't I have a pint? "Thanks," I said and flashed him a bright smile. Tara looked at me, bewildered.

"Ya want a pint?" she asked.

"I sure do," I said with a slap on the bar.

"Okay." She shook her head and handed us both our pints.

I raised mine with the Irish toast, "Sláinte!"

He returned the toast, and we both drank. It was disgusting, but I was determined not to show that. I took a second gulp and wiped the foam from my lips as I'd seen others do.

"Yer Brenna?" he asked.

"Yep. What's your name?"

"Conor. Nice to meet ya, Brenna."

"Thanks for the pint, Conor." I smiled and took another horrific swallow. The taste was awful, but the warmth spreading down the back of my throat was kind of nice.

"Do ya go to UCC?" he asked me.

"No, I work here, actually," I replied. "You?"

"Aye, my last year!"

We talked through another pint, and I was feeling quite good. He was a nice guy. I liked the attention, but when he asked me if I wanted to go home with him, I laughed. "No, thanks, Conor. It was nice chatting with you, though." I got up and headed toward the other end of the bar where Tara was talking with John.

"Hi, Brenna, how are ya?" John asked and offered me his seat. I normally wouldn't have accepted, but tonight I did.

"Great, John, yourself?" I asked.

"I'm well, thanks. Are ya here alone?" He looked around.

"Yeah, I just wanted a night out, ya know?" I answered.

Tara was counting out her drawer; she was probably done with her shift. I noticed a couple girls in the middle of the bar doing shots of something. They seemed to be taking turns or trying to outdo one another.

"Tara, what are they drinking?" I asked her.

"Short o' whiskey," she replied.

"Okay, I'll take one of those," I said with confidence.

Tara looked at John and then back at me. "Are ya okay, Brenna? Yer not actin' normal."

"I'm fine. Really. I just want to try what they're having—just one. It's okay; I'm legal. Wanna see my passport?" I joked. She eyed me for a moment and looked back at John for help.

"Aw, let her have a short, Tara. One won't hurt her," he reasoned.

Tara relented and poured my shot of whiskey. I had been watching the other girls, and I mimicked them. Down the hatch, all at once. *Woo, that burned!* And it would stain too, since it dribbled down my chin and onto my shirt. I saw both John and Tara chuckling at my expression, and then Tara's eyes widened as she looked behind me.

"Now, Brenna, I thought ya didn't drink!" Luke slid smoothly into the newly vacated seat next to me.

Wow, he was gorgeous. "I thought I didn't drink too!" I said and laughed at myself. He signaled to Tara that he wanted a pint and one for me too.

"Thanks, Luke," I said as I took a long sip of the beer. This one didn't taste as bad. "That the same kind I had before?" I asked Tara.

"Aye, the same. Probably just gettin' used to it," she answered.

"Are ya ready?" John asked her.

"Aye. Brenna, I'm done. Do ya need a ride home?" Tara asked.

I wasn't ready to leave. I hesitated, and Luke jumped in. "I'll make sure she gets home safe," he assured Tara. She nodded and headed out with John.

I had tried two more shots with different crude names when Luke flashed his wicked smile and said, "Wanna dance?"

"Absolutely." I took his hand, and that was a good thing, because I got a head rush as I jumped off the barstool. There were still so many people here that I couldn't even see the dance floor from where I stood, swooning.

"Whoa, careful there," Luke said as he put his arm around me and led me through the swarm to the dance floor. The music was a little fast, but Luke was such a good dancer, he was able to keep pace with it as he led me around and around. I heard the bartender call for last round as the song changed to a slow-moving one.

"I love dancing with you," I told him as he changed his hold and moved us into a different, slower dance pattern.

He pulled me closer and held me tighter as he whispered in my ear, "I dream about dancin' with you, Brenna." He sent shivers down my spine, and then he kissed my neck without missing a beat, and I felt an intense heat surge through me.

He wanted me, and I needed to be wanted. I disarmed the warning bells screaming through my brain, until all I heard was the sound of his breath, hot on my neck. I turned toward him, and he crushed his lips to mine, and I responded with an equal intensity. My body hadn't felt this particular sensation in over a year, and suddenly my legs went weak. It seemed as if we were instantly outside the back door and on our way up to his flat. I knew I shouldn't go, but I also knew I didn't care.

Chapter Twenty-One

I did care when I woke up in a strange place. It was early morning, and as I opened my lead-filled eyes, I knew I was not home. I slowly turned my head, afraid of what I knew I'd see. Luke was asleep next to me, and immediately the previous night came flooding back to me. I'd made a *huge* mistake. I'd never done anything like this before. What had felt so good in the cover of dark night, now felt *so* wrong in the clear light of day. What had I done?

I lay there for several minutes, trying to figure out what to do next. I did *not* want Luke to wake up. I didn't want to talk to him; I just wanted to get out. I moved a few times as if moving in my sleep to see if he would stir, but he didn't. So I painstakingly eased my way out from under the covers and onto the floor. I recovered my jeans and shirt, trying not to remember how they'd been separated from me, as my head pulsated with every heartbeat.

I made it out of his flat without a noise, only to realize that I hadn't thought about what to do next. I looked out the small window in the stairwell to make sure Ryan's truck was not there and then flew up the stairs and into his flat. I locked the door and lowered myself to the floor. What had I done? I closed my eyes, willing myself to wake up from a nightmare. But the jackhammer in my head told me it was all too real. *How could I have been so stupid?*

159

I replayed the night in my head, trying to figure out at what point I went flying off the rails. Probably going down to the pub at all had been looking for trouble. I'd been angry, and I had wanted to play it a little fast and loose … just not that fast and loose. Would I have gone with Luke if I hadn't had three pints and as many shots? Probably not. I didn't think so. I should have just gone home when Anna offered to pick me up.

I desperately wanted a shower but couldn't bring myself to use Ryan's. I threw my hair up into a ponytail, washed my face, grabbed my purse, and left Ryan's flat. I locked the door from the inside and pulled the door shut on my hopes of ever being with the man who lived there. I swallowed the lump in my throat as tears of remorse started to well up. I quietly crept down the stairs, and as soon as I was clear of the parking lot, I ran all the way home.

I hoped I could get to my room without being seen. It was early enough that I had a chance. Every sound was magnified as I crept through the kitchen. I'd never noticed how many squeaky steps the back stairs had. I closed and locked my door. *Safe.*

I ran the shower as hot as I could stand it. It was so hot that it hurt, but that felt right. I wanted to punish myself for being so stupid. I *knew* Luke was dangerous. Anna and I had even talked about it! Why did I let my guard down? I stayed in the shower until the water ran cold and I began to shiver.

I towel-dried my hair and crawled into bed. I couldn't get warm. Even with two extra blankets, I fell asleep, shivering. My head was still pounding when Anna's knock woke me.

"Brenna, can I come in, love?" she asked.

"Yeah," I said.

She came in and sat down on my bed. "You look horrible."

"Thanks," I said, unable to even fake a smile. I didn't want to talk. I didn't want to see anyone right now. I just wanted to sleep until it all went away.

"What happened last night?" she asked.

I knew she was referring to what had happened with Ryan, but fuzzy thoughts of what had happened with Luke assaulted me. I closed my eyes. "Sorry, Anna. I just really don't wanna talk right now. I know that's not fair, but can you just let me sleep?" I asked in a weak voice.

She felt my forehead the way mother's do when kids are trying to get out of school. "No fever, but ya do look awful. Aye, I think sleep is what ya need. Come down when ya get hungry. I'll fix y'some tea and toast." She smiled a warm smile that I knew I didn't deserve.

"Thanks," I mumbled as I pulled the covers over my head and rolled onto my side. I slept until it was dark. I had no idea I was capable of so much sleep. I got up long enough to go pee and get a glass of water, and then I went right back to bed. I was hoping that somehow I could keep this up until I no longer remembered what I'd done.

Surprisingly, I was able to sleep again and did not wake until the next morning. I knew I would not go to church. God knew what I had done. I understood that, but going to church would make me that much more aware of what a mess I was. No, I would stay in my bed until Anna got fed up dragged me out. That was my new plan, my new strategy.

Sunday afternoon, Megan came to my rescue. She knocked and opened my door tentatively. Taking one look at me, she closed the door and sat next to me on my bed. "What happened?"

I turned away. I didn't want her to know. I didn't want anyone to know. I was so embarrassed and ashamed.

"Brenna, yer scarin' me. What's wrong?" she pleaded.

"Don't wanna tell you," I admitted without looking at her.

"This isn't about Ryan, is it?" How did she know? I turned over and looked at her with tears now filling my eyes. Just the mention of Ryan hurt me deeply.

"No. Ryan doesn't want me anyway. I mean, he does, but he won't do anything about it. That's just hopeless." I sighed.

"Why?" She was temporarily distracted from her previous inquiry.

I sat up and told her about what had transpired between me and Ryan. I told her about the movie, the argument afterward, and the kiss. Telling her about it, I re-lived it and was staggered by the contrast between kissing Ryan and kissing Luke. With Ryan, it was like we were both giving each other something, but with Luke it was all about taking something.

"Geez, Brenna, that sucks!" Megan said angrily. For the moment she was angry with Ryan for his lack of explanation. That would change when she found out what I'd done in response. "What in the world could have happened to him that he'd swear off datin' forever?" She asked the question I'd asked myself a hundred times.

"No clue. I wish I knew. Father Tim knows, but he can't tell me … clergy oath or whatever."

"Well, maybe he'll come around, friend," she said hopefully.

I shook my head. "Doesn't matter. He won't want me anyway," I said in despair.

"What happened with Luke?" she asked, and my jaw dropped open.

"How do you know?" I was bewildered. Did I have a sign on my forehead or something? That would be very inconvenient.

"I didn't, but you've been AWOL all weekend, and I did know ya were drinkin' with him on Friday, so I put two and two together. Wasn't hard for a brain like me," she offered with a smile. Maybe she wouldn't hate me.

"John told Jamie?" I asked.

"Aye. Said you were actin' really odd, orderin' whiskey and pints, and just not yerself. John actually thought you were pretty comical, but Jamie was worried about it, so he told me."

I nodded. "Jamie was right to worry," I confirmed.

"Just tell me what happened, Brenna." She wanted the truth.

I took a deep breath. "Promise you'll still be my friend?"

"Of course I'll still be yer friend, ya eejit. Just tell me!"

My hands were shaking, and my heart raced as I confessed what had happened with Luke. She kept an indecipherable look plastered onto her face. That made it worse. It was like talking to a wall, but I spilled it all and waited for her reaction.

"Oh, friend, I'm so sorry that happened." She reached over and gave me a warm hug. I was not expecting that. I was waiting for condemnation and punishment of some kind.

"I messed up," I said through fresh tears.

"Yes, ya did," she replied matter-of-factly.

"You're not mad at me for being such a screw-up?"

"Course not. I'm sad for ya, but I'm not mad at ya. Why would I be?" She was truly puzzled by my question.

"I don't know. Maybe I just think everyone should be mad at me. I want a punishment for being so stupid."

"I have a feelin' you've been punishin' yerself plenty in the last day and a half," she said with a wry smile. "Ya look like y've lost a half-stone! Ya haven't eaten a thing, have ya?"

She was right, and I hadn't even realized. "No, guess I haven't."

"I figured as much," she said as she pulled a granola bar out of her bag. "Here, this is for you. It'll do for now, but yer gonna eat dinner as well." She was taking control, and it was a relief.

"Megan?" I took the granola bar from her. "What should I do now?"

"Well, ya know what ya did was wrong, aye?" she asked.

"Absolutely." No question.

"Okay, so have ya asked God to forgive ya?" she asked me.

The thought hadn't even crossed my mind. I just assumed I'd be on His bad list now. "No, I wouldn't even know how," I confessed.

"Just ask Him," she replied.

"Why would He forgive me?"

"Why wouldn't He?" she countered.

"Well, I don't know. I mean, I was drunk, I guess, but it's not like I didn't know what was happening. It's not like I was date-raped or anything. It's my fault."

"Not only yours," she said with a look that might have killed Luke had he been in her sights. "But yes, you are responsible, and just the fact that ya know and admit that is part of why God will forgive ya. Yer not lyin' about it or denyin' it. Yer confessin'. Have ya heard the word 'repent' before?" she asked.

"Yeah, like 'Repent and be saved'?" I replied.

"Exactly. If ya aren't sorry and ya just say y'are to get forgiven, well, yer not really repentin'. It's not sincere, and I have a feelin' ya wouldn't be forgiven. But you are sincere. Yer not only sorry, but ya wouldn't do it again, right?" she confirmed.

"Right!"

"Okay, so that's repentance. Yer sorry, yer turnin' away from what ya did."

"Yeah, but this isn't like I lied about something or screamed at someone. I had sex with someone I'm not married to, Megan. Someone I wouldn't marry, even if he asked me. That's got to be harder to get forgiveness for."

"No." She shook her head adamantly. "*We* rate sins. We give each sin a different value, but God doesn't. To Him, all sin is sin," she assured me.

"So, wait, you're saying that if I murdered someone, it's no different than if I told a lie about them?" I said, incredulous.

"Not in the fact that both are sin. Yes, there's obviously a difference in the consequences. If ya murder someone, ya go to jail, ya ruin yer life and the lives of their family—all that stuff. So the natural consequences for that sin may be greater, but the eternal consequence is the same. All sin separates us from God."

"So what do I do to make up for it?" I asked.

"You can't do anything except ask Him to forgive ya, and He will," she explained.

"How do you know?"

"Well ya know, I don't know what yer background is. Did ya grow up in the church?" She switched gears on me.

"No, not really. Ben did, but I didn't really go to church until we'd been dating for quite a while. He was smart about it, like you. He knew all kinds of stuff. He could quote verses and everything. I don't know all that. I know God's real. I know Jesus died for my sins." As I said it, I saw what she was getting at. If I didn't think God would forgive me for this, was I saying that what Jesus did wasn't enough to cover it? "Okay, I see, He is able to forgive me. But how do I know He will?"

"Do ya believe the Bible is true?" she asked me.

"Um, I've never really thought about it before," I admitted. "I guess so."

"Well, I do, and I have very good reasons for doin' so. That's a whole other conversation we can get into later, but I asked because the Bible says—I think it's in First John—"If we confess our sins, He is faithful and just to forgive our sins and purify us from all unrighteousness." Now, it doesn't say *some* unrighteousness. It says *all*. That includes gettin' drunk and sleepin' with a loser, Brenna," she said with a smile on her face.

I laughed at her insult of Luke. He was a loser, wasn't he? He knew exactly what he was doing. I was angry with him for taking advantage of me. But that didn't negate my part. No, I needed to ask for forgiveness. Because I knew I'd made a mistake and because maybe it would take away the constant churning guilt that was eating me from the inside out.

"So all I have to do is ask God to forgive me, and because I mean it, He'll forgive me?"

"Right. And what's even more amazing is that he doesn't forgive like we do. We forgive, but we don't forget. We keep a record of things people have done to us, even if we don't mean to. But not God. He completely strikes it from the record. It's as if it didn't happen. Jesus took all the punishment for it already."

"Seriously?" I asked. How come I didn't know all this stuff? I'd been coasting on Ben's coattails, that's why. I had said the prayer asking Jesus to save me, but then I had taken Ben's faith as my own without really learning about it myself. And then when he was gone, I latched on to Anna's faith. It was about time I grew up and learned about the faith I professed. "So, should I pray right now?"

She smiled. "Sure. Why wait? Ya don't have to pray aloud. This is between you and God. Would ya like me to leave the room?"

"No, stay!" I felt better with her there. I closed my eyes, and I did just what she'd suggested. I asked Him to forgive me for messing up. I asked Him to purify me like the Bible said He would, and I thanked Him for it. I was crying again, but these were tears of relief. I immediately felt better. All the junk I'd been carrying for the last day and a half seemed to float away from me, and I felt ...peaceful. "Wow, Megan. I really think He forgave me!" I said, surprised.

She laughed at me. "Of course, He did."

"So what now? Do I have to tell Anna?" I worried.

"Hmm. I don't know. But I don't think so. I'm no theologian, but I think yer supposed to confess and ask forgiveness from whomever ya sin against. So in this case, that's God; I mean, sin is always against Him. But it's not like yer married anymore, and as much as you'd like to be, yer not datin' Ryan. Technically, I guess it could be said that you and Luke sinned against each other, so ya could ask him to forgive ya, but I think we both know how he'd respond." She smirked.

"Yeah, he'd probably offer me a drink, hoping to repeat the sin."

"Aye. Probably," she said.

"Megan, how did you learn all this stuff?"

She chuckled. "Well, I don't really know all that much. But I've been a believer since I was twelve, and I've been blessed with a great teacher. Father Tim is not yer typical priest. He's more … I don't know how to put it. He's really good at helpin' us grow in our relationship with God. I know that a lot of people got their feather's ruffled when he came in and started doin' Bible studies for the teens and just doin' things differently than the status quo. So I've learned from him. But let me ask ya this: if Ryan wrote ya a letter—" Again, the mention of his name hurt physically. "—would ya read it?" she asked.

"Of course!" I answered.

"Okay, so that's what God did for us with the Bible. It's one huge love letter. It's the best way to get to know Him. Read it."

"That's it?" I asked.

"That's the place to start," she answered. "From there y'can study it, but it starts with just readin' it. Just like readin' a letter from Ryan would help you get to know him better."

Wow, I'd never thought about the Bible in that way. I'd seen Anna reading it, and Ben too. He'd given me a Bible for my eighteenth birthday, actually. I decided I'd add reading my Bible to my nightly journaling time. "Thanks, Megan. You've been awesome. I might never have left this room if you hadn't come to see me."

"Well, let's put that to the test, shall we? You look like you've been in bed for two days." I cringed at the thought of what I must look like. "So why don't ya freshen up, and I'll go put the water on for tea. Anna invited me to stay for dinner, so I'll let her know you'll be down in a few."

"Thanks. Will do," I said. I slid out of bed and headed toward my bathroom as Megan headed downstairs. After a dismal attempt at making myself look better, I changed out of my wrinkled pj's and took a few minutes to write in my journal.

Lord,

I feel so clueless when it comes to knowing about you and how I should act. I'm thankful you've put people like Megan and Anna in my life to give me some advice. But I want to know more myself. I want to know you more than I have. Help me do that. Help me understand what I read in the Bible and help me grow closer to you. Thank you for forgiving me.

In Jesus Name, Amen.

Chapter Twenty-Two

I was up very early Monday morning. I had slept enough to last me a week, so I went for a run back up into the hills. I stopped to rest at the same poplar stand I had last week. I felt different now, though. Stronger, maybe? I remembered the panic I'd felt when Ryan wasn't going to come back, and it still hurt to think about him; but I felt like no matter what he decided to do, I'd be okay. So when the caller ID said his name, I didn't know what to feel.

"Hello?" I said, tentative.

"Brenna," he said in a warm, rich voice.

"Hi … are you all right?"

"Am *I* all right?" He laughed heartily. "Yes, I'm all right. Are you?" I panicked for a second. Did he know?

"I'm okay, thanks," I said, completely unsure of where this conversation was heading. "Where are you?"

"On my way into Millway. Can I see ya?"

My heart leaped into my throat. "Why?" It was the only response that came to my head.

He hesitated. "I understand if ya don't want to see me. I've been rotten to ya." He sounded sad, resigned.

I was completely confused. "Is this the same Ryan who left me at his flat Friday night?" At the mention of Friday night, the feeling of guilt tried to rear its ugly head, but Megan had warned me that would happen. She

169

assured me that I was forgiven, and if I started feeling like that wasn't true, I was supposed to repeat the verse she'd made me memorize, "If we confess our sins …" I did this quietly in my head as I waited for his response.

"Aye, it's me. I'm so sorry for that. I had so much to think about, and I just should have stayed away until I got it sorted out. But ya broke my heart when ya begged me to come see ya. I don't think anything could have kept me away." What was he saying? Who was this Ryan on the other end of the line? I didn't even know what to say. "Brenna, are ya there?"

"Sorry, yeah. I'm just confused," I answered.

"Can I see ya today?" He repeated his original question with a vulnerability that melted me.

"Of course you can see me. When?"

"Are ya workin?" he asked.

Crap! "Yes." *Double crap.* I was going to have to wait the whole day to see him!

"Will ya come up when yer done?"

"I'll be there as soon as I can," I promised with my heart racing.

"I can't wait to see ya," he said before he hung up, and I flew down the hill toward home. I was trying to figure out if I could get someone to work for me. When I caught my breath outside the B&B, I dialed Brigit to see if she'd pick up my shift.

"I've got an appointment this mornin; otherwise I would," she said.

"You wanna split the shift then? I'll even give you all my tips from breakfast," I pleaded.

"Geez, Brenna, where's the fire?" she joked.

"I just have something important to do, and I don't want to wait all day to do it," I explained without giving any real information.

"Okay. I'll come in at eleven, all right? And ya don't have to give me yer tips, ya crazy Yank," she added and laughed.

"Thanks, Brigit. I owe you big-time!" I dialed Ryan's number.

"Brenna," he answered. "Yer not cancelin' on me?"

"No." I laughed. "I got Brigit to come in at eleven. Is that too early?" I suddenly worried that he wouldn't be available, and then I'd be stuck waiting with nothing to do.

"No, that's perfect! I'm goin' to see Father Tim at nine, so I'll be sure to be back in time." He sounded so alive, so excited that he was contagious. I hung up and practically floated into the kitchen.

"What happened to ya on yer run?" Anna asked when she saw the huge smile on my face. I had told her the night before about what had happened with Ryan on Friday. I let her assume I'd stayed in bed all weekend because of that alone.

"Ryan called," I beamed.

"And?" She waited.

"And … I don't know. But he wants to see me, and he sounds really happy." My heart was racing all over again and not from the run. I couldn't wait for eleven o'clock to come. "Gotta go get ready for work!" I said as I ran up the stairs and into my room.

I arrived at Rosie's and my high was instantly flattened when I came out of the kitchen and saw Luke sitting in my section. The reality of my situation with him hit me like a bucket of ice water splashed in my face. He was smiling at me like he knew a secret. I sat down across from him and whispered, "Luke, Friday never happened. I don't want to talk about it, okay?"

"Brenna, it definitely happened. I was there, remember? I'll give ya this; yer no tease!" he said with his wicked smile that now made me want to vomit. His beauty had so quickly turned repulsive. What had I seen in him?

"Luke, listen to me. I know it did actually happen. What I mean is that I did not *intend* for it to happen, nor will it happen again. I had way too much to drink, and you knew that."

"Come on, ya weren't that drunk. You had a grand time, and I know ya did cuz ya told me so. Lay off on the good-girl routine. You are no good girl." He smirked and got even uglier.

I pulled out the big guns hoping to scare him. "Actually, Luke, I don't remember much of what happened. I was so drunk that I blacked out. I'm not even sure how I got to your apartment, and I have witnesses to how much I drank. Someone even said that they saw you slip something in that pint you ordered for me." I paused, staring at him to let it sink in what I was saying. "Now, date-rape drugs, cops take that stuff pretty seriously nowadays, you know?" I was bluffing, but I was giving it an Oscar-worthy effort, so afraid of what would happen if he talked.

He looked at me shrewdly. "You wouldn't," he said.

"You won't be bragging to anyone about your Friday night conquest, now, will you?"

He stood up and leveled a hateful stare at me. "I'm not hungry," he said as he stalked out the door and left me shaking with adrenaline.

"What happened with you two Friday night?" Tara asked as I approached the bar.

"We danced," I answered flatly. "But he's a jerk, and I told him I don't want to go dancing with him anymore." She didn't catch my double meaning, which was as I intended.

"Brenna, yer the only girl I know who's strong enough to resist those chocolate-brown eyes," she remarked. *If only that were true!*

"I prefer blue," I said, feeling ill, but throwing her completely off the scent.

"Ryan?" she asked with excitement.

I nodded. "I'm meeting him at eleven. I have a good feeling." That was all she was going to get from me right now. Besides, I had two tables to take care of.

Unfortunately, it was a slow morning that crawled by. Tara was busy doing her paperwork for Sam. Katie and I took turns on the few tables that did come in and got everything ready for the lunch crowd. We'd been warned it was a tour bus day so we were expecting to get a big hit. Thankfully, I wouldn't be there to see it.

I watched the clock strike 11:00 a.m., and by 11:05 a.m. I thought I'd lose my mind; but Brigit came strolling in two minutes later, and I thanked her as I ran past her and out the door. I took the back stairs two at a time and then took a moment to compose myself before knocking on Ryan's door.

Suddenly the weight of what was happening hit me. By the sound of his voice and the things he'd said on the phone, Ryan was finally admitting how he felt about me. I felt so sick to my stomach. Why had I gone with Luke? I was such an idiot. I couldn't have waited three days? I might have ruined the whole thing before it started! I decided then that I couldn't tell Ryan what had happened. Not right now. I'd let him have his say first, and then I'd figure out what to do.

I had taken my apron off on the way up, but I still looked and smelled like a greasy kitchen. Not exactly what I would have chosen for this moment. Oh, well. He'd have to look past it. I knocked, and before I could put my hand down, he had the door open. The sight of him standing there in a stark white shirt and jeans, with his bright, blue eyes lit up like a Christmas tree, took my breath away. I wasn't sure how to act. I wanted to go in, but I held back.

"Come in!" He laughed as I hesitated. Then he did something that I'd longed for him to do ever since I'd met him. He opened his arms in invitation. Why couldn't he have done this three days ago? I still wasn't sure what to think. I tentatively stepped into his embrace. Was this real? Was he going to kick me out the door in a minute? After a hesitant moment, I relaxed in his arms. "I'm sorry, Brenna," he said tenderly. That cut to the quick. I was sorry too. So sorry, but I couldn't tell him.

I pushed away and looked up at his face. "You seem so different. What's going on with you?"

"I'm a new man," he smiled. "I promise, I'll tell ya everything. But it's gonna take a while. Do ya want to freshen up or anything first?"

"Do I need to?" I was already self-conscious. Maybe I should go look in mirror.

"No, I just thought since you've been workin' all mornin', ya might want to freshen up. That's all. Honest!" He held his hand up in a scout's-honor pose.

"Well, okay. I think that's a good idea, anyway. Now, if I go into that bathroom and clean up, will you be here when I come back out?" I was only half teasing.

"I'm not goin' anywhere. You would have to pick me up and throw me out," he said with a chuckle at the idea.

Still, I was gun-shy. "You promise?" I looked him in the eyes.

He got serious. "I promise."

I took my ponytail out and ran a brush through my hair. I put on some lip-gloss and that was about all I could do. I came out as he was

173

setting down a cup of tea for me on the side table. He sat on the couch and motioned for me to sit next to him.

"Okay, first … I want to tell ya I'm so very sorry for how I've treated ya," he began.

"Ryan, you don't—"

He put his finger over my lips to silence me. "Wait, ground rules. Some of what I'm goin' to tell ya is gonna be very hard for me to say, so do me a favor and just let me say it. I promise, I'll give ya time to ask me questions or argue with me afterward, okay?"

"Okay," I promised.

"So, I have been unfair to ya. I assumed that since ya had lost Ben, ya wouldn't be interested in me, and selfishly I took advantage of that. Ahht!" He held up his finger as I tried to interrupt.

"Okay!" I promised again and reminded myself to keep my mouth shut. That would be hard.

"I wanted to get to know ya … ever since I first saw ya in the pub and made ya blush." His mischievous smile tempted me to speak, but I'd promised not to. Instead I looked at him with wide eyes. He *had* been smiling at me that day. I knew it! He continued. "It wasn't just that yer drop-dead gorgeous, Brenna. It was the way ya were so oblivious to that fact." I knew my cheeks were burning yet again. "Ya didn't notice the heads turning as ya walked by. Ya didn't realize the effect that yer stunning smile had on the men in the room. Yer cluelessness made ya that much more … well … intriguing. Ya have to understand; Patsy has been tryin' to set me up with someone for years. I knew why I was bein' invited for dinner, and I knew who ya were when I saw ya in the pub. Ya weren't what I expected, though." He paused.

"Why—oops!" I slipped.

"Okay, I'm havin' fun watchin' ya try to avoid an aneurism not interruptin' me, but it's okay; we're not to the critical part yet. I'll let ya know when I really need ya to just let me talk." He laughed as I smacked his chest.

"So you knew who I was and then pretended not to have seen me when you came for dinner?" I asked.

"Aye, sorry. But I knew I'd embarrassed ya when I waved at ya from the bar, and then ya were completely flustered when ya discovered I was

Anna's cousin just before dinner. I was really trying to be helpful. Honest," he assured me, and I believed him.

"Okay, go on then."

"Well, okay, so ... I know ya talked with Father Tim." I looked down, embarrassed. "It's all right. I was drivin' ya crazy. I would have done exactly the same thing."

"Really? You *were* driving me crazy! You still are. Keep going," I demanded with a smile.

"So ya know that I sort of took a vow of abstinence. I'll explain why later, I swear. But after spendin' the whole evenin' talkin' with ya at dinner, I was just so intrigued by ya. Before I even got to yer place, I had repeated to myself over and over that you were like a sister to me. I did my very best to think of ya that way all night long. It's a defense mechanism I've picked up to keep me on the straight and narrow, so to speak."

"That's a good trick," I commented. I could have used that tip, I thought sourly.

"So, after dinner I didn't want to leave. I was havin' too much fun, but eventually I had to make my exit. But I still thought about ya constantly after I got home, and to my great frustration, I was not thinkin' of ya as a sister. I couldn't even sleep." My heart was beating so hard I thought I might have a heart attack. I had no clue he'd felt all this. He was a frighteningly good actor.

"Are you serious?"

"Ya have no idea. You were a bigger challenge than anyone I can remember. I had to see ya that next mornin'. I told myself I just needed to get some breakfast, but I knew it was all about seein' ya again. And there ya were, all adorable and funny, jokin' with me about gettin' in trouble with the boss." I laughed as I remembered that conversation.

"Wait, you told me you didn't know who I was when you'd seen me the day before," I recalled.

"Yeah, I know," he said sheepishly. "I was tryin' to cover my tracks. I didn't know how to explain why ... I just didn't want ya to know I'd been there checkin' ya out, y'know? Sorry 'bout that."

I nodded. "Okay."

"So, where was I? Oh, yeah … so I saw ya at breakfast, and then I came back up here and checked my e-mail and wasted time until lunch. Once again, I rationalized. I didn't have any groceries in the house. I needed lunch, right? But I knew it would be too obvious if I sat in yer section again, so I didn't. It was easier to watch ya that way anyway."

"You're horrible," I teased, still slightly stunned by all he was sharing.

"Brenna, seriously, I was so torn between wantin' to be around ya and knowin' that I was playin' with fire. I came up with my little plan to drive Patsy and Anna crazy, just so I could spend time with ya, guilt-free. But that was so unfair to you. I honestly didn't think you'd have feelin's for me. I thought I was the only one I was puttin' at risk, and I fooled myself into thinkin' I could handle it." My heart was literally about to burst out of my chest. I couldn't believe what I was hearing.

"You are a really good actor, you know," I said.

"Aye, been told that before," he said with a wry smile.

"So what happened next?" I asked as if he was telling me a fairy tale. It felt like a fairy tale!

He looked up like he was trying to remember the chain of events. "Next was Sunday dinner … no wait, that's wrong … next was Veritas, the night I sang with Megan."

"Right," I confirmed. "I saw you looking at me."

"Aye, well, this was before I came up with our little plan, so I was still tryin' to avoid ya. But that was impossible. I knew I was in trouble then, because all through the worship I was sneakin' glances at ya. My mind was definitely not where it should have been, and I was embarrassed by that," he admitted.

"You blushed!" I remembered. He blushed again as I brought it up. It was so cute, I just couldn't resist him anymore. "Ryan, I don't want to scare you. I know I've upset you before when I've rushed up and hugged you or kissed you on the cheek or whatever, but you're driving me crazy right now. Can I please just give you a little kiss?"

He looked at me with an unsure look. "Can that wait until I'm done explainin'?" he asked. "I mean, ya need to know that I definitely want to kiss ya." My stomach did a flip. "But I need to finish my story, and if I let ya kiss me right now, I might not be able to finish." He blushed again.

Geez! He was killing me. I couldn't take this much longer. "How about a compromise? Can we take a short break, and can you just hold me in your arms? I just need you to hold me for a little while. I'll be good, I promise." I looked into his eyes to get my point across.

"It's not *you* bein' good that I'm worried about, Brenna," he said with a grin.

"Okay, I'll make sure *you're* good, then. Please?" I begged. I couldn't stand sitting still, listening to him tell me all the things I'd been wanting to hear, without touching him. I couldn't even explain it, but I just needed him to hold me so I would know this was real.

He opened up his arms, and I cautiously leaned over and let him pull me into a strong embrace. I could have died happy right at that moment. There was nowhere else in the world I wanted to be. I could hear his heart beating rapidly as I laid my head on his chest. I listened as it slowed to a steady, even pace, and I said a prayer of thanks as I lay there listening. I was overwhelmed with gratitude that God had brought this amazing guy into my life.

At the same time, I was distraught over what I knew he didn't know. I couldn't tell him right now. I just couldn't. He was finally talking to me, finally telling me everything, and I wouldn't chance ruining that, even if it would relieve the guilt I was feeling. No, I'd just swallow those horrid feelings every time they crept up.

I was dying to hear the rest of his story, but I didn't want to move. Still, after a while, I grudgingly pulled myself away from him and moved over to the chair. I thought that might make things easier.

"See, we did good," I said.

"Aye, that was a very good idea. Thanks." He smiled a beautiful smile. "Now where did we leave off?"

"Sunday dinner?" I offered.

"Right. No, actually, I came in for lunch with Father Tim."

"Yeah! I remember. You guys were arguing—about me, weren't you?"

He nodded. "Oh, yeah. He was pushin' me. He's been tryin' to get me to see things differently for years now. I'm just really stubborn. When I get somethin' in my head ... well, I'm gettin' ahead of myself. So, yes, we were arguin'. He was tellin' me I should give things a chance with ya, and

I was insistin' that I couldn't do that. Plus, I still thought ya wouldn't be interested." I rolled my eyes at him.

"So now we're up to Sunday dinner?" I asked.

"Aye. By that point I knew it was hopeless to try avoidin' ya, so I came up with the idea to let us hang out as friends while keepin' Patsy off our backs."

"Which was brilliant, by the way," I added.

"Aye, thanks. It was, wasn't it?" He grinned. "So from there, we just hung out and got to know each other better, which just made it harder and harder for me to get out," he explained. "Then Anna's birthday came. Remember, we were out on the bridge and you were upset?" he asked.

"Yeah, I remember, because you kept saying how much you just wanted to be friends. It was like being constantly rejected," I admitted.

"That's why y'were cryin'?"

"Yeah. I know you thought it was about Ben, but you were way off. I didn't think you liked me in that way, but I knew I was falling for you." I blushed as I explained. "I was afraid if I told you how I felt, you'd stop being my friend."

"Really?" This was all news to him. "Ya may have been right. I might have bolted sooner."

"So why *did* you bolt?" I asked the all-important question, and he took a deep breath.

"Do ya want more tea?" he asked hopefully.

"No, thanks." I would not let him off the hook.

"Okay, then. Here goes. This is the part where I need ya to let me say it all, okay?"

I mimed locking my lips. He laughed a nervous laugh and then dove in.

"When I was younger—ya know, seventeen or eighteen—I was not really livin' right. I'd made a bit of money, and let it go to my head. I bought a fast car and all the things that came with it. Drank too much, drove too fast, and went out with way too many girls."

I had trouble picturing Ryan like that. It sounded like he was describing Luke, actually. *Ugh.* I felt sick again. *Stomp it down!* I told myself.

"So that continued for a couple years," Ryan went on, "and then ..." He hesitated and seemed like he couldn't continue. I moved back over to the couch and took his hand to try to encourage him. He smiled a sad smile and continued.

"So, I was datin' this girl in Limerick. Her name was Kelley." I couldn't help it; I looked at him and giggled, but I didn't speak. "I know, Kelley Kelly if we'd gotten married. Yeah, everyone joked about that. But anyway, Kelley and I had been datin' for a couple months when she told me she thought she was pregnant." He looked at me to gauge my reaction, and I did my best to remain calm and encouraging, although I wondered where this was leading.

"She *was* pregnant," he admitted. "And I was a total jackass. Told her I didn't believe it was mine. I hurt her really bad with that. But I knew she wasn't lyin'; it was mine. Neither of us knew what to do." He paused, and I saw tears welling up in his eyes.

"She ... I ... well, I guess we agreed that we weren't ready for a baby ... so ..." Now there were tears streaming down his face, and my heart was breaking for him. "I gave her the money, and I drove her up north where it was legal." The realization of what he was telling me hit me like a ton of bricks. He saw the change in my face, and I could see he was worried about what I thought. He looked away.

"Do you want to tell me more?" I asked tenderly.

He nodded. "I told myself it was the best for everyone. Told myself it wasn't really a baby yet anyway. I told myself every lie I could to make it seem okay. Kelley got scared when we got to the clinic, but I pushed her to...to go through with it." He broke down at this point. He began to sob, and I pulled him close and held him.

"Shh, it's okay. Shh ... oh, Ryan, I'm so sorry." I didn't know what else to say. He had been carrying this for so long. Punishing himself for so long. I couldn't imagine. He took a deep breath and continued.

"So, needless to say, our relationship ended very soon after. Neither of us could stand to look at each other, much less touch each other. I think we both blamed each other. It was horrible," he said.

"For a while, I dealt with it by drinkin' more. I definitely dealt with it by datin' more and more women, odd as that sounds. I ended up with another girlfriend. We weren't real serious, but she had a scare one month. She thought she was pregnant, and I lost it. I mean, really lost it. We got into a huge fight, and I said all sorts of horrible things to her. I told her I didn't want to see her again. It was bad."

I knew he expected me to look at him differently after hearing all this. But I now knew firsthand how easy it was to make such stupid mistakes. He was probably thinking I wouldn't like him anymore, but it all had the opposite effect. I wanted to protect him. Knowing he had been through so much pain just made me so sad.

"Yer doin' a really good job at bein' quiet," he said softly.

I smiled. "Do you want to keep talking?"

He took another steadying breath. "Aye. Let me just get it all out," he said and continued. "So, she wasn't pregnant, but when she thought she was, she said she would get an abortion. That was when I lost it, and afterward I knew that I had really screwed up my life. I came back here to talk with Father Tim. I needed big-time help. He was great. He helped me come to a place of askin' God to forgive me, and I made huge changes in my life. I stopped drinkin', more importantly, stopped datin'. That's when I made a vow to myself that I wouldn't date anymore," he explained.

"So, like forever? Did you think you'd never date, never get married?" I asked.

"I don't know. I thought I was doin' a really good, holy thing, ya know? Kind of like a priest. I never made any official vow in the church or anythin'—just to myself. But what I didn't realize was that even though I knew God had forgiven me, I wasn't livin' a full life in Him, because I never actually forgave *myself.* I've been punishin' myself all this time … in the name of self-sacrifice and penance."

"Wow," I said.

"After a few years, Father Tim figured out what I was doin' and tried to make me see things in a better light, but I had grown used to the protection from temptation that my vow afforded me. I didn't ever want to put myself in a position to get a girl pregnant again, and the easiest way to do that was to avoid datin' altogether."

"How'd you do that for all this time?" I asked.

"You'd be surprised how easy it was to do," he responded. "I worked a lot. I built a very good business as a result. Of course, I've certainly been lonely

WHERE THE PINK HOUSES ARE

at times, and I've been tempted a few times, but never so strongly as when I met you." His eyes twinkled. "I knew ya were trouble from day one."

"Why?" I asked, truly curious.

"Don't know. Fate? You were almost impossible for me to resist. Father Tim thinks it was God's doin'. That He brought ya into my life to wake me up to what I was missin' by stubbornly refusin' to be fully forgiven. It still hurts a lot to think about it, ya know? I would have a ten-year-old kid," he said in a thick voice. "But I finally understand that, although what I did was horrible, nothin' I do can make up for it. I can't punish myself enough. I just have to accept it for what it is and live like a man who's been forgiven, cuz I have been. I don't deserve it, but I am forgiven, and if I continue to live like I'm in prison, I'm never gonna be who God wants me to be." I understood that.

"So that's why you ran—because I was too tempting for you?" I giggled at the thought.

"Aye, that's why. I was still tryin' to hold on to my vow, but I knew I couldn't do that and be around ya at the same time. When I saw ya dancin' with that joker downstairs, I lost my head." Another stab of guilt. *This was so hard.* "Then, dancin' with ya, holdin' ya like I'd been dreamin' of—it was too much. I went back to Limerick just to be safe while I tried to figure it all out. By puttin' you in my life, was God tellin' me to let it go? I didn't know. But then bein' away from ya was killin' me, and I just wanted to hear yer voice, so when I called ya and ya begged me to come, I just couldn't say no."

"But then you were so angry with me when you came," I said, puzzled.

"Well, I told myself I could come and see ya and keep my distance. But ya never make it easy to resist ya, y'know? Jumpin' in my arms as soon as ya see me. Dancin' with other guys, makin' my blood boil. I was tryin' so hard to resist ya, that I can see how it came out like I was mad at ya. Wasn't you I was mad at; it was me. I was disgusted that I couldn't be stronger. Not to mention that ya did everything ya could to get me alone on Friday, which was the exact opposite of what I wanted. Well, not really, but the opposite of what I needed, anyway."

181

I felt like such a jerk. I had been so focused on myself, on how I felt, that I'd pushed this poor guy to the breaking point. "I'm so sorry, Ryan. I had no idea! I was just so confused by you,"

"I know. I don't blame you at all. How could I? I was confusin' you. I was confused myself. But then we came up here, and ya started tellin' me how ya really felt. It was too much for me, so I did get angry. Still, not at you—probably at God. I felt like He was rubbin' my face in it, y'know? I know now that He was tryin' to help me. But it didn't seem like it at the time."

"No, I'm sure it didn't. Then I go and cry all over you," I added.

"Aye, that really did me in. Ya pierced my heart. You were so sad, and I was makin' it worse, and then ya told me it was the anniversary of Ben's death. What else could I do? I let my guard down, and then I did what I'd been wantin' to do for weeks. Kissed that gorgeous mouth of yers, and it was all over. I knew if I didn't leave then, I'd be sorry," he explained.

I tried hard not to think about how sorry I was that he had left. *If we confess our sins, he is faithful and just to forgive...*, I repeated in my head.

"So how did you end up here today?" I asked.

"I spent the weekend literally on my knees. I prayed a lot. I read the Word a lot, and I talked to Father Tim a lot. I finally saw the mistake in what I was doin', and I had to come see ya to tell ya the whole story. I know I've acted badly, but I'm askin' ya for a second chance."

I wasn't sure how to respond. I wanted to jump into his arms, but I wasn't the same person I'd been three days ago. No matter how much I wanted to forget what I'd done, it was there in the back of my mind, dampening the joy of this moment. "Ryan, I ..." I tried to tell him, but I faltered.

"What is it?" He was concerned.

"I just, I don't ..." I couldn't put the words together. I was afraid of hurting him. I was afraid he'd walk away again. I paused to try and gather my thoughts. He completely misread my hesitation.

"Listen," he jumped in, "ya don't need to give me any kind of commitment right now. I know you've been through so much this last year. All I'm askin' for is the chance to spend time with ya and see what happens."

I still didn't speak. I couldn't even look at him. I was wrestling with what to do. Should I tell him about Luke? Would he even want to know? Should I just take it one day at a time?

My silence was making him nervous. "Ben was yer first boyfriend, right?" he asked.

He'd done some homework on me, apparently. "Yeah," I said, puzzled by the subject change.

"Here's the thing. I've been around awhile, but yer still so young. I know ya may want to kind of see what's out there, and as much as it would kill me, I'd understand if ya wanted to date other people. But I want ya to know that I'm not goin' anywhere. I'll wait for ya."

I was floored. Did he seriously think my affection for him was so small that I'd date other guys while he waited around?

"No!" I cried. "No, you don't have to wait for me. I don't want to date anyone else. I want to be with you!"

He grinned, visibly relieved. "I'm so glad y'said that. Does that mean I can have that kiss now?" He didn't wait for my answer. He reached over and gently pulled me toward him, kissing me sweetly at first and then suddenly so passionately that I'm sure I forgot to breathe for a while. My heart raced as he pulled back and looked at me with smiling eyes. "I have t'say, Brenna … that was worth the wait."

I giggled and threw myself into his arms. I didn't want to leave. "Can I stay here forever?" I asked sleepily.

"Aye, fine with me," he said, hiding a yawn. We'd both been up very early. He grabbed a blanket from the back of the couch and laid it over us as we snuggled up close and fell asleep in each other's arms.

Chapter Twenty-Three

I opened my eyes, unsure of where I was. The room was dark, but I knew I was not in my own room. I blinked to wake up more fully and realized where I was. It was not a dream. I was nestled in Ryan's arms, waking up from a long afternoon nap that had obviously stretched into the evening. I looked around slowly, trying to see the clock on the wall. Ryan stirred.

"Hello, beautiful," he said as he opened his eyes and looked down into mine.

"That was wonderful." I smiled and hugged him.

"Aye, it was, but I'm starvin!" he said as he scooped me up and set me down again on the couch. He turned on the lights, and once my eyes adjusted, I saw that it was after 6:00 p.m.

"Wow! We slept for a long time!" I was shocked. "That had to have been like four hours?"

"Aye, my stomach woke me more than once, but there was an angel in my arms, and I just couldn't wake her." He winked. "Wanna go downstairs and get some dinner?"

"Absolutely. I'll be ready in a minute." I tried to freshen up, but without my toothbrush and a change of clothes, there wasn't much I could do. Ryan noticed my small pout.

"Do y'want me to take ya home to change?" he offered.

"No, then I'll get stuck telling them what's going on. I'd rather just make this day with you last as long as I can." I grinned.

"Oh, I know …" He took off into his bedroom and came out with a small box. "These are some of my sister's things. She's not too much bigger than you. Maybe somethin' will work?"

I sifted through and found a sweater that almost fit and smelled way better than my work shirt. I wore jeans to work anyway, so they were fine. I felt much better except for one thing. "Do you have any mouthwash I can use?" I asked, feeling slightly embarrassed. "Tea breath." I pointed to the cup sitting on the side table.

"Right. I can do ya one better, actually." I followed him to the bathroom, where he produced a brand new toothbrush still in its package. "I keep a few extras here and in Limerick in case I forget to bring mine," he explained.

We both took a moment to freshen up, and when Ryan came out of his room, I took advantage of the fresh-breath moment and reached up on tiptoes for another kiss. He obliged, literally lifting me off the floor.

"Okay, no more. I need food!" He chuckled as he set me back down.

The pub was fairly empty; normal for a Monday night. We took turns answering each other's random questions while we ate. We probably laughed more than we talked, and I hated to leave the bubble of this amazing day, but I knew I needed to get home. Anna would be dying to know what was going on. I was surprised she hadn't called me.

As we pulled up to the B&B, I dreaded having to say good-night. It felt like this was a dream, and if I went inside and went to bed, I'd wake up in the morning and it would all be gone.

Ryan wasn't coming in. We agreed that I would be the one to let the matchmakers know that their mission was officially a success. After a long kiss at the door, I said good-night and headed in.

"Brenna?" Anna called from the front room. "Is that you, love?"

"It's me," I called back. She pushed through the swinging kitchen door with a cautious smile on her face.

"Can I assume that since you've been gone all day long, yer talk with Ryan went well?" My beaming smile told her more than words, but she still wanted the words. "Come on, then; spill it. What happened?"

"He's amazing; that's what happened," I replied, giggling. There was no way I could or would recount the whole day's conversation. But how to summarize, I wasn't sure. "He apologized for leaving like he did. He has his reasons, and they're good ones; but I don't think it's my place to share them." She looked disappointed that she wasn't going to get the full scoop.

"Well, what did he say, though. Did he tell ya why he's not dated in all this time?" she asked.

I hesitated. "Yes, he did. But I'm sorry; it's not stuff I feel okay to share, you know?"

"Aye, I understand. What can ya tell me then?"

I giggled yet again. "That he's amazing." She rolled her eyes and grinned. "That my heart feels like it's going to explode."

"Yer gonna be useless for a while, aren't ya?" she asked, shaking her head.

"Probably," I replied. "I don't know how long this vacation of his will last, so I plan to spend every minute I can with him. I'm so happy." I knew my eyes were glistening.

"I can see that, love. You deserve that."

"Will you fill Bettie and Patsy in for me? I want to go upstairs and take a bath."

"Sure, but what am I tellin' them? Are you two officially together?" she inquired.

I thought about it for a moment. "Yeah, we are officially together." I beamed. How awesome was that? Anna reached over and gave me a quick squeeze, and then I headed up to draw a steaming bath.

Megan called while I was soaking. "Brenna, I'm dyin. You've got to tell me what's goin' on," she said. I had left her a quick message in the morning, telling her I was meeting Ryan.

"Sorry, Meg. It's been a long crazy day—but very good."

"What are y'doin right now?" she asked expectantly. I knew she wanted an invite.

"Just turning into a prune. You're next door, aren't you?" I guessed.

"Aye," she said sheepishly.

"Okay, give me ten minutes to dry off and get dressed, and then come on over," I said.

"Can't wait to hear about yer day!"

She wasn't kidding. I had just finished pulling on my sweats when she knocked. "Come in," I called from the bathroom. "Geez, Megan, that was barely five minutes." I laughed as I came out, towel-drying my hair.

"I know. Sorry. I've just been waitin' all day to hear, and it's gettin' late, and I need to be home soon," she explained.

We both flopped onto the bed. "So what do you want to know?" I asked.

"Everything, obviously." She chuckled. "But just tell me what ya can."

I proceeded to skim through the conversation I'd had with Ryan without divulging the details I felt I should keep to myself.

"So," she asked, "did ya tell him what happened with Luke?" It was a perfectly reasonable question, but it irritated me.

"I tried a couple times. I just couldn't get the words out," I admitted. "Do you think I have to tell him?"

"That's a tough question. I don't think I can answer that for ya."

"I feel so torn. I wanna put it behind me, but it just happened, and it's still affecting me, even if I don't want it to. Officially, Ryan and I weren't together yet, so I don't know. Do I hurt him more if I tell him or if I don't?"

"Geez, I really don't know."

"Megan, I'm not asking you for the answer, just for your opinion." I needed some advice.

She was quiet for a moment, thinking. "Okay, well, let's just talk it through then. Like ya said, it's not like ya were cheatin' on him, right?" I nodded. "So, from that standpoint, it's not like ya need to ask him to forgive ya," she paused. "But he's just shared all these details with you, which I assume were very personal and hard for him to tell ya?" I hadn't given her the details, but she had the gist of my conversation with Ryan.

"Yeah," I admitted.

"So, from that angle, I guess it would be good for ya to tell him, just so there's no secrets between ya, right?"

She was right. I was hoping I could get off on a technicality, but I could see that her point made sense. "Crap. I think you're right," I told her.

"So how are ya goin' to tell him?" she asked.

"I don't know. He's so happy and upbeat, and I'm afraid to squash that. I have no idea how he'll react, and that makes me really nervous." Terrified was more accurate. "He's taking a huge step here, dating after ten years? What if he can't take it, and he leaves? I don't know if I can handle that now." I knew I couldn't.

"Well, all I can suggest is to pray about it then. Ask God to give ya wisdom. He promises to give it to us when we ask with pure motives. You want to do what's right, and I believe He'll help ya do that."

I nodded. "Good idea. I'll do that. In the meantime, I'll wait for a time that seems right. I can't just spring it on him while serving him an omelet, ya know?" Megan chuckled. "Even if I wait a week or two, that would give us more time together as a couple, and maybe he'd be less likely to hate me for it."

"I'll pray for ya, friend," she said as she rose to go. "I do have to get home. But I'm really happy for ya."

I smiled. "Thanks. I am too."

Just after Megan left, my phone rang. It was Ryan.

"Hi there," I said.

"Hey, I was just thinkin' about ya. Wanted to say good-night." His voice made me smile.

"We said good-night on the back porch," I reminded him.

"Aye, and it was fun. That's what I was thinkin' about." He chuckled.

"How is it possible that I saw you an hour ago, and I already miss you?" I asked.

"It's taken all the self-restraint I have not to drive back there just to kiss ya good-night again," he admitted.

"I have tomorrow off," I told him hopefully.

"Brilliant. I'll be there for a run at 8:00 a.m.," he said.

"I'll be ready. Good-night again," I said quietly.

"Good-night, love," he said and hung up. I lay there listening to the sound of my heartbeat slowly returning to normal. I slept very soundly that night.

We were running up the trail Ryan had shown me. It was a gorgeous autumn morning. The leaves had begun turning colors. It wasn't quite as spectacular as it had been in western New York. I missed the vibrant reds and oranges. The leaves here were more of a yellowish color, but it was fall nonetheless, and I loved fall. It had always been my favorite season. Of course, I also loved warm weather and summer fun. I had enjoyed going to the beach as a kid or swimming in friends' pools. But there was always something magical about fall. When September would hit and the air turned crisp and clear, it was invigorating. This was one of those days. When we reached the poplar stand, we sat down for a breather.

"This is fine weather," Ryan said as he settled himself in the crook of a low branch.

"This is my favorite weather," I told him.

"Was it like this where ya grew up?" he asked.

"At this time of year, yeah. The weather was more varied, though—like, summer was really hot, and winter was really cold. It seems like here you have mostly spring and fall and not much in the way of extremes."

"Aye, that's about right. And it's fairly wet here too. That's why it's so green," he explained.

"It's breathtaking."

"So do ya miss home?" he asked.

"Hmm. I don't think so. I mean, I miss certain things—good pizza, good peanut butter, stuff like that. But I didn't leave much behind, ya know?"

"Ya have no family left there?" he asked.

"I have two half-brothers. Mike is in Boston, and Jake is in Texas somewhere. They're quite a bit older than me, and I never really got to know them well," I explained.

"Why not?" he asked.

"I don't know. I guess because my dad left their mom and eventually married mine. I always kind of felt like they blamed me somehow, even though I wasn't even born yet when it happened. I don't know what the full scoop is. I just know their mom didn't like me and didn't want them coming to visit or anything. She's the reason that I went to Gram's house instead of moving in with one of my brothers after my mom and dad died."

"They wouldn't take ya?" he asked.

"Well, they kind of offered, but it was clear that I would have been a big inconvenience. We get along better now, but at the time, things were awkward. The only one who welcomed me with open arms was Gram. She was my dad's mom and the only grandparent I knew. I didn't see her a ton when I was a kid, but we were both in New York, so I'd go to visit her on school breaks and stuff. She was funny. A real independent, fiery kind of lady until she got sick. Patsy kind of reminds me of her, actually," I said.

"Aye, how's Patsy doin' these days? I haven't seen her out and about as much," he said.

I shook my head. "I'm not sure. She seems to sleep so much more than when I first got here. Her memory is definitely worse. She forgets names a lot. I mean, she knows who people are—or at least that she's supposed to know them—but the names are really hard for her. She's a good actress, though."

"Ya think it's worse than she's lettin' on?" he asked.

"Oh, I know it is. But most people wouldn't know there was anything wrong. She's smooth. She's figured out ways to fool people into thinking she knows what they're talking about or who they are. Isn't there some verse in Proverbs about the person who says little being thought of as wise?"

"I believe there is. So, she just keeps quiet and people don't notice how bad it's gettin'?"

"Yeah. I mean, Anna and Bettie certainly know. Tom knows. But anyone who doesn't see her every day would think she's just fine."

"What's Bettie gonna do?" he asked.

"I don't know what she can do. We're just doing our best to keep her safe. The LifeSave bracelet helps."

"The what?" He looked puzzled.

"You didn't hear about her wandering off?" I was surprised.

"No! When? What happened?" he demanded.

"Wow. I guess it was almost two months ago now. Maybe a couple weeks before I met you." I moved to sit on the ground, as the tree branch was getting uncomfortable. Ryan sat next to me as I continued, telling him the story of that night and how Patsy had agreed to wear the bracelet in exchange for a little more freedom.

"I can't believe I didn't find out about that. Of course, it's usually Patsy who calls and keeps my mum up to date on things. I imagine she wasn't real keen to share that particular story."

"That would explain why you didn't know," I agreed.

"So this is serious, then. It's really good that you and Anna are there to help out," he concluded.

"Yeah, I'm glad we stayed," I answered.

"Why did ya decide to stay?" he asked.

"Well, I guess because Anna was staying. She's home here, ya know? I didn't realize how powerful the pull to come back here was for her. I understand it now, having lived here. It's like this place gets into your soul. I think it would have been too painful for her to leave again. She has friends back in New York, but mostly her life there was about Ben and Joe."

"Aye, there wasn't much callin' her back there, then … just painful memories."

I took a deep breath. It was difficult to talk about, because it was the same for me. When I thought of New York, I thought of Ben. Sometimes I dreamed he was still there, waiting for me to come home. I think Ryan saw a look of pain cross my face, and he pulled me into a warm embrace.

"Sorry. Is it hard to talk about?" he asked.

"No, not really. It's getting easier most of the time. It just comes on suddenly, though. A memory will come up, and the sadness hits like a wave." I wiped a solitary tear from my eye. "Sorry."

"Brenna, look at me." He lifted my chin. "Ya never have to apologize when thinkin' of Ben makes ya sad. Ya have every right. I mean, I've known ya such a short time, and I already know that if I lost ya, I might lose my mind. I can't even imagine goin' through what you've gone through. You amaze me."

"I do?" I didn't see why. I was such a basket case sometimes.

"Aye, yer such a strong woman, and ya don't even realize it," he answered.

"I don't feel strong," I confided.

"I know." He squeezed me tightly. "But ya are."

"Thanks." I smiled and laid my head on his chest. It was becoming one of my favorite places.

Chapter Twenty-Four

OCTOBER

For the next week, we spent every free moment together. Ryan drove me to a few places in Cork City that he had renovated and then sold. He was a true craftsman. His work was beautiful and distinctive. I could see why he'd been so successful. My favorite, though, was when he showed me his first project: his grandma's place on the outskirts of Millway. It was a charming, thatch-roofed house. The outside was a white stucco-type surface with green-trimmed, lead-paned windows. There were flower boxes filled with plants outside the front windows and a stone pathway that wound through the quaint flower garden to the front door.

"Oh, Ryan, this is beautiful! Do you have "before" pictures?" My HGTV obsession kicked in.

"Aye, somewhere," he chuckled. "Would y'like to see inside?"

"Really? Who lives there?" I asked.

"The current owners are friends of mine, and they're away on holiday. They don't mind, I promise. They gave me a key." He grinned while brandishing a shiny silver key.

The inside was not at all what I expected. In this case, what you saw was definitely not what you got. On the surface it appeared to be an old-fashioned, craftsman-styled interior. Many details looked to be original, such as the tiles in the bathroom or the backsplash in the kitchen, but they

193

were actually newly done. The whole thing was so well done, it looked like a perfectly preserved blast from the past—at first glance.

The cool thing was when you looked closer. Behind what appeared to be antique hutch doors was a state-of-the-art refrigerator. All the cabinets looked antique on the outside and twenty-first-century on the inside. I loved it. It was so creative and clever.

"Ryan, this is amazing! Is this how you do all your homes?" I was thinking about Bettie's country kitchen that had been combined with the most up-to-date kitchen appliances.

"Well, no, this one was definitely more special. But I do add a touch of this kind of thing wherever I work. I like the look of the past combined with the convenience of today."

"I love that. I'm so impressed." I beamed at him, and he blushed. Too cute.

"Thanks," he replied as we locked the front door and headed back to the truck. "Okay, this time yer drivin'." He tossed me the keys. My stomach flipped. I was nervous, but he was right. My test was coming up in less than two weeks, and I'd gotten no practice at all since he'd taken me for my theory test.

"Okay, just say your prayers," I said as I turned the key in the ignition. Thankfully, it was a Monday afternoon without much in the way of traffic. Ryan directed me to take us out into the countryside where we'd go for long stretches without seeing other cars. By the time we got back to Millway, I was feeling much more confident. It was really mostly the same while I was driving straight down the road—other than being on the opposite side of the car and the street. But the turning, that took some getting used to.

We drove through the town at least four times to give me lots of turning practice. Everyone waved as we passed by. Apparently we were the talk of the town. I'd heard all the rumors and speculation that was whispered about us in shops and beauty salons, Tara and Brigit being my most trusted informants.

"He's way too old for her." I'd heard that one the most.

"Didn't her husband just die?" That was just rude.

"I think they're perfect for each other." That was my favorite.

"I told ya he wasn't gay!" That was the funniest and the first one I shared with Ryan. He laughed heartily at that one. Evidently, that had been the prevailing rumor for years, and he'd done little to squash it, since it helped keep the girls at bay. He'd also done nothing to encourage it, he was quick to point out.

"Well, anything that helped keep you off the market until I got here is good with me," I told him as I suddenly swerved to avoid an oncoming car. I had accidentally switched to autopilot and drifted to the wrong side of the street.

"Brenna, why don't ya pull over, and I'll get us back home," he said, clutching his heart in a feigned heart attack.

"Fine … one tiny mistake." I pouted playfully and smacked him on the chest. I pulled over but refused to hand over the keys. "I think I did a wonderful job, and you haven't said so yet," I told him, still pouting.

"Aye, ya did a fabulous job—right till the part when ya almost killed us." He grinned and proceeded to tickle me until I cried, "Uncle!" and handed him the keys.

We could hear the argument from outside as we walked up the back steps. It was Patsy and Bettie again, and I wasn't sure we should go in.

"You stole my shoes!" Patsy screamed.

"Mum, don't be ridiculous. Why would I take yer shoes?" Bettie yelled back. From the sound of it, this had been going on awhile. Bettie had been doing a great job of remaining calm around her mum lately, so something must have happened to rile her up.

"That's what I want to know! Why did ya take them?" Patsy said.

"Mum, I don't have yer shoes. Ya can look in my room if y'want. I don't care. I don't even know what shoes yer talkin' about!" Bettie sounded exhausted. This was so hard on her because Patsy was the worst with her. She'd increasingly been accusing Bettie of random grievances that mostly made no sense.

"You know exactly which shoes I mean. Ya always wanted them b'cause they reminded ya of Dorothy's ruby slippers," Patsy explained, still raising her voice.

The kitchen was silent so long, we almost went in to check on them. Then we heard Bettie say quietly, "Aye, Mum, I'm sorry I took them. I'll get them for ya, okay?" That was odd. I opened the door and walked in to see Bettie sitting at the table with her head in her hands, and Patsy was no where to be seen.

"Bettie, what was that all about?" I asked.

She shook her head. "It's gettin' so hard, Brenna. She's goin' on about some shoes, and then I realize she's talkin' about shoes she had when I was a kid! She hasn't had those shoes for some forty years!"

Ryan walked over and began giving Bettie a light shoulder massage. "What can we do to help?" he asked.

She chuckled. "What yer doin' right there is brilliant."

"What's the doctor say?" I asked.

"Well, I couldn't get her to go for the longest time. I finally tricked her by tellin' her we both had to have our blood checked for a new strain of smallpox." She chuckled sadly.

"That was clever," Ryan commented.

"Well, it got her there. He confirmed that it's mid-stage Alzheimer's. I've all these pamphlets he gave me over there in my desk. If ya want to read 'em, be my guest. I'm gettin' so tired."

"Did he tell *her* that?" I asked.

"No, she won't listen to anything about it. He said we're lucky we got her to wear that bracelet. Denial is very strong at this stage; so is paranoia. It's not a pretty picture, and I don't know how to help her."

"I'm sorry I've been gone so much, Bettie." I felt really guilty.

"Nonsense. You two should be enjoyin' this time together. Y'only fall in love once!" she said and then chuckled. "Well, twice for some of us," she added with a wink at me.

"Yeah, I'm twice blessed," I agreed, giving Ryan's hand a squeeze. "But seriously, how can I help?"

"I don't know, dear. Y'can read through those pamphlets. Just havin' everyone on the same page would be good. The doc suggested I go to a caregivers group. They meet once a month and share ideas for carin' for Alzheimer's patients."

"Let's do that together, then," I suggested.

"Aye, that'd be nice," she agreed, and it was settled. The next meeting was Thursday night. I'd miss Veritas, but this was more important.

"I'll tell Anna when she gets home. She'll want to come too," I said.

"Ah, but there's the rub. We can't leave her alone, right?" she said sadly.

"I'll come spend the evenin' with her," Ryan offered.

"Thank you, Finn. That'd be really helpful; plus, she adores ya. She won't give you a hard time," she said. "Are y'stayin' fer dinner then?"

"No, actually I have a meetin' in Cork tonight. We're just gonna visit for a while until I have to leave," he explained.

We headed upstairs, but it felt awkward going into my room and closing the door. "Wanna go hang out downstairs?" Ryan asked, obviously feeling the same.

"Yeah, good idea," I agreed. We headed down to the front room and sat on the couch. He had spent many years exercising self-control in the area of physical attraction, but he admitted he was finding that to be very difficult with me. I knew that I was obviously not the queen of self-control and didn't trust myself to stop if things progressed too quickly. So Ryan suggested we agree on some ground rules.

First, we would part company by 11:00 p.m. each night … a sort of curfew. *Nothing good happens after midnight* was the old saying, and in the week we'd been together, we'd found that to be true. Second, Ryan suggested we stop kissing altogether, but that was not going to fly with me. I offered a compromise. "How about if we only kiss standing up?" Kissing while snuggling on the couch quickly led to other things, and that was not good. But standing up, that would help, wouldn't it? We agreed. And third, no bedrooms; the only place to sit was the bed, and there was no need to be stupid.

Although Ryan was on vacation, he still had business to attend to at times, so he would be spending the next three days going between Cork and Limerick. He kissed me goodnight and promised to be back in time to spend Thursday night with Patsy while the rest of us went to the caregivers meeting in Cork.

He'd been gone for approximately two hours, and I was already missing him. It was incredible to me that I'd grown so attached in such a short time. But I knew occasional distance was a healthy thing. I didn't want to make the mistake with Ryan that I'd made with Ben. Ben had been my whole life. I never realized it until he was gone, but it was probably the one aspect of our marriage that had been unhealthy. I was intentional now about making sure I still called Megan and Tara; and knowing Ryan would be gone for a few days, I had arranged to meet them for tea the next day.

"How about we get a group together to go to Cork for dinner and a movie?" Tara suggested as we waited for Megan at the Tea Shoppe. It was Tuesday after work, and Tara and I had just sat down.

"That sounds great. Who should we ask?" Megan walked in and joined us. "We're talkin' about doing dinner and a movie at the mall in Cork tomorrow. Are ya in?" I asked.

"Sure! Who's goin'?" she asked.

"Well, so far, we are," I answered. "Who should we invite?"

"The girls from work, right?" Tara said.

"That's Katie and Sarah?" Megan asked.

"Aye, and Brigit," Tara answered.

"What about Shannon?" I asked. "I haven't seen her in so long."

"Aye, great idea. She can meet us there. I'll call her right now." Tara stepped outside to get better reception.

"So, how are things with Ryan?" Megan asked.

I knew my eyes went dreamy, but I couldn't help it. "Really good," I answered. "He's helping me learn how to drive here; I'm taking my test next week. And he showed me his grandma's place that he renovated. It's beautiful."

"I've heard. I haven't seen it on the inside, but even from outside it's lovely," she replied.

"He's really talented, you know? I think he's gonna take me to Limerick soon to see some of his work there. I can't wait. He even has 'before-and-after' pictures in his office there. I love that kind of stuff," I gushed.

"Isn't it cool that ya have similar interests?" she said.

"We have so much in common ... at least in how we view things and what we enjoy. The age difference doesn't really seem to affect us," I said.

"How much older is he?"

"Well, I'm almost twenty-one, and he's twenty-eight, so, barely eight years," I answered.

"Wow, I didn't realize he was that much older. But it doesn't bother ya, right?"

"No, not so far. I don't see why it will. We get along so well; we have so much fun together. I don't see it being an issue."

"When do ya turn twenty-one?" she asked.

"Saturday," I replied.

"*This* Saturday?" she cried.

"Yeah."

"Why didn't ya tell me sooner? I don't have time to put a party together," she said, distraught.

"I don't know; I didn't think about it. I don't need a party. I'm not even sure what I'm doing that night. I figured either Anna or Ryan would want to go out for dinner."

"Did ya tell Ryan?" she asked.

"No, Anna did."

"Well, let's make tomorrow night a birthday celebration then!" she said. "Where's Tara? She's takin' forever." She looked toward the door. "I'll be right back." She left to find her. I took a minute to try and wipe the newest tea stain out of my shirt. Pointless. *Another one bites the dust.*

They came back moments later but said they had planning to do now, so they wanted to drop me off at home.

"No, it's okay. I'll walk. Anna's working late, so I'll stop in and see if she's ready to walk home," I said.

"Good. We'll pick ya up tomorrow at 4:30, okay?" Megan asked.

"I'll be ready. We're still doing dinner and a movie, right?"

"Aye, still the same plans." Megan replied as I gave her a quick hug and headed toward the church on foot.

Anna was happy to see me. "What a pleasant surprise. I'm glad ya caught me. I almost left ten minutes ago, but then I got stuck on the phone."

"Good! I'm glad I caught you too," I replied. "I feel like I never see you anymore."

"Aye, me too. But it's to be expected, right?" she added as she grabbed a sweater and we headed out the door.

"Yeah. I guess … but I need your help with that." She looked at me, puzzled. "Remember how we talked about when Ben and I got married and you wanted us to wait so I would have more time to meet new people and all that?" I asked.

"Aye."

"Well, I want to be careful that I don't focus so much attention on Ryan that I leave all my other relationships in the dust, you know? Cuz it would be extremely easy to do. I just want to spend every minute with him," I explained.

"How can I help?" she asked.

"Just help me keep it real," I said. "Let me know if I seem out of balance?"

"I'll do my best, love," she answered with a smile. "So I take it all is well?"

"Yeah. I'm falling fast and hard. You're sure you're okay with it? I mean, it's not weird?" I had to ask.

"Brenna, even if it were weird for me, should that change how ya feel about Ryan?" she asked.

"You didn't answer me, though. Is it weird for you?" I pressed.

She sighed. "Yes and no. It's weird in that for so many years I looked forward to the day you and Ben would get married and then eventually start a family." She got quiet for a moment. "It still makes me sad, love. I won't have grandchildren. I won't ever get to see my son become a dad. That's hard. But that would be hard regardless. Seein' ya happy again, seein' ya with a very special man, that's not weird at all. That's fabulous."

"Anna, there's no question who will be grandma to my children. I know it's not the same, but I want you to know that anyway," I assured her.

"Thanks, dear," she said. "That means a lot to me, and I'm truly thrilled that you and Ryan have hit it off. Truly. Aunty Pat mentioned him to me not a week after we had arrived, but I convinced her to hold off a little in her matchmaking. I'm glad she was right."

"Yeah, speaking of Patsy, did Bettie mention Thursday night?" I asked.

"No, what's goin' on?"

"Well, the doctor suggested a support group thing for caregivers of Alzheimer's patients," I explained.

"Aye, she did tell me that."

"Well, the next one is Thursday night, and I told Bettie I'd go with her. Wanna come?" I asked.

"Sure. Let me consult my busy social calendar first, though." She was teasing, but it made me sad. I wondered if she would ever allow herself to fall in love again. "But wait, that leaves Auntie Pat alone for the night," Anna suddenly realized. "That won't do."

"No, Ryan's gonna hang out with her."

"What a gem that boy is," she said with a wink.

"Aye, that he is, love," I imitated her with an almost perfect Irish accent. I was getting good!

Chapter Twenty-Five

Megan picked me up, and then we headed next door to get Tara where she had been visiting John. "Are we picking anyone else up?" I asked.

"No," Tara answered. "Brigit is drivin' the others, but they had to wait for Sarah to get back from an appointment. We're gonna go early to make sure we get a table."

I eyed the gift bags in the back seat next to Tara. "I told you guys I didn't want a birthday party," I scolded.

"Actually, ya said ya didn't *need* a birthday party," Megan corrected. "There's a difference."

I rolled my eyes and gave her a playful push. "What did you two cook up?"

"Nothin' big, don't worry. Just a girls' night out with presents and maybe a little cake. Ya can't complain about that. It's yer twenty-first birthday, for Pete's sake!" Megan insisted.

"Okay, thanks. That's really thoughtful, guys," I admitted.

"Yer welcome," Tara replied. "Besides, we're always up for a party."

Most of the remaining forty-minute drive was spent with me answering questions about Ryan. What did his apartment look like? What was he like? Was he a good kisser? I wondered if I was in junior high again, but I obliged them because it was fun—and even more so because I'd been away from him for a couple days now, and I missed him.

"Yer completely gone, aren't ya?" Tara asked as I sighed, missing him.

"Yep. I don't think there's any question," I answered. "So, what's happening with you and John?" I changed the subject.

"Eh, hard to tell." She was vague. "He's not very talkative. I guess we're together, but he doesn't ever talk about it. We just hang out a lot."

"I know he likes ya," Megan added.

"Aye, I know. I mean, he's shown that, if ya get my meanin'." She smirked. "But we don't go out on dates or anythin'. We just hang out. It's weird."

"Well, he is young," I offered. "Is Jamie like that, Meg?"

"No. He's quiet, but he's very deliberate about our relationship," she answered.

"So it's probably just a maturity thing. He's what … nineteen? That's young—for a guy anyway. You know it takes them longer to catch up," I said.

"That's why you go fer older men?" Tara teased.

"Funny," I smacked her. "But yes, that's one way to avoid immature boys." I grinned.

They had made reservations at a quaint little Italian restaurant near the movie theater. We sat down in the small lounge to wait for the others. The ambiance was warm, and the room was softly lit.

"This is really pretty," I commented. "Have either of you been here before?"

"No. Shannon suggested it," Tara replied. "And here she is!" She jumped up from her seat and hugged Shannon in greeting.

Hugs went all around, and Shannon sat down as the cocktail waitress approached. "Can I get you ladies somethin' t'drink while yer waitin?" she asked.

"Aye, I'll have a sangria," Tara responded.

"I'm fine," Megan and I said in unison and then giggled..

"I'll have a red lemonade, please," Shannon added.

As the waitress walked away, Tara pouted. "What, I'm the only one drinkin'? I thought this was a celebration!"

"Ya know I don't really drink, Tara," Megan said.

"And I rarely do either," I said. But Tara was having none of it.

"That wasn't yer attitude that night at Rosie's!" She laughed as she told the tale of my drinking 'binge' at Rosie's. I think she made Conor sound even better-looking than he was, but overall, the retelling was accurate.

I cringed when she got to the part about Luke buying me a pint. Megan gave me a quick look of sympathy as Tara continued on. I did notice that Shannon was intently watching me instead of Tara, and I thought that was weird.

"Okay, I admit I did drink last week, but you know that's not the norm for me. I think I had more that night than I ever have in my life," I said with a blush creeping up my cheeks. The waitress was back with our drinks, and I took advantage of Tara's momentary distraction to change the subject.

"So, how are you liking school, Shannon?"

"Fine. Actually, I really do like it. I'm enjoyin' bein' on my own but not fully on my own, y'know? Classes are okay. Some are better than others. I'm mostly takin' general courses right now. Not much to do with nursing, but that will come."

"I have to give you credit," I said. "I don't think I could be a nurse, but I really admire people who can. I think it takes a very special person to do that."

"Thanks." She smiled. "I think I've always wanted to do it. My mum said I used to set up doll hospitals in the back yard, and I'd bandage them up and give them medicine. Apparently I made a big mess, but I had so much fun she let it slide," she explained.

"Katie!" Tara called as she saw the others come inside. And then her eyes popped wide. I followed her gaze and saw why. Brigit had brought a friend—Char. My stomach dropped at the sight of her. This was no longer a fun night. I looked to Megan and Tara in a panic. Tara knew we couldn't stand each other, and Megan instinctively understood that I was afraid Char knew about what happened with Luke. I imagined bolting from the restaurant, but that wasn't really an option. No, I'd just have to grin and bear it.

We all stood up and said our hellos. "Ya all know Char, right?" Brigit asked, and everyone nodded. I stood there trying to figure out if Brigit was cruel or clueless. My gut said the latter. She had no clue what a can of worms she'd just opened.

Our table was ready. Brigit explained that Sarah couldn't make it, but Char had stopped by, so she asked her to join us. I smiled and nodded, afraid to open my mouth. I had a dreadful feeling that Char knew exactly what she was doing and was relishing every second of my inner turmoil.

We had barely been seated when she started. "So, Brenna, I hear you and Ryan are a thing now. Isn't he a lot older than you?" She said this with a practiced sweetness that would fool anyone who didn't know her. She made her question sound innocent, when I knew it was anything but.

"Yes, he's eight years older than me, and we just started seeing each other last week," I answered politely.

"Oh, okay. That explains it," she said coyly.

She was so smooth. "Explains what?" Katie took the bait.

"Well, I had just heard she was out drinkin' and dancin' and stuff with Luke the Friday before last, so I was confused," she said offhandedly. But I knew she'd done what she intended. She had started the wheels turning.

Katie continued taking her bait. "I didn't know you and Luke had gone out." She looked at me, puzzled. "I mean, don't get me wrong; everyone knew he was totally into you. He was constantly flirtin' with ya, but you seemed to be able to resist him like no one I've seen."

I enjoyed watching Char seethe beneath the surface as Katie went on about Luke's interest in me. "No, we weren't out together. He just came up and bought me a pint when I was at the bar. We went out once a couple months ago, but that was it." I tried to end it there. "Katie, what happened to Sarah?"

"Oh, she had a hair appointment, but it got moved back. She was in the middle of gettin' her hair colored when she was supposed to be meetin' us, so she said to go without her. She said to tell ya Happy Birthday, though." Katie smiled her contagious smile.

"Oh, no problem," I said as the server came over to present the menu. Once we had all decided and placed our orders, Char started up again.

"So, someone told me you and Luke were dancin' pretty hot and heavy that night, though."

I knew my face was beet red. Megan came to my rescue. "Char, Brenna had a little too much to drink that night, and Luke knew it, so if he took some liberties with her on the dance floor, I don't think anyone is surprised, knowin' the kind of guy he is. Did ya really come to Brenna's birthday dinner to talk about Luke?"

"No," Char quipped and then shut her mouth. She sat there quietly fuming, and I squeezed Megan's hand as a thank-you. If she hadn't stepped in, I don't know what I might have done. Even Brigit was looking at Char with irritation.

We finished a delicious dinner. Of course I ended up wearing some sauce, but they no longer even laughed at me when I spilled stuff. It was fully expected. They had all—except Char, obviously—chipped in and bought me a couple of birthday presents. One was a trendy little purse filled with assorted lip glosses, eye shadows, and liners. *Hint, hint?*

I laughed immediately as I removed the tissue paper from the heavy, second bag. Inside was a bottle of bleach surrounded by at least ten stain-blocker pens. "You're so funny!" I teased, but I loved it. These were my friends, and they knew me. I actually was very excited about the pens. I immediately took one out and rubbed it over the red sauce marks on my sleeve. Time would tell if it helped at all, but it was the thought that counted.

The rest of the night went smoothly, with Char put properly in her place. She essentially became a tagalong, and I did my very best to ignore her completely, as did most of the others, leaving Brigit to handle her alone as we walked into the movie theater. I decided that she probably did know about me and Luke, but she also seemed to have been warned not to say anything directly about it. I took some comfort in that, but not much. I knew she would gleefully tell Ryan if she got the chance, just to spite me. I had to tell Ryan before she did. My stomach hurt as I sat through yet another movie without watching it.

"I can't believe Brigit brought her!" Tara said as soon as we pulled away from the cinema.

"Yeah, that was not cool," I responded. "Megan, thanks so much for stepping in."

"I wanted to strangle her," Megan said through gritted teeth.

"Well, you put her in her place, and that was awesome." I chuckled, remembering her face as Megan lit into her. "I don't think she's used to people standing up to her."

"No, I've never seen anyone do that to her," Tara agreed, "although I know plenty of girls in school who wanted to—right, Megan? She was the popular girl who everyone wanted to be friends with but no one really liked. Y'know?"

"You went to school together? How old is she?" I asked Tara. I thought she was closer in age to Luke.

"She's Meg's age. We were all in the same secondary school, but they were three years ahead of me, in Liam's class, so I heard plenty," she explained. "There was this big fuss when she started datin' Luke. She was in third year, and he was in sixth. I remember Liam was jealous, and that's when he decided he didn't like Luke."

"Okay, wait. I need you to translate that for me. Secondary school is like high school, right?"

"Aye." Megan joined in. "We start secondary at age thirteen. You have junior high, I think?"

"Yeah, seventh grade. That's 'first year' for you guys?" I was catching on.

Megan nodded. "So third year would be ninth grade and sixth would be twelfth grade," she explained.

"Okay, so that would be like a freshman dating a senior," I said. "Wow. She must have been one gorgeous freshman."

"Aye," said Megan. "It was the talk of the school when they got together. They were like the two prettiest people in secondary." Against my will, I began to feel sorry for her. I knew firsthand how persuasive Luke could be. He got a hold on her very young. No wonder she couldn't get over him. I imagined how I would have felt if Ben had started dating other girls when we got to college. It would have been horrid.

"Okay, let's stop talking about her, cuz I'm starting to feel sorry for her and I don't want to," I admitted, and they laughed. The rest of the ride was a little awkward for me, because I desperately wanted to talk with Megan. I wanted to know if she thought Char knew. But I couldn't ask until we'd dropped Tara off.

"So, do ya think she knows?" Megan beat me to it as soon as Tara's door closed.

"Tara or Char?" I asked.

"You think Tara knows?" she said, surprised.

"No," I said. "I think Char does, though, don't you?"

"Aye, I got that distinct impression." She nodded.

"Great," I said flatly. "Did I tell you I threatened Luke not to tell anyone?"

"No! What did ya say?" she asked with wide eyes. I recounted my "date-rape" conversation with Luke, and she laughed like I was a comedian.

"Oh, Brenna, yer awesome. I wish I could have seen his face. No one stands up to him either. No wonder you and I get along so well."

"Yeah, we make a good pair, don't we?" I smiled.

Megan brought the conversation back. "So, are ya worried Char will tell?"

I took a deep breath. "Geez, I hope not. But I don't trust her. I have to tell Ryan now. I certainly don't want him hearing it on the streets, you know?"

"I agree. You've gotta tell him," she said, and my chest felt heavy. I had been so excited to see Ryan again. Now I was dreading it.

Of course my shift the next day flew by when I would have preferred it to go slowly. Ryan got in around lunchtime and stopped in to order lunch for us for after my shift. The queasy feeling started as soon as I saw him and didn't stop by the time I was climbing the back stairs. He heard me coming and opened the door before I could knock. He then swooped me into his arms for a strong embrace. "Geez, I've missed ya," he said into my hair as he kissed the top of my head. "It was all I could do not to kidnap ya when I came in at lunchtime."

"I'm glad you didn't do that; my boss would have gotten really mad," I joked.

He chuckled and took a look at my face. "Are ya feelin' okay? Ya don't look good," he said, concerned.

"Thanks," I quipped with a forced smile.

"Cut it out, Bren. Ya know what I mean. Seriously, are y'sick?" he asked.

"No, I'm just really tired." *And I have to tell you something horrible.*

"Well, come sit down." He picked up the bag of to-go food I'd brought up and motioned for me to grab a seat on the couch. I sat there, trying to muster the courage to speak while he was busy in the kitchen. Minutes later, he brought me a hot cup of tea and the sandwich from Rosie's. "Eat something; that will help."

I did take a bite, and it did help. I felt less weak and took advantage of the momentary boost to launch into what I needed to talk about. "Ryan, I need to tell you about something, and I don't know how to start. Remember when …" I stopped. Looking into those concerned blue eyes, I faltered. Did I really have to tell him? Char's sneering face popped up in my mind, and I knew I did.

"What is it?" he asked.

Suddenly the sandwich seemed like a bad idea, as I felt it threatening to come back up. I pushed the plate away, took a sip of hot tea, and tried again. "Okay." *Deep breath.* "This is so hard." I could see he was completely worried now. "Remember the night we went to the movie?" I said.

"Aye." He looked down. I knew he felt bad about how he'd acted that night.

"Well, you told me I could stay here, and that's what I did—at first. I was so upset when you left. I called Anna and told her I was staying so she wouldn't worry, and then I tried to fall asleep in your bed." I paused as he stared at me intently, waiting for me to go on.

"So, I couldn't sleep. The music was so loud downstairs, it was like the bass was being played in my head," I explained.

"Aye, that can be a problem on the weekends. I forgot to warn ya."

"Okay, remember when you told me about you and Kelley, and you asked me not to interrupt?" I reminded him.

"I remember," he said.

"This is one of those times," I responded, and he nodded cautiously.

"So, I tried for quite a while to fall asleep, but I couldn't. And then I started getting madder and madder. Why was I alone? Blah, blah … feeling sorry for myself."

"I'm so sorry I did that, Brenna," he interrupted, and I leveled a no-nonsense look that had him pretending to zip his mouth shut.

"Anyway, I did something really stupid." *Deep breath.* "I need you to know, though, that it was probably the hardest day I've had since Ben died." I was stalling, and Ryan was looking ill himself now. I continued, with a lump in my throat. "I went down to the pub, and I let a guy buy me a couple pints. Then he asked me to go back to his place with him, and I laughed at him and went to go find Tara." I felt bad letting him be relieved when I knew where the story was going. "It gets worse," I warned him, holding back tears with every word I spoke. "I was really angry and emotional and stupid. I saw some girls doing shots of whiskey, so I had Tara pour me one." Ryan's eyebrows shot up, but he stayed quiet. I didn't know if I could actually say what had happened. Tears were springing to my eyes at the thought.

He took my hands in his. "It's okay, Brenna. Just tell me," he said quietly. I continued, all the while thinking I might vomit.

Deep breath. "That's when Luke came up to the bar." Ryan's face went white as a sheet, and I knew he could figure out where this was leading. I pulled my hands away from him and covered my face, unable to continue.

"Brenna, what happened?" he asked with a dangerous edge to his voice. I shook my head.

"I'm so sorry. You didn't want me, and I was such a mess, and I'd had more to drink than I ever have." I began crying again. It was excruciating, hurting him like this. "I didn't mean to, and I never wanted to hurt you. I've never done anything like that before. I didn't think about it. I just acted on impulse."

"Tell me what happened, Brenna," he said again in a louder, scarier voice.

"You know what happened. It's what you're thinking." I tried desperately to not have to say out loud what I had done.

"I want to know what that snake did to ya," he said, almost in a whisper.

"It's my fault, Ryan. I was drunk, but I still went along with it. We were dancing and I just … I missed the feeling of being wanted." There, that was really what it was all about. "So I went up with him to his apartment, and I woke up there in the morning." I was barely whispering by this point and that was as close as I would get to telling him what happened.

Ryan bolted off the couch and headed for the door. It was my worst nightmare come true. He was leaving me. "Ryan, wait! I'm so sorry. Please forgive me!" I begged, and he stopped in his tracks. He turned around, and a look of fury was simmering on his face. He put his hands over his face and whispered something and then walked back toward me.

"Brenna," he said tenderly and wrapped his powerful arms around me. "I am so, so sorry."

"What?" I pounded on his chest and backed up. "What are you talking about? I make the biggest mistake of my life, and *you* say you're sorry?"

"I don't blame you," he said honestly. Then his face darkened. "I blame *him*." He spat the word as if it were poison. "He had no right to take advantage of ya." His anger was simmering once again.

"Wait a minute. I agree that he did that … he took advantage of me. But I *let* him. I should have just gone home. *I* was wrong."

"Aye, but why were ya stuck in that position? That was *my* doin'! I left ya here like a coward. If I had just been strong enough to take ya home like I should have, then nothin' would have happened." He was incredible. Not only was he taking the blame, but it was beginning to make sense to me.

I shook my head. "Ryan, look at me. You can be mad at Luke; you can be mad at yourself. But that doesn't change the fact that I did something extremely stupid and wrong. I need to know if you can forgive me for that. I mean *truly* forgive me—not gallantly put all the blame elsewhere."

He closed his eyes and visibly calmed down. "I don't have a right to be angry with ya, Brenna. If the situation were different … if we had been together and this had happened, well … yeah, I'd be furious with ya. I hate that it happened, but the truth is that you and I were not together. And that was *my* fault. I'd made that impossible and given ya nothin' to go on. I put ya in a vulnerable situation and left ya there. If ya need to hear that I forgive ya, then aye, I forgive ya." He paused and took my hands. "But I need to know if you forgive me for abandonin' you that night. It was cowardly, and whether ya think so or not, I am partly to blame for what happened."

I looked up into those genuine, blue eyes and melted with relief. Tears came again, unwelcome, but there nonetheless. I nodded. It was all I could do, and he wrapped me in his arms again. He kissed the top of my head and whispered, "I love ya, Brenna. This doesn't change that. I will not abandon y'again; you can be sure of that."

He'd said "I love you." I squeezed him as hard as I could. "I love you too, Ryan," I whispered into his chest. He tilted my chin up toward his face and pulled me into a soft and tender kiss. "You are a prince, Ryan Kelly," I told him. "I don't know if I'll ever deserve you, but I'm never letting you go."

"Even when I'm usin' a walker and ya have to go to support meetings about takin' care of me?" he joked, not for the first time, about our age difference.

I smacked his chest yet again while stifling a yawn. "You're ruining the moment," I said with a smile, looking up at him.

"You really are tired, aren't ya? I was up early, and I'm kind of tired too. Wanna take a nap on the couch?"

"That's one of my favorite places." I grinned. I think I was asleep before he had the blanket on top of us.

Chapter Twenty-Six

"How was the meeting?" Ryan asked as I filed into the kitchen behind Bettie and Anna.

"It was very good," said Bettie. The Alzheimer's support meeting had had a powerful impact on her. Just to see others going through the same things she was with Patsy was comforting.

"Aye, very informative," Anna agreed.

I gave Ryan a hug. "How was Patsy tonight?" I asked.

"Fine. We played cards. She beat me." He grinned. "She went up to bed about an hour ago."

"Thank you so much for stayin' with her, Finn. It was great havin' the girls with me." Bettie gave him a kiss on the cheek and headed upstairs to check on Patsy.

"I'm puttin' the water on. Would ya like some tea?" Anna offered.

"Aye, that'd be great," Ryan answered, and I nodded. "We'll be in front," he said as he pulled me through the swinging door. I started to sit down on the couch, but he stopped me.

"Oh no ya don't." I looked at him, puzzled. "If ya sit down, I'm not allowed to do this." He bent down and kissed me until I couldn't breathe.

"What was that for?" I asked while trying to catch my breath.

"Ya didn't like it?" he pouted.

"Of course I liked it!" I laughed.

215

"Good." He went for a second round, but I was giggling so much it didn't really work. "Fine, sit down." He gently pushed me onto the couch where I continued to laugh. "So," he said, sitting down. "Someone has a birthday in two days."

"Ooh, ooh, I know … it's me!"

"Aye, and do ya know what we're goin' to do for yer birthday?" he asked.

"No, what?"

"Well, part of it's a surprise, but we're gonna go to Limerick." He smiled.

"Yay! Do I get to see where you work?"

"Sure, if ya like," he agreed. "But here's what I was wonderin', because it's yer day and I want to do what you want. What would ya say to meeting my mum and da?"

"Really? I'd love to meet them," I said, but cautiously. It made me nervous. What if they didn't like me? "Do they know about us?"

"Oh, they've heard all about ya." He grinned.

"Great," I said sarcastically.

"Stop it. They love you already and can't wait to meet ya."

"Okay. Sounds like a plan to me," I said as Anna brought in two steaming cups of tea.

"What's a plan?" she asked.

"We're makin' plans for Saturday," Ryan answered. "I thought I could come over and make breakfast for ya all, and then if it's okay with you, I'd like to steal Brenna away for the weekend."

Anna raised her eyebrows in a look I couldn't read. "Oh, okay. Sounds good. I'm always into someone else makin' me breakfast," she said. "I'm headin' upstairs. Will ya lock up?"

"Sure," I told her. "Ryan will be heading home soon." Our self-imposed curfew was over an hour away, but I was tired and knew I had an early morning. He looked at me sideways as Anna said good-night.

"Are y'kickin me out so soon?" he asked with a fake wounded look.

"No, not yet." I giggled at his goofy, sad face. "But soon. I have to be up early," I reminded him.

"Aye, I hear the boss is comin' in fer breakfast, so you'd best not be late."

"Exactly. He's a slave driver, and I don't want to get on his bad side," I teased.

"Ah, ya can try, but I don't think it's possible." He cuddled me and kissed my neck.

"Hey!" I slapped him. "Cut that out, rule breaker!"

"Sorry. I'll be good," he repented.

"Snuggle," I said, and I curled up in his arms.

The next thing I remember was him tucking me into my bed. "I fell asleep?" I asked, groggy.

"Aye." He kissed my forehead. "Good-night, love. I have a key; I'll lock up," he assured me and left the room.

True to his word, Ryan was sitting there in my section, smiling, when I walked in. He was my only customer as of yet, so I sat down with him.

"Mornin', beautiful," he said.

"Mornin', boss," I replied.

He laughed. "Okay, you can cut that out now. Sam's yer boss anyway, not me."

"Yeah, but you're the big boss," I corrected him.

"Aye, yer right. So it's come to this. I guess I'll have to fire ya so there's no conflict of interest."

"You wouldn't!" I was pretty sure he was joking.

"Course not. But no more 'boss' talk, okay?" he replied.

"Okay," I agreed. "Omelet?"

"Aye, the usual," he answered, and then his face turned to stone.

"What is it?" I asked, alarmed, and followed his gaze to the door. *Luke.* "Ryan, look at me." He didn't look away from Luke, who now saw him staring. Ryan was quite a bit bigger than Luke. "Ryan, please," I begged while holding on to his now bulging arm. He finally broke his laser stare and looked at me.

"Sorry," he said quietly.

"Are you okay?"

"Aye, I'm okay now. He's gone," he answered, staring blankly at the door.

I looked, and sure enough he had left. He was smarter than I thought. "Good. Listen to me. I don't care about him, but if you did something to him, *you* could get in trouble, and *that* would kill me. Ryan, look at me." He did. "Please, don't do anything. You could probably kill him, you know?" I knew it wasn't in his nature to do anything of the sort, but I also knew that at this moment he hated Luke.

He nodded. "I'm okay. Sorry," he said again.

"No, don't apologize. Just be careful," I warned. I kissed him quickly and headed into the kitchen.

Tara was talking to Liam and laughing. "Brenna, remind me never to get on Ryan's bad side!" she said with a grin. "Really, Liam. Ya would have loved it. It was almost like one of those nature shows where there's like this face-off between two wolves or somethin', and then the bigger one growls, and the other one runs away with his tail between his legs." She laughed and so did Liam.

I smiled at her analogy and pictured Luke running away. It was funny, but it still worried me. "Yeah, well, in the wild that big wolf wouldn't get arrested for beating the crap out of the smaller wolf, you know?"

"Good point," Tara said.

"The usual for Ryan," I told Liam and went back to the dining room, which was starting to fill up.

Ryan had a meeting in Cork City, so I walked home after work. My phone rang, and I thought it would be him, but it wasn't his number.

"Hello?" I answered.

"Hey, Brenna, it's Shannon."

"Oh, hi, Shannon. How are you?"

"Fine, thanks. Do y'have a minute?"

"Sure. Are you okay?" I wondered if something was wrong. She'd never called me before.

"Aye, I'm fine, really. I'm gonna be in town on Monday, and I wanted to see if we could meet for a cuppa tea."

"Oh, sure. That'd be nice. What time?" I asked.

"Are y'workin'?"

"Yeah, till around two."

"How about after work then? We can meet at the Tea Shoppe?" she suggested.

"Okay, I'll see you there, say, two thirty to be safe?"

"Two thirty it is." She hung up.

That was weird. I thought to myself and shrugged.

I went to bed early and woke up with the birds. I tried to go back to sleep, but I couldn't. My mind was racing. What would Ryan's parents be like? Would his sister be there too? Would they like me? I didn't usually worry about meeting new people … I mean, it wasn't a favorite thing of mine, but it didn't usually keep me awake, either. But this was big. This was "Come meet my parents" big.

I gave up on trying to fall back to sleep and instead put on sweats and grabbed my comforter, my Bible, and my journal. I slipped out onto the terrace and snuggled into my comforter. I sat there watching the sunrise on my twenty-first birthday.

Once it was light enough, I read a couple Psalms and then pulled out my journal.

Lord,

Thank you for this new day. Thank you for blessing me with Ryan. Please help me as I go meet his parents today. I'm nervous, but I know that you are with me. And Lord, thank you so much for helping me tell Ryan about Luke. Please help Ryan not to kill him.

Amen.

I always thought my prayer attempts were a little feeble, but they were heartfelt, and I knew that counted for something. On the days that I started my day by reading and writing in my journal, I had an inner peace that stayed with me. I felt that peace as I headed into the shower and got myself ready for the day.

Both Bettie and Ryan were working in the kitchen when I came downstairs. We had an elderly couple staying over, and Bettie was making breakfast for them while Ryan was making a birthday breakfast feast for the rest of us.

As I sat down, Ryan presented me with a huge plate. I would never be able to eat all the food that was piled on it. He had made scrambled eggs, sausage and bacon, potato bread, and soda bread—as well as a heaping pile of fried potatoes.

"Ryan, this is enough breakfast for me for a week! Do they not have food in Limerick? Are we stocking up?"

"Just eat yer breakfast, young lady," Patsy chimed in.

"Yes, ma'am," I answered with a salute.

"Just cuz it's yer birthday doesn't mean you can get cheeky with me," she said with narrowed eyes, trying to hide a twinkle. She had good days and bad days. This appeared to be a good one, which was a birthday present in itself. I missed her when she stayed in her room or moped about. This was the Patsy that I was used to, and it was good to see her acting herself.

As I pushed away my half-full plate, Anna handed me a heavy, rectangular present. As usual, it was so beautifully wrapped that I didn't want to wreck it.

"Oh, Anna, it's lovely. I'll go hang it on my wall right now!" I said before opening it. Anna laughed, but Ryan was lost. "It's an old joke," I explained. "Anna can make wrapping paper made from a paper bag look elegant. I never want to open her presents because they look so gorgeous."

"Ah, I see. Well, have no fear of that with me." He set a modestly wrapped gift on the table in front of me. It was a flat, rectangular box about the size of a pack of gum. I looked at him with a sideways smile. "What is it?" I asked, knowing he wouldn't answer.

"Ya know I'm not gonna tell ya. Open Anna's," he reminded me.

I looked down at the Martha Stewart wrapping job and sighed. "Okay, here goes." I tore into it. It was the only way to go. I'd tried to do it delicately before, but there was no point. I could never make my presents look like hers, even if I used her paper.

Castles of Ireland. It was a magnificent coffee-table book. I loved castles and Anna knew it. "I love it!" I cried, and I jumped up and gave her a hug. "We should make a plan to go visit all of them, you know?"

"I'd love that!" she agreed.

"We're next," said Patsy. "We're not stupid enough to go after him." She pointed at Ryan who feigned offense.

Bettie and Patsy had chipped in and bought me three new shirts. Bettie often did my wash without me asking, and she knew my tendency for stains. I had more stained shirts in my closet than she had shirts in total.

"Now ya can get rid of some of those old blouses of yers," Bettie said firmly. It was more of a command than a suggestion.

"Okay, okay," I agreed. "Thank you. These are perfect."

Ryan's eyes were practically glowing sapphires by this point. "Go ahead, open it." He nudged the box toward me. I looked around, and they were all beaming.

"So, you all know what's in this box?" I asked.

"Just open it," said Anna.

I tore off the wrapping and opened the box to reveal a gold key with a black handle sporting gold wings. I was in shock. "You did not," I said to Ryan.

He was grinning from ear to ear. "Oh, yes I did," he said as he bounded toward the front door. "Come on!"

I looked at the others. They were grinning. "He didn't buy me a car?!" I was in disbelief.

"Get out there." Anna grabbed my hand and pulled me through the house. There, parked right in front, was the most adorable red Mini Cooper I'd ever seen. Ryan was leaning on it beaming.

"Oh my gosh!" I just stood there, staring.

"Come see it!" Ryan beckoned.

I stumbled down the stairs and walked around it, afraid to touch it. "You can't buy me a car, Ryan!" I scolded him. I couldn't accept a gift like that. As much as I was dying to, it was way too much. Any car would have been way too much, but this was just over the top.

"Yes, I can," he argued. "I already did." A smug grin appeared as he watched me run my hand along the black stripes on the hood of the car.

"Ryan, it's gorgeous. But I can't accept it," I told him.

"Why not?" he asked confidently.

"I … because … I don't know. It's just too much," I stammered.

"Ya need a car, right?" he asked.

"Yes, I was saving to buy one."

"Okay, so ya needed new shirts, and Bettie and Patsy got ya some. Ya needed a car, and I got ya one. Same thing." He laughed as I punched his arm.

"It is not the same thing, and you know it, crazy person!"

"Brenna, seriously, look at me." I looked up at him. "This really isn't a big deal. I mean, I got a great deal on it, and trust me … it's not a big deal." I knew he had a lot of money. I didn't have a clue how much, but I was beginning to suspect it was more than I imagined. Still, I hesitated. "Okay, how about this," he offered. "For now, we'll say yer borrowin' my car. Fair?"

I gave in and threw my arms around his neck. "Deal," I whispered before kissing him. When he set me down, I slid into the driver's seat. It was so sleek and elegant inside. It was all black leather with silver controls and red accents. Of course, it was not an automatic. I'd have to brush up on my stick-shift driving. Ryan came around and sat in the passenger side.

"How did you know I always wanted a Mini Coop?" I asked him with tears glistening in my eyes.

"I didn't. I just saw it, and it was you," he explained.

We both knew I would accept it. He was right; it was so me … like it was made for me. "I love it," I told him.

"I'm glad." He grinned.

"How rich are you?" I asked, and he burst out laughing but didn't answer.

Anna, Bettie, and Patsy were now standing outside my door wanting to see inside, so I obliged them. Ryan came back around to my side, and we took a quick walk while the ladies examined the car.

"Now for the second part of yer present, we need to get our stuff and head out toward Limerick," he said.

"Second part? I don't think that needs a follow-up," I assured him.

"No, but I already made plans before I decided to get ya the car, so I still want to do the rest," he explained.

"Where are we going?"

"I'll show ya. Let's go inside," he answered as he turned us up the back driveway. Once inside, he picked up my new *Castle* book and said, "Page twenty-seven."

I turned to the page that read, "Bunratty Castle, County Clare." I looked at him, excited. "We're going to visit a castle?"

"Aye, one of the best in Ireland," he said. "They have a village right next to it that's all done up like Victorian times. We're gonna go meet my folks for lunch, and then I'm takin' ya up to Bunratty after. So we should get goln'."

"I'm so excited! Anna told you I love castles, huh?" I asked.

"Aye, she told me. But she didn't tell me ya loved Mini Coopers. I came up with that one on my own," he insisted.

Ryan wanted me to drive. I wanted to drive. But I didn't want to screw up the transmission on my first day with the car, and I hadn't driven a stick shift in years. We compromised. He drove us out of town up onto N72. From there, I took over until we got close to Limerick. The ride was smooth and fast.

"It's like driving a sports car!" I said, delighted.

"Aye, it is," he agreed. "This baby is little, but she packs a punch."

"So, where are we meeting your parents?"

"Terrace Cafe, in the hotel next to my flat," he answered.

Limerick wasn't especially beautiful. It was a typical city, but where Ryan lived at "The Strand" was very pretty, right on the river Shannon. His company had something to do with the building of the luxury apartments, and he'd just moved in about a year ago. It was a totally upscale bachelor pad—very sleek, modern, and minimally furnished.

"It doesn't look like you spend much time here," I remarked as he took me on a tour of the two-bedroom flat.

"No, I don't. When I'm in town, I sleep here; but otherwise I'm workin' or visitin' my parents or sister. That's why I sold my house. There wasn't much point in keepin' it when I was hardly there, and it was just me, besides. This is easier. No upkeep, no maintenance—not as fun and kind of boring, but definitely easier."

"You mean not as fun because you don't get to build up or tear down anything?" I clarified.

"Aye," he said with a grin. "So I just help friends with their renovations when I get the urge."

"Come here." I motioned to him. "I have an urge." I stood on a small, leather ottoman so I could stand eye-to-eye with him. "Now, don't get me wrong," I said. "Looking at your chest is very enjoyable, but I just wanted see what the view was like from up here." I giggled as he took advantage of the nearness of my lips.

"And here I'm doin' my best not to look at yer chest," he whispered in my ear. "We should probably go down to the restaurant before I break some rules with ya," he warned. I didn't want to let go. I forced myself to think of the pain on his face as he told me about getting Kelley pregnant. It was as good as a cold shower, and I pushed away.

"Good idea," I encouraged him. "I'll be ready in a minute." I took a moment in the bathroom to fix my hair and touch up my lip gloss. "All set," I said, and he escorted me to the elevator.

The butterflies in my stomach started to riot as the elevator doors opened on the lobby. I had felt like this the first time Ben took me to meet Joe and Anna, too. Not that meeting the parents is a make-or-breaker for a relationship, but it certainly helps if the guy's parents like you. I breathed deeply.

"Nervous?" he asked as we stepped out onto the sidewalk.

"Mm-hmm ... a little," I admitted.

"We still have a little time. Wanna walk along the river?" he offered, and I nodded. "You really don't have to be nervous. My parents are cool. Truly, Brenna. Look at me. I don't think there's a person in Millway who's met you that doesn't love ya. What are ya worried for?"

I could name a few—Char, Patricia—but overall, he was right. I got along with most people. "I don't know. It's just cuz they're your parents. I don't so much care what other people think, but with them ... I just want them to like me."

"They will," he assured me.

"Ryan, you haven't brought anyone home in ten years. That's a little bit of pressure, you know?" I tried to explain.

He laughed. "Actually, at this point I could probably bring home a toothless beggar, and they'd be thrilled. Trust me; when they meet ya, they'll be ecstatic. But they'll also see what I've been waitin' for all these years." He squeezed my shoulder, and I began to relax.

"Oooh, look! Is that the castle?" I pointed to a huge stone fortress with three round towers that rose high above the river.

"Well, that's King John's Castle. Probably won't have time today, but we can visit soon. The one we're goin' to is about twenty minutes east of here."

"Do you think King John's is in my book?" I asked.

"Aye, I'm sure it is."

"How many castles are there in Ireland?"

"Has to be over a hundred in all of Ireland. Of course, many of them are ruins. Bunratty is restored, just like King John's over there."

I clapped my hands like a little kid. "I'm so excited!"

He laughed at me. "Aye, I can see that. We should get to the restaurant." He took my hand as we walked back toward the Hilton where the restaurant was located.

"Are your parents more likely to be early or late?" I was curious.

"Depends on who's drivin'. If my da drives, they'll be late, because unlike most of the world, he believes the speed limit is a limit, not a baseline." He chuckled as he explained. "Now, my mum has a lead foot, so she'll get them here early if she drives.

His mom must have driven. They were waiting for us when we walked in. Ryan continued to hold my hand, which was comforting. "Mum, Da, this is Brenna." He let go of my hand so I could shake theirs, but he put his arm around me instead. "Brenna, this is my mum, Mary Catherine ... and my da, Ryan."

"It's a pleasure to meet you," I said, and they replied in kind. Mary Catherine was taller than me but probably of average height and pleasantly plump. She had black hair pulled into a twist that left wispy grays escaping on either side. Her smile was wide and genuine, and her green eyes were warm and welcoming. The senior Ryan was very tall but lanky. He reminded me of Abraham Lincoln in build. A few remnants of his former black hair remained, but his short hair was mostly gray and curly. He had a crooked smile and calm, deep-blue eyes.

"Brenna, Ryan has told us so much about you. It's great to meet ya, finally," his mom said with warmth as Ryan pulled back the chair next to his dad for me to sit in.

"I'm really glad to meet you too," I said, although at the moment I was definitely feeling more sick than glad.

"So, how are ya likin' Ireland?" she asked.

"I love it. It's like it gets inside of you," I answered, and they all nodded as if they understood.

"You don't miss yer home in the States?" she asked.

"No, surprisingly I don't," I replied. "I guess I look at home as more of a feeling than a place, if that makes sense." She looked a little confused, so I continued. "Well, you know my husband died last year, right?"

"Aye, we're so sorry to hear that," she said. I really wasn't good at small talk. I preferred real conversation and sometimes got to it too quickly, but giving shallow answers just wasn't me.

"Thanks. Well, he and his parents were the only family I knew. With him gone and Anna leaving, it wouldn't have been home anymore," I finished.

"Aye, that makes sense," she agreed.

"Have you ever been to the States?" I attempted small talk in return.

"No, but Finn has," she answered.

"Really? I didn't know that." I looked at him in surprise.

"Aye, the one year I went to university, I did a summer abroad with the Fulbright program in Philadelphia," he explained.

"He won a spot in the program. It was very competitive," Mary Catherine said in a way only a mother could.

Ryan rolled his eyes in a way only a son would, and I suppressed a giggle. "Did you enjoy it?" I asked.

"Aye, I guess," he said. "It was quick. Just a five- or six-week business course, but it was interesting. I spent my free time studyin' some of the construction techniques that were more advanced than what we were usin' here. It was very educational in that way. Not all that much in the academic aspect."

"He was a very bright student but easily bored with academics," she complained slightly.

"Well, it turned out all right now, didn't it?" his dad said, finally joining the conversation. He wasn't sitting back with his arms crossed or anything. He had been actively listening to the banter, but he was obviously the type who only spoke when he felt like it.

"Aye, that it did. We're very proud of the business Ryan's built for himself," she agreed readily.

We ate our lunch amid amiable conversation, mostly between Ryan and his mother. I was relieved that his dad was quiet, because it made it easier for me to just hang back and listen. As we stood to go, Mary Catherine gave me a big hug and whispered in my ear, "We're so glad Ryan's found ya."

I blushed, of course, and told her I was glad too. His dad gave me an awkward hug, and they left by the front door, while Ryan and I headed through the hotel to the adjoining apartments.

"Now that wasn't so bad, was it?" he asked as we took the elevator to the top floor.

"No, they're very sweet," I assured him as I stifled a yawn. The excitement of the day combined with my very early morning had me crashing, now that it was early afternoon. Ryan eyed me with a crooked smile.

"We have time for a quick nap if y'like," he said.

"I'm sorry. I'm really excited to go to the castle, but I woke up early and couldn't get back to sleep. Maybe I just need some caffeine," I offered.

"Aye, that might do the trick, but it's nowhere near as enjoyable as cuddlin' with ya on the couch." His eyes glinted mischievously.

I appraised him through narrowed eyes as he opened his apartment door. "I'll have to go with the caffeine if you can't agree to stick to the rules," I warned him with a grin.

"I promise." He held up his hands as if to surrender.

"Good. A nap it is then." I was relieved. Caffeine never seemed to work on me, anyway.

Chapter Twenty-Seven

It was getting dark when I woke with a start. "Ryan!" I turned and shook his shoulder. "Wake up!"

He opened his eyes and looked around, confused for a moment. "Oh."

"This is becoming a bad habit," I said.

"Aye, you've turned me into a lazy, nappin' bum," he joked.

"The castle …" I pouted.

"No worries. We can go tomorrow after church," he assured me.

"Church?"

"Aye, ya want to go to church, right?" he asked.

"Yeah, I just didn't think … well, I never thought about where you'd go to church when you weren't in Millway. What's your church here like? Is it like Sacred Heart?" I asked as he got up and put the water on for tea.

"Well, no. No one is quite like Father Tim, ya know?" he said with a smile.

"I know. I was hesitant to go to a Catholic church in the first place. You do know I'm not Catholic, right?" Would that make a difference?

"Aye, I know. I'm not really, either," he said.

I was surprised. "You're not? But you and Father Tim are so close." I had totally assumed he was Catholic.

"Aye, he's been a great friend and mentor, and I grew up Catholic, but I'd guess I'm not officially a Catholic anymore in the eyes of the Roman Catholic Church," he said.

"Why not?" I asked.

"Well, as a Catholic, I would be required to go to Catholic Mass every week, and I don't. I go to a Protestant church here in Limerick," he explained.

I was shocked and relieved. I loved Father Tim, and I loved the people at Sacred Heart, but I didn't have a desire to convert to Catholicism. I knew many wonderful catholic people but I just didn't think I could fully embrace all that the Catholic Church taught. Hearing that Ryan was not a Catholic lifted a weight I didn't know I'd been carrying. "How did you end up going from one to the other?"

"Well, when I was young, I just went to church because it was what we were supposed to do, ya know? I wasn't into it; I just survived it like all my friends. Then when Father Tim came along, it was suddenly interestin', and I started actually listenin' and payin' attention."

"Yeah, he's an incredible communicator," I agreed.

"Aye, but by the time he came, I was startin' to head in the wrong direction. I liked what I heard, but I didn't live it. Then we moved here, and I stopped goin' to church altogether," he explained.

"That's when everything happened with Kelley?" I asked.

"Aye, not right away, but there was about a two-year period where I was really a mess. When I realized I needed help, Father Tim was the first person I thought of, so I started goin' home to visit him and get some wise counsel."

"Were you still considered a Catholic then?" I wondered.

"I guess, yeah. Just one who had been gone and was now comin' back. But I couldn't move to Millway. My business had taken off here, so I looked for a church here, but nothin' was even close to Father Tim—not in the Catholic Church, anyway."

"So Father Tim's church is not your typical Catholic church then?" I had suspected as much by things I'd heard Anna say.

"No. Just like in Protestant churches, some are more appealin' than others. I think in any church group ya must have that. But I ended up doin' a construction job for this church here called New Life Christian Fellowship. They had been meeting in a secondary school on Sundays, but they'd outgrown it and had been savin' for years to build their own building. As I was workin' on it, the youth pastor came in every day to help. He had worked in construction and knew what he was doin', so I let him help."

"I want to learn carpentry," I told Ryan, completely interrupting his story.

"Ya do?" He was surprised and entertained at the same time.

"Yeah, I love watching all the shows where they do room makeovers and stuff, and I want to be able to build things. Like bookshelves and tables and stuff." I was blushing at my admission. I'd never told anyone about my secret ambition.

"I'm picturin' ya in jeans and a tool belt. I like it." He grinned. "Yer always surprisin' me. I love that. I'll gladly teach ya!"

"Thanks. Sorry I interrupted. Continue."

He just looked at me for a minute with an adorable grin on his face. Then he continued. "So Danny started comin' in and talkin' to me while we worked. He was a lot like me. His story was even similar to mine, so I guess I trusted him, and we became good friends. Then once the building was done, I started goin' to church there."

"What was it like?" I asked.

"Well, very different from what I was used to." He smiled. "There was a full rock band playin' worship, and there was none of the traditional stuff that I knew."

"Like the up-down stuff?" I asked, and he laughed.

"Aye. They didn't even do communion every week. That's one of the biggest differences. The Eucharist is a huge deal in the Catholic Church. They believe that is it a miraculous experience of Christ's actual flesh and blood and that by partakin' in it every week, we are stayin' connected, I guess, to God. It's as if we are physically takin' Christ into our bodies every time, literally communin' with Him. So that's why it's required to attend Mass every week."

"Wow, I didn't know that. But it's still a big deal in the Protestant church," I commented.

"Aye, I didn't mean to imply that it wasn't. It's just viewed a little differently. It's more symbolic. Holy Communion is probably one of the biggest disagreements that Father Tim and I have."

"Do you argue about stuff?" I asked.

"No, not really. We both really respect each other. We often debate things, but we basically agree to disagree. So I go to Sacred Heart when I'm in town, because I love the teachin' and seein' everyone, but I don't partake in Holy Communion, because Father Tim knows I see it differently. I wouldn't have a problem takin' Communion there but he would have a problem with me doin' so."

"So it's okay for a Protestant to go to a Catholic Mass but not for a Catholic to go to a Protestant service?" I was trying to understand.

"Aye," he nodded. "I mean, a Catholic is not forbidden to go to a non-Catholic service, but he would still be required to go to a Mass that same week. So because I don't go to Mass regularly and don't partake in Holy Communion, I don't think I can be considered Catholic anymore. But I still have great respect for Father Tim and his church."

This was a lot to digest, dispelling many of my preconceived notions. I was excited to hear it, though. "So we're going to New Life church tomorrow?"

"Aye. If ya like."

"Absolutely. I'd love to. It sounds like the church I went to back home," I said.

"Really? Good. I think you'll like it."

"Do your parents go?" I asked.

"No." He chuckled. "No, they're still prayin' for me to come back to the 'true church.' They go to St. Greg's in their neighborhood. But my sister and her husband go to New Life."

"So I'm gonna meet your sister?" I asked, a little nervous.

"I'm assumin' she'll be there. She'll love ya; don't worry." He knew me.

"Okay, I won't worry. So, what do ya wanna do tonight?"

"How 'bout we watch a movie, pop some popcorn, and just hang out?" he asked.

"Sounds perfect," I agreed, and it was. We relaxed and laughed and cuddled until the movie was over. Ryan insisted I take his room, even though

I told him he was ridiculous. I fit on the couch much better than he did, but he wouldn't listen, so I eventually gave in and went to sleep in his comfy bed.

New Life was located on the outskirts of Limerick. It was a large, brick-and-stone building with a stunning circular window at the front, which displayed a cross etched in frosted glass.

"It's pretty," I said as we parked the car. He'd made me drive. Even though it made me nervous, I knew I should drive as much as possible—partly because I loved driving the Mini Coop but mostly because my test was coming up in three days.

"Aye, the architect is a friend. He's very good," he replied. "We have a fifteen-minute mingle time before service. There's coffee and pastries. I'd like to try and find Darcy beforehand so we don't have to stick around afterward. We've a castle to visit, right?"

"Yes!" I clapped my hands. "Darcy's your sister?"

"Aye. I've never told ya her name before?" He laughed at himself.

"No, I don't think so. I would have remembered. It's a cool name."

"Well, she'd agree. She loves her name. Wanted to name her daughter the same, but Pete wouldn't go for it." He chuckled. "She's not really full of herself. She just pretends to be," he warned.

Great. Now I was nervous again. "Well, let's find her then. I don't want to feel nervous all through service," I said.

"Yer so silly. Are ya normally nervous when ya meet new people?" he asked.

"Nope. Just your family," I assured him. In response he pulled me to him in a side embrace and kissed the top of my head.

"Just be yerself, Bren. I promise she'll love ya. Darcy!" he shouted suddenly. He waved to a raven-haired beauty who looked to be in her late twenties. She had the same stunning smile that he did—and the same sapphire eyes.

"Are you twins?" I whispered as she walked toward us.

"No." He chuckled. "But people have asked us that our whole lives. Don't ask her. She's my big sister, and she likes it that way. Easier to boss me around."

Darcy gave him a hug and kiss and then turned to me expectantly. "So, this is the beautiful Brenna I've heard so much about?" she said with a smile.

"Hi, Darcy. I'm so glad to meet you." I extended my hand, which she found funny. She playfully swatted my hand away and enveloped me in a warm hug.

"It's about time someone snapped this guy up," she congratulated me. "I'm glad to finally meet ya. I figured he was lyin'," she teased and punched Ryan in the arm.

"Yeah, cuz I'm such a liar." He smirked. "Where's Pete?"

"Ah, Trevor's got a fever, so he stayed home with him. Erin's here, though. Come on; she's dyin' to see ya, Ry." Darcy ambled through the crowd of people, waving and stopping to exchange greetings with several people along the way. Ryan was just as popular. "Ryan, yer back!" "Ryan, where've ya been?" "Welcome back, Ryan!"

"Does everyone know you?" I asked with eyebrows raised.

"I've been here a long time." He grinned. "No, not everyone. I've never met that guy over there." He pointed to a random man, and I rolled my eyes.

"Funny," I said sarcastically, but it *was* funny.

Darcy had gone into a side room and now came back holding an adorable, chestnut-haired little girl. She looked to be about two or three, with wide chocolate eyes and rosy-red lips. "Unk Ry!" she cried, holding her hands out for Ryan to hold her. His eyes lit up at the sight of her, and he grabbed her and swung her around in his arms.

"Ah, wee baby Erin, how are ya, love?" he asked.

"I'n not a baby, Unk Ry. I'n tree yers old!" she said with a perfect pout.

"Aye, yer absolutely right. I forgot ya were 'tree' now. Erin, remember I told y'about my special friend, Brenna?" he asked her. She nodded, looking suspiciously at me. "This is she. Brenna, this is Erin," he said.

"Hi, Erin!" I said, stepping closer to her. She hid her face in Ryan's neck at my approach. He whispered something to her, and she shook her head. "It's okay," I said. I could see she didn't want to meet me, but I didn't take it to heart. I'd babysat enough to know that kids are fickle. I turned to Darcy who was looking embarrassed. "She's adorable."

"Thanks," she said with a relieved smile. "Sorry. She's stubborn like me. My mum always said I'd get one just like me." She rolled her eyes and took Erin from Ryan. "I'll see ya inside." She nodded toward the large doors that led to the auditorium.

The service was very much like the one Ben and I attended. I got choked up as the worship band played. It reminded me so much of my home church. The pastor was funny but to-the-point. He spoke on repentance, which I found humorous, because much of what he said was identical to what Megan had explained to me.

"Has Megan been to this church?" I whispered.

"No, not that I know of, why?" Ryan asked.

"Cuz, she's told me most of what he's saying," I explained. "It's weird."

"Ah, well, no, not really. Pastor Joe wrote a couple books, and I put them in the Veritas library. I believe much of what he's sayin' today is taken from his first book, *Woman at the Well*."

"That explains it," I agreed.

We heard the peals of thunder toward the end of the service. Next, we heard the rain pounding on the roof. I looked at Ryan and motioned toward the noise.

"We can still go visit," he said. "We can drive over, and maybe it will clear up."

I shrugged. "We'll see."

At the end of service we looked out the front windows and saw the torrential rains slashing almost horizontal lines through the parking lot.

"It looks like I'll be taking a literal rain check," I said sadly while staring at the few brave umbrella-bearing souls crossing the parking lot. At the same moment, the wind changed direction, and all three umbrellas turned inside out. I couldn't help but laugh.

"I'm sure they don't think it's funny," Ryan whispered with a chuckle. "But it sure looks funny."

I laughed in agreement. "Now what?"

"Well, we could wait for it to die down, but from the looks of those clouds, I don't think that's gonna happen any time soon." We eyed the enormous, inky clouds stretching miles into the distance.

"I think you're right."

"Okay, I'll go get yer car, and I'll pick ya up here." He took the keys and made a run for the Mini Cooper. I watched and laughed. He was so sweet—and so drenched. He pulled right up onto the sidewalk, so I didn't even have to leave the cover of the awning.

"Thank you!" I said. As I slipped into the passenger seat I cracked up. "Oh, I'm so sorry." He looked like a drowned rat. His hair was plastered to his head, sending streams of water down his cheeks, and his clothes were soaked through. I secretly admired the view through his shirt, but all I could do was laugh and say I was sorry.

"Yer welcome," he said grumpily at first, but as I couldn't stop laughing, he eventually joined in.

"Let's get you home so you can dry off," I suggested.

"You'll need to dry off too." He smiled mischievously.

"Why?" I asked.

"Because," he said, and then he shook his head like a sheep dog after a swim.

"Aaagh! Ryan!" I held up my hands to deflect the sudden shower, but it was pointless. He was now laughing heartily, and I joined in, once again smacking his rock-hard chest and hurting my hand in the process. This only made us both laugh harder. "Okay, stop making me laugh!" I cried. "I have to pee!" It was suddenly urgent that we get to his flat.

"Really?" he asked. "Oh, I thought we'd stop by this really cool waterfall on the way back," he teased.

"Stop!" I cried.

"Sorry. Look at the rain. It's just pourin' down in buckets," he said, still taunting as he intentionally took us over the speed bumps in the parking lot.

"If I pee my pants, I'll never forgive you!" I warned.

"Okay, okay. I'll be good." He chuckled, thoroughly amused by my panic.

Back at his flat, I changed into jeans and a T-shirt, while he dried off and changed in his room. I knocked and walked in, thinking he was done, but he came out of his bathroom with just his jeans on. I'd never seen him without his shirt, and it had me gulping. My heart started racing at the sight of his bare, muscular torso, and I looked at him like a deer in the headlights. I couldn't read his face, but he walked toward me, and I couldn't resist putting a hand on his bare chest. That was stupid. It was getting harder and harder to resist our natural desire for each other. We immediately broke two rules without even thinking. We were in the bedroom, and we were not standing up.

"Nothing happened," I reminded him. Ryan was sitting at the table with his head in his hands.

"I know, but it was close," he countered. We had been very close to the point of no return. I was disgusted with myself for not being stronger. He was the one who had stopped it.

"I'm sorry, Ryan. I'll try to be stronger," I promised.

"Could ya try to be ugly too?" He chuckled.

I smiled. "I could stop bathing. Would that help?" I teased.

"Aye, and I'd prefer if ya dressed in a potato sack from now on," he said.

"Deal. And you … never, ever take your shirt off again if I'm within a fifty-mile radius," I commanded.

He blushed, and I kissed his forehead. "You should take me home," I said.

"Aye, but yer drivin'." He grinned.

Chapter Twenty-Eight

🌸 "Hi, Shannon!" I waved as I strode into the Tea Shoppe. "Sorry I'm late. Of course, I always get out on time unless I have plans." I sat down and caught my breath. I had run all the way from Rosie's.

"No problem. I just got here meself," she admitted.

"Good," I said, relieved. "So how is everything?" I asked, unsure of why she'd asked to meet me but figuring a bit of small talk was expected.

"Still good," she said.

There was an awkward silence that we both tried to break at the same moment. "You go first," I laughed.

"Okay. I know yer wonderin' why I called, right?" she asked.

"Yeah."

She took a deep breath. "When we got together for yer birthday and Tara was talkin' about you and Luke ... I just felt like I should talk to ya."

"Okay?" I asked, my stomach lurching.

"Well, I guess a better way to put it is that I felt I should warn ya," she amended. "Did I ever tell ya I have a sister in Cork City?"

"Yeah, I think you mentioned her when we first met."

"Okay, yeah. Remember that night ... the street festival?" she asked, and I nodded. "Remember how ya asked me about Luke, and I kind of avoided yer questions?"

"Yep, I remember. You looked upset when you saw him in the pub," I recalled.

"Well, I didn't feel like I could share with ya then, but I've talked to my sister, and she says it's okay. See, she grew up with Luke, and he was always tryin' to get her to go out with him, but she never would. For some reason, she just didn't trust him. I know it drove him crazy. Very few girls tell him no, ya know?"

"I've heard." I rolled my eyes.

"So, he tried all through secondary, and she never gave him the time of day. She went off to Cork for University and ended up movin' there. Then five or six months ago, she threw a birthday party for her roommate, and Luke showed up. I think he came along with one of the guests. So, Emily says she only drank one beer, and it was one Luke handed to her. She remembers talkin' with him for a while, and the next thing she knows, it's mornin', and she's in her bed half-dressed."

"No way. Does she think he drugged her?"

"Aye, she knows he did. She wasn't sure at first. She couldn't remember what had happened, but she had a really bad feelin' about it. That night I met you, I had only heard about her suspicions," she said.

"But now she knows for sure?" I asked.

"Aye. She heard rumors that Luke was braggin' about havin' his way with her. But that's not why she knows. Brenna, she's pregnant."

"Oh, Shannon. Does Luke know she's pregnant?" I asked.

"Aye. Says it's not his." She rolled her eyes. "Problem is, Em hasn't had a boyfriend or been with anyone in over a year," she explained.

I shook my head. "How is she?"

"Doin' okay. She's adjusted. My brother Tom lost it, though. When he found out, he drove here from Germany, lookin' fer Luke. I think he might have killed him, but Luke must've been warned cuz he skipped town. Tom's a big guy," she explained.

"I remember Luke disappeared for a month," I said.

"Aye, he waited 'til he was sure my brother was long gone, I think. Hid out in Limerick with his friends. Tom went there on his way home but didn't find him."

"Geez. The poor girl is pregnant, and Luke's hiding out like some coward."

"Aye, probably had the next girl all lined up," she said flippantly.

I imagined the color draining from my face. As she continued to talk, I was trying to figure dates in my head. If I was right, I was officially one day late. That was unusual for me, but it had happened a couple times before. I forced myself to be calm and listen to what Shannon was saying.

"He denied everythin', of course," she said with a grimace. "My family is keepin' this all quiet, but when I heard Luke was buyin' ya drinks, I just had to tell ya, to warn ya to stay away from him."

I couldn't speak. I was in complete shock and just sat there like an idiot. "Brenna, are you okay?" she asked.

I shook my head. "It may be too late to warn me," I whispered. She looked horrified.

"That night? At the pub?" she asked.

I nodded. "I don't think he drugged me, cuz I remember what happened, but he definitely knew I was not myself, and he did order me a pint," I said.

"Oh, Brenna, I'm so sorry. I should have warned ya earlier. I knew he was after ya. Emily's just so embarrassed. She didn't want anyone to know."

"I won't tell anyone," I assured her.

"What happened?" she asked.

"I was angry and upset. It was the one-year anniversary of my husband's death. I was stupid, and I had more to drink than I ever have, and Luke just happened to be there. We danced and … well, you know. I woke up in his flat," I admitted.

She looked at me, concerned. "Yer not pregnant, are ya?" she whispered.

"Oh, God, I hope not," I said. "Honestly, it didn't even cross my mind until now. Ben and I weren't very careful, but I never got pregnant in the four months we were married. So I just didn't even think about it." My heart was racing, and I was beginning to sweat.

"Yer probably not then, right?" she said with a face that was looking paler by the minute.

"Shannon, I'm one day late. I'm rarely ever late," I said with a heaviness pressing my chest.

My head was spinning as I trudged home. I'd promised Shannon I'd let her know as soon as I knew anything, and she'd promised me she wouldn't tell a soul. *Lord, please don't let this happen. I can't be pregnant.*

Please, God," I begged silently. I told myself that I'd been so stressed lately that I probably just pushed my cycle off by a day or two. It was certainly possible. By the time I got home, I'd convinced myself that was the case. Ryan came over after dinner, and we watched a movie.

"Bren, are ya all right?" he asked. "Y'don't seem yerself."

"I'm fine. I'm just tired is all." I tried to brush it off.

"You've been tired a lot lately," he commented.

"Have not," I argued. He was right, but I refused to admit it. There were other factors that could have made me more tired than normal. Wisely, he dropped it.

"Are y'working tomorrow?" he asked.

"Yep."

"Come over after?"

"Sure."

"You should go to bed." He pulled me off the couch and into his arms. "Are y'sure yer all right?"

"I'm fine. But I need a kiss," I said.

He grinned and obliged me. Then he headed out the door, and I went straight to bed. Before I fell asleep, I wrote in my journal.

Lord,

Please hear me. Please let me wake up with my period tomorrow. Things are going so perfectly right now. Ryan is awesome, and you've brought us together, and I'm so thankful. Please, Lord. Please let me just be late.

In Jesus name, amen.

Tuesday came and went without an answer to my prayer. Wednesday was my driver's test. Ryan arrived early, ready for a run.

"Sorry, Ry. I don't feel very good," I explained.

"Are ya nervous about yer test?" he asked.

"I guess so. I think that's why my stomach is upset," I explained.

I was terrified that there was another reason for it, but I pushed that out of my mind long enough to get through my test. I passed without issue, and we filled out all the necessary paperwork. I was now a licensed driver. The thrill was tempered by my queasy stomach. Ryan wanted to go celebrate.

"Sorry. I think I should just go home," I said with little enthusiasm. "Would you mind driving?"

"No problem. Let's get ya home," he said with obvious concern for my well-being.

Before we left Cork, I made a plan. "Ry, could you pull in there?" I pointed to a drug store. "I need to run in and get some stuff for Bettie. I'll be quick."

"Want me to come in?" he offered.

"No, I'll just be a minute," I assured him.

I grabbed four random things for Bettie off the shelf and two pregnancy tests. I couldn't exactly buy a pregnancy test in Millway without it being front-page news. Before I left the store, I put the tests in my purse.

"All set," I said as I got back in the car. "Thanks."

"Sure." He smiled and squeezed my knee.

At home, I said good-bye at the door and wanted to sprint to my room, but Bettie and Patsy were in the kitchen.

"How'd it go?" asked Bettie.

"Great. I've got my license," I said with forced enthusiasm. "I'm not feeling well, though. I'm gonna head upstairs. Oh, Bettie, these are for you," I handed her the bag of randomness, and she looked inside and said thanks with a puzzled expression.

I knew early morning was supposed to be the best time to take a pregnancy test, but I couldn't wait that long. I locked my bathroom door, followed the package directions, and waited as the seconds ticked by.

The longest three minutes of my life were up, and now I couldn't look. I stood there with my eyes closed, terrified to open them. "Please, Lord, please," I chanted in my head. One eye open ... *plus sign.* "Oh, God, no!"

Chapter Twenty-Nine

I'd turned off my phone and stayed in bed the whole night. I cried quietly. I didn't want to be heard. Anna had knocked, but I told her I was sick and just wanted to sleep. I'd saved the second test for the morning. Maybe it had been a false positive?

Another plus sign. "God, why? You could have prevented it, couldn't you?" Either the horrid truth or the morning sickness drove me back to the bathroom, but either way, I couldn't go in to work. Sam was grumpy about it, but I didn't care. At that moment, I didn't care about anything. Honestly, I wanted to die. I still hadn't turned my phone back on. So it wasn't surprising when Ryan showed up at my door around 10:00 a.m.

"Brenna, unlock the door. What's wrong?" he said.

"Sorry, Ry; I'm just sick. I've been throwing up, and I don't want to get you sick too. I'll be fine," I yelled from my bathroom.

"Can I get ya anythin'? Chicken soup?" *Ugh, chicken!* Back to the toilet. "Brenna, I don't care if I get sick. Let me help ya," he said in his best authoritarian voice.

"No. Sorry. I'll be fine. I just need to rest!" I insisted.

"Well, at least turn yer phone on!" he said as he stomped away. I felt guilty for lying, but there was no way I was telling him anything right now. My mind was still reeling, and I couldn't think straight between trips to the bathroom. I slept the rest of the morning and woke up ravenous. What was the acrostic word for what you could eat when your stomach was upset?

245

I remembered Anna telling me when I was in high school, but I couldn't remember what she'd said.

"Sacred Heart of Millway," Anna answered on the first ring.

"Hey, Anna, it's me." My voice sounded weak.

"Brenna, how are ya feelin', love?"

"Uh, not great. Got a stomach bug. What was that thing you told me about what to eat when your stomach's upset?" I asked.

"The BRATT diet," she answered. "Bananas, rice, applesauce, tea, and toast."

"Right! Thanks," I said and hung up.

I could manage tea and toast. Bettie was at the market in Cork, and she must have taken Patsy with her because the house was empty. One small blessing on this horrible day. Megan caught me in the kitchen, so I couldn't hide behind my locked bedroom door.

"Brenna?" She had let herself in. "Anna said you were sick, and since ya aren't answerin' yer phone ..." She leveled me with a frustrated stare.

"I don't feel good." I wouldn't be able to lie to her face. "Thanks for stopping, but I'll be fine. I'm just waiting for my tea to steep and then heading back to bed." I tried my best to brush her off while avoiding looking at her.

"Brenna, look at me, please?" She stood right in front of me. I took one look at her face, and mine crumpled. I had felt so alone for the last twenty-four hours. I just cried, and she hugged me until I was done. "Oh, friend, I was waitin' to see," she admitted.

"What do you mean?" I asked. She just looked at me with a sad look on her face and shook her head. "How did you know?" I was astonished. "I had no clue!"

"Well, you've had so much on yer mind. Remember that first time we had dinner ... we were talkin' about PMS-ing?"

"Yeah, we were on the same cycle," I remembered now. "We said that people had better watch out if they caught us together on the wrong week."

"Aye. So when you and Luke ... well, I did the math for myself, and I knew it would be close," she explained.

"Why didn't you say anything?" I asked.

"Are ya kiddin'?" She looked at me like I was crazy. "If there was the tiniest chance it wouldn't happen, that's what I was hopin' for. But when Anna said you were throwin' up all mornin'."

"You don't think she suspects?" I interrupted.

"No, I don't think so. She said ya had a stomach bug. Besides, she has no idea there's reason to suspect, right?"

"Right. What about Ryan? Meg, what am I gonna do?" I started crying all over again. She grabbed my tea and toast for me and ushered me up to my room.

"Well, what are yer options?" she asked.

"Megan, I don't want his baby inside of me," I admitted. "I hate him, and I don't want it!" I was beginning to feel hysterical.

"Shhh, it's okay. We'll figure somethin' out." She smoothed my hair as I lay down.

"I think this is the worst thing that's ever happened to me," I cried. "And that says a lot!"

"Okay, let's just think it through. If ya keep yerself up here in yer room, everyone's gonna know somethin's wrong. Ya need to try and pull yerself together, okay?" She was right. I wiped my eyes and sat up. A bite of toast. A sip of tea. Just one thing at a time.

"Thanks. You're right."

"Brenna, this is hard to ask …" She hesitated.

"Come on, out with it," I pushed her. "You know more about me than anyone else. Just say it."

"Yer not considerin' abortion, are ya?" She looked at me through tears.

"No," I answered. "I won't lie; the thought went through my mind. But I couldn't ever go through with it. As much as I hate this baby right now, I still believe it's a living thing."

She was visibly relieved. "Thank God. I mean, ya know I'm here for ya, but that would have been …" She didn't finish. She just shook her head. "I mean, it's certainly not God's will for ya to be pregnant when yer not married, but once that little baby is conceived, well, then it is His will for that baby to live, right?"

"Yeah, I know. It's not the baby's fault."

"Okay, so that's off the table. So what are yer options then?" she asked.

"Well, let's start with the best one. I can go back to the States—make up some reason, like I have to finish school or something. I'll have the baby and give it up for adoption." This was the front-runner by far in my mind.

"What about Ryan?" she asked.

"I can't tell him. I have to end it with him. I don't want him to know, understand?" I said firmly.

"That's in scenario one. The other option is, ya can tell him. I know ya love him, Brenna. Ya can't just walk away."

"Yes, I can. He'll never see me the same. He hates Luke more than I do! This is too much. I'd rather leave and have him hate me than have him know I'm carrying Luke's baby." I was adamant. Honestly, I had no idea how he'd react. The thought of leaving him was incredibly painful, but my feelings were slowly numbing. Surprisingly, I had felt very much the same after Ben died. Just numb. Like I was just going through the motions to please everyone else, but I was lost deep inside somewhere. Right now, what I wanted—Ryan—was far less important than what was best for everyone involved.

Megan looked so sad. "Brenna, ya can't go do this on yer own. Think about it. You've already said that Anna is yer only family," she reminded me.

"Yeah, but I do have two brothers," I explained. "We keep in touch through Christmas cards and stuff. They were actually pretty cool when Ben died. They even came to the funeral. I think their mom has less of a hold on them now. I'd rather face them than tell Ryan."

"Okay, how about this. Ya have time before ya have to decide what to do. Just don't make any decisions yet. You've just found out. Ya need time to process. Ya won't be showin' for another three months," she said.

I shook my head. "I can't fake it with Ryan. I have to go right away, or he'll know." My voice cracked as I thought of actually leaving. In theory it seemed best, but my emotions weren't numb enough yet.

My phone rang. "Did you turn my phone on?" That was uncalled for. She unashamedly grabbed my phone and showed me the caller ID. Ryan.

"Answer it," she commanded.

Against my better judgment, I answered. "Hi, Ry."

"Hey, yer phone's on. Thanks." Just hearing his voice was killing me. "Feelin' any better?" he asked.

"Yeah, I am. Thanks," I lied.

"Good. I have to go back to Limerick for a couple days. They're havin' trouble with one of our jobs, and I need to check in," he explained. "Are y'gonna be okay?"

"Yeah, I'm feeling better, really." And I was, now that I wouldn't have to see him face to face.

"All right, so can I come say good-bye then?" he asked.

"Ryan, you have to go take care of stuff at work. Do you really want to risk having to puke at the job site?" I was convincing, I knew.

"Aye, yer right. Well, I'll be back tomorrow night, okay? I'll call ya when I get in. Love ya, Bren." He sounded concerned. He knew something wasn't right, even if he couldn't pinpoint it.

"Love you too," I said without losing it. I was proud of myself as I hung up.

"He's goin' away?" Megan asked.

"Just for a day. I have twenty-four hours to figure out what to do," I said. "I have to come up with a good reason to leave. Something even Anna would buy." I chewed my lip. This was impossible.

"I've got nothin'." Megan looked almost as miserable as I felt.

We sat in silence for a few moments. "I've got it! At the funeral, my brother Mike's wife had just found out she was pregnant. First baby. And she has some high-powered executive job, so I can say that they've asked me to come back and nanny for them!" It was perfect, actually. I could use that as a way to get out quickly. I had saved most of my income over the last few months because I was gonna buy a car. Suddenly, in my mind I saw Ryan standing in front of the Mini Coop on my birthday. Could I really walk away from him? *I had to.* I couldn't tell him!

"So, what, yer gonna leave tomorrow?" Megan asked incredulously.

"No, I'm sure I can't put it together that fast. But at least I have a plan. I need to look at flights and stuff. Megan, you have been such a good friend to me. You're the best. Thank you." I had to do this before I changed my mind. I had more people that I cared about here in Millway than I had back in the States. Maybe this was insane.

"Brenna, whatever ya do, yer not gettin' rid of me, y'hear?" she said through tears.

"Thanks." I hugged her as the tears dripped off my nose.

Megan left, and I went into planning mode. It was extremely useful in taking my mind off of the fact that I was pregnant. I found a decent flight leaving the next Monday that would take me straight to Boston. I could go visit Mike and then figure out what to do from there. I was confident he'd let me stay for a little while. I sent him an email to let him know I'd be in town. I was about to book the flight when Anna knocked. I closed my computer.

"Come in."

"You look better," she commented.

"Yeah, I feel a lot better," I answered.

"Good. Would y'like some tea?" she asked.

"Sure. Um, can I talk to you for a minute?" I had to do this now while I still had the nerve. My stomach was stirring again. She set her bag down and took a seat on my bed.

"What's up?"

"Well, something really unexpected came up. I think I'm gonna go visit my brother for a while." There, I'd said it. She looked shocked.

"Which brother?" she asked.

"Mike. See, Michelle is going back to work, and they need a fill-in nanny, so I offered to go help them temporarily. Their baby is a few months old now."

"Their baby?" she said with a very strange look on her face.

"Yeah, remember at the funeral, Michelle said she was pregnant?" Even that word made me want to throw up.

Anna stared at me for a moment. "Brenna, what's goin' on?" she asked in a stern, motherly tone that would make anyone squirm.

"What do you mean?" I continued to play. "I won't be gone too long. I'm just gonna play it by ear."

"What about Ryan?" she asked coolly.

"Well, I haven't told him yet, but … I just feel like this is something I need to do." I should have thought all this through better before I talked to her. *Dummy.*

"So, yer goin' to nanny for Mike. Goin' to watch his baby?" She said slowly as if I were new to the language. I nodded. I was sensing a trap, but I couldn't fathom what it was. "Which one?"

"Which one what?" I was totally confused.

"Well, ya keep sayin' *baby.* I'm wonderin' if yer goin' to watch the boy or the girl?" Sirens in my head. Something was definitely wrong.

"They had twins?" *Uh-oh.* "How do you know that?" I asked. She reached into her tote and pulled out a stack of mail held together by a rubber band.

"Sue sent another package. There's a couple birthday cards for each of us—and this." She handed me a postcard with a picture on the front of twin babies. I looked at her, stunned. "Read it," she ordered.

I turned it over and read.

Hey, Brenna,

You're an aunt twice over! This is so much harder than going to work, but I'm loving it! Let us know if you're gonna be in town any time soon. I'll be home with the babies for at least six months.

Love,
Michelle & Mike

I was so incredibly busted. I sat there looking at the postcard long after I'd finished reading it. Finally Anna reached over and tilted my head up to look me in the eyes. "Brenna, I want to know exactly what is goin' on with you. Please, don't lie to me anymore." She looked so hurt and so serious. I couldn't lie anymore. Instead, I started to cry. Anna remained where she was, expectantly waiting.

"I'm so sorry. I'm so messed up. I don't know how to begin to tell you."

"Did somethin' happen with Ryan?" she asked.

"No." This surprised her. She clearly had thought Ryan and I were fighting.

"Then what on earth would make ya leave?" she asked.

Deep breath. Deep breath. "This is really hard to tell you."

"Brenna O'Brien, how many times do I have to tell ya? You can tell me anything."

"Easier said than done," I said. "Okay, here goes—oh, sorry …I'll be right back." I rushed to the bathroom. So much for the BRATT diet. Anna came to the bathroom door.

"Are y'all right?"

"Yeah, I'm done now." I washed my face and brushed my teeth, which almost started me puking again.

We sat back down and I tried again. "Remember on the twenty-fifth when I went to Ryan's and he left?" I asked.

"Aye, ya called and said ya were stayin' over."

"Right. And after I called you, I went to bed. But I couldn't sleep. I tried really hard, but I was very angry and feeling sorry for myself and …" There was no way to tell her I was pregnant without admitting what I'd done.

"And …" she prompted.

"And I was really stupid. I went down to the pub and got myself drunk." Her eyes popped open wide.

"Brenna, I've never even seen you drink!" she said.

"No, cuz I never do. This was the first time I'd ever had more than a sip. I had three pints and three shots, all in about an hour," I explained. "That's when Luke found me." I couldn't look at her as I continued. "He bought me the last pint, and then we danced. That led to other stuff and …" I peeked at her through my lashes. She was angry. I couldn't continue.

"Brenna, please tell me you did not sleep with him," she insisted.

I shook my head. "I didn't mean to. I was drunk and lonely," I tried to explain.

"But ya *knew* he was dangerous for you!" she cried.

"Anna, have you ever been drunk and lonely?" I asked, and she blinked.

"No, I guess I can't say I have," she admitted. "Does Ryan know?"

"Of course. I told him. That's why he hates Luke so much. I know it was incredibly stupid. Believe me, I know; but it's so much worse than that," I admitted.

"What could be worse—" She stopped mid-sentence. She'd figured it out, and I buried my face in my pillow, unable to look at her. "Oh, God, no. Brenna, yer not pregnant." As if saying it wasn't true would change it.

"Please, don't tell anyone," I begged, my words muffled in my pillow.

"Of course I won't. This is a lot to digest. I'm sorry I'm not bein' very comfortin'. I just need a little time, love. I'll ... I'll come back in and check on ya soon. But yer not goin' anywhere, young lady. Just try to rest. I'll be back." She left. Part of me wanted to be offended at her commanding attitude, but most of me was too exhausted to care. I closed my eyes and drifted off to a dream world where nothing bad was happening.

Chapter Thirty

"Come in," I said. Anna was back, carrying a steaming mug of something.

"It's broth," she said as she handed it to me. "How are ya feelin'?"

"Okay, I guess. Hungry, actually," I said.

"Well, drink up, and if ya keep that down, we'll get ya somethin' else," she promised.

"Thanks." I sipped, and it was good. No nausea at all. I downed it while she sat patiently next to me. "I'm sorry I lied to you," I said softly.

"Yer forgiven. I don't blame ya. I don't know what I'd do if I were you," she admitted. "So explain to me what ya thought ya would do with this whole silly Mike-thing."

"I can't tell Ryan!"

"But ya said he knows what happened," she clarified.

"Yeah, but this will be too much for him. I'd rather he hate me than let him know. Can you understand that?" I asked.

"No, I can't. I'm sure he won't like it, but he loves ya, Brenna. He'll stand by ya no matter what," she assured me.

"I know. I know he'd stand by me, but this changes everything. Every time he sees my expanding stomach, he'll think of me and Luke. I can't handle that. Plus, there's other stuff about Ryan that you don't even know about that makes this even worse," I explained.

"What other stuff?"

"Well, I'll tell you, cuz I don't know what to do, but please keep this between us. I shouldn't be telling Ryan's secrets." I paused for her to stop me, but she didn't. "The reason Ryan stopped dating ten years ago is cuz he got a girl pregnant and then paid for the abortion." She inhaled sharpley. "I have no idea how he'll react to this, Anna. I don't want to hurt him, but I will any way I go about it. I'd rather not hurt him in this way. I'd rather he just think I'm a jerk who left him."

"Wow. What a mess." She shook her head. "I don't know how he'll respond, but I think ya owe him honesty. Ya have to do what's right, Brenna. Runnin' away is not the answer. Ya have to face this," she said tenderly.

I put my head into my hands. I was at a loss. The slight freedom I had felt with the idea of escaping to the States evaporated as I realized I'd have to face this head on. She was right, and I knew it. But how could I possibly tell him this. I thought it was hard to tell him I'd slept with Luke. This was a hundred times worse.

"You're right. I know I have to face it. He's gone to Limerick, but he'll be back tomorrow night. I'll tell him then," I promised, and the queasy feeling returned. Anna leaned over and hugged me.

"I know you'll do the right thing. And no matter what, I love you, and I'll be here for ya, okay?" She let go and looked me in the eyes to make her point. "Okay?" she repeated.

"Okay. Thanks." I smiled weakly.

"Do ya want me to bring ya some dinner or are ya gonna come down?" she asked.

"I'll come down," I decided.

I picked at my dinner and was scolded by Patsy. I would have much preferred to eat in my room, but Megan was right. The longer I holed up in there the more talk there would be, so I had to put in an appearance. Megan called to see if I wanted to go to Veritas to take my mind off things, but I couldn't do it. Instead I watched a movie with Bettie and then went to my room. I was exhausted again, but I'd read that was normal. Being overly tired was one of the earliest signs of pregnancy. Well, that explained the last week. I had been ridiculously tired, constantly taking naps. Ryan had noticed, but I don't think he suspected the real reason.

I grabbed my journal and flipped through the last couple months. My gaze landed on a verse that Anna had told me about. "Trust in the Lord with all your heart and lean not on your own understanding. In all your ways, acknowledge him and he will make your paths straight" (Proverbs 3:5–6). I wasn't sure how to live that out. I had heard Father Tim quote a verse that said if you lacked wisdom, you could pray and ask God for it. I definitely lacked it and praying couldn't hurt. I flipped to a clean page and began an earnest written prayer:

Lord,

I need your wisdom. I read that verse and it seems so simple. Trust you and you'll show me my path. But how do I trust you when everything looks so bleak. I know it's my own fault. Sin has consequences, and this is mine. But it's not Ryan's fault. He shouldn't have to deal with this.

Trust you. With all my heart. And don't lean on my own understanding. The trust part doesn't come easy for me. But I guess there is no such thing as "kind of" trust. Either I trust you all the way or I'm not really trusting you at all. As far as the leaning on my own understanding? Well, that's not hard because I don't have any understanding! I don't understand this at all. But I have to make a choice. Either I believe that you are big enough to help me, or I don't.

Okay, Lord. I'm gonna trust you. I'm gonna tell Ryan the truth and trust you to help me deal with the consequences, whatever they are. Please prepare him somehow, Lord. And help me have the words. Give me your wisdom. I don't know what else to pray. I choose to trust you.

In Jesus name, amen.

I slept surprisingly well. I woke early and, lying in bed, I thought I might even be able to go for a run. But as soon as my feet hit the floor, my stomach began heaving. There was no way I could wait tables like this. I had to call in sick again.

"Sam, I'm sorry. I'm still throwing up, and I know you don't want us near the place if we're throwing up, right?" I explained.

"Aye, damn it. Ya can't come in if yer pukin, cuz if people catch it, they'll blame the food. Then we'll have a whole food-poisonin' rumor goin' 'round. Fine, stay home. I'm gonna cover yer shift for tomorrow, too. Feel better," Sam said gruffly.

I would have preferred to work just to take my mind off of everything. Instead, I had all day to sit and think. Megan stopped in after worship practice to check on me.

"Oh, thank God," she said when I told her I wasn't planning to leave. "I totally agree with Anna. Honesty is the best way."

I nodded. I agreed, but I didn't have to like it. "I'm gonna go see Ryan tonight and tell him," I explained.

"Geez, I'll be prayin' for ya both," she said.

"Thanks. I'm trying to do the right thing and trust God to take care of the rest," I said.

"Good plan." She smiled.

Ryan had called and said he'd be home around 7:00 p.m. The plan was for him to call me when he got there, and then I was gonna drive over. He didn't know I wanted to talk with him, though. I didn't want him worrying all day. I was able to act very natural and casual on the phone. So as far as he knew, this was just an ordinary night. I was eager to get it over with, so I drove over at 7:00 p.m. He called while I was driving.

"Hey, I'm runnin' about five minutes behind," he said. "Ya wanna just meet me there?"

I chuckled. "Yeah. I'm already on my way. I'll wait for you upstairs."

I had been sitting at his doorstep for about a minute when I heard footsteps below. But it was Luke. I backed into the corner, hoping he wouldn't see me. I was in no mood to deal with him right now. But he looked right up at Ryan's door.

"Brenna, that you?" he asked.

"Yes, it's me Luke. I'm just waiting for Ryan," I explained. He continued up the stairs.

"Ryan ... isn't he a little *old* for ya?" I realized as he stumbled that he was quite drunk. I stood up and thought about running past him.

"Luke, you should go home. You don't look good." I was trying to distract him, but it wasn't working. He backed me into the corner.

"Ya know ya want me, Brenna. Everyone knows ya want me." He grabbed me and kissed me hard.

"Luke, stop! You're hurting me. *Stop!*" He slammed me against the wall, knocking the wind out of me. I couldn't even yell. When he ripped my shirt open I knew I was in big trouble. I tried to kick him where it hurt, but he was too close, and I was pinned. I took a razor like, deep breath and found my voice. "Luke, please don't do this. Luke. Let me go!" I screamed.

Then everything happened so fast. I heard a guttural cry, and suddenly I was free. I slumped to the ground, my legs unwilling to work as I watched Ryan beat the crap out of Luke. I may have enjoyed that part. I sat there taking ragged, shallow breaths while Ryan dragged Luke down the stairs and shoved him into his apartment. I heard the tail end of what he said to him: "—ever touch her again, you'll pay." And then I blacked out.

Chapter Thirty-One

"Brenna?" Ryan was saying my name softly, but I couldn't see him. "Brenna, wake up, love." Oh, my eyes were closed. I opened them slowly, trying to remember what was going on. Was it morning? Did I take a nap at Ryan's place?

"Ryan," I said softly. He smiled in relief.

"Thank God," he said as he helped me sit up on the couch. "Are ya okay?" He looked so strange.

"What's going on?" I asked him, confused and sore.

He looked puzzled for a moment. "Ya don't remember? Brenna, ya passed out on my doorstep," he reminded me.

Oh! Everything came back at once. Why I was here. What Luke had done. And then my knight in shining armor. "You saved me," I told him. "Thank God, you came."

"Aye, and that jackass is lucky I didn't kill him," he said with a fury bubbling just below the surface.

"You didn't, did you?" I worried.

"No, of course not. I could have, but I'm not stupid. No, don't worry. I won't get in trouble," he assured me, and I relaxed—until I remembered why I was there in the first place. "What's wrong? Are ya hurt?" he asked, seeing the change in my expression.

"No, I don't think so." But as I took a deep breath, there was a shooting pain in my side, and I gasped.

"Yer hurt!" he cried. "What hurts?"

"My side. I think it's a rib," I said in a rising panic as the pain continued stabbing at me.

He pulled up my shirt and touched my ribs where I indicated. "Ouch!" It killed.

"That asshole broke yer ribs!" I'd never seen him so angry. He looked as if he would go back downstairs and finish Luke off.

"Ryan, wait. It'll be okay. You're here with me now, and you can't leave me, okay?" He looked at my fearful face and agreed.

"Aye. I won't. I'll call Doctor Rowan. He'll know what to do." He dialed and waited.

"Hi, Rob, this is Ryan. Sorry to bother ya on a Friday night." Pause.

"Aye. Do ya have a few minutes ya could come see me?" Pause.

"No, I'm fine, but I think my girlfriend's rib is broke." Pause.

"Thanks." He hung up. "He's on his way. He said to ice it. I'm just gonna go in the kitchen and get an ice pack for ya, okay?" he said as I held on to his hand, not wanting him to leave my side.

"Okay," I let go.

Dr. Rowan was younger than I expected. Apparently he was the third Dr. Rowan to serve the fine folks of Millway, and he'd grown up with Ryan.

"Aye, definitely a break. Can you breathe deeply for me, Brenna?" he asked as he put a stethoscope over my chest. It hurt to breath, and I gasped again. "I know it hurts. I just need to hear how yer breathin' sounds," he explained. "One more time for me." He moved the stethoscope to my back. "Okay, sounds good. I don't think anything's been punctured. Keep icin' it, tonight. Twenty minutes on, twenty off."

"Okay," I said. "Should I wrap it with an elastic bandage or anything?" I asked.

"No, better not to, actually. We used to do that, but we want you to be takin' deep breaths. That's important, so wrapping it is no longer recommended. You'll need to take it easy for the next several weeks. It'll probably take a good six weeks to heal up completely."

He turned to Ryan. "Make sure she's takin' a deep breath or coughin' at least once per hour. That helps prevent a collapsed lung or pneumonia," he explained. "I'm tellin you this, cuz she won't want to do it. It's gonna hurt, and she'll avoid it." He eyed me. "But she needs to do it, okay?" He looked at both of us, and we both nodded. "Oh, and this may seem counter-intuitive, but you should probably lie on that side. It will make breathin' easier."

"Okay. Thanks, Doctor," I said.

"Please, call me Rob. And it's a pleasure to meet you, even under these circumstances," he said with a wink, and Ryan walked him to the door. As they stepped outside the door, Ryan kept his hand on the door so I could see he was still there, but I couldn't hear what was being said. He was probably telling Rob exactly what happened. They seemed to be fairly close friends and he was definitely someone Ryan trusted. Finally he came back inside.

"Do ya want me to call Anna and let her know yer stayin' here?" he asked.

"I don't have to stay here. I can go home," I said with confidence I didn't feel. I really didn't want Ryan out of my sight. It was irrational. Nothing would happen to me at the B&B, but I definitely felt safer with him.

"No, please stay here," he pleaded. "I don't think I'll be able to sleep unless ya do."

"Okay. I'd like that better anyway," I admitted, and he smiled for the first time since I'd opened my eyes.

I called Anna. She didn't even say hello. "Brenna, did ya tell him?"

"Hi, Anna. I'm at Ryan's." I ignored her question, and she got the hint.

"Ya can't talk?"

"No, not right now. Listen, I'm okay, but I've had a bad night. Ryan's with me and I'm gonna stay here, okay?"

"What happened?" she asked.

I was done lying to Anna, so I told her the truth. "While I was waiting for Ryan to get here, Luke came home drunk, and he … he … well, he kind of attacked me." I heard Ryan say, *"Kind-of?"* from the other room, and I suppressed a smile.

"What!" Anna cried.

"Yeah, he was drunk and he tried to … you know. He had me pinned to the wall, and then Ryan got there, and he took care of him." I smiled at the recollection. I wouldn't have figured myself for the type to enjoy seeing someone get the crap beat out of them, but it really was a wonderful thing to see, in this case.

"Good Lord!" Anna replied. "Are ya okay?"

"Yeah, I'm okay, but I have a broken rib," I admitted.

"He broke yer rib? Geez. Is Luke still breathin'?" she asked, only half kidding.

"Yeah, but Ryan gave him what he deserved. You should have seen it. It was awesome."

I giggled as I heard her say, "Good!" She took a deep breath. "So, ya can't tell him tonight then, right?"

"No. Not a good idea, right?" I said cryptically.

"I agree. So are ya comin home?" she asked.

"No, I'd feel better just staying here tonight. You understand?" I asked.

"Aye, but be careful," she warned in a motherly tone. "I'll see ya tomorrow, love."

I'd had every intention of telling Ryan that I was pregnant. But I couldn't do it now. Not after what had happened. He just might kill Luke, and then I'd never see him except through prison bars. No, I would wait for a better time.

We watched a movie, pausing it regularly for Ryan to refresh my ice pack or insist that I breathe deeply. He was a good taskmaster. I grew sleepy halfway through, and he noticed.

"Let's just go to sleep," he said. He still had a smoldering look in his eyes, like he was replaying the night in his head.

"Okay, but I think it's safe to break the rules, tonight. Can you please just sleep with me? Obviously, nothing's gonna happen, and I'd feel better if you were right there with me," I explained.

"Aye, I would have snuck in with ya later if ya hadn't asked," he admitted.

I curled up beneath his down comforter, safely tucked into his arms. My side hurt, but I could tell the painkillers were starting to work. Although I had the feeling Ryan wouldn't sleep for quite some time, I closed my eyes and was probably out within five minutes.

I woke up in a great deal of pain. Ryan was still with me, but I could tell by his breathing that he was awake. I wondered if he'd slept much at all. "Ryan?" I tried to roll over to look at him. I had to grit my teeth to keep from crying out.

"How did ya sleep?" he asked.

"Good. I like sleeping in your arms. You know that," I said.

"And I like it too." He smiled briefly. "Brenna, I think ya should file a complaint with the police." He got right down to business.

It hadn't occurred to me. "Should I?'

He sat up. The movement jarred me, and I grimaced automatically. "Sorry, love. It hurts a lot, huh?" I nodded. "I'll go get ya some more painkillers."

He returned with a glass of water and two pills. "What will happen to him if I complain?" I asked.

"He broke yer rib! He has to pay for that," he said angrily.

"I think he's probably paying right now, after the beating you gave him," I said with a grin.

"Listen, I'm glad I could get him off ya, and I'm glad I stopped before I really hurt him, but that's not enough punishment for what he did—or what he almost did." He was practically growling. "If he'll do it to you, he'll do it to someone else. Maybe you can stop that." As he said this, I thought of Shannon's sister. This wasn't just about me.

"You're right. Let's call the cops," I said. I could see that he was surprised at how quickly I agreed, but he didn't know the full story.

"Good. I'll call right now." He left the room, and I slowly got up and freshened up in the bathroom. He'd given me an old T-shirt and sweats of Darcy's to wear to bed. Now I sifted through the box of her stuff to find a more suitable shirt for the day, since the buttons were torn completely off mine.

The police came by to take a report. I recognized them both from the day Patsy went missing. They looked at the bruise that had since formed on my right side. It was nasty-looking. Ryan told them what Rob had said and gave them his phone number. He was expecting their call. That was probably what Ryan had been talking to him about outside the door.

265

I heard the cops banging on Luke's door after they left. It only made sense they'd question him or even arrest him. I had mixed feelings. I knew that he should be punished, but part of me felt sorry for him. There was no good reason for that, and I kept it to myself for obvious reasons. I looked out the window and saw that Luke's car was gone. "Coward probably skipped town again," I thought to myself.

"Are you okay?" I asked Ryan as I caught him staring out the kitchen window.

"Me? I'm okay. Are you?" he asked.

"Yeah, I'm fine," I said. "But you're not. I can tell."

He looked at me and then looked down. "I'm sorry. Yer right; I'm not fine. I'm so angry." His fists were squeezed into tight balls. "When I saw him on ya like that … I couldn't help but think of the night you were with him," he admitted.

I closed my eyes. This would never go away, would it? "I'm so sorry, Ryan. If I could go back in time, I would make sure it never happened. You know that, right?" I stepped closer to look at his face.

"Aye, I know. Understand, I meant everythin' I said when ya told me. I don't blame ya. It was my fault too. All of that. But it doesn't mean it's not really hard for me. Whenever I see him, I have to force myself not to see the two of you in bed together," he said with a flush of anger on his cheeks.

"Really?" I'd had no idea. "I don't know how to change that," I told him sadly.

"No, ya can't. I've prayed about it a million times. The only thing I can come up with is that I have to forgive him. I think I was close, and then he goes and attacks ya. Geez! I can only handle so much, ya know?"

I shook my head and resigned myself to what I had to do. I knew I had to just rip the band-aid off all at once. "Ryan, you know I love you, right?" I asked.

"Aye, I know. I'm not questionin' that. I know this was all before we were even together. I know that. It's just hard to stop the thoughts," he answered.

"Well, I think that maybe we should just stop seeing each other for a while." There. I'd said it.

"What?" He looked completely blindsided.

"It's not fair for you to have to deal with all this. I'm not good for you. You deserve so much better than—"

He interrupted by kissing me hard. "No, I've waited all this time for ya. I'm not giving ya up, Brenna. That is not the answer. I'll get this under control. Don't worry," he promised.

"Ryan, let's sit down," I suggested. We sat on the couch and I tried again. "Listen to me. This will get worse. You deserve better," I said.

"It won't get worse. I know I can conquer this. And he'll be locked up or long gone, so we won't have to see him," he said.

"I'm so sorry to hurt you." I looked into his eyes and said the last thing I wanted to say. "Ryan, I'm pregnant." Shock. Hurt. Disbelief. Pain. Anger. It was all there in his eyes. Tears sprang to my eyes and I knew I was about to lose it. "I have to go," I said, and I left him staring straight ahead in shock.

Chapter Thirty-Two

"He hasn't called?" Megan asked. I shook my head. It had been a week, and I knew he'd taken off. He'd left me a message to say he'd call me, but that was last Sunday. No one had heard from him since, not even Father Tim. I had a feeling he was okay. I just prayed he hadn't gone in search of Luke. But the police hadn't been able to find Luke, so hopefully Ryan wouldn't either. It was one thing to lose Ryan. It would be another thing altogether if he lost his freedom because of me. I'd prayed a lot in the past week, and although I was a wreck, somewhere deep inside I felt a peace growing.

"I don't think he will," I admitted. "I think he must have realized it was too much for him to deal with."

"I don't know. I'm surprised he hasn't called ya. But I guess you know him better," she said. "Yer handlin' this amazingly well," she added.

"You know, what else can I do?" I asked. "I said I was going to trust God no matter what, so ... I don't know. Right now my next eight months are pretty much planned out for me, ya know? After that, I don't know." It felt good to not have to make any decisions right now. I couldn't work at the moment because of my broken rib. Word had spread that Luke had attacked me—probably through the cops. I was glad I wasn't at the pub every day having to answer questions.

"I'm proud of ya, though. I know this has to be harder than yer lettin' on," she said.

"Well, for one, I guess I've developed a thick skin. I see people whispering and staring when I'm out in public. It doesn't bother me like it would have before. I don't know why. Wait till they find out I'm pregnant!" I laughed.

Megan had been checking in on me every day. I was able to keep a brave face on most of the time, but she still suspected I was not doing as well as I said. She was right, but it was easier to fake it than to talk about it right now. We watched a movie, and then Megan headed home. She had to be up early for church, and I was glad to be left alone. Nighttime was when it hit me hard. I was solid as a rock all day, but once the lights were out, I lost my steely exterior and crumbled. Most nights I cried myself to sleep. I missed Ryan so much, it hurt physically. I didn't blame him for leaving. I wanted him to leave. That was easier than seeing him in pain every day. It was the best thing, but I didn't know if I'd ever get over him.

I drove the family to church the next morning. I was beginning to find amusement in the whispers and stares. Every time I noticed someone doing it, I'd look directly at them and smile. Sometimes I'd even wave. They didn't mean to be rude. Small towns loved gossip, and this was a scandal. The situation might have been looked at differently, but my broken rib made my claim more legitimate, which meant that Luke was clearly out of favor. His friends had left town too, so there was no one left to defend him. I knew Char and Patricia would privately trash me, but in public even they didn't dare go against popular sentiment.

Father Tim caught my eye from the front. His eyes were sad, and I knew he knew. I smiled briefly, and he nodded in response. After church we headed home, and my heart leaped into my throat as I pulled behind the house. Ryan's car was there. I looked at Anna in shock. "He's here?" I said.

"Go!" She shooed me out of the car.

I ran through the back door. "Ryan?" I called.

"In here," he called from the front room. *Breathe, Brenna; breathe and remain calm.* I forced myself to walk through the swinging door and down the hall. I restrained myself as I rounded the corner and saw him standing there.

"You came back?" I asked. Obviously he was back, but he knew what I was asking.

"Aye," he said with a smile. "I've told ya before, I'm not goin' anywhere. I needed time to sort through everything, but I'd never leave ya, Bren."

I ran and jumped into his arms without thinking. "Ouch!" I cried and then laughed.

"Geez, yer ribs, Brenna. What are ya thinkin'!" He laughed as he gingerly set me down.

"So, you're not leaving me?" I asked.

"No, I'm not," he said. Then I punched him hard in the arm. "Ouch!" we said simultaneously.

"What was that for?" he asked as I nursed both my hand and my sore rib while he rubbed his arm.

"Why didn't you call me all week then?" I asked, getting angry in retrospect.

"I'm sorry. I know I should have, but I went completely off the grid, Bren. I left my cell phone at home, and I went hiking. I was gone the whole week. I needed time to process and pray and yell at God and stuff," he explained. "Then I came straight here. I didn't even stop back in Limerick, so I still don't have my phone."

I was still pouting at him for putting me through a week from hell, wondering if he was okay. "Don't ever do that again," I said.

"Ah, I can't promise that," he said, and I stared. "See, I deal with things best by gettin' away. I have a temper, and if I stay too close to a situation, I'll do somethin' I regret, so I know I need a sort of time-out. Does that make sense?" he asked. "But I'll never leave ya, Brenna. I just may need time-outs from time to time."

"Okay. I can handle that. But next time, bring your phone, okay?" I asked.

He shook his head. "I leave it on purpose," he explained. "If I have my phone, it's too easy to call someone and talk to them instead of waitin' for God. If I have no other options, I hear from Him more clearly."

"Geez. Okay, that makes sense," I agreed.

"Thanks. So, can we go back to my place?" he whispered and motioned toward the kitchen where three pairs of shoes were visible beneath the swinging door. "I want to talk with ya more about all this, but I'd rather do it in private."

I giggled. "Let's go."

We heard the shuffling of feet as we headed back toward the kitchen. "Hi, ladies," Ryan said as we strode toward the back door. "Bye, ladies!" We stepped outside and headed to Ryan's place.

Ryan made us tea, and then we sat on the couch to talk.

"So, what happened when you went hiking?" I asked.

"I was angry at first. Angry that God would allow somethin' like this to happen. Angry that Luke was born. I spent the first two days just fumin'. It's lucky I didn't run into anyone up there, because I was not fit to be around anybody."

"Then what?" I asked.

"Then, slowly, He got through to me. If God can forgive me for what I did, who am I to hold anything against anyone else. Luke's an ass, but then so was I."

"It's not the same thing," I said.

"Sure it is. What I did is worse, Bren. I took a life!" He said it with an ache still evident in his eyes. "I just pray that Luke wises up before he does the same, because I wouldn't wish that pain on anyone." I thought to myself that I wouldn't be surprised if he'd already done the same. I felt sorry for him again.

"Yeah, he's one screwed-up guy," I admitted. "They haven't found him yet."

"I know," he said sadly. "Bren, I know it will be harder for you than for me, but you need to forgive him too," he encouraged.

"I don't know," I said slowly.

"Well, no one can force ya, but I'll tell ya what I know from experience. If ya don't forgive, yer not punishin' Luke; yer punishin' yerself."

I nodded. "I know. You're right. It'll take me a while, I think."

"Aye." He kissed my forehead. "That's understandable. Can I ask ya somethin'?"

"Sure."

"What are ya gonna do about the baby?" he asked cautiously.

"I decided I'd put it up for adoption."

He nodded. "That makes sense. How're ya doin'?" he asked.

"Sick, actually. The morning sickness isn't as bad as it was last week. It's not all the time, but it's not pleasant."

He nodded again. "I mean, how are ya doin', like, emotionally with all this."

"Oh. Yeah, well, it revolted me at first. Are you sure you're okay to talk about this?" I asked.

"Positive. I'm sure. Go ahead. I want to know what yer goin' through."

"Okay. Honestly, the thought of having Luke's baby inside of me disgusts me," I answered.

"But ya wouldn't ever consider endin' the pregnancy, right?" His eyes were so vulnerable.

"Oh, no, Ryan. I wouldn't do that. Don't worry."

"I didn't think ya would, but I had to ask, ya know?" he said quietly.

"I thought about it." He looked up at me. "I'd rather not have to deal with this. It would be the so-called easier way in the short term. But I could never do it," I assured him. "Adoption is the next easiest, I guess."

"Well, regardless of what ya decide, I need to know somethin'," he said with an unreadable expression.

"What?" I asked him.

"Okay, so, it comes to this …" He took a slow, deep breath and continued. "Brenna, I'm madly in love with ya." I swallowed hard at the way he said those beautiful words. He took my hands in his. "I've wasted so many years just existin', not livin'—but I'm glad because, if I hadn't, I probably wouldn't have ended up knowin' ya. I've made some serious mistakes in my past, and I'm still screwed up in so many ways." He took another deep breath and then blew me away as he slid down to the floor on one knee. "I know this might seem sudden, but I don't want to waste any more time. I don't care if yer havin' a baby or could never have a baby. I want to be with ya for the rest of my life. Yer a gift that I can never thank God enough for. If you'll have me, Brenna, I'd so like to be yer husband." He pulled a ring out of his pocket and held it up, but I couldn't even look at it. All I could see were his breathtaking, electric-blue eyes, and I threw myself at him, knocking him into the chair and completely ignoring the pain in my side. I didn't answer with words; I just kissed him until he pushed me away and started laughing. I joined in, and we laughed together until he finally said, "So, I take it that's a yes?"

Chapter Thirty-Three

"So, a New Year's wedding?" Anna grinned.

"Yep. And get this: we booked Glin Castle!" I was beaming. It had been two weeks since Ryan had proposed, and we'd gotten so much accomplished. It was going to be a small wedding. Just family and a few friends. Anna would give me away, and Megan was my maid of honor. If I was lucky, the baby bump wouldn't even be evident in the pictures. The morning sickness was getting easier to deal with, and I was scheduled to see Dr. Rob in fifteen minutes for a follow-up on my broken ribs. I planned to ask him for a recommendation for an obstetrician.

Anna replied, "You get yer castle wedding after all. God sure works in mysterious ways."

"Yeah." I heard Ryan pull up. "Gotta go. Be back later," I said as I slipped out the door.

"Hey, Ry." I climbed into the passenger side. "Got a kiss for me?"

"Course I do." He leaned over and said "good morning" in his own way. "How are yer ribs feelin'?"

"Good. I think they're healing up well." There was a faint bruise left and a slight ache, but I was much better.

Dr. Rob shared an office with his dad, Dr. Joe. However, according to Bettie, Dr. Joe was seen more often on the links than in the office.

"Brenna, how are ya feelin'?" Rob asked as he stepped into the exam room.

"Much better, thanks," I said.

He examined my ribs and agreed that I was on the mend. "Keep up the good work." He smiled.

"Um. I have a favor to ask," I said hesitantly. He would be only the fourth person who knew about the baby. "I need a recommendation for a good obstetrician in Cork."

He looked at me with obvious surprise. "Yer pregnant?" I nodded and saw him glance at Ryan, who sat there tight-lipped. He was letting me say as much or as little as I wanted. I didn't want his friend to think it was his fault, though. Geez, this sucked. But it would only get worse before it got better. "It's complicated," I said. "It happened before Ryan and I were together."

"Oh. Well, none of my business anyway. Sure, I can give you a couple good names. I'm guessin' you want to keep this out of Millway, then?" He understood.

"Yes, at least for now." Until I started to show. "Do you know anyone in Cork?"

"Absolutely. A couple good friends, actually." He wrote down their names and numbers and handed them to me. "Do you know how far along you are?" he asked.

"No, not exactly. I mean, I know when it happened." I felt my cheeks blazing. "But I don't know exactly how the due date is figured and stuff." I had tried to figure it out at home but just got confused. "It seems like the way they figure it is off. Like the day you get pregnant is already considered your third week of pregnancy?" I shook my head.

"Aye, that's the conventional way of countin' it. Officially, it goes from the start of yer last menstrual cycle, so yer right, it's like addin' two weeks on at the beginning. Do ya know when yer last cycle started?"

I nodded. "September 13th." He pulled out a small, cardboard wheel and began sliding the outer circle around.

"Okay, are you fairly regular?" This was getting embarrassing with Ryan in the room. I refused to look in his direction.

"Yes, twenty-eight days," I answered.

"Looks like yer due date is … June twentieth." He smiled. "Yer startin' yer ninth week."

That shocked me. It was almost a quarter of the way through. "Really?" I asked in disbelief. I had calculated that I was about six weeks. So the official word that I was starting my ninth week just threw me.

"Really. In about a week or two, you should be able to hear the heartbeat. If ya want to stop back in next week, we can give it a try." He smiled.

"Thanks," I said as I rose to go. I just wanted to get in the car. I let Ryan take care of the paperwork, and I sat in the car waiting.

"Are ya okay?" he asked when he got in.

"No! I'm eight weeks pregnant!" It was actually sinking in that I was going to have a baby. "I don't want to have a baby. I'm too young." I looked at him for reassurance.

"You'll be okay, Bren. You can do this," he said in his best soothing voice.

"I'm scared," I admitted for the first time. "Actually, I'm freaking out!"

He pulled me over the center console and sat me in his lap so he could hold me. "I know." He stroked my hair as I buried my face in his neck. "I'm goin' to be here with ya every step of the way."

And he was. He even called and made the OB appointment for me: November twenty-third. I didn't want to go back to Dr. Rob to hear the heartbeat. I could wait for the OB. I did my best to put it in the back of my mind as we continued to make wedding plans. I knew I was pregnant, but I didn't feel pregnant—especially with the morning sickness fading away. If I didn't think about it, I could almost pretend it was a bad dream.

Ryan picked me up early on the morning of the twenty-third. We were going to make a day of it in Cork. There were a couple of castles in my book that were near or in Cork City, so those were first on the list after a quick breakfast on the fly. I didn't enjoy seeing the sights as much as I would have on an ordinary day. I was distracted. This appointment was like I was admitting to the world that I was pregnant. I realized it wouldn't be on the evening news, but still, it was making it official in my mind.

The OB's office was located next to Mercy Hospital, where I'd probably deliver. We stepped into the waiting room, and it was filled with pregnant women of varying sizes. *Would I really get that big?* I thought as I watched one of them waddle to the bathroom. "Thank you for being here with me," I whispered to Ryan as we sat down to wait.

"Yer welcome, love." He held my hand. "Do ya want me to wait out here or come in with ya?

"Come in. Definitely. I don't want to go in by myself. When it's time for the physical exam, you can leave the room, okay?" He relaxed visibly when I said that. "You didn't think I wanted you to stay in for that, did you?" I chuckled.

"Geez, no. I'm here for ya, Bren, but I have to draw the line somewhere." He grimaced.

"Brenna O'Brien?" A nurse called my name and we followed her. "First visit?" she asked as we walked.

"Yeah," I answered.

"Oh, a Yank. Where ya from?" she chatted.

"Uh, New York," I answered.

"Oh, I love New York. My sister and me took a holiday there a few years back. All the lights …" I let her voice fade into background noise and nodded when necessary. "Can ya pee in a cup for me?" she asked with a way-too-cheery voice. I nodded and took the cup, not looking at Ryan's face. I suspected he was probably trying not to crack up.

I delivered the cup and stepped on the scale as directed. Once all my vitals were duly recorded, she led us to an exam room. Ryan took one look at the stirrups and I thought he might pass out. When the nurse left the room, I started to laugh. "Don't worry. You won't be in here when we use those." This was embarrassing. I should have had Megan come with me! The nurse came back in and took a full medical history as well as some of my blood, and then she was off again. She instructed me to get undressed and put on the flimsy robe folded on the exam table.

"Should I leave now?" Ryan asked.

"No, not yet. Stay to meet the doctor. Just turn around, and I'll pull the curtain while I change," I did so quickly and opened the curtain once I'd crawled up onto the exam table. "Well, I hope you wanted to know every medical detail about me." I noticed he was looking pale. "You okay?"

"I'm fine. Just not big on the blood thing," he admitted.

"Seriously?" I asked. "Big strong construction guy like you?" I teased.

"Actually, it's really more the needle than the blood," he explained.

"Oh. Sorry you had to see that then." There was a knock at the door, and then it opened.

"Brenna? I'm Dr. O'Grady." A thin, redheaded woman entered and shook my hand.

"Nice to meet you. This is my fiancé, Ryan," I said. It still thrilled me to introduce him that way.

"Ryan," she nodded. "Would you like to step outside while I do the exam?" she asked, and he accepted.

Five minutes later, the stirrups were put away and he was back in the room. Dr. O'Grady had confirmed the due date and said everything seemed to be progressing nicely. "Would you like to hear the heartbeat?" she asked.

I nodded. She pulled out an instrument that looked like a large remote with a telephone cord attached to a tube.

"Ahh! That's cold!" She had squirted a clear jelly on my tummy, and it shocked me.

"Sorry, sometimes it's cold. I should have warned ya," she said. Then she moved the tube around on my abdomen listening for the heartbeat. All I heard was a swishing sound at first. Then it was there. A very strong, very fast heartbeat. I looked at Ryan and saw tears in his eyes. He leaned over and kissed my forehead as the doctor wiped the jelly off. "Sounds great. Good strong heartbeat. Do you have any other questions for me, Brenna?" she asked.

"Nope."

She nodded. "We'll see you in six weeks then." She left the room.

"Oh my gosh, Ryan. Did you hear that?" I was still in shock. "There's totally a baby in there!" I giggled.

"I know." He smiled and wiped the tears from his eyes.

"Are you okay?" I asked, knowing this must have been so hard for him.

"Aye, course I am. Let's go have lunch." He handed me my clothes. "I know you'd probably like to keep that lovely gown, but it's best if ya put yer own clothes back on," he teased.

"Get out of here." I swatted him, and he slipped out the door. I stopped smiling and sat down. *Lord, this is gonna be so hard. Please help me get through this.*

There was a little café across the street, and we were both ravenous. It was unseasonably warm, so we took our sandwiches outside and sat on a bench.

"Brenna." Ryan looked at me. "I need to tell ya somethin." He looked so serious.

"What?" I asked.

"I've been thinkin' about this for a few weeks now, and I'm not sure how to explain it." He paused.

"What is it?" I had a sinking feeling in my chest. What now? What else could go wrong, I wondered.

"Well, it's just that … I know yer plannin' on givin' the baby up for adoption, right?" He knew that. Why was he asking?

"Yeah," I said.

"What if ya didn't?" he asked. "Because I want ya to do what you feel like ya need to do," he said quickly. "But … I also want ya to know that—" He faltered. He was crying!

"Ryan," I pulled him close. "What is it?"

He wiped his eyes. "I don't want to guilt ya into anything, understand?" He looked at me with an intensity that frightened me. I nodded. "But I hear that heartbeat, and all I can think of is the baby I would have had." He took a deep breath. "If ya decide to keep this baby, I want ya to know I would raise him or her as my own."

I was speechless. I hadn't even considered asking such a thing of him. I just looked into his brokenhearted eyes, and tears streamed down my face. I'd known the moment I heard that heart beating that I was in trouble. This was Luke's baby, but it was also mine. I was already doubting that I'd have the strength to give the baby away—and now this?

"You would do that?" I whispered as tears continued to fall. He nodded, unable to speak. "Are you sure?"

He took a deep breath. "Brenna …" He faltered again. "Brenna, I feel like maybe this baby is God's second chance for me." His lip was quivering, and it was more than I could take. I climbed onto his lap and looked him directly in the eyes.

"Ryan, if you want to raise this baby as yours, there's no way I'll give it up for adoption."

He laid his head on my chest, and I put my arms around him while he wept. I knew these were tears of relief. He'd been wanting to ask me this for a while.

"It was good that you waited to ask me," I admitted as we drove home.

"Aye?"

"Aye," I said with a smile. "I needed to hear the heartbeat. That changed everything."

"When I heard it, I couldn't wait anymore to tell ya," he said with a grin. "Hey."

"Hey, what?" I asked.

"We're gonna have a baby."

"We are!" I laughed until my ribs hurt.

Chapter Thirty-Four

DECEMBER

"I'm getting married in one week!" I said for the fifth time that day. We had declared a "wedding-free day" since it was Christmas Day. No plans or talk about the wedding was supposed to be allowed. But I couldn't help myself.

"Shhh. I know, Brenna. Yer gonna get in trouble." Megan motioned toward Patsy, who was the initiator of the wedding-free day.

"This is the Lord's day," Patsy had said at breakfast, "and I don't want to hear about dresses or shoes or somethin' borrowed or somethin' blue. Yer day is next week. Give Him His day!" We had agreed and promised not to talk about it for one day.

"She won't hear me," I whispered. "So how's Jamie?"

"He's doin' great, but I miss him." She frowned.

"How long will he be in London?" I asked.

"Well, his uncle can't run the dairy with a broken pelvis, ya know? He's bringin' in a hired hand for the next week so Jamie can come home tomorrow and stay through the wedding." She glanced at Patsy and began whispering. "He'll be here for the wedding, and then he'll go back and help until his uncle is back on his feet ... literally."

"He couldn't get back for Christmas?" How sad.

283

"No. No ferry service, and even if there was, it's a ten-hour trip from London," she explained.

"Sorry. Your first Christmas together and you can't be together. What a bummer."

"Aye, it's okay. There'll be others. I'm just glad he'll be here for the—" She mouthed the word *wedding* and I rolled my eyes. Then I caught the mouthwatering aroma wafting from the kitchen. Ryan and Bettie were in there, creating their Christmas masterpiece.

"Mmmm, do you smell that?" I asked.

"Aye, smells like mince pie." She grinned.

"Is that dessert?"

"'Tis, and it's yummy," she promised.

She was right. Everything was delicious, from the turkey to the potatoes to the—well, not the brussels sprouts—but everything else, including the mince pies, was fabulous. It was hard to satisfy my hunger these days, and even I was full.

"Bettie and Ryan, that was delicious!" Anna began a round of applause. "Brenna, how lucky you are to have a man who will cook." she pointed out.

"He cooks, I eat. A match made in heaven," I joked. I hadn't really gained much weight, thankfully. But that wasn't for lack of eating. There was nothing in particular that I craved. It was just that if I did crave something, I couldn't rest until I had it. One night I was craving a burger so badly that Ryan and I drove all the way to Cork so I could get an American-tasting burger. And it was well worth the drive.

As we all sat around feeling too full to move, the doorbell rang, and Bettie went to the front door. We could hear her enthusiastic greeting but had no idea who had come until Char and Patricia followed her into the dining room. Ryan and Megan both looked at me, concerned. Nothing public had happened since my birthday, but they both knew how I felt about Char.

"Look who's stopped for coffee." Bettie smiled, oblivious to the frost that had settled on the room. We all politely greeted each other, and I was shocked when Char made a beeline for me. Patricia began telling a story, but I didn't hear it.

"Merry Christmas, Brenna. Can I talk with you in private for a moment?" Char asked. I was unsure. I looked at Megan who appeared ready to block and tackle. Something about Char's demeanor told me it would be okay.

"Sure, we can go in the kitchen," I offered. I saw Ryan make a move to follow, but I waved him off and smiled to ease his concern.

We sat at the kitchen table. "What's up, Char?" I asked. No small talk here.

"Um, I wanted to tell ya I'm sorry. For what I did on yer birthday … and for everythin' else," she said without looking at me.

I was stunned. This was the last thing I expected. "Uh, okay. Thanks, I guess." *Very eloquent Brenna.*

"I know you may not want to forgive me, but I'm still sorry. It's taken me so long to see Luke for what he really is, and I was so rotten to you. I really am sorry." She was sincere … or she was an incredible actress. I tried to figure out what her endgame could be, if she was bluffing, but I was coming up empty.

"Char, I tend to get along with most people. You haven't made that easy in your case." I was completely honest with her.

"I know." She looked down at the floor. "I'm tryin' to make some positive changes in my life. This is one of my first steps—comin' to you and admittin' I was … well, ya know."

I laughed softly. "Yeah, I know." She looked at my face, trying to read me. "I forgive you, Char. I dealt with Luke for a few months. I can't imagine what you've gone through having to deal with him for years."

Her eyes held pain and sadness. "Ya did the right thing, havin' him arrested." She was full of surprises today. Once he'd been located, he'd been arrested, and on the advice of his lawyer, pled an "assault with bodily harm" down to a lesser offense. He'd gotten six months in jail and a fine.

"You really think it was good that I filed a complaint against him?" I knew it was the right thing to do, but I was shocked that she agreed.

She nodded. "Brenna, he's been gettin' away with so much for so long. No one's ever stood up to him like you did. He needed the wake-up call."

"Have you seen him?" I was curious.

"Aye, I went today," she said.

"Char, if you know what he's like, then why do you keep going back to him?"

She took a deep breath. "I don't know. I guess I love him, even though he doesn't deserve it. But I'm not goin' back to him. Not really. I'm just bein' a friend. He doesn't have many now, ya know? Everyone wanted to be his friend when he was the big man in town, but not now."

"How's he doing?" I asked.

"He hasn't hit bottom yet." I figured that was code for *"He's not sorry and he blames you."*

"Well, maybe he'll get a clue while he's in there," I said.

"Aye, I hope so. Father Tim's goin' to see him this week."

"Good." Awkward silence. "Well, thanks for coming by, Char." I stood to go back to the dining room.

"Thanks for bein' forgiving," she replied. I offered her a tentative hug, which she literally embraced. I knew we'd never be close, but I was glad she'd had a change of heart, and it felt good to let go of the anger I'd had toward her.

After everyone had left for the night, I put on my new pjs from Anna and snuggled under the covers with my journal in hand.

Lord,

Today was a good day. Thank you for loving us enough to enter this crazy world two thousand years ago. Thank you for Ryan. Thank you for Megan and Anna and Bettie and Patsy. Lord, help Patsy as she goes through this dark time and help us all to be a support for her. And I pray for Char too. Wow ... she really surprised me today. Whatever she's going through, I ask that you'll help her. And Luke, Lord. I know I need to forgive him. Help me do that. Help me want to forgive him. Cuz a big part of me wants to hold on to the hate. But I know that's not what you want from me, so help me to change.

In Jesus's name, amen.

"Six days and counting," I said as Ryan gave me a good-morning hug. "You have to push me. I want to make it up to the poplar trees and back, okay?" I was determined to keep running as far into my pregnancy as I could.

"Okay, but don't yell at me when I push, agreed?" *The voice of experience.*

"Me? Yell at you? Never." My hormones were not always as kind to Ryan as I would have liked. He still put up with me.

We set off at an easy pace. I was going more for marathon than sprint at this point. "So, ya said you'd tell me what Char wanted," he prompted. There had been too much commotion the night before for me to explain.

"Yeah, it was so weird. She asked me to forgive her," I revealed.

"Seriously?" He was as surprised as I had been. I relayed the conversation between me and Char, and he listened patiently. "I'm proud of ya for bein' so nice to her."

"Thanks. She was sincere. I couldn't hold a grudge. What would be the point?"

"Wouldn't do y'any good, anyway," he agreed.

"Yeah. I think I'm ready to forgive Luke," I admitted. "But do I have to *tell* him I forgive him?" That might be a deal-breaker.

"I don't know, Bren." We ran in uncharacteristic silence.

"What are ya thinking?" I finally asked.

"Ya gonna tell him ... about the baby?" he asked quietly. I'd wondered when this conversation would happen.

"I don't know. Guess I should. But I don't want to. What do you think?"

"I don't want ya to," he admitted. That surprised me.

"Why?" I asked. He was silent for a long time and I was having trouble keeping up. I pointed toward the poplar trees up ahead. "Take a breather?"

"Aye." He nodded, and we collapsed under the trees.

"So, I'm surprised you think I shouldn't tell Luke," I said.

"No, I didn't say y'shouldn't. Just that I don't *want* ya to," he explained.

"Okay, so why don't you want me to?" One thing I'd discovered about Ryan was his unwavering commitment to do what was right. Deep down, I knew it was the right thing to tell Luke he was the biological father of the child I carried. I had expected Ryan to be adamant that I tell him.

"Because I'm selfish," he answered. "I want ya all to myself. I want the baby all to myself. It should be my baby, not his. That's why."

I nodded. That was exactly how I felt. "If we had been dating and gone too far and I was carrying your baby, I'd feel guilty for having messed up, but I'd feel so different about this whole thing," I admitted.

"Aye, but that's not what we're dealin' with. I don't want ya to tell him, but I still think y'should. I want to adopt the baby, Bren. Can't do that if he doesn't relinquish his rights," he said.

"Then why don't you want me to tell him?" I was confused.

"I'm afraid he won't agree. I'm afraid he'll try to take y'away from me."

"Whoa, he could never do that, Ry. You know that, don't you?" How could he even think such a thing? He nodded but wouldn't look me in the eye. "Ryan, look at me." He was breaking my heart. "You know he could never do that, right?" He looked away. "What is it?"

"I know y'were drunk, and I know ya weren't yerself, but there's still some part of you that wanted to be with him." I felt like I'd just been sucker punched.

"I thought this was all behind us?" I asked, hurt.

"I'm sorry. I thought it was too. But when I think of you goin' to talk with him, I can't describe how it makes me feel. I've been prayin' and askin' God to help me deal with it." He was frustrated. "He will. I didn't mean to bring it up. I'm sorry, darlin. Just forget it."

"Okay, let's just get this all in the open, okay? Attraction and commitment are two totally different things. We'll both have times in our lives that we're attracted to someone other than each other. You do know that, right?" I asked, thankful that Anna and I had discussed this before.

He looked shocked. "What are ya sayin'?"

"I'm saying that, for a time, I found Luke attractive. I made stupid choices that put me in a vulnerable place, but I learned from that. I won't ever put myself in that kind of place again. I'm stronger now than if I'd never met him. You don't have to worry about Luke or any other guy taking me away from you. I love you, Ryan. I'm committing myself to you for life, and nothing will change that. Got it?" He looked at me with a crooked smile and nodded. "And I expect the same from you, mister.

I'm not a fool. I know at some point you'll meet another woman that you find attractive. I don't expect you to gouge your eye out. I expect you to protect yourself from vulnerable situations and honor your commitment to me. Make sense?" I asked.

"Yer amazin'," he said, and he kissed me. For a long time.

Once I regained my breath, I added, "As far as telling Luke, I don't want to tell him. I'd rather never have to talk to him again, but legally, he has rights. If we don't deal with this head on, it'll always be hanging over our heads. Don't think I haven't considered just putting your name on the birth certificate."

He looked at me with wide eyes. "Ya have?"

"Yes, I have. But we both know we wouldn't feel right about that." He nodded. "So, I guess we do the right thing, which is to tell him the truth and trust God to take it from there, okay?"

"Okay. Yer right, love." He stood and pulled me up. "Have I told ya how much I love ya, t'day?" he asked with a wide grin.

"Well, not in words," I teased, and he pulled me close and hugged me tightly.

"I love ya so much more than I can say," he whispered into my hair.

I pulled back and looked into his eyes. "I love you too ... but I bet I can beat you down the hill." I took off in a sprint. I had a lead but it was short-lived. He overtook me within seconds and then toyed with me all the way home. I knew I had no chance of beating him, but it was fun trying.

"Four days and counting!" I repeated my daily mantra when I slipped into Ryan's car. He had been to Limerick to visit his lawyer. "So, paperwork is all ready to go?" I asked.

"Aye." He handed me a large envelope. Inside was a bunch of stuff I didn't really care to read.

"So, if Luke signs this, then you can adopt the baby when he or she is born?" I asked and he nodded. "And if Luke doesn't agree?"

"Then he doesn't. I can't adopt, but it doesn't mean I won't be the baby's father, ya know?"

"I know." I felt better. He was right. It would be nice to make it all legal and tie a bow around it, but that wasn't going to change our lives in the day-to-day. I was so nervous to see Luke. I hadn't seen him since Ryan had pulled him off of me that night in the stairwell. Sometimes I had nightmares about it, and that wasn't helping to ease my nerves.

"Are ya okay?" Ryan noticed me chewing my lip.

"Yeah. It's awkward," I admitted. "Let's talk about something else."

"Okay … four days and countin'," he said with a grin. The drive to the county jail passed quickly as we discussed last-minute details for the wedding. Ryan had arranged for my brothers and their families to fly in for the wedding. I was so excited. Something about being pregnant had made me really want to get to know my family better. As a kid, I had little control over seeing my brothers. But I was an adult now and determined to change that. I was thrilled they wanted to come.

"Here we are," he said as we pulled up to the Cork Prison gate on Rathmore Road. Once we were parked and ready to go, Ryan took my hand. "I'm gonna pray for ya." I nodded. "Lord, please give Brenna the courage t'forgive and the words t'say. We put this all into yer hands and trust you to help us deal with the results. In Jesus name, amen."

"Amen. Thanks, Ry."

Fifteen minutes. That was all that was allowed. I took a deep breath as we waited. *Lord, help me,* I whispered. The guard ushered us into a common room filled with tables. There were a number of prisoners visiting with families. Luke was seated by himself at a far table. His eyes met mine and then looked away. *Breathe deep.* Fifteen minutes.

"Hi, Luke," I said as I sat down. Ryan hung back, unsure of whether he should join us or not.

"Hi, Brenna." He smiled coolly. Had he always looked at me like I was a piece of meat? How had I not recognized it before? I didn't have to look to know Ryan was watching like a hawk. I saw Luke's gaze flick toward Ryan before resting back on me.

"How are you doin'?" I asked.

"Grand, Brenna, how are you?" His voice was hard.

"Listen, we don't have a lot of time, and there's a lot I need to say, so let's just drop the pleasantries, okay?"

He was surprised. "Fine. Why've ya come?"

I didn't need his understanding for why I'd called the police, but I thought I'd try. "First, do you remember what happened that night?"

He looked away. "Some of it." His gaze flicked back to Ryan again and then away.

"You scared me, Luke. You wouldn't get off me. If Ryan hadn't come …" I was starting to get upset. This was not in my plan. "You were crushing me. I couldn't breathe, and you slammed me so hard against the wall, you broke a rib! I *had* to make a formal complaint. Can you understand that?" He studied the table and shrugged. Well, at least he wasn't defending himself. "Listen, I want you to know—" Deep breath. "I want you to know that whether you're sorry or not, I forgive you, Luke." Wow. I'd said it. And I had actually meant it. And I'd shocked him.

He looked me in the eyes, and all defenses were down for just a moment. "I'm sorry, Brenna," he said quietly.

"Thanks," I said. "I wanted to tell you that, but it's not the reason I came."

He looked puzzled. He looked back to Ryan again. "I hear yer gettin' married this week," he said with some of his swagger returning. The vulnerability was gone.

"Yes, Friday," I said.

"Congrats," he said without emotion.

"Luke, that night when I went up to your flat with you …" There was that smile again that used to drive me crazy. Now it made me feel sick. *Deep breath.* "I'm pregnant," I whispered.

He recovered quickly from the shock. "Brenna, y'made it clear that nothin' happened that night." He smirked.

"Listen to me. I want nothing from you, but I felt it was only right to tell you."

"How do ya know it's not his?" He motioned behind me.

I leaned in and answered as quietly as I could, wishing Ryan didn't have to hear any of this. "Luke, I've been with two men in my life: my husband who's been dead over a year and you. Do the math." He looked away.

"So y've told me. Is that all?" He was so cold.

"No. I told you I want nothing from you, and I mean that. I'd like to make it official. As the biological father of the baby I'm carrying, you have rights and responsibilities. If you don't wish to have those responsibilities, I'd like you to relinquish your parental rights."

I slid the paper and a pen toward him. He gave me a calculating look. *Please, Lord, let him sign it.* I continued to look him directly in the eyes. I refused to look away before he did. It felt like forever. Finally, he looked down at the paper in front of him.

He picked up the pen and signed. *Thank you, God!* I could hear Ryan exhale behind me. "Good-bye, Luke," I said as I rose, took Ryan's hand, and strode out of the room.

Chapter Thirty-Five

My hands were trembling. *Seriously? Trembling? Ridiculous!* "Megan, why can't I calm down?" I whined.

She giggled. "It's actually funny to see ya like this."

"Thanks," I said with a killer look in her direction.

"Sorry, Bren. You'll calm down. One look at those dreamy blue eyes, and you'll float down the aisle," she assured me. "Say a prayer?"

"That's good. You're right." I closed my eyes. *Lord help me calm down. I want to enjoy this day, not hyperventilate through it.* Deep breath. "Okay, that's a little better," I said as Anna and Patsy slipped into the room.

"Just a couple more minutes!" Anna said, grinning. "Brenna, this is it. Yer castle wedding. Who would have thought a year ago ..."

"I know. Patsy, just imagine if you hadn't sent that gift!" I said with a smile for the irony as I pulled her into a heartfelt embrace. I wasn't sure if she even remembered her generous wedding gift to me and Ben. But I was so grateful that it had allowed me and Anna to make the trip to Ireland after everything had turned upside down in our lives. "Thank you so much."

"Yer welcome, love. I'm glad to have had a part in bringin' you and Finn together. "

"You helped me find my home before I even knew I needed to." I kissed her on the cheek as she smiled wide.

"But just so we're clear, I won't be makin' such a contribution this time around. Finn can pay for *me* to take a trip! I'm gonna go take my seat." She winked as she left the room and we all laughed.

Anna took my hands and held one up for me to twirl around. "Ya look stunning, love." I had chosen a delicate, ivory dress with an empire waist and a hem that fell just above my knees. I guess it could be called a "baby doll" dress. I paired it with the tallest heels I could find in ivory. It took a little practice to walk in them, but I was getting there. *Just make it down the aisle*, I'd repeated to myself. Ryan wanted me to get a real wedding dress, but I felt like that was over the top. I wanted simple and beautiful. I'd done the full wedding thing before, and it was nice but not necessary.

"Are ya nervous?" Anna asked. My hands were freezing.

"A little, I guess. I don't know why, though. I'm so ready for this," I said.

"Aye, it's probably just adrenaline," she said.

Megan answered a light knock at the door. "It's time," she said as she turned toward me, grinning. Jamie was playing a classical tune on the guitar for me to walk down the aisle to. Everyone I loved was in the room as I stepped through the door. The fifty or so chairs were set up in the castle hall. The sunlight filtered through the two-story windows along one wall, casting rainbows through the crystal chandeliers. The colonnades at one end provided the perfect spot to perform the ceremony. As I glanced at the rich tapestries that covered the walls, I thought of my visit to Boldt Castle when I was a girl. Here was my fairy-tale wedding. I took a steadying breath and sighted Ryan. He was so incredibly handsome in his black tux. My heart was beating double-time. But Megan was right. I just fastened my gaze on his glistening eyes, and he drew me right toward his waiting hands. Anna held my arm as we walked together toward my prince.

We had asked Ryan's friend, Danny, to marry us, and Father Tim would do a reading.

"Who gives this woman to be married?" Danny asked all officiously.

"We all do," Anna replied, and the audience applauded. This was not going to be a typical ceremony.

Ryan's warm hands enveloped mine, and I instantly calmed.

"We are gathered here today ..." Danny said all the necessary words leading up to the declaration of intent.

"Will you, Brenna Tanner O'Brien, take this man, Ryan Finn Kelly, to be yer lawfully wedded husband?"

"I will." I grinned. This was easy.

"Will you, Ryan Finn Kelly, take this woman, Brenna Tanner O'Brien, to be yer lawfully wedded wife?"

"I will." I could tell he wanted to kiss me right then, and I tried not to giggle.

Father Tim stood to read. I had requested Proverbs 3:5–6, my new theme verses. "Trust in the Lord with all yer heart and lean not on yer own understanding. In all yer ways acknowledge him and he will make yer paths straight."

Megan left my side and sat down on a stool next to Jamie. The first night I'd gone to Veritas, she and Ryan had sung a song that had become one of my favorites because it was so true in my life. I was thrilled when she offered to sing it at my wedding.

Deep in the heart of the struggle
There is a hope that will shine
Up from the ashes, the song of your glory will rise

Higher than every mountain
Deeper than all of my fears
Over my brokenness, this is the truth that I hear

You have been so good, You have been so good
Faithful forever and ever you are
Through every season, in every trial
There is no question about who you are
You have been so good.

Savior, we've seen the power of your hand
Grateful, here in your presence we stand.

I winked at Megan. What a blessing she was in my life. Next were the vows. That would be the hard part. I hadn't gotten through them yet without crying. Neither of us had heard each other's completed vows yet.

"Brenna?" Danny prompted me.

Deep breath and a gulp. "I, Brenna, take you, Ryan, to be my husband. I promise to walk alongside you through every valley and on every mountain top. I promise to seek God's wisdom to help me be the wife you need. And I promise, with God's help, to be a faithful mother to our children." I made it through without a tear, but I saw them welling up in Ryan's eyes.

"Ryan?" Danny prompted him.

Deep breath and another gulp. "I, Ryan, take you, Brenna, to be my wife. I promise to be yer provider and protector. I promise to be yer friend, but most of all I promise to love ya with everything I am." His voice cracked. Deep breath again. "I promise to ask for God's help, daily, to love ya like Jesus loves you, and I promise to be a lovin' father to our children." Now it was my turn for tears. *God, you are so good to me.*

We exchanged the rings, and Danny announced that we were official. "You may kiss the bride."

Ryan didn't even wait for him to finish, but he did show restraint. He kissed me tenderly, when I knew he wanted more. I had a feeling we wouldn't stay long after dinner and that was fine with me.

Before long the sounds of Irish dance music floated on the air and as the song changed to a slow but happy tune, Ryan pulled me out to the middle of the small dance floor. I remembered our first and only dance together. How far we'd come in such a short time. All eyes were on us as we spun around the room. This time my eyes were open and fixed on his. The song ended too soon, but I saw my brothers gathered off to one side, so we headed over to say hi.

"Ryan, this is my brother Mike and his wife Michelle," I said as Ryan shook his hand. "And this is my brother Jake and his wife Heather—and their daughter is around here somewhere." I looked around. I had met my twelve-year-old niece, Emma, for the first time the night before. Ryan hadn't met any of them, because Patsy had insisted he could not see me the night before the wedding. She wouldn't even make an exception because it was New Year's Eve.

"I'm so glad ya came," Ryan said. "Yer stayin' for a few days, right?"

"Absolutely," said Mike. "We're making a vacation of it. Well, as much as we can with twin six-month-olds." He winked at his wife.

"Good. Brenna and I aren't leavin' for our honeymoon till Wednesday, so we'll have some time to visit, right?"

"Definitely," Jake responded.

"Brilliant," Ryan said. "Then I don't feel guilty stealin' her away from ya right now." He smiled mischievously and took me by the hand as my brothers both nodded with understanding.

"What are you doing?" I swatted him.

"I have an urge." He grinned as he pulled me into a side room and shut the door.

"Ryan, we have guests." I giggled.

"I know. They'll still be there in five minutes. I just wanted a couple minutes alone with ya before dinner. Ya look beautiful, Bren. Yer breathtaking." He bent down and kissed me until I pushed him away.

I caught my breath and then wiped my lip gloss off of his mouth with my fingers. "Now look what you've done. I have to go fix my hair and makeup, silly man." I laughed, fully enjoying the moment.

"I just couldn't wait until dinner was over. Sorry. Call me weak." He grinned.

"You've waited ten years, you can wait another hour." I reached up and kissed his cheek.

"If I must, but not a minute more. Ya have sixty minutes, startin' … now," he teased.

"Seriously, though, I can't go back out there looking like this. I need to fix my hair," I could see my reflection in the glass frame on the wall. It wasn't pretty.

"Okay, here." He sauntered toward the bookcase. Unexpectedly, he moved it, and I realized it was a secret door to the double staircase beyond.

"How cool!" I giggled.

He handed me our room key. "Run upstairs and freshen up. I'll go mingle." I hesitated long enough for him to add, "If y'don't go now, Bren, I'm gonna show ya the way, and we won't be comin' back down t'night."

He looked like he might be serious, so I laughed, took off my heels and sprinted toward the staircase.

"Time's up." Ryan whispered in my ear, sending chills down my spine. We had visited with every friend and family member except for one.

"I was just about to thank Father Tim," I said.

"Aye, let's do that together," he suggested. "Then yer mine," he promised as we caught Father Tim's eye.

"Ah, just look at the two of ya. The Lord sure does work in mysterious ways. I'm so glad I was here to see His plan unfold," he said.

"Thank you for everything." I gave him a hug and a kiss on the cheek.

"My pleasure, Brenna. My pleasure." He grinned. When he looked at Ryan, I could see that both men were fighting to keep their emotions in check. If anyone knew how long this day was in coming, it was Father Tim. "Ryan, I'm so proud of ya …" He couldn't say more.

"Thanks for bein' here, and I don't just mean today," Ryan said as he gave him a hug. "Now, if you'll do me one more favor?"

"Aye, name it," Father Tim replied.

"Run interference for me. I'm takin' my wife upstairs, and as much as I love 'em all, I don't want to talk to another person in this room. Tell them we'll see 'em in church on Sunday, okay?"

Father Tim laughed heartily and said, "Aye, get goin' already!"

Ryan grabbed my hand and pulled me back into the library with the secret door. This time there was no kiss; he was on a mission to get me up those stairs as quickly as he could. I was surprised he didn't hoist me over his shoulder.

When the door to our room was closed and locked, he said, "Thank God. Alone at last."

"At long last," I agreed. I took off my three-inch heels and stood up on the four-poster bed. "Come here, Mr. Kelly." I crooked my finger toward him. "Now *I* have an urge."

With two steps, he was standing in front of me, his arms wrapped around me. But as I leaned down to kiss him, he stopped me. "No, wait.

I don't have to kiss ya standin' up anymore, Mrs. Kelly." And with that, he picked me up, tossed me on the bed, and we enthusiastically broke all the rules.

Epilogue

The hospital clamor faded into white noise as I stared at him. His tiny little fingers were hooked around one of mine. He had a full head of black curly hair and dark blue eyes. Of course, I guess most babies have blue eyes when they're born. But I considered it a gift that he looked so much like Ryan.

"He's beautiful," Ryan said as he tenderly stroked the soft, newborn cheek.

"He is. But don't wake him," I whispered. "I need to sleep." Ryan looked at me with admiring eyes.

"Yer remarkable, Brenna," he said. "I'm in awe of what ya just did. Are y'okay?"

"Yeah, I'm just tired and sore is all," I admitted. It had been both the hardest and the most amazing thing I'd ever done in my life. "That's a miracle," I whispered, nodding toward my son. My son! *Oh, Lord, forgive me for ever thinking, even for a moment, that I didn't want him.* My heart was overwhelmed. A solitary tear escaped as I closed my eyes with a smile on my face. "I'm so blessed," I said with a yawn. "And tired."

Ryan bent over and kissed my forehead. "You go to sleep, love. I'm not goin' anywhere. I'm just gonna sit here and watch our little Benjamin Finn Kelly while he sleeps."

Author's Note

I love to read. When I get ahold of a great novel, I usually restrict myself to reading only before bed. Otherwise my four kids would be left to fend for themselves while I read all day long. So I'm honored that you have taken the time to read my book.

For years I had thought it would be cool to take one of the love stories in the Bible and write a modern day love story. But I was afraid. I love stories that tell truth through fiction. But what if I wrote it and it was terrible? It was safer just to sit on the idea. Until the day my husband challenged me to stop dreaming and start writing. I had read a popular book series in less than a week. (Okay, I didn't read only before bed that week!) A few weeks later, we were going on a trip and I told my husband that everything I'd tried to read since was boring so I would probably just read the series again since I knew it was so good. I'll always be thankful for his response. "Babe, instead of reading that again, why don't you just write what you've always wanted to write?"

So I did. First, I wrote the scene where Brenna meets Ryan. From there I started at the beginning and wrote to the end in about three months, often staying up till four a.m. because I couldn't stop writing.

My inspiration for "Where the Pink Houses Are" is the book of Ruth. I love that story and wish we knew more about what happened between Ruth and Boaz. Bill Cosby would say "it's in the missing pages." My story is not a re-telling. I didn't try to draw exact parallels. I just wanted to take the basic themes of Ruth; loyalty, trust, love and redemption and show them in a modern context.

I hope that Brenna and Ryan's story has encouraged and challenged you. I hope that you found yourself somewhere in the story. I've heard it said that fiction shouldn't be about learning a lesson. It should just be for fun. I don't necessarily agree. I like it when fiction makes me think. I believe that God can teach us truth through stories. I believe that's why Jesus told parables. So, I hope that you've heard something true in this fictional story.

Every author wants to hear, "I couldn't put your book down!" It's the greatest compliment I've received and I hope that if you've made it to this point in my book, it means that at some point you had trouble putting it down, too. Thank you for reading my first novel. Feel free to look me up on facebook, where I may post discussion questions for book clubs, if there is an interest. God bless!

Rebekah Ruth

P.S. The song that Megan sings at the wedding in the last chapter is a real song sung by Benji and Jenna Cowart called, "You Have Been So Good," off their EP called "Letters to the Church At Buffalo." It's one of my favorite CDs. Check it out on iTunes!

CPSIA information can be obtained at www.ICGtesting.com
Printed in the USA
BVOW071456220712

295875BV00004B/19/P